GIRL
IN THE
STORM

THE GIRL IN THE STORM

CERI A. LOWE

bookouture

Published by Bookouture in 2018

An imprint of StoryFire Ltd.

Carmelite House
50 Victoria Embankment
London EC4Y 0DZ

www.bookouture.com

ISBN: 978-1-78681-527-9
eBook ISBN: 978-1-78681-526-2

Prologue

Carter

The shock of what he saw almost killed him.

If he hadn't been holding onto the rusted rail, it was likely that fifteen-year-old Carter Warren would have fallen directly into the empty ruins of the overgrown city nine storeys below. The communal council garden beneath him was now an ugly jungle, but there was one corner that had been carefully cultivated. He could clearly make out the words written in blocks of stone:

THERE ARE OTHERS

Inside the walls of the Community, he had heard stories. But they were just that – stories. The wild imaginings of children that were extinguished as quickly as they began. Ideas of terrible creatures that roamed outside the Barricades had always been there to stop the little ones – and often the older ones – approaching the fences. Carter had never believed there could really be anything else – anyone else. Not anyone real who was still alive. It was forbidden, impossible. A thrill of the unknown coursed through his veins.

Others.

*

In the quietness of the landscape, Carter could feel the bass of his heart thumping in his chest. The words were real. And, although they looked like they had been there a fair amount of time, the growth over them had been cleared – and recently.

'Where are you?' he yelled. 'Where are you?' His voice sounded strained and thin and he couldn't remember when he had last spoken out aloud. It felt much longer than the day or so since he'd left the Community and been declared dead.

His words melted into the air. A crow circled above him, papery wings flapping in the breeze.

No response.

Carter scanned the empty landscape. The person who had stacked the stones up into a precise order and had cleared the way to ensure people would find the message had gone. There was nothing. No one.

To the west, the lights of the Community glowed within the tight vein of the river. He felt an ache of nostalgia for somewhere that felt like it was a world away. There were distant lights within the Barricades, like the pale resonance of a machine recently switched off. But any nostalgia for that place was pointless. To most, if not all, he was dead – and had died a traitor, putting the whole existence of the Community in jeopardy; the Industry would be sure that everyone knew that.

Then there was Isabella – the school sweetheart he had adored and shared so much with – he hoped the end had been quick for her. And his son, Ariel – the son he had only just begun to know. He hoped there had been no repercussions for him. His heart sank and he felt his soul swirl around the depths of his body. And then there was his daughter Lucia, murdered by a woman he had trusted. A sliver of anger speared him when he thought of them and how he'd been forced to leave them all.

Carter watched the tail of a Transporter, carrying its load of Community travellers, crawling silently in the distance before it looped underground and disappeared. He wondered whether they were on their way to work in the deep underground factories, or perhaps headed towards the Industry to be frozen for the next stage of their lives. Somehow, he would have to let the people of the Community know the truth about what was outside the Barricades.

It seemed impossible that anyone else could have survived the Storms – or the aftermath – without the protection of the Industry. Five years of biblically punishing rain, hail and flooding that had destroyed everything in its path. Having to build a whole existence up from scratch without the power of the Industry – without the skill and the knowledge of how to create a new world? But someone, it seemed, *had* done it. And they were out there, looking for more like them. The spill of exhilaration came again, mixing his emotions.

If there were something other than the Industry then he, Carter, would be the one to find it. He would show the people of the Community the truth and honour the memory of Isabella and Lucia. And maybe the Others would help him.

Far beyond the Community, against the white line of the horizon, stood the melancholic shape of the Drakewater nuclear plant and beyond that, nothing. He picked a point in the distance and followed the line of land, his eyes scanning for any sign of human habitation. He knew he needed to find the Others, but he couldn't take off out into the Deadlands without a plan.

The blackness of the river wound tight around the floodplain like a noose. Further into the distance the land widened out, scratched through with trees and overgrowth and peppered with small groups of decaying houses that disappeared into the distance. Carter stared out, waiting as the day crept slowly on. The quietness got quieter.

His eyes scanned backwards and forwards.

Left.

Right.

He watched birds gust across the valley and through the remains of buildings, their wings clipping the breeze and lifting them higher. He traced each one as it circled down and then up and down again. Then suddenly, in the darkness of a clump of trees, there was a flash of light: a sliver of something glinting in the distance.

'Hello!' Carter leaned across the edge of the building as far as was safe and screamed as loudly as he could. The piercing call of his voice bounced off derelict buildings and pavements, echoing until it bled into silence. He listened, but there was nothing except the sound of the wind and the birds overhead.

'Hello.' He watched the trees intently.

There was nothing and then the flash was there again.

And again.

This time it was not completely random in its intervals and deliberate enough to be intentionally catching attention. He looked at the position of the sun and the direction of the flash. It was in the opposite direction to the Community. In the absence of anywhere else to go or any other sign, for Carter, that was good enough. He checked the distance between the tower and the flashing and drew a path in his mind. Now he knew where to begin his journey.

Carter held up the crumpled, faded map he'd found in the flat, covered in words and names that didn't mean anything to him. It was different on both sides. He ran his finger over the contours, reading

place names and directions and traced the outline of three words
scrawled over where the thick, circled block of the Community was:

DANGER - KEEP OUT

After he had watched the rays of the morning sun lift off the Black
River, Carter pulled the rucksack he'd found in a cupboard in one of
the apartments over his shoulders. Stuffed inside were the remains of
the map, some old clothes that were falling apart and the books and
rusted scissors he had arrived with. He looked himself up and down – if
this constituted prepared, then he was.

The stairway was covered with a soft, slippery moss that formed a
thick green line of carpet down the inside of the steps leading from the
top of the building to the bottom. Another crow, perched on one of the
banisters called a sharp warning as Carter passed, snapping its beak in a
tight black smile before unfolding feathery ebony wings and flying towards
the open door at the bottom of the stairwell and out into the white sun.

By early afternoon, Carter reached a group of outbuildings around
a courtyard where there were containers filled with enough clean
rainwater that he could drink from. The square that had once been
covered in grass was now dotted with trees and bushes, save for the
pathway Carter had beaten his way through the night before. The leaves
on the trees were blackened around the edges with a deep, juicy green
colour at the centre and firm yellow fruit that hung in clusters at the
ends of the branches. Up towards the top of the stout, round tree sat
a creature with big, blackened eyes staring down from the branch with
one of the fruit clasped between black claws.

It eyed Carter carefully, opening its mouth a little to reveal two rows of sharp teeth, white against its dark reddish-brown fur. It rolled the fruit around slowly and, for a second, Carter thought that it was going to throw it at him and he ducked. But instead, the creature twitched on the high branch, steadying itself with a thick, bushy tail and bit deep into the fleshy fruit. A trickle of juice spilled onto its fur. There was moment while they watched each other and Carter wondered who would attack first.

A thin wind blew softly through the branches and two of the fruit that hung from the branches fell at his feet. The tree-rat nibbled away and kept its eyes directly fixed frontwards.

Carter picked a small globe from the branch and it broke off easily, cool and round in his palm. He held it in his hand for a while and felt the bumpy edges of its skin. The hunger inside him was unbearable, yet the thought of eating something that was still growing, still alive, disgusted him. His stomach groaned desperately and he paused for a second, opening his mouth slowly. And then he took a bite. Although the taste was sharp, it was better than he had expected, a little like the faupples that the Industry filled up the corners of the ration baskets with that were good for snacking on. He felt himself retch at the thought of what he was doing but still, he opened his mouth and took another bite, his teeth crunching into the fruit. Then the flavour hit him – sweet, delicious and incomparable. His stomach suddenly craved more and he leant towards the tree pulling the leafy branches closer to pick some more. As he shook the branch, handfuls of fruit fell to the floor. No manufacturing required. They were just there, growing in front of him. It seemed unbelievable and almost lazy.

He picked up as much as he could carry and put them in the rucksack. In the distance, there was the crackle of leaves and the soothing shush of the wind through half-empty branches. The rat-like animal scampered to a higher position in the tree then launched itself to a neighbouring conifer and across an adjoining flat roof. Then, in a rush of rustling and a soft thumping of fruit, it scouted the upper branches, sniffed the air – and was gone.

At the next fork, Carter wiped the sweat from the lids of his eyes and squinted through the branches of the trees and up into the canopy. A rustling in the bushes behind him made him turn quickly.

'Who's there?' he called, his heart beating fast. However, nothing but the wind whispering through the trees responded. To his left, he could just make out the crumbled needle of the church on the hill in the distance and, to his right, nothing but thick creeping plants with a thin path that, at some time, had been a roadway through the darkness. Bright purple flowers filled with sunshine-yellow pollen curled around the trees and chunky soft insects buzzed around them, stopping to rest on the petals.

A crack of twigs in the bushes startled him.

'Hello?' he said nervously. 'Who is it?' The almost-silence magnified every sound and, while Carter dismissed it as paranoia, he got the distinct uneasy feeling he was being followed and quickened his pace. Patches of clear ground remained where the last vestiges of man-made resistance fought against the forest, but the road was cracked around the edges and scattered with rotten fruit from the trees, leaving a deep musky scent in the air. As he neared the entrance to the wood, Carter passed underneath an archway choked with ivy and creepers that tangled their branches around a sign. From the other side he could just about make out the name:

SIMMONS STREET PLAYGROUND: KIDZ ONLY!

Through the archway and into the scrubland, the outlines of metal structures glinted in the distance and a trail of leaves swirled around through the air. There was something familiar in the dampness and the smell of the leaves that made his heart beat faster and he looked upwards at the clouds gathering above him. It was about to rain. And it was going to be heavy. That was the last thing he needed.

Suddenly, a small object spun past his head, missing him by millimetres. He threw himself to the ground.

'What the hell…?' He started as a flash of colour bled out through the patchwork of trees and disappeared again. He felt a shiver of fear, snapping his head back and forth at the movements either side of him.

'Hello,' he called. 'Is there someone there? Show yourself!'

Another snap of a twig and he swore he heard a cough. He focused his gaze on a leafy bush to his left. Another cough.

'Hello?' He felt his blood run cold as he became increasingly aware of a presence near him. 'Hello?'

The last thing he heard before the soft drops of rain started to patter down was the crack of a wooden bat against the side of his head and the distant echo of a strange voice that came from behind him. It sounded just like the voice of the assistant in the Catacombs that had pushed the thin sliver of anaesthetic into his veins before he'd been sent to sleep.

'That's it, he's gone,' it said, and the light of the afternoon faded to a muggy shade of black as the dark rain started to fall.

Chapter One

The Preparation

Alice

The dreams had woken her early, as they often did. And, in the last few weeks, they had been more frequent than ever.

They were lucid, terrifying dreams of Prospect House, of stabbing Hutchinson as he had climbed on top of her and of finding Richard Warren, the boy she and Filip had discovered in their first voyage above ground when the Storms subsided. She thought of Richard often – the one person she had met who had survived outside of the sterile, perfect underground world created by the Industry. She often wondered what the world had been like then, after she had left it, and what Richard could tell her about what had happened to all the other people – and whether there were more like him. When she tried to ask him in her dreams, he was blood-drenched and incoherent, speaking words she didn't understand. These were the dreams where the faces of everyone she knew melded into one – dreams that left her heart racing and her skin clammy.

The sun filtered through the skylight, empty of glass, and cast thin white shadows on Alice as she lay next to her co-leader, and partner, on the mattress in the attic of the building on Morristown Row that they now called home. It had been just over two months – but it seemed like forever since they had been back in the world and away from the order of the underground.

As the brightness of the new day pulled her from her slumber, Alice looked over at Filip, lying on his back, his mouth firmly fixed in a determined line. He looked as intriguing and striking as he always had, but in the days since they had left the Ship, something between them felt different. The softness with which he had once spoken to her had hardened, and the semi-romantic dreams she'd had of a family, a garden and a home of her own had all but evaporated in a functional mist of the day-to-day hard work of building the new Community. There was still something inside of her that felt the teenage pangs of desire when he held her hand tightly but there was something that she couldn't place that made her feel less of a whole person now that she was a part of someone else. Somehow, less equal.

'We need to get up,' she whispered gently, pushing away the thoughts of doubt. 'Today's a new day.'

Filip rolled over and threw one arm across Alice's chest, pulling her into him. His physical strength made her feel so secure and yet there was something about the way he held her that made her feel owned, possessed even. She shook herself free, confused by the mixture of emotions she felt.

'Five more minutes,' he mumbled. 'Just five more. I was awake until four a.m. working on the constitution updates for today.'

'You can sleep when you're frozen,' said Alice with a half-smile. 'Come on, we need to go. People are already up and about.'

Outside in the street, the morning was crisp and Alice blinked in the light. A few of the other new residents had started to gather in the centre of the town, most at work carrying things from one side of the central square to another. The most recent arrivals who'd come from underground just a day or so before stood out clearly with their freshly laundered workwear and almost bewildered fascination with the world outside. Alice always found it reassuring to see the original Scouts amongst them – Jayden or one of the First Generation of pioneers, helping the new arrivals understand their new life and how the Community would function.

She spotted Kelly Simons and Quinn Fordham across the square, Quinn's arm resting on the smaller girl, who had her arms full of papers. At fourteen and fifteen respectively, they were two of the youngest of the Scouts – but had proven themselves as two of the bravest when they'd had to retrieve the body of Jonah from the other side of the Black River. Quinn waved to Alice, and then whispered something to Kelly. She kissed her cheek and disappeared into one of the houses.

Alice waved back and beckoned Kelly over towards her. As she moved out of the shadows of an old building, Alice could see her skinny arms were heavy with partly water-damaged photographs of a long-gone life.

'What have you got there?' asked Alice.

Kelly carefully placed the piles in the dust and brushed the hair out of her eyes. Alice could see she had been crying.

'Nothing really,' said Kelly. 'Just some old pictures. Holiday snaps and stuff – it's really sad that all these people are gone. Quinn told me to take them to the burn pile. This one here looks like it might have been taken in Spain.' She paused and fingered a blotchy picture of white sand and a faded azure sea. 'Did you ever go to Spain?'

Alice shook her head. 'No,' she said slowly. 'I never actually left England. We were…' She hesitated for a second. 'We didn't have a lot of money and my mother was always working – so we mostly took day trips around the city during the holidays.'

'I want to go to Spain,' said Kelly, staring out towards the old city. 'Especially if it still looks like these pictures. There was so much of the world I wanted to see.'

Alice opened her mouth in response but, as she did so, another group of people appeared across the square. Kunstein easily stood out amongst them, her long black robes wrapped around her.

'Alice,' she said, striding towards her. 'I assume you're ready for today and your speeches are all prepared. Now, there's someone here I would like you to meet properly; I don't believe you've had the pleasure, formally.'

Alice guarded her eyes from the sun as Kunstein beckoned over a short young woman in bright white laboratory coat. A clutch of sample bottles bulged from both her lower pockets and a stethoscope hung around her neck. The woman thrust out her hand to be shaken.

'Doctor Barnes,' she said. 'And you must be Alice.' Her voice held the slight trace of a Russian accent; her words clipped carefully short and like a well-manicured hedge. She was serious-looking with thin-rimmed glasses. Her coat was filthy – but everything else about her was perfectly in place. Every single hair immaculately groomed.

Alice pushed back her own fringe. 'Pleased to meet you,' she said with a smile. 'I believe you've been doing some teaching with the children? Thank you for your help.'

The doctor nodded then flashed a large smile, pulling her lips tightly together a little too early.

'It's a very small part of my work,' she said. 'That and researching new viruses at present, managing our repopulation efforts and so forth. I know we have an appointment scheduled to discuss that soon, don't we?'

'When I'm ready,' said Alice, 'which I am not yet. I will let you know when.'

'Of course, running things above ground – very, very busy work. Now, are you ready for today? It's very important to get this absolutely right.'

Alice nodded. 'Of course,' she said the sun glaring into her eyes. 'But…'

'We can't have any doubts or nerves,' said Barnes, quickly. 'If we have any, they'll feel it.'

Alice bristled. 'Absolutely none,' she said. 'Everything's under control.'

'Barnes is also going to be responsible for integration topside,' interjected Kunstein. 'People are going to find things very strange at first, until they get used to our new ways of living.'

'They are,' Barnes agreed, nodding and rubbing the side of her glasses. 'And I don't want my new hospital filled up with anxiety cases and idiots who think they can find long-lost members of their family out there.'

Alice swallowed deeply. 'Jonah was a mistake,' she said, pinpricks of sunshine from between her fingers making her eyes water a little. She cleared her throat. 'Anyway, we have this all under control, right Kunstein?'

'Of course you do.' Barnes smiled and tapped Alice's shoulder. 'I'll be seeing you very soon, Alice,' she said, 'now I'm up here much more often…'

She nodded a goodbye at Kunstein and Alice watched her march across the square.

'Who appointed *her*?' said Alice, irritated. 'I thought Filip and I were in charge of recruitment?'

'You are,' said Kunstein. 'But she's proved herself to be invaluable in the labs and fantastic with conditioning the younger children and preparing them for life above ground. Wilson and I believe you're going to need some help with the detail – there's going to be a huge amount to do and you can't do it alone.'

A gentle trickle of people emerging from the Industry building had started to gather in the square. Alice looked from face to confused face gazing towards the small plinth that had been erected in the centre.

'I know,' she said, biting her lip in annoyance. 'But why does it have to be Barnes? I already find her a little controlling and I'd like to be involved in decisions about the structure.'

Kunstein smiled. 'Yes,' she said in a comforting voice, but one that held a certain bite to it. 'But remember, you are an Original Scout and you have very important work to do helping to repopulate the Community. Your children will be direct Descendants and will be the next leaders of our Community. Barnes has developed a very comprehensive strategy – and it involves you, Alice. We need to rebuild, just like you and Filip planned.'

'That doesn't mean I don't get a say in how and when it happens,' said Alice defiantly. 'You trusted me to lead people up here, so trust me in the decision making. As one of the Original Scouts, I deserve that.'

They both fell silent for a moment. Through an upstairs window came the sound of movement, the shifting of furniture and then the intermittent whoop as they began work clearing the next set of homes for habitation. The clank of metal and a rise of dust filled the air. Alice knew she needed to determine what had happened to the boy she had found in the flat that had once belonged to her and her mother.

'How's Richard?' she asked, turning to Kunstein again.

Kunstein narrowed her eyes a little. 'He's almost recovered – at least physically. He's still in the infirmary, in isolation for the time being. Barnes is taking care of him – she's one of our best. She'll be working closely with Quinn to determine who will fit best up here with us. She has some excellent selection criteria and...'

Alice frowned. 'I don't understand why Barnes is making all these decisions. Richard belongs here...'

'We've taken him through some of the initial rehabilitation steps and he's made some progress but... you took a risk with him. A big risk. Bringing a Storm survivor into our Community was a gamble – he hasn't been through the same process that we all have. There's no telling how he's going to react when he comes back up top. Or what infections he could have brought. We're going to have to keep him down there for longer – you know that, don't you?'

Alice held Kunstein's glance. 'Yes,' she said. 'But I'd like to speak to him. I have some questions about the outside that need to be answered. I brought him in and I need to see him.'

'Not at the moment. Barnes is dealing with him and that's actually a decision for her and Wilson. As the outgoing Controller General, he has to sanction anything that happens below ground until we finalise our new management structure. He's going to stay down there with some of the others to take care of things. Going forwards, Barnes will be your main link between the Ship and up here, rather than Wilson.' Kunstein let out a curt laugh. 'Wilson's not interested in coming back up here. He says there's nothing up here for him any more. This world does not appeal to him.'

Alice shrugged. 'The world from the Ship probably makes sense to him – sometimes it does to me. Things have felt—' she paused for a second '—well, different up here in the last month or so.'

Kunstein nodded. 'It's a perfect world underground,' she said. 'Everyone and everything is equal. You know you're going to have a job to maintain that up here. Some of the rules are going to be unpopular.'

'I understand that,' said Alice, wanting to change the subject. 'So, when will Richard be back up here?'

'Richard survived five years outside in the world while the Storms tore everything apart. He's either going to be a great asset to us or an absolute liability. His mental state could be... well... precarious. We'll be monitoring him carefully.'

'I still want to see him.'

'All in good time. And, when he's needed to come back up here will, of course, depend on Quinn's model, and Barnes's assessments. The work they've done alongside some of the other Industry technicians is quite, quite impressive.'

'I've seen it.'

Alice had sat for hours as Quinn had explained everything with exceptional enthusiasm, pointing at the screen with graphs and charts, outlining the population of the Community as it stood and the projections for years to come. Her eyes had looked tired and her skin pale from the long days and nights she'd spent back underground.

'We have people frozen down here,' she'd said to Alice. 'We're pioneering it now but they can remain in stasis without any physical or mental development for ten, maybe twenty years. As long as they're frozen while they're still alive, nothing changes for them. We can ensure we have the right number of people above ground at the right time; we can feed them all, clothe them all...' Her voice had trailed off and Alice had smiled.

'And this... computer programme will tell you all of this?'

Quinn had nodded.

'We know how many males, females, children, ages, skills based on their genetic profiles, everything we need to make this work. We know when we need to bring them up from underground and how we can disperse people to ensure stability. And—' her voice turned to a dark whisper '—if anything like the Storms were to happen again, there would never be a risk of losing everything if we maintain our underground and overground populations.'

Alice shivered.

'And you're sure this will work? You really believe that this will be the best way to start again?'

'Without a doubt,' said Quinn. 'I've run everything past Barnes and she's agreed. We have one chance to redesign and this is it. The groundwork has been done. Now all we need to do is to let people know about it.'

As morning turned to afternoon on that first official day of the new Community, the crowds gathered in Unity Square, jostling towards the front, some staring open-eyed at the white ball of sun that hung high in the sky.

Alice and Filip spoke first, both calm, eloquent and relaxed as they talked first about the creation of the Community and then about the dangers of the Deadlands. Across the crowd there were questions, laughter, tears and, above all, a sense of overwhelming commitment to be a part of their new world. Kunstein stood at the back, nodding slowly as Alice spoke, her eyes glittering in the sunlight.

'What we have here is a new beginning,' said Alice. 'Something we could never have dreamed of in the old world. This is a world where hope does not exist. It is a world where we already have what we could never have hoped for. Whatever went before is now gone. What we create here is what we want for ourselves and our new lives.' She paused. 'We are the Community.'

When the clattering of cheers and applause had stopped, Quinn took Alice's place on the small, hand-carved podium in the centre of Unity Square. Her eyes were glistening in the sunlight as she held one hand high in the air to calm the crowd.

'Thank you all,' she said in her voice, as cool and soft as vanilla, and immediately the throng moved closer. Kelly sat on the edge of the podium punching numbers into a tablet. She passed it to Quinn who motioned for the crowd to sit. Alice edged onto the side of the raised platform next to Filip and Kelly and waited until Quinn was ready to speak. Barnes stood behind them, her coat flapping in the breeze.

'As most of you know,' said Quinn, 'I've – we've – been working hard over the last few months to bring you a solution to the problem that our communities have faced many times across the years. And we now have that solution.'

The crowd cheered as Quinn stood, cheeks flaming with pride, in front of the group explaining the Model and how it worked. The freezing, the thawing, the waiting.

'It doesn't mean that you definitely won't see those members of your friends and family groups who are not here today again. You may do, and they will become an important part of our future generations.

A woman with lank blonde hair stood up, her voice faltering. 'My children are down there,' she said slowly. 'When are they coming back here?' She started to sob quietly. 'It's only been a day and I miss them so much.'

Quinn moved forwards and addressed the woman directly. 'Marnie – it is Marnie, isn't it?'

The woman nodded.

'Marnie, as we talked about before, the families that formed on the Ship were temporary. They were always going to be temporary. We all thank you so much for your kindness and work to take care of them but now, we may need to form new families – new groups to make our new Community work.'

There were some cheers from the crowd but the woman, Marnie, began to protest.

'You can't give them to me and then take them away... they're mine. They're MINE.' Her voice was raised to a shout and Alice felt a chill whisper across the back of her neck. As Quinn began to speak again the woman started to wail.

'I want my children!'

Barnes swept from behind the group and down into the crowd. Within seconds, she was next to Marnie and whispered in her ear. Alice watched as the woman nodded and the two of them left the square and disappeared into the main Industry building. Before she could speak, she realised that Quinn was already re-engaging the crowds.

'We know there will be some who find this difficult, but we have the opportunity today to create something amazing, something incredible that our civilisations have never seen before: something beyond our wildest dreams. Those who are chosen to stay within the Ship for the time that is right for them will be doing the greatest service to all of us that we could ever imagine.'

A shout came up from the crowd. 'Will they suffer? Is it painful?'

Quinn smiled. 'Not at all – it's just like going to sleep and waking up again twenty years later when we'll have all the facilities to be able to support the type of community we want to be.'

Alice looked across the square as huddles of people began to whisper to each other. In amongst them was Barnes, her eyes flitting from one group to the next. Alice scanned the faces for Marnie, but she was nowhere to be seen. One man stood out from the others, his arms folded.

'Sounds like a good deal for those still down there. Coming back into a world that's all hooked up again, rather than this junkyard. Can I volunteer to go back down there?'

Quinn addressed him directly. 'No,' she said firmly. 'You're here because we need your particular skills now. But the way we live our lives may no longer be linear. In years to come, we could be younger than our children or older than our grandparents. We could experience two, maybe three different generations even. We will do what we need to do to ensure that what we create is sustainable and works for every single one of us and all of us at once. And your job now is to make that happen. In the future, you may be able to choose to return to the Ship.'

'But why do *you* get to choose?' The man stood firm, his hands now on his hips.

There was an ever-so-subtle nod of Quinn's head and Barnes was at the man's side immediately, whispering in his ear.

Quinn smiled. 'We want a Community that works for everyone,' she said. 'And we'll do the best to ensure that we *all* get to choose what we want.'

The man raised his eyebrows and then addressed Quinn directly. 'I see,' he said quietly and gestured to the crowd. 'It seems that we have an answer to everything here,' he said, this time more loudly, and gestured again to the crowd, encouraging mass applause. The cheers were deafening as Quinn thanked the crowd and bowed to an excited bout of whooping and screeching. The man melted back quietly and stood, arms still folded, watching Alice intently.

As she took the stage again and began to speak, a stillness descended over the crowd.

'There's so much we want to achieve here and there's still so much that can go wrong,' she said. 'But for those of us who are old enough to remember and young enough to understand, we can learn from that past. What has been done is now done. We are complete with that. That time is over and we have carved our place in a new history to reinvent what it is to be human.

'We will grow and we will develop but we will never go back to what we were or try to recreate that world in any way. Today is just the start of what we can achieve together.'

A roar rose from the crowd and hands were interlinked and palms touched in alliance. Alice took a deep breath before she finished.

'This is not the first stop on our journey or the last stop on our journey. This is where the old road ends and another one begins – not just for us but for the whole of humankind.'

She paused.

'You are the First Generation,' she said. 'And this is just the start of things.'

As the crowds melted back to their clearance work, Kunstein approached Alice and put one hand on her shoulder.

'Beautiful,' she said. 'Utterly captivating.'

Alice turned to her. 'What happened to that woman, Marnie?'

Kunstein took her arm away. 'What do you mean?'

'Well, Barnes took her away and she never came back. Where is she?'

Kunstein smiled. 'She's fine, just a little upset – Barnes took her down to the infirmary to see her children.'

'Will she be coming back?'

'She'll be back when she's ready, Alice. You know just as well as I do that we can't take any risks up here.'

Alice felt a growing concern. 'And what did Barnes say to that man? Did she threaten him?'

'Those who have been in the Ship will have a lot of reservations,' said Kunstein. 'They haven't seen what you have seen. They need to be guided – this new world will require a new way of thinking and we have to remind people of that.'

Alice nodded slowly, but couldn't help but feel unsatisfied with her answer.

Filip, who was directing a group of people clearing out the last few houses on Morristown Row, called to Quinn and she sped off to join him. They carried armfuls of toys, books and other junk and were hoisting them into the disposal containers. A young girl sat perched at the edges of the street shooting at rats with a pellet gun while a boy trudged around gathering up the carcasses in a large brown sack, his head hanging low.

'Pretty good aim for a kid,' said Alice, distracted by the pop-pop of the pellets.

'Well-trained,' said Kunstein. 'School has taken on a very different meaning in the Ship, as you well know.'

Alice thought back to her first few days at comprehensive school and the mindless history lessons and home economics classes she'd taken that meant nothing to her any more. Learning to build a shelter or start a fire with just some tinder and a couple of sticks would have been more useful than memorising the kings and queens of England. And yet, somehow, she still remembered some of them. Useless knowledge that stuck lodged in the recesses of her brain, to resurface one day when it meant nothing to anyone any more.

'We'll be bringing more people up in a few weeks,' said Kunstein, 'and then, apart from the odd individual that we'll need to fill the gaps, that will be the last batch.'

'Quinn has this all figured, doesn't she?' said Alice. 'I mean, the numbers are perfect, aren't they?'

'As right as they can be,' said Kunstein, twisting her robes. 'Obviously there's a need to start building the population up from here and, on the projections we have to date, taking into account the impact of any genetic malfunctioning due to Drakewater, Quinn believes we have the right mix of stored bodies underground and people up top. But there weren't as many births during the five years in the Ship as we'd have liked so we'll need to make sure that we start the new generation strongly. I myself won't be able to participate in that kind of activity, of course, but you know, Alice, you are going to have to start preparing yourself for your role in this – we have agreed to start the process from next week.'

Alice nodded slowly and watched as the piles of the old world grew higher in the disposal bins. She remembered the pact she and the others had made in the desperate confines of the underground bunker they'd grown to know as the Ship. In the days after they had come back above ground, they had resolved to destroy everything that reminded them of the life before. That had been only a few months ago.

'We are the future,' she had said to her team. 'And it is our responsibility to take the next generation back out there into the world.' She'd looked straight ahead at the team, bravely. 'While we may be young, we have everything we need to make this a success.'

Quinn, Filip and Jayden had nodded seriously.

'What does that mean?' Kelly had called out. 'Does that mean we have to have babies?'

'Yes,' Filip had interjected. 'But we won't be doing it the traditional way, of course.' Kelly had looked relieved and smiled back at him.

'While we have abandoned the old-world traditions, we should respect the fact that the age of consent has not yet been determined. And as a result, anyone under the age of sixteen who will be required to produce children will be not be *expected* to have physical relations with their partner until they reach the appropriate age.'

'So how *will* it happen?'

Filip smiled at Jayden. 'We will each choose a partner for this process and allow our medical professionals to guide us through the artificial process. Work is already underway to source the medical supplies required for that and the doctor will speak to each couple to determine when we commence.' He'd smiled again. 'It may sound a bit clinical but we're suggesting we do it this way to ensure maximum success and also the maximum respect for our younger Scouts.'

Grenfell had nodded wisely. 'That sounds very fair,' he'd said. 'I agree that's the right approach.'

Alice had smiled. 'So, when the time is right, we'll all be called upon to participate. You'll need to select the person with whom you'll participate in this programme.' She'd glanced across at Filip who'd stood officious and bold, his jaw strengthened and determined. He'd winked at Alice, his crooked smile making her heart melt.

But, now, back in the bright light of real sunshine, she wondered if all of what they had discussed had been agreed with the best of intentions. A family – a real family – had been what she'd always wanted. And Filip, she was sure, was a good person.

'Next week, Alice,' repeated Kunstein.

Alice took a deep breath. 'Next week?' she said. 'I know we talked about it, but so soon? I'm not even sure I'm parent material.' She paused for a second. 'At least, not yet. I've got a Community to build.' She smiled. 'And what if I don't want to?'

As the words left her mouth she was acutely aware, for the first time in years, of how child-like she sounded. She felt angry, and in some ways conflicted. It had been what she had agreed but now, when it was all becoming real, she felt something almost similar to the violation she'd experienced with Hutchinson. She shivered as she remembered the way the old army captain had ordered her around when everyone had disappeared. How he made her believe that her very being belonged to him and how he'd climbed on top of her, his heavy stinking body, pushing against her. An internal claustrophobia overwhelmed her. Some of the decisions made in the Ship seemed almost banal now that they were above ground. All the years of wishing she could grow up and be an adult flashed past her in an instant. Her face flushed red as Kunstein smiled awkwardly, her arm back around Alice's shoulders.

'It's not about what we want, Alice, remember. It's about what we need. You and Filip will make fantastic parents – you've both been tested so you know it's possible. Kelly has already started treatment – she and Quinn have agreed to raise the child together with a donation kindly provided by Grenfell. And like I said, Barnes has already booked in appointments for the next week.'

'Kelly?' Alice thought of the serious, shy girl who doted on Quinn. The gentle optimist who still clung to dreams of Spanish sunsets and butterflies. 'Do you think she's ready right now?' she added.

Kunstein nodded and looked out across the river. 'We all have to be ready for whatever challenges the new world sends us. It's an exciting time, Alice, very exciting indeed. Although I have my concerns – our team has some weaker members. We don't want another Jonah incident, do we?'

Alice felt a shard of guilt pierce her heart as his name hung in the air between her and Kunstein. Jonah, the boy with whom she had shared that first delicate, childlike love. The boy she had known would not have been able to survive in the outside world. A deep ache welled inside of her as she remembered how she'd agreed – no demanded – that Jonah become part of the initial team that she'd led out into the Deadlands. He had been a test – a test of how those who had been afraid underground would react to the outside world. And, as expected, he had failed. She had almost felt the bullet of Filip's gun herself as it had pierced her friend.

'No,' she said. 'Jonah was a mistake. I…'

'You're not to blame,' said Kunstein, interrupting her. 'But we need to be sure that everyone is focused on creating the future. Our new future. Otherwise all of this—' she spread her cloak wide '—will fall apart. Clear leadership is what we need now, Alice.'

Her words tailed off as the sound of jubilation rang through the square.

'We will all have to make sacrifices,' Kunstein continued. 'For the good of the new Community there will be things we all have to do to make this work. And as a leadership team, we all need to be aligned on this. It's what we agreed before we came back up here. It's how we will survive. You want this world to be different, don't you? And really, you should be one of the first. *Setting a good example.* It's not a suggestion, Alice, it's your duty. Lead by example. Remember, these were your ideas.' She smiled. 'I'm sure Barnes will be delivering your treatment pack in the next few days and then you can get started!'

'I know,' Alice said, then kicked her feet in the dirt. 'I know.'

Something stuck tight in her throat as she thought about the promises she had made underground and what would have to happen next. She rubbed her stomach softly and felt anxiety wash over her as she watched Kunstein walk away into the brightness of the sun.

Chapter Two

The Others

Carter

'Who are you?'

When the cloying smell of wet soil and the bellowing voice in his head woke him, Carter was sure that he was back in the Catacombs. But he wasn't. This was different. The events of the last few days – losing Isabella, being sent to storage to being awoken, fleeing from the Community, the betrayal by Lily, the realisation that he was not alone and finally, the hailstorm – all swirled around inside his head. They repeated themselves and then went in reverse. He hoped he was dreaming as eyes closed again.

When he awoke for the second time, there was a clump of heavy footsteps, then the rush of ice-cold water in his face. Drips slid down his cheeks like tears and he caught some between his lips, licking enough to keep his thirst away. All the time he kept his eyes tightly screwed shut. As he tried to move his arms and legs he realised three of his four limbs were secured fast to whatever it was he had been sleeping on. Panic set in.

'Who are you?'

The voice that spoke to him was loud and very close. Breath like stale carrotina forced its way into his face. Carter coughed.

'Are you the Others?' he asked. 'Where am I? What's going on?'

'We ask the questions,' growled a voice.

His head pounded. He opened one eye briefly and saw two people standing over him. One, a woman, had long hair tied back and grimy dirt smudged across her forehead. As she scanned him intently, Carter realised there was something in her face that was different and misshapen. The other, a man about his own age or maybe a few years older, had an ugly scar running the length of his cheek.

She spoke more softly than the man but her voice was still loud in his ears. 'Where's the woman you were travelling with?' she said. 'What happened to her?'

'Did you make that flashing light? Where am I?' Carter tried to focus his eyes – his throat felt gritty and sore. In the background, somewhere, there was the sound of light rain.

He forced his other eye open. It was encrusted with blood and it hurt when he pulled back the lashes. When he did, he could see the girl properly. Her hair, blonde and braided back, framed the openness of her face, her left eye a blank, cloudy grey, empty of colour or features. The other, deep blue and sharp, caught him looking at her. He pulled at the straps that held down both legs and his left arm.

'It's him,' said the girl quietly to her companion who held Carter's bag between his legs and rifled through the contents. 'I'm sure of it.'

'Then it's true.' The man cut a short, squat figure with a thin brush of wispy hair above his upper lip. The deep violet scar that ran from one side of his cheek to the other seemed to move like an extra, angry mouth.

'Now what happens?' The woman shook her head. 'They're going to be looking for him.'

The man grunted and kicked the side of the rester that Carter lay on. 'And how exactly did he get out? They don't let anyone out voluntarily. It could be a trap.'

'Possibly,' said the woman, eyeing him intently. 'But he would be the first to get out in, what, twenty years? More?' She put two fingers on the side of Carter's cheek and turned his head slightly to one side. Her one bright-blue eye scanned behind his ear while the other eye sat motionless like frosted glass, the paleness of the inside glowing dully like a clouded moon. Carter had never seen anyone who looked like her.

'He's chipped,' said the woman. 'We'll need to get it out. He doesn't have his card on him, which is a start. We can't travel far if—'

'We must do it before we leave,' said the man. 'But we haven't agreed we're going to take him with us yet.'

'How can you say that? It *is* him, isn't it?'

'Only one way to find out.'

The girl looked thoughtful and pulled her ponytail tightly as she faced Carter. 'Now. Tell us your name and how you got here?'

Carter hesitated and tried to sit up again. This time he succeeded in moving his body free a little and leaned upwards on the pillows behind him. 'My name is Carter Warren,' he said. 'I'm from the Community.'

There was a silence while the two beside him looked at each other.

'Told you,' said the woman.

'You have to let me go,' Carter added desperately. 'I can help you. I can tell you things. There are other people, a whole Community of them.'

Both of them laughed and Carter felt a crimson rush hit his cheeks. His throat was parched and his head hurt.

'He looks just like the picture,' said the woman to the man who nodded at her with a smirk.

'What happened to the woman you were travelling with?' he asked.

'What picture?' said Carter. 'Let me go and tell me where I am first.'

The woman handed Carter a glass half filled with water. He assumed that the other half had been what she'd thrown at him to wake him up. She gestured to him to drink and, as he did, the groaning of hunger began in his stomach again.

'Your head is going to be a little sore for a while,' she said. 'You'll need to rest for a while before we get moving.'

'You're not taking me anywhere.' As angry as he was, Carter couldn't help feeling sorry for the woman and her disfigured face. His pity did not, however, extend to the man that reeked of filth, making him want to retch. He rattled the arm that was still bound in the strap. 'Tell me where I am.'

'Right now, you're in Outpost Three.' The woman carefully decanted a liquid substance from the candle and the flame spat and flickered.

'I'm still in the Deadlands?'

The woman cleared her throat and the man grinned slyly, crooked brown teeth showing in both corners of his mouth. 'Ain't nothing dead about out here,' he said and the woman nodded.

'Samuel's right, Carter Warren. Inside your Community you may have called this the Deadlands but while you're out here, that world and all it has to offer is, well, defunct. We call this area something different. And yes, you're still there.'

The man – Samuel – pulled the map from Carter's rucksack and handed it to the woman.

'So, you're the Others?'

'Ah, someone found our sign,' said the man, and again they both laughed. He held up the map. 'This is the world, Carter Warren,' he said handing it to the woman. 'The whole of the old world. Did you really think this might help you to find your way around out here?' He laughed; a throaty mean chortle. His face was lined and drawn, and his mouth had a cruel sharpness. Where there were teeth, many had chips and a few were a dark yellowing colour. The woman put an arm on his shoulder and, for a moment, his eyes softened.

'Samuel,' she said in a calm tone. 'Go a bit easier on him. He has absolutely no idea what's going on.'

'What *is* going on?' said Carter. 'And who are you? Why am I attached to this rester?' An arc of white light trickled through the door at the other end of the room and Carter could just distinguish the outline of a huddle of trees scraping the skyline.

'My name is Angel Stanton,' said the woman. 'And you were staring at my face.' She ran her fingers across the lid of her moon-eye. 'I was born like this,' she said. 'But I was not born here. I was brought to the Village because here our individual differences are celebrated and we are not cast out or eliminated because of what you may see as a defect. Normal is not just what you think it is. How you live in the Community is not normal.'

Carter tilted his head, puzzled. 'Were you born near Drakewater, is that why your eye...?'

'No,' said Angel vehemently. 'What happened to me has nothing to do with Drakewater.'

'Then what...?'

Samuel pulled off a thick leather boot that stank deep of years of wear. He thrust his foot up onto the rester. All six toes were loosely joined together by leaf-thin white webbing. Through the skin mesh of the splayed open toes, Carter could make out the other side of the room. It was disgusting and unsettling. The room was silent, except for the regular pattering of hail on metal somewhere in the distance.

'That's vile,' he said with revulsion on his face.

'It's just different,' said Angel and smiled briefly, turning to look at Samuel. 'And different doesn't always mean bad. You're going to have to get used to that.' For a second, Carter thought that he saw her dull, lifeless eye glow into life but when her face was level with his again, it was blank.

'Tell me,' he said. 'What did that to you?'

'We don't have much time,' said Samuel. 'We need to make a choice whether to take you with us or leave you for the wolves. Tell us where the woman is and we might be able to help you.'

Carter sipped on the glass of water. 'You tell me what happened. You seem to know everything.'

The volume of the pelting rain above increased and the shape of Angel disappeared. There was the sound of feet on stairs and then a sharp slam. When she returned the fringe of her hair was damp and there were tiny rivulets of rain running down her neck. They cut vein-like lines through the grubby dirt.

'Storm,' she said. 'It's going to be a severe one today, worst one this season so far. You're lucky we found you when we did.'

'I'd have found somewhere,' said Carter. 'I'm used to the rain and I can make shelters. In the Community…'

'Yes, in the Community you have your electronic weather warning indicators,' said Samuel. 'They tell you when there's going to be a red storm or a blue storm so that you can get to safe haven. We don't have that here, there's something better we've developed to manage our meteorological assessments. It's called intuition. Clueless, that's what you are.'

'What would someone like you know about the Community?' said Carter, feeling a sudden rise of defence. 'It's wild out here – what with the creatures and the pollution. At least in there it's civilised, they don't treat you like animals.'

'Civilised?' Samuel snorted and rolled his eyes. 'Your idea of civilisation is to lie to your people and murder anyone who gets in your way. You don't even know the meaning of the word civilised.'

Carter felt a surge of anger at his dismissal and pulled his arm hard from the strap. With both hands free he quickly released his legs and expelled himself from the rester onto the man next to him. He pinned Samuel to the floor.

'You think I'm clueless now?' he breathed at Samuel, looking him deep in the eyes. 'You have no idea what I've been through to get here. Tell me what's going on and who you are.' As he looked at Samuel there was a glint in his eyes that scared Carter, and as hard as he tried not to show it, he felt the man's eyes boring into him.

'This one's dangerous, Angel – you should have secured him properly,' said Samuel, struggling underneath Carter. He was strong, muscular and skin-weathered from spending much of his life out of doors, but as Carter looked into his face there was something familiar about him: something disarming. Without meaning to, Carter eased up and Samuel slid from under him and backed away towards the other side of the room.

'He'd better be worth it after all this,' he said, dusting himself down. 'Every second we keep him here, we're risking everything.'

'*I'm* not asking you to keep me here,' said Carter. 'I won't be a risk to you if you just let me out of here. So just do that and I can find the Others.'

Angel put her hand gently on his shoulder. 'Carter, friend, it's not that easy. You're weak and injured – and Samuel won't hurt you. We've got a long way to travel today, as soon as the rain stops and there's something we need to tell you. But you need to promise to stay calm.'

As they sat around the table, Angel handed Carter a cup of something hot that smelled like sweet grass and leaves.

'Drink,' she said. 'It will make you feel better.'

Carter sniffed the rim of the heavy brown cup. 'What is it?'

'It's herbal tea. I made it myself and it will make you feel better, give you some strength.' She paused. 'But Carter, there are many things outside here that you won't know or understand. You have to trust that we will help you through this and then you can choose whether to believe us or not.'

He sipped at the tea. 'Why should I believe you?'

Samuel grunted from the other side of the room. 'Well, you trusted the Industry and look what happened there. You people in that Community are just like sheep.'

Carter creased his forehead and looked at Angel. 'What is he talking about? Is he always this stupid? Why would people be like an animal that doesn't even exist any more?'

Angel laughed. 'We forget that you in the Community forgot the old ways of speaking.' She poured herself some of the thin, dark liquid and sat down next to Carter. 'I know this must be very difficult, but I need you to tell us exactly what happened and then we can help you. And before you do that, there's something you need to know. Carter, you were a Contender for the position of what they call Controller General, correct?'

Carter nodded. 'I guess that doesn't mean much out here, does it?' he said.

'Actually, it does,' said Angel. 'It puts you – and us – in serious danger. Take this off.' She pulled at his sleeve and lifted his jumper over his head. The cut on his shoulder from the scissors that Lily had thrown at him was still weeping a little blood, traces of sticky red tapered down his arm.

'How did this happen?' Angel asked, dabbing at it with a cloth.

'The woman I was with, Lily, tried to stab me with a pair of cutters.'

Samuel made a low whistling sound. 'She's good,' he said. 'Better than we thought.'

'She's not good. She's a murderer.'

Angel put her one eye close to the wound and looked deeply. 'She almost managed to disable it too,' she said. 'This will take less than a second.' She whipped a needle from behind her back and dug it into the cut, pulling it back sharply. Carter screamed but before he could move, she pulled a thin thread of black out of the wound, and immediately burned it above a flame.

'Tracking line,' she said. 'It doesn't last forever but if it's still functional, the Industry will know exactly where you are – and that you are still alive. It looks like our friend Lily tried to help you out there.'

Carter grimaced. 'She was no friend of mine,' he said. 'She betrayed me, killed my daughter, tried to kill me and left me to die out here. Then she went back to the Community – she's a traitor.'

Samuel raised his eyebrows and looked over at Angel. 'Well, she has been busy, hasn't she?' he said. 'It's no wonder she's not even had time to send us a postcard.'

'You *know* her? How can you possibly know her – she's from the Community.'

'We don't have time to explain everything now, it's not safe to stay here,' said Angel, kindly. 'But you can rest assured that what you think you know about your Community might not all be true. She won't have killed your daughter.'

Carter shook his head. Lily – the woman he had, at first, trusted, the woman who had mentored him to become Controller General, who had then killed his daughter and cast him out into the Deadlands. He stopped for a second. For someone so accomplished, her attempts at attacking him *had* been pretty pathetic – and while he hadn't seen her kill Lucia, she *had* admitted it to him. He tried to work through all the implications.

'What about…' he started but Angel was already busying herself around him.

We need to move from here,' she said, 'now, just in case this thread has transmitted anything already.' She started to pack things into a small bag and pulled out a stretcher from behind one of the resters.

'Carter, your shoulder is going to start to burn from the line removal in a moment – the tea will help with the pain but soon your body will go into shock. It won't last long – less than twelve hours – but we're going to need to carry you the rest of the way.'

When Carter awoke for the third time that day it was only for a brief moment. There was a sweet smell of fresh grass as he gazed up at the forest canopy. The leaves were bigger here, he remembered. Large, red and yellow leaves patterned with intricate brown swirls that made his head ache. He longed to launch himself off the edge of the stretcher and run back to where he had come from, but the sharp pain in his shoulder stopped him moving any further – as he glanced across at it, he realised that it was bandaged tightly and blood was now seeping through. He needed a plan to get away from these people – when they next stopped to eat he could launch himself off the stretcher and out into the forest. He flexed his leg and thought through his strategy but in moments his eyes glazed again and his body gave way to a sleep that enveloped him.

It was dark again by the time they reached the Village in the depths of the forest on the hillside. Many of the homes were slung up into the trees, covered by something thick and dark that kept out the light of the stars. It afforded the Village a level of warmth that was different from the rest of the forest. As they made their way underneath the huge canopy, the pinpricks of light above them disappeared and a delicate heat radiated. Small outbuildings covered the forest floor – old and squat, built of bricks.

As they moved closer, Carter could make out figures – hundreds of them – gathered in a wide circle that opened up as he, Samuel and Angel approached. Their whispering unnerved him – like the shushing of soft rain on grass. The crowd stepped backwards as they came closer, the movement of shadows folding outwards into the wide clearing surrounded by flaming torches. As they set down the stretcher and helped him onto a bench at the edge of the clearing, Carter saw face after face step in to peer at him, then move away to let others in. There was a hum of conversation that lifted upwards into the air that stopped suddenly as Samuel began to speak.

'Move back,' he said. 'There's much to be discussed here, but it will not happen this evening.'

'Who is he?' someone shouted. 'Is it him?'

Then Carter heard: 'Someone bring her, bring her now.'

Samuel held his hands up to the crowd. 'There's no need,' he said. 'Tomorrow will be soon enough.'

'She should be told,' said Angel. 'She must be told. Someone bring her.'

Carter looked up at her face. There was something kind and honest that reminded him of Isabella, who he'd left back in the Community, the one person he should have protected. The Lab Made that had meant the world to him. He felt an ache in his arm under the bandage, an ache that resonated deep inside him and wound its way outwards. Part of him felt desperately sad for the simplicity and security of what he no longer had.

'I want to know where I am,' he said calm, yet despondent. 'I can tell you a lot about the Community – and the Industry. They're not what you think they are.'

'We know that,' said Samuel. 'We know exactly who they are. The question is – are *you* who you say you are. We need to be sure.'

In the light of the flames that surrounded the circle, a woman pushed her way to the front. The people parted immediately when they saw her coming. Carter could barely make out her features, except for the greying strands of white hair that covered her face, but he could tell by the hush of the crowd and the way that they moved that she was respected. Samuel took a step to the left and immediately the woman was almost astride Carter as she peered down at him, blocking out the light.

Aside from the flutter of night birds in the trees above, there was no sound at all. The crowd fell completely silent. Carter opened his mouth to speak but, before he could, came a voice that he had heard many times before, but in the last few years, that voice had only been inside his head. A voice that had sounded so sweet and melodic, but was now cold and emotionless. Before she had even finished her sentence, he felt himself falling into her words as they dropped downwards like leaves from a tree.

'That's him,' said the woman, nodding her head gravely. 'Yes. That's Carter Warren. That's my son.'

Chapter Three

The First Generation

Alice

Each night on her way back to the place she now called home, Alice stood for a while and watched as the pink dusk had gathered across the rooftops of the Community. It had been a week since the speeches in the square, and already the skyline was beginning to change. Some chimneys that had previously stood crumbling into the growing darkness had been torn down while others – satellite dishes still intact – looked almost untouched by the floodwater that had swept across the land.

As she approached the core of the Community, she saw Kunstein, surrounded by a bunch of younger children who ran and chased their way across the edge of Unity square. She frowned at the disruption then felt a jolt of irritation as a plastic football sailed across the square, brushing the edge of Kunstein's robes and grazing Alice's knee.

'Where the hell did they get that?' she said, pointing at the football and turning to Kunstein. 'I thought we'd got rid of everything.' Her eyes sparkled a dangerous black colour as she felt her anger compounding.

'They probably just found it,' said Kunstein. 'You've got to be prepared. Things like this are going to happen. This is what Barnes was talking about.' She smiled briefly as Filip strode over towards them. 'It's up to you both to be clear about that today. These next few months will be the most challenging you will ever have to face. You have to be firm. People will have to learn.'

'I think we both knew this wasn't going to be easy,' said Filip, but Alice was already walking over to where the children were playing.

'Give it to me,' she said, holding out here hand. 'Now.'

Immediately, but with some sad reluctance, one of the youngest looking of the group, around nine years old, kicked it in her direction. Alice picked it up and passed it from one hand to the other before pulling a knife from her pocket and slashing the plastic into pieces. Then, balling the pieces into one fist, she dunked them into one of the disposal carts that sat despondently at the edge of the square.

'It was only a ball,' said the boy and brushed long hair from his grubby face. Underneath the dirt, his skin was pale and he squinted up into the sun. 'I haven't played football since before.' He kicked his feet in the dirt. 'I'm real sorry, Alice.'

'It's not about the ball, Marcus,' said Filip, joining Alice. 'You know that.'

'I told you not to play with it,' said the girl next to Marcus. 'You're so stupid. Rules are rules.' She was a few years older, eleven or so with blonde hair cropped short, and she held her lips in a defiant pout.

'You know why,' said Alice, firmly. 'We made these procedures for a reason.'

There was a tense silence before Marcus looked down and reluctantly smudged out the makeshift goal line that had been chalked into the lines on the square. The others picked up two ragged jumpers, one humped on each corner while the girl watched. Just as Alice had done with the football, they rolled them up and threw them into the disposal cart. One miserable red arm of a jumper remained draped over the side. There was a further moment of silence as the children acknowledged Filip and held their hands in the air as a sign of apology. The boy, Marcus, swiped his palm along Filip's and looked at Alice.

The girl smiled a toothy grin.

'I did tell them,' she said defiantly. 'I told them the old ways were bad. They don't listen in conditioning classes like I do. Marcus is stupid anyway, he's just a baby.' She kicked her feet in the dirt.

'Just behave yourselves,' said Filip with an edge of danger in his voice. 'You both are only up here topside early because you're my siblings,' he said. 'Remember that, otherwise you'll go back down there with the rest of them. You're smart – the Industry will be able to use you in the future. Now say sorry.'

The children both looked at Alice silently.

'Say sorry,' repeated Filip, sternly.

'Sorry; said Marcus, his head hanging low.

'Yeah, sorry,' said the girl, distracted by movement in the opposite direction. 'Look there's Barnes! Hey Barnes!'

She looked up at the group and waved back. Alice nodded in response and turned back to the children.

'Come on, there's work to do at home,' she said to Marcus and Izzy, guiding them towards the house, but they turned towards Barnes and dragged her with them all the way home. Izzy ran towards Barnes and threw her arms around her waist. The woman patted her head gently and they walked towards Alice.

'Hello, Alice – lovely to see you again so soon,' said Barnes, once she was free of the children. 'I was just performing some visits – home study check-ups and medical deliveries,' she said, smiling. 'And I need to make sure that young Izzy keeps up to date with her education now she's topside.'

'She studies every night,' said Alice, shepherding them all inside the house. 'I think I can make sure she completes her homework.'

'I had an idea already,' interrupted Izzy from the kitchen as Alice and Barnes walked through the living area. 'About my Contribution. I'm going to…'

'Contributions are meant to be a surprise,' said Barnes, narrowing her eyes at the girl. 'I'm sure Alice doesn't want to hear your idea before it's fully formed now, does she? Remember what we talked about…'

'We need to work hard and become the best citizens of the Community we can be,' recited Izzy.

The doctor nodded approvingly at Izzy.

Alice scowled. 'Filip and I are still developing how Contributions will work. How does Izzy know about them?' She and the others had dreamed up with the idea while in the Ship as a way to help all members of the Community have their ideas heard and as an entry criterion to the more senior positions within the councils.

'Well, it was such a brilliant idea, we already adopted it for the new Academy, Alice. All students will have the opportunity to have their ideas, theories and acts of selfless bravery recognised. It's such a motivating way of bringing out our students' strengths.'

Alice seethed quietly and gritted her teeth at the doctor.

'Sounds great,' she managed, breathing deeply.

'I'm already selfless and brave,' said Izzy smiling. 'Aren't I, Barnes?'

'You're as bright as a penny.' Alice pulled her hair packed and tapped Izzy on her head.

'Don't say that,' shouted Izzy. 'That's a stupid phrase. There are no pennies. Barnes says we're not allowed to talk about things like that any more, didn't you, Barnes?' Then she looked upwards at the doctor. 'A threat to our rules is a threat to us all, isn't that right?'

Barnes nodded and gave a wide smile. 'She's going to go far, this one, Alice. Very bright.' Her voice danced delicately, cutting tight the edges of her words.

Alice frowned. 'You should really be in bed,' she said, trying to make her voice sound kind. 'You have an early start tomorrow.'

'No, I don't,' said Izzy, defiantly. 'I can do what I want. And besides, Barnes says that if I study really hard, I can do my own experiments in the labs with her. I have really good ideas.'

Barnes laughed deeply. 'Come on now, Izzy, Alice might be right. There will be plenty of time for studying and thinking about your Contribution tomorrow. Remember what I told you about listening to your new parents.'

'They're *not* my...' began Izzy and then looked at Barnes. 'Okay, fine,' she said and then scampered her way into the house.

'It's late,' said Alice, moving past Barnes and through the doorway. 'Shouldn't you be making your way back down to the lab?'

'Not this evening,' she said. 'Another visit to complete after yours, I'm up here topside on official business. I need to perform a few more *visits* before making my way back down in the morning.' She held up her bag and bared her teeth. 'Important things to collect and deliver.'

Alice nodded. 'Insemination supplies?' she said, looking back inside the house. 'I haven't authorised my start date or...'

'No authorisation required,' said Barnes. 'It's written into our constitution as a critical activity, as you declared. We will all be required to participate when required, as already agreed. You and Filip are in a very privileged position having been tested as eligible parents and having chosen each other.' Her stress on the words privileged and eligible were over-pronounced.

'Yes,' said Alice. 'Yes, I suppose we are. We're very lucky to have Izzy and Marcus living with us.' She paused and was about to start again but the look in the pools of Barnes's eyes made her think twice.

'You know that's not what I mean,' said Barnes, handing her a small bag. 'Everything you need is in here for the next stage in your process. Do you understand?'

Through the twilight, the silence echoed with pregnant intent and Alice nodded her head slowly, her fists clenched tight. 'Yes,' she said, pushing tight the door. 'Good night, Barnes.'

Filip sat at the table, leafing through some papers, his focus intent and unwavering.

'I don't know what to do with Izzy,' said Alice, sinking down next to him. 'She's... unmanageable.'

'It's her age,' said Filip, without looking up. 'But on this issue, she – and Barnes – are right. We do need to be extra vigilant in this new world. We don't know what we're facing out there or how our people will react when they come outside and we can't take any chances. You know all this.'

He pulled his chair around to face Alice. 'Look, Izzy will be fine when she's settled in here. It's all new to her too, remember? Maybe you should make more of an effort with her?'

'In what way? I make her food, I set out her clothes, I help with her homework...'

Filip looked at her closely. 'I don't know, maybe be a little more *maternal* towards her. Show her some affection in the same way you do Marcus. You're going to need to practise that so that you're ready.'

Alice pulled back her hair into a ponytail. 'What do you mean?'

'You know exactly what I mean.' He stood up and kissed her shoulder and let her hair down again. 'I believe Barnes dropped our materials off today so we can start trying for ourselves.'

Alice felt a cool shiver run down her spine and glanced at the bag she'd thrown onto the counter top. 'I'm still not sure.'

She kept her eyes focused on Filip. There was a crookedness to his face that had made him intrinsically attractive, dark and somehow intriguing when they had been locked in the intense negotiations deep in the Ship. The Alice who had so desperately wanted to be the builder of a new world, the creator of life and a figure that everyone had looked up to had been the girl who had been attracted to everything he'd had to offer. He was still the most attractive of the Scouts and there was no reason why she shouldn't want what she had promised, but everything now seemed to be happening so quickly. And somehow, outside of her control. Filip's determination and commitment had once matched hers equally – in both content and voracity – but now he seemed more commanding. Controlling, even.

'There are things I need to do first,' she said firmly, touching Filip's arm. 'Things we need to do first before we become parents.'

'You agreed, remember. It's what we both want, isn't it?'

Alice looked into his eager expression. Back in the Ship, deciding what they were about to do had been easy. Now it felt so real, she wasn't sure if she was ready. 'Yes,' she said. 'I suppose it's what we agreed. But maybe we should wait.'

Filip pulled her in close to him. 'We really should start trying soon. If we want to be one of the first, it's important that we're…'

'You sound like Barnes,' said Alice, pushing him away. She took a deep breath and exhaled slowly. 'Like I said, it's not that I don't want to have children of our own, it's just that I thought we'd have more time.' She kissed Filip gently on the cheek, shrugging off his wounded look. 'I'm going to get some air.'

In the quiet of the square, Alice lay on her back, watching the moon. Tiny pinpricks of stars filtered through the darkness, intermittent flashes in the sky. Her hands were tight at her sides, holding down her dress and her body was rigid.

'Shooting star,' said Filip, breaking the silence of the square as he walked across to join her.

'It's just a meteor,' said Alice without moving. 'Not even a star – just a small piece of rock hitting our atmosphere from space. They've been doing that for thousands, no millions of years. It's nothing special.'

Filip lowered himself back down onto the blanket. 'And that's exactly why it *is* special,' he said. 'Out there, nothing's changed. It's all just the same. The sky didn't fall and the earth didn't explode. Terrible things happened, yes, but we're alive and it's special that we are. The threats that existed in the old world will still be there – murder, famine, the propensity of people to rise above each other and persecute the weak. Which is why we are developing something different, something equal. We have let old world go and we're doing something different already. Look at what you're doing with the children. You've shown them what it is to have a home with us – how to live a life that isn't like before.'

Alice shook her head. 'I don't know *how* to be a parent,' she said, looking up at the stars.

He took her hand but it offered no warmth, just a limp coldness.

'Nobody does,' said Filip. 'It's new to everyone the first time. There's no training for it – we just have to go for it. And the sooner the better.'

A cold silence shifted out from between them and upwards into the darkness of the night sky and then further out into the depths of the atmosphere to where freezing rocks of ice drifted between the planets and the stars. Alice almost didn't feel Filip's finger tracing the line of her spine gently, his palm resting against her shoulder.

'I'm going to speak to Richard,' she said. 'I want to know why he was in my flat and what he knows about what happened there. About what happened with…'

'No,' said Filip firmly. 'Hutchinson is dead and his body is gone. You don't need to relive any of that or discuss the details with anyone else. Richard's recovery is Barnes's responsibility, not yours.'

'But…'

'It's for your own good, Alice. No.'

Filip's voice was authoritative and clear. At the sound of her own name, Alice felt a stab of frustration at her chastisement. Her mind was immediately made up, but she bit her lip and kept silent.

'We'd better go in,' said Filip, finally. 'There's a storm coming, I can feel it.'

In less than the time it took them to get back to the square, there was the dark creak of thunder in the distance, followed by a silver flash of lightening that cast white shadows across the dirtiness of the river. Halfway across, the miserable spire of a church loomed from the blackness.

'I wonder if they got out of there,' said Alice, looking at the crooked outline as they picked up speed and headed towards the row of houses on one side of the square. 'I doubt it. Maybe they were the lucky ones. Sometimes I wish I'd stayed there in Prospect House. Richard managed to survive on his own.'

'Don't ever say that,' said Filip, sternly. 'We were the lucky ones. And Richard was even luckier that we found him when we did. The Industry saved as many people as they could – but they didn't save them all. They saved *us* – some by chance, some by design. Did Wilson ever tell you the story of how he found me?'

They ducked inside the first building they came to and listened as the rain hammered down around them. The house was one of the earliest cleared when they had initially come above ground. Alice remembered the stickers on the door and the way that, somehow, there had still been picture frames hanging on the walls. The photographs inside the frames had disintegrated, just like the owners of the house, but the remnants of what had once been still remained.

'No,' said Alice. 'You never told me.' There was so much that had happened between them but, in some sense, so little that they had talked about. There was so much that even Alice didn't want to remember and so much that clung to the memory of her body like wet clothing in the rain. But in that moment, any distraction from the designated task of the evening was a welcome one.

'It's not a great story,' said Filip, clearing a space the floor where they could sit. 'But it's one you probably should know.'

Alice had so many questions for him about what had happened when the rain had stopped, whether her mother had returned and how the world had looked when the water started to subside. When there were so many other places he could have gone, why had Richard gone there?

'I should have been at school,' Filip started. 'I wanted to be an engineer and I was pretty good at science, so it would probably have happened. I didn't go to a very good school, not like Izzy, but I never skipped classes. The night before the Storms I'd been working on a scale model of London until three in the morning and the day the rain really started, I slept late.

'I loved making models – the other kids in my class all had the latest games consoles but my family couldn't afford much so I collected bits and pieces from around the house and made models. Izzy helped sometimes – she was the one that put in the matchbox that was her school. That morning, my foster father forgot to wake me – I guess he thought I'd left already. Izzy had gone to school and I was alone in the house when the hail came.'

Alice remembered how she had been all alone for the first few days – the cold, echoing sound of her own voice seeming empty and hollow.

'What about Marcus?' she said. 'Where was he?'

'Marcus wasn't with us then,' said Filip. 'Izzy and I were brought up together – we had the same mother but Marcus, well…' He stopped for a second. 'He came later.'

As they looked up through an open window at the sky, another comet slid silently across the blackness, and Alice folded her arms across the coldness of her stomach and felt the softness of her own skin.

'I was only on my own for a few days,' she said. 'But I remember being calm mostly, although very, very lonely – and scared. And then when Hutchinson came…' She shivered at the thought of the man who had forced himself upon her and what she'd had to do to save herself.

'You did the right thing at the time – if you hadn't have killed him, you wouldn't be here today. He tried to force himself on you Alice – you were, what, eleven, twelve years old? The same age as Izzy is now. What's past is past. There's nothing you can do about it."

Alice nodded slowly. 'I know,' she said. 'But it doesn't make it right.'

'When the hail started later on, I knew I had to leave. The only things I took with me were my phone and my army knife. It killed me to leave the model behind, it was the best thing I'd ever made but I knew if I didn't leave the house then, I'd never leave alive. I took a photograph on my phone so that I could remember it. I still had it right up until Kunstein made us give up all our personal belongings. The water had already started coming in under the kitchen door, I knew I didn't have that long – and all the windows had been smashed by the falling ice, so there was rain coming in from all angles.'

'How did you not get yourself killed by the hail? My neighbour…' Alice remembered the woman with the pink hair that Hutchinson had described as lifeless after getting pelted relentlessly.

'I made a helmet from a metal colander and some other stuff I found in the garage and then I dodged between buildings. It wasn't as hard as I thought it would be but I do have some scars to prove it.'

He smiled and held up his right hand. Alice could see that the middle finger was significantly shorter than all the rest.

'Apart from a few scratches, this was the only injury I got the whole time I was out there. We lived just outside the city, in the suburbs, so I didn't know central London that well – but I knew that I had to try to find Izzy. She was only six at the time and she'd be terrified and wouldn't be able to get home. So, I hitched a ride with anyone who would take me, walked – even ran part of the way. Then, when the water started to get deep, I went up into a department store and got as much food as I could and spent the night there. The next morning, the water was so high I couldn't leave so I made a raft. That bit was the hardest – launching it – but it worked just like the movies.'

'Were you on your own the whole time?' Alice thought about the people she had seen fleeing the city, the gunshots, the fires and the terrible stench of death all around her.

Filip shrugged. 'Not all of the time. Before I got into central London, I found this dog, shivering on a roof. He was whining constantly, and starving. I tried to feed him some chocolate but he wouldn't take it. I knew he'd never survive on his own and it seemed cruel to leave him there. He was licking my hand and staring at me with huge brown eyes filled with cataracts and his matted tail kept flopping back and fore slowly.'

Alice remembered her puppy Charlie Davenport and the long summer evenings she had spent playing in the garden before she and her mother had been forced to move into Prospect house. She shivered as she thought about the bullies who had cruelly hurt him but, for the first time, she was glad that he was already gone and hadn't had to go through the trauma of the Storms or the devastation that had happened next. She warmed to Filip's compassion.

'So, you took him with you?' she said, rubbing her arm against his and pulling him close to her. 'What happened to him?'

Filip held her hand in his.

'No,' he said firmly. 'There was no way domesticated animals were going to survive, Alice. I did the only thing I could do in the circumstances.'

'You…?'

'I drowned him. He struggled and I held his head under the water until he stopped moving. Then I let him float away with the others.'

Alice felt her eyes fill with tears – even with the scale of destruction, she couldn't bear to think about some of the terrible things that people had done during the Storms. She shivered. 'How could you?' she said. 'How can you live with yourself?'

'How can any of us?' said Filip. 'We all did what we had to at the time to survive, you know that. Compassion for the suffering of others is just a part of that.'

The house they were in creaked as a soft patter of rain began to fall on the roof and, as the clouds came across the sky, one by one the hard, white stars were snuffed into darkness.

'Was there…' Alice wasn't sure she wanted to know. 'Was there anything else that you did, that you haven't told me?'

'There's a lot, Alice. Too much for tonight, but for all the years I'd spent in school learning about engineering and every book I'd read… all that hadn't taught me anywhere near as much about the world and construction and survival as those couple of days in the Deadlands.'

'Did you see anyone?'

'Not really. Almost everything out there – out here – was dead. I saw the odd person clinging onto something, but mostly I avoided them. The old people were the worst – they weren't even trying. I watched three people jump off buildings into water that was only a few feet deep. When I passed the hospital, it was tragic – some had made it outside, still all hooked up with wires and tubes but they couldn't make it any further, you know, didn't have anywhere to go and they were just stood there, waiting. Nothing prepares you to see anything like that.'

'So how long did it take you to get to the school?' said Alice. The pain of remembering was sometimes too much to bear.

'I used the model of London on my phone to find my way there mostly,' said Filip. 'I'd been there a few times and later I found a map but it felt good to be able to use something I'd made. After a couple of days, I found the school – it was signposted. That was where I saw him.'

'Wilson was at the school?'

'Yes. Well, sort of. He was picking out candidates to survive.'

Alice wasn't sure whether it was the gentle thrumming of the rain or the heavy blanket of sleep that was beginning to fall over her that had been clouding the conversation but she suddenly felt alert and more awake than she had done in weeks.

'You mean he didn't rescue *everyone* he found? That people were *chosen* to survive? What was he doing at the school?' Her questions came like bullets; fast and hard. Filip pushed his back up against the wall and picked up a small piece of plastic that had been left on the floor. He twirled it around in his fingers.

'Some things, some people became disposable, Alice. The Industry took as many as they could but, ultimately, not everyone could be saved. There wasn't a test for who could survive but there were some people that just wouldn't make it longer term – you saw that on the Ship. And those were the ones taking up the space of someone who, well, could contribute to building this whole thing back up again.'

After just weeks underground the suicides had started – Alice remembered how the first few had shocked her and then how it gradually became part of life beneath the surface. Not everybody had been cut out for the dramatic change in lifestyle. Those over thirty had found it the hardest.

'The school was on slightly higher ground so there were others there, not just the children – some were parents or teachers, but there were also neighbours and passers-by. Wilson had brought a boat as far as he could and sent two Industry officials to select those he thought would be best suited to the facilities and the life he could offer. He waited with the other officials on the boat to make sure nobody took it or tried to climb aboard. By the time I got there, Izzy was already on the boat and most of those who were stopped from coming were already dead or had left. It was chaos.'

'The officials killed them?'

'Some – but not many. Most of those that refused to allow their children to go with the Industry eventually realised that it would be their only chance at any sort of life for their kids. A few parents ran with their younger ones– the Industry let those go – but there were a couple that Wilson specifically wanted, ones he had named, whose parents insisted that they accompany them. But there just wasn't enough room for everyone.'

'Why did they let you go with them? I mean, if there wasn't enough room, how come you made the cut?'

'I was on the list. I didn't know it at the time but they had already sent for me. Wilson guessed I'd try to come to find Izzy but he'd already made arrangements for his people to go my house. They were called back as soon as I could tell them who I was.'

'You were on a list? How did Wilson even know who you were?'

'His wife was Izzy's teacher. And my foster father worked for him. Like you, I was easier to work with, easier to mould. My family situation wasn't the best and he knew I would welcome the opportunity. I got onto that boat, Alice, while Wilson's wife stayed with the others that didn't make it, those that would find it too difficult to leave the old world.

'That almost killed Wilson there and then. He couldn't bear to leave her but she refused to go, not while there were still children at the school who hadn't been chosen. She stayed with them right until the end – or at least until Wilson lost communication with her. The last he knew was that she was heading for higher ground with the one remaining teenage girl. They both had some form of infection from drinking dirty water. Everything went down not long after that. He blamed himself for not going back, even after it wasn't safe any longer.'

Alice sat in silence listening as the rain gradually came to a stop outside. She shivered in the darkness, trying to separate what she knew from what Filip had just told her. He put one arm across her shoulders, making her shiver even more, as she tried to make sense of what she was hearing.

She opened and closed her mouth several times to speak before the right words would come out. 'What about me? Was I just some random pick up that they made on their rounds? Nobody actually came looking for me.'

Filip twisted the piece of plastic he was holding until it broke into two pieces. 'But they did, Alice. Kunstein had been looking for someone just like you for months and then she found you, riding the underground on your own. She'd been watching you for days, when they first determined that this Storm was going to be the one – I think she spoke to you once – in a library or a museum or something. It just happened that they almost didn't make it to you in time.'

He flicked the pieces of plastic into the corner of the room and took her hand, guiding her back to their house.

In the quiet of their room, Alice watched the clouds part and the stars prickle the sky again as a final comet shot past the skylight. She had almost forgotten that this was what they were there to do. There was a crackling of paper and cellophane as Filip opened the package that Barnes had left and he knelt down beside her.

'Are we really going to do this now?' she said, watching as Filip unwrapped a large syringe.

'We can do it the other way if you like?' said Filip. 'You know, the way they used to? You're almost sixteen. Or we can wait until morning.'

Alice shook her head. 'No,' she said. 'We'll do it the way we agreed and we'll do it now.'

Her hands felt clammy and in the heat of the room she felt significantly younger than her fifteen years. She counted each birthday before the baby and then imagined each one afterwards. Her legs started to shake as she moved them apart.

As the moon shifted from their sight and the room grew dark, she closed her eyes and listened to the shuffling and movement in the darkness. Thoughts of the Ship, of motherhood and leadership and her life before the Storms shifted and melded until there was nothing but a huge wave of silence and the regular tick-tick-tick of rain hitting the roof as she breathed deep and closed her eyes.

Chapter Four

The Family

Carter

As Carter woke with a jolt, the anger from the night before came flooding back. Having been half-carried, half dragged through the Village and locked in a room high in the trees, it had taken him a long while to get to sleep. He'd demanded to speak to his mother, Jacinta, but instead two men had roughly hoisted him along a walkway and upwards through a wooden entrance into the darkness of the room.

The sharp knock that had woken him came again and Angel appeared through the trapdoor.

'Where is my mother?' said Carter, angrily. 'What is she doing here? I need to know what exactly is going on. I demand to see her.' Through the haze of waking up came the chirrup of insects from somewhere in the grassy roof of the room.

'I know you want answers,' said Angel, pushing a small plate full of red, green and yellow food in front of Carter. 'But so do we. And right now, you're going to need to wait. You mother and Samuel are busy meeting with the Village Council to agree your right to stay here. It isn't simply a done deal. When that has been authorised, and that council have agreed, you can meet with her. Plus, there are a number of other important things happening at the moment.'

'A meeting with my mother has to be authorised? What kind of place is this?'

She gestured to the plate. 'Eat this, while it's fresh. I know you're used to all that processed stuff but you won't get any of that out here. This is all real, genuine. You'll need to get used to that now. It doesn't last for ever – and make sure you keep the flies away from it.'

She put down some water and smiled at Carter. 'Stay here where it's safe and I'll be back for you soon,' she said. And then she left, lowering herself into a hole in the floor and onto a ladder. She swung around and disappeared.

Carter moved the plate and crawled along the smooth wooden floor to where Angel had vanished. He peered through the opening that had a small ladder attached, leading down onto a sturdy platform. The landing had a set of carefully carved wooden railings connecting to a network of other raised walkways through the trees. Each one led to other houses, some two storeys tall, all neatly wrapped up within the safety of the trees. From where he was, Carter counted as many as he could and stopped when he got to a hundred. There were many more, at all different levels, in the trees that surrounded the clearing below.

Two children pelted across the walkways and slid down the ladders, darting across the open forest floor, singing to each other. When they reached the treeline at the edge of the clearing, one of them pointed upwards at Carter, while the other ran and hid in the bushes. Amongst the huts below that had been built from things from the old world, other people milled around, occasionally glancing up and then looking away. He spotted Samuel from across the clearing, glaring up at him from behind a brick building. Carter glared back and pulled himself back inside and picked at the plate of food that Angel had brought him. The sight of Samuel had all but ruined his appetite.

Carter couldn't quite make out exactly what the food was supposed to be but it smelled strong and all the different components were irregular in shape. It was so alien and different to the neatly cut blocks of chicker and carrotina he was used to in the Community. He pushed his finger into the edge of something and licked at the juice. It was hot and sweet and tasted more strongly than anything he'd ever eaten before. He delicately picked at the different coloured mounds– there were traces of something similar to the peapod slices he'd eaten so many times in the Community, carrotina and a piece of whiteloaf. It was overpoweringly rich and strong in taste, but with his stomach churning in hunger, in seconds it was gone.

The edges of the room were jammed with books, artefacts and pictures of the old world – most well preserved and in much better condition than those he'd seen when he'd escaped with Lily from the Industry. Spines of deep crimson, ochre and green lined the rooms on thick wooden shelves and, above those, photographs of people and places from the world before the Storms. Some of the places he recognised from the sparse history lessons in the Academy – old London, bridges, castles and towers – but others seemed alien, distant and strange. The shelves creaked with the sheer weight of things stuffed on top of them.

On one wall there was a picture, hand-drawn, that included some people he recognised. It had been dark when he'd arrived and he'd been too angry and tired to explore. In the picture, there were four people in total – his mother and father were definitely two of them, standing at the back. His father had his arm around a boy of about ten. Carter ran his finger over the jawline of the boy.

'That's me,' he said softly to himself.

His mother looked older, more like herself now than the person she had been back then. She had her arm on the shoulder of another boy, about six years old, with thick black hair and a scar that ran from one side of his cheek to the other. There was no mistaking the sneering look in his eyes. Even as a child, thought Carter, there was something not right about him. Silas. Samuel. The brother he thought was dead. Why were his mother and brother here and why he had been left behind in the Community? Confusion and anger wracked his body.

Through a square window in the wall of the dwelling, Carter could hear the noises of the Village. He looked past the clearing to a path that wound deep into the forest. He had to know what was going on. He could easily make it down to the clearing and find his mother himself. No one, especially not Angel nor his brother Samuel, had the right to tell him what to do. He needed answers.

Outside he could see children playing with sticks, banging them against small plastic pots in a rhythmic beat while others strummed strange instruments and the smallest of them sang. As the sounds covered the tap of his feet on the walkway, he slipped out of the room and crept down the planked paths until he was on the last walkway before the base, at the ladder that led down to the clearing. A squat, dark-haired man with a sharpened stick stood guarding the tree. Carter pulled himself back behind a branch and waited but the man didn't move, other than to scratch his feet into the ground. He crept back up the walkway to the opposite side of the tree and gauged the height from the walkway to the ground. Silently, he pulled himself over the handrail and dropped to the floor, cursing as his ankle jarred against a rock half-buried in the grass.

Limping a little, he moved from tree to tree until he had made his way around the edge of the clearing, at the back of the stone hut and behind the group of children. As he peered from behind a tree, one of the boys pointed and backed away.

'You're that one from outside, aren't you?' he said, dropping the tin cans he was holding. 'Samuel told us we're not allowed to talk to you. He told us to stay away. He's your brother, isn't he?'

His voice sounded strange and then Carter realised that the child was missing both of his ears.

'Erm... yes...' said Carter slowly and loudly, walking towards them.

'He can't hear you, stupid,' said a girl, sharpening a stick. 'But he can read your lips. So, don't shout at him.'

The boy smiled. 'They're talking about you in there,' he said, motioning towards the hut. 'She told me.'

The girl scowled at him. 'My brother has a big mouth for someone who can't hear,' she said and clipped him across the back of the head. The boy lunged towards her legs and Carter left them there play-fighting and crept across to the building across the clearing.

Inside, the talking was animated and he pushed his face against the door to hear more.

'*Your* guilt at having left the boy is one thing,' said a loud voice, 'but you can't expect us to believe that he's on our side. And certainly not that he's going to be in any position to lead our rebellion.'

'I have always been reconciled in my decision,' came his mother's voice. 'I may have felt some guilt, yes, but you know my reasons. And this is not about my feelings on the matter. Carter has more information to give us than we could ever have achieved alone. This is just a variation on the plan.'

'I agree,' said another. 'But I thought McDermott was keeping an eye on things in there – and that we had some more time before the Controller elections.'

'McDermott did what she could. No one could have predicted this. And we don't know the full story. When we had Mendoza…'

'Mendoza's gone. She's been gone for years. McDermott's the one we need now. What the hell happened? Why hasn't she made contact?'

Carter frowned. Mendoza gone? And Lily? He shook his head trying to make sense of her place in all this. He heard his mother's voice above the general growling of the crowd.

'As you well know, we haven't heard from Lily since the incident. There was a message, but not from her – all we knew was that the boy had made it past the Barricades. I can only assume she has concerns that her cover has been compromised.'

'What was the message?'

'The last we heard was that there were big plans to cause trouble for us out here. We also know that there's a delivery tomorrow to the sluice gate, for which we're already putting together a collection team.'

Further rumbling came from the crowd and Carter heard a number of people begin to speak at the same time.

'We need to move forward with the main plan,' a clear voice said finally. 'With or without your family's support, Jacinta. And we need to move fast. We need to know what they're planning.'

'I did not watch my husband die at the hands of those monsters at the Barricades all those years ago to sit back and let them try to take over what we have here. Of course, we're on board, it's just a case of making the right move at the right time. And my boys will lead that.'

There was another flurry of disgruntled chatter from behind the door and Carter pressed his body closer to hear more.

His mother spoke again. 'We've waited long enough. The boy's expulsion is only going to inflame the mood inside the Community. The perfect time will be within the next two months but no later – until then they'll still be in disarray and confusion. We use the boy's knowledge to get into the Catacombs and free our people. Samuel can lead.'

A cheer rose from the crowd as Carter backed slowly away from the door. Individual voices could no longer be heard, just the boom of conversation amidst the crackle of disagreement. A banging brought the calamity to order and over the grunting and shouting Carter could hear his mother's voice.

'We cannot survive without a source on the inside so we will send them in to find out exactly what's happening with regard to the greater threat. But this decision is not for today. When it is time, we will address you all to discuss plans further. Right now, we need to focus on the recovery mission.'

'And what about Lily McDermott?'

Carter felt his anger rise at the thought of what Lily had done to his daughter. He yanked open the wooden doors and stormed inside.

'Yes,' he said loudly. 'What about that murderer?'

The scraping of chairs preceded the sound of each Villager turning around to look at him. There was a rumbling noise and then a hushed silence. Jacinta placed a hand over her own mouth.

'I want to know about Lily,' said Carter, his voice wavering. 'She killed my daughter. I want to know what's going on here.'

The crowd looked first towards Jacinta and then at Carter. His mother held up her hand. 'I think this meeting can be closed,' she said to the Villagers. 'I will take this from here.' Grumbling, the group consulted with one another and then gradually spilled out of the door. When the last had left, Jacinta closed it and turned to Carter.

'It is not your place to interrupt Village business,' she admonished. 'Lily is a prized asset and not an enemy.'

'She said that she killed my daughter.'

Jacinta's face brightened with anger. 'Your daughter, from what I hear, is a rebel herself and it would not have improved our cause to kill her. Lily is with *us,* Carter.'

'But she said—'

'Lily is on our side,' repeated Jacinta, exasperated. 'Her role was to protect you and ensure your safety. The only way to keep you away from the Community was to tell you enough that would have made you leave there for good once you were out of the running for Controller General. Sending you out here to us was the only option left to her. And from what Samuel has told me, Lily attempted to remove the tracking device from your arm so that you could make your way to us without being followed. If she had wanted to kill you she had ample opportunity to do so.'

Carter stared at her. Jacinta was right in some ways – Lily had been alone with him many times and could easily have taken him off guard if she had really wanted to. But… He shook his head as Jacinta snapped back at him, annoyed.

You were told to stay at home until I was ready. Get back there and wait until I can explain everything more fully.'

'But what's going on here?' he demanded. 'What's this all about? Why were you talking about Mendoza?'

The door opened and Samuel strode into the room. Carter glared angrily at him and the look was returned.

'You!' Carter glared. 'You could have told me you were my brother.'

'Shut up,' sneered Samuel, pushing past him. 'We have important business to attend to. And like Mother said, you'll stay inside the house if you know what's good for you. You're not supposed to be out here.'

'Don't touch me,' said Carter, pushing him back. You disgust me, treating me like this. Did you even care that you were my brother?'

Samuel shoved him roughly to the ground. 'We're trying to protect you, you idiot,' he said, his face clouding with anger. 'You can't just turn up here demanding answers – you need to wait. There are some things that are more important than you. Right now, *most* things are more important than you. And no, I didn't care.'

'Why didn't you tell me? I deserved to know. You owed me that at least.'

'I don't owe you anything.' Samuel looked at Carter with disdain. 'I don't even know you.'

'You should have told me,' said Carter, wiping his hands and his clothes. And you have no right to tell me where I can and can't go, keeping me under guard.' He looked at his mother. 'I want answers,' he said. 'And I want them now.'

Jacinta shook her head and glanced away. 'Samuel is right,' she said. 'We have important work to do. But I will talk to you this evening. Now go back to the house.' She turned to Samuel. 'And try to be little more civil to our guest. He is your brother after all.'

Then, pushing her hair backwards, she headed out into the afternoon sun.

'Stay at home,' said Samuel again, dangerously. 'If you know what's good for you. Or at least, stay away from me.'

*

Carter wandered through the Village, watching as one by one the people he encountered whispered and turned their heads downwards as he walked past. On the other side of the clearing, a group led by Samuel packed up rucksacks with blankets and food and headed out into the darkness of the forest. He walked over the trodden down grass where they had stood.

'Where are they going?' he said to a man who stood waving them off.

'Retrieval mission.' The man looked old and tired, his bones withered to stumps; one leg had been replaced with a wooden peg.

'Retrieval of what?'

The man rubbed his eyes and shook his head sadly at Carter.

'Your people,' he started. 'They are cruel and evil. If only you knew…'

'Then tell me,' demanded Carter, impatient.

'It's not my place,' said the man, looking away. 'You people all disgust me.' He picked up a pair of sticks from the ground and hobbled away.

In the distance, the last of Samuel's party cast shadows through the afternoon forest. As he caught up with them, Carter heard the tail end of the conversation. The smell of sweat and the stench of men's boots leaked a trail behind them.

'I hope this is going to be the last one,' said a woman next to Samuel. 'I hate this. It's heart-breaking.'

'If we can get inside the Barricades, we can stop this once and for all,' replied Samuel. 'Stop *them* once and for all. Every last one of them.' His voice was menacing, personal even.

'Yeah,' said a man towards the back of the trail. 'They are beyond evil. I don't know how they could do this. You know, it's not the crying that gets me, it's when it stops.'

There was the crackle of a twig underfoot and Carter ducked behind a tree, his heart beating fast and his mind racing.

'Sssh.' Samuel held his hand up to the men and they all stopped. He looked up at the sky and then out through the trees.

Carter listened as they traced their steps back towards him.

'Probably just a squirrel or something,' said one woman. 'We need to move on if we're going to catch the light. Carter held his breath and pushed his body tight against the tree. He heard the sound of Samuel grunting in agreement and then a silence before the crunch of leaves as the group headed away from him. He waited a while before peering out from behind the barky trunk and watched as they headed out into the distance of the forest.

For a moment he thought to follow them but then decided against it. He thought about what the man had said to him. Retrieval mission? And then his outburst against the Community? He tried to make sense of it all but every new thing he found out made what was happening less and less clear. But he was determined to get to the truth.

He trudged back to the tree house, avoiding as many insects as he could. There had been some forms of flying creatures that had dared to make their way across the Black River but most took only seconds to rest on a leaf before moving on. Very few living things had stayed for very long. His skin itched with bites and welts, due to the fact that none of the food had been treated with the anti-infestation medication he was used to.

The place was wild – largely untended, full of old world detritus and, more than anything, desperately uninviting. He was furious with Samuel – how dare he talk to him that way? Days ago, he was destined to be the most important person in his world and now? He took a deep intake of breath. If the Community could see him now. He belonged nowhere and had nothing – except a family who didn't believe in him. His strengthened his jaw – his resolve had always come from his own self-belief and the desire to do what *he* knew was right.

He pulled back his shoulders from the stoop he had started to slump into. He would show them – the Villagers and the Community. He would bring the truth to both of them. And the best place to start was by learning more about where he was right now. He nodded to himself – Jacinta's house in the trees was full of books, tomes full of knowledge of this strange new world he was inhabiting. This would be where he would start.

A woman, her stomach swollen with pregnancy and carrying a huge log on her shoulder walked past him and spat at the floor next to him, her eyes glaring in anger.

'We don't want you here,' she said. 'Go back to your own place.'

'I have just as much right to be here as you,' he said with a little more clarity than he had before.

'No, you don't, you're not like us.' She smirked. 'You're a First Gen, aren't you? So, I suppose life is very different for you.'

'I'm a Descendant actually,' said Carter, defensively. 'My ancestors built the new world.'

The woman shook her head. 'You're no better than anyone else,' she sneered. 'Those poor people who were born out of the chemistry your ancestors created – what do you call them?'

'Lab Mades,' said Carter, sullenly, thinking of Isabella. 'They have the same rights as everyone else.' He felt his argument slipping as he remembered the true reason why he wanted to become Controller General.

'The Lab Mades, that's right – they didn't ask to be born as part of your sordid underclass, did they? Your people are savages – evil people that destroy anything they can to maintain that...' she struggled for the word '...that prison that they keep you all in.'

'It's not a prison,' said Carter, defensive until he remembered the thick metal walls. 'Well, it's a lot more civilised than here,' he added.

'Civilised?' The woman laughed and thumped the log down next to her. 'If it's not a prison, how many times have you been outside and seen the rest of the world? How many times have you eaten real food that's not grown in a lab? When did you ever swim in a lake or play with a ball?'

Carter shook his head. 'It's not that bad,' he said, looking at the dirt on his hands, struggling to find something to say. 'At least it was clean.'

The woman picked up the log again and put it over her shoulder, then walked over until she was close to Carter. 'If it's not that bad then why are you here?' she said. 'More importantly, why are you *still* here, *Carter Warren?*' Then, with an angry toss of her head, she stalked off.

As he walked around the edge of the clearing, children backed away from him and scuttled up into the trees. At one edge, the grass had been razed to stubble and a row of sculptured trunks framed the boundary between village and forest. Across the wood that had been scraped free of the gnarly bark, words had been carved, deep and indelible. He ran his fingers over each of them in turn, from the last to the first. There were many of them, too many to count, and all of them names:

Lazarus, Constantine, Davie, Sephora, Joshua, Victoria, Angel, Samuel.

Even the sight of his brother's name made Carter feel angry but he calmed himself with the desire to learn. He hiked his way back to the house in the trees to envelop himself in the books that lined the walls of his new, albeit temporary abode. That evening he skim-read most of the books in his mother's house, picking through each of them one by one. Old, incorrect science, historic engineering, fiction that was desperately confusing and children's books that made no sense at all. Some of the books were similar to those he'd picked out in the house that he and Lily had stopped at in the Deadlands and the intricate detail of the old life consumed him for hours with a renewed vigour to discover the truth.

He looked around the room. Everything was stained, dirty and archaic. Frothy water came in jugs hauled up through the trees or from a plastic barrel, hooked on the side of strong branches. It was ingenious, thought Carter; you had to give them that. Not particularly sanitary, but it was some sort of life.

Then, there was a sharp clack of footsteps on the walkway. Jacinta climbed into the room and stood in the doorway.

'It's time for us to talk,' she said, calmly. 'It's time for you to know the truth.'

Chapter Five

The Community

Alice

'We need to keep trying.'

Filip stood with his arms folded, above Alice, as she pored over some papers on an old couch covered in plastic wrapping. The thick, pungent smell of damp hung in the air. He sighed deeply. 'Especially if Barnes says it's the right time. It's going to be important to bring as many new lives into the Community as quickly as possible.'

'Not every second of every day, Filip. There are other things to do too.'

'Nothing as important as this. We could go and see Barnes; maybe she has something that could help you? Maybe make it easier for you?' He looked a little uncomfortable with the conversation but persistent nonetheless.

'No!' Alice threw her papers onto the floor. 'I don't *need* help. Anyway, what is it with everyone's obsession with Barnes?'

'She's a doctor, Alice, she might be able to give you something, speed up the process, I don't know.' He put his arm gently around her waist and kissed the crown of her head. Alice felt her muscles tighten under his touch and she moved into the kitchen.

'It's not optional, Alice,' Filip called after her. 'We need to make it happen.'

'I know,' she hissed through her teeth. 'But I don't want that... doctor... involved – not any more than she has to be.'

'What do you mean?'

Alice picked at some carrotina from the counter and walked back towards him. 'This is a personal thing, Filip, something between us. I don't want everyone else interfering.' She crunched down on the food she had become so accustomed to, and yet still despised. 'Especially not her.'

'But it's not a personal thing, Alice, it's between all of us. We *all* agreed, remember?'

'I remember,' said Alice angrily, wishing things were very different. 'But I want to do this my way.' She looked out of the window at the fractured buildings and weather worn landscape. There were hundreds – no thousands – of dwelling houses to be developed, a whole infrastructure to be built and a Community that depended on her. She ran her hand over her stomach and remembered the brief and somewhat ineffective sex education she had received in one of the few days she'd been at school before the Storms.

'My body, my rules,' the teacher had made them repeat after her. 'You get to decide who you allow to touch you and what happens to you. And remember, if anyone asks you to do something you don't feel comfortable with you must tell someone in authority – the police, a teacher, your parents...' Alice remembered how one of the boys in her class had remained silent but had stayed behind after class to speak to Miss Johnson and hadn't been back to her school after that. 'My body, my rules,' she said to herself quietly.

*

A dull thump and a bang heralded Izzy's entrance into the room, making her frown. The girl turned three backflips in a row and landed on the heap of papers that still lay creased on the floor.

'Izzy! I've told you before, not in the house!'

Alice gathered up the papers from under her as she sat grinning a perfect white smile at Marcus who turned quickly and ran up the stairs. Izzy jumped up laughing and punched Filip playfully in the chest just as a sharp knock sounded at the front door.

Barnes bustled through into her living room. 'I shall not be stopping,' she said, icily as the air fell silent. 'Just a few vitamins to help with your conception.' She looked straight beyond Alice and out into the kitchen, placing a bag of medication on the floor. 'Filip tells me you've not had a great deal of luck so far.' Her face broke out into a smile. 'Don't give up, it will happen soon but you must take care of yourself.' She tapped Alice's stomach, making her flinch.

She glared at Filip, a dark, vibrant anger rising in her chest.

'Barnes!' said Izzy, wrapping her arms around the doctor before Alice could speak. 'Can I show you my experiments – I've been working really hard, like you told me.'

Barnes peeled the small girl out from underneath her lab coat. 'Not this morning, Izzy,' she said, her voice laced with a sugary sweetness. 'But maybe later you can show me everything, okay?'

'If it's good enough can I still come down to help you in the Infirmary? Please? I've got some really good ideas that will help with your work.'

Barnes twitched. 'Only if you've done what I asked, okay?'

'Yes, yes,' said Izzy and jumped up onto the couch, bouncing hard and giggling at Alice who stood unmoving, her body rigid, a cold cut of a stare directed towards Filip. He placed his arm on Barnes's shoulder.

'Thank you again,' he said, ushering her back out onto the street. 'We do appreciate all your help.'

As he pushed the door closed, Alice turned on him, fury burning in her eyes. 'You spoke to her?' she shouted. 'About me... about THIS? Without talking to me first?' Her throat felt scraped and raw and her hands shook as she felt her anger rise again.

'She's a *doctor*, Alice. There's no need to get upset – it's her job, it's what she does. You're overreacting and look...' He picked up Izzy who was uncharacteristically quiet. 'Now you've upset the children. You're going to have to start controlling yourself.'

Marcus, who had crept back down the stairs, stood with his eyes wide and frightened.

'Don't fight,' he pleaded, blinking up at her and, gradually, she let her rage subside for the moment.

She ruffled his hair softly and turned to Filip. 'We'll talk about this later,' she said stiffly and threw the bag that Barnes had placed on the floor into the kitchen.

'Do I have to go on duty today?' said Marcus quietly. 'I'd much rather stay here and search through the old houses.'

'You have to do whatever it says on your rota,' said Filip. 'Now get yourself to work.'

Marcus looked at Alice. 'Can I help you today please?' he said with an almost pleading tone in his voice. His wide eyes and tousled hair reminded Alice of Jonah.

'Not today,' she said in a gentle voice, her anger dissipating slightly. 'We've all got to do what needs to be done to rebuild this place as we're asked to. Even I have to do things I don't want to sometimes.'

Filip shot her a glance and bundled both Marcus and Izzy into the hallway 'I'll see you on site later,' he said and with the thump of the door, they were gone.

Alice sank back down onto the couch that creaked and leaked a hiss of damp air each time she moved. She ran her fingers over her stomach and listened to the faint lilt of birds in the distance. On the Ship, she thought, everything had been disinfectant-clean and there had been an order that was unquestionable. There was little that needed to be questioned.

But now, she knew there were questions that needed to be answered. Everyone who had been her friend on the Ship seemed different. No one was like they used to be. But maybe it was Alice who wasn't like she used to be. She wanted so desperately to speak to someone who wasn't on Barnes' side, someone who could talk to her about the world before she made any decisions, who could help her make sense of what was happening.

Her resolve stiffened. She was going to see the boy she had saved.

By the time she made her way out into the square, a cluster of butterflies had gathered around the small plinth and danced in the morning sunlight. Quinn sat engrossed amongst them, her tablet on her lap, eyes fixed on the screen. Since the night she had burned the violin, Quinn had become almost obsessively mathematical and cold to the point of indifferent towards her.

'Hey,' said Alice, sitting down next to her. 'I'm glad I've seen you. What's up?'

'Not a lot,' said Quinn. 'Running some diagnostics on a set of samples for Barnes.'

Alice stiffened. 'I thought you were supposed to be up at the Barricades today. Marcus has left already.'

Quinn looked up briefly and squinted at the sun, her eyes sparkling with a dark urgency. 'These diagnostics are more important,' she said. 'Barnes needs them by lunchtime.'

Alice thought back to the meeting in the square, to the woman who disappeared. 'Since when has Barnes been directing your actions?'

Quinn carried on tapping at her screen. 'I do what's required,' she said. 'As we all do. This could be a major breakthrough in managing our numbers. Life is different now, Alice.'

Alice shook her head. 'I know that. But *you* seem different. Has Barnes said something to you, you know, about me? You're being so...' she struggled for the word '...I don't know, *cold*.' The mechanical tapping continued at the same pace although, to Alice, it seemed to get louder.

'Change is constant,' said Quinn, focused. 'We all have to be different. Always. I answer to whoever is in charge.'

'That's still me, Quinn. I don't know who Barnes thinks she is but...'

Quinn frowned. 'It was never just you, Alice. You need to keep in line with us all. There is no one leader, we are all equal now.' She paused. 'Are you having *doubts*, Alice?'

The clicking on the screen stopped and there was silence. Alice thought she could almost hear the flutter of the butterflies' wings.

'No,' said Alice, slowly. 'I just feel like things are happening very quickly.'

'Alice,' Quinn began, the tapping restarting, 'Barnes is incredibly talented – if you're jealous, that has to stop. I'm not the only one who has noticed it. Up here, things *are* different. And we all have a part to play. We aren't who we were before the Storms, and we aren't who we were in the Ship. When I burned that violin, part of me died. Part of me had to. We all have a part to play – and I suggest you play yours.' She glanced up at Alice. 'Look, I don't have to report to you – I'm in Settlement and Readjustment. My direction comes from Barnes now.'

Alice felt the anger rise inside of her. 'Barnes doesn't run things around here.'

'Well, she certainly has the right ideas about how we're going to repopulate this broken mess of a city.' Quinn ran her finger over the screen. 'I suggest we just stick to the plan we agreed underground and let Barnes make it all happen.'

There was a suffocating silence as Alice struggled to maintain her composure. She looked out towards the half-ruined buildings across the Black River that looked a thousand miles away. She let her eyes trace up and down over the spires and domes, the high-rises and the low-rises across the desolate city, calming herself through clenched teeth.

'How's Kelly?' she said, her eyes still focused on the buildings. 'She's seemed a little distracted lately.'

Quinn shook her head and traced her finger across the screen. 'I'm sure she's fine,' she said. 'She's been quite emotional but Barnes has been giving her some supplements to help her a little. She's quieter than usual but I guess it's just the hormones, you know.'

'What kind of supplements?'

'Just some herbal remedies from the lab. Barnes is brilliant, considering she did the majority of learning while we were in the Ship. We're very excited about the prospect of bringing a new life into the world. Barnes says it's just a matter of time before her magic works and we can start preparing.' Quinn paused and smiled, her cheeks looking flushed.

'Is Kelly excited? Prepared?' Alice asked through her growing anger, desperately trying to keep her tone smooth, neutral. 'Ready?'

'Of course, it's what we've been planning for. I think she's just nervous but of course she'll get over it. It's such a big thing and I guess our lives will change forever when the babies come.'

'They certainly will,' said Alice quietly.

Quinn turned back to her tablet. 'I need to get these numbers finished,' she said, 'before I head down to the lab. I'll be meeting Barnes down there in an hour.' Her skin, as white as porcelain, gleamed in the sun and her hair was perfectly groomed. Alice felt tired and messy in contrast, sticky with the heat and her head felt unusually disorganised and chaotic.

'Yes,' she said, 'I've a lot to do too; I should get on my way. I wasn't expecting to see you here, but I was hoping to catch Barnes. Is she here or down in the Ship?

'She's doing her rounds here before she goes back underground,' said Quinn looking up briefly without a smile. You'll probably catch her near the new Academy.'

'Great,' said Alice, already out of the square. 'See you later.'

She walked halfway to the Academy, glancing behind her, before heading back towards the opposite side of town. Climbing down the stairs to the Ship was faster than Alice had remembered but by the time she had made her way down to the Infirmary, she felt tired and slightly uneasy, like she had crept into the house of someone she had once known without invitation. She pressed her body against the walls of the tunnel, sneaking through the dimly lit corridors pausing at each corner to check that there was no one around.

Alice pushed open the door.

'Hello?' she said quietly. 'Is there anyone there?'

Silence confirmed she was alone. Relieved, she pushed the door tight behind her. The Laboratory had been completely redeveloped since she'd last been there. Various sample jars lined the shelves and there were stacks of equipment all over the benches. Towards the back, on the right, a separate door with a double lock separated the Lab from a room that was signposted 'Infirmary Isolation Room'. She glanced through the tiny slat-like aperture in the door.

The interior square room was small and cell-like. A large screen took up most of one wall. There was a table, a bed and very little else. Three pictures had been stuck on the opposite side of the room; two were of herself in the crumbling waste of the Deadlands and the last one was of Jonah, face down and bloody, his body broken and shot after his fall from the supermarket roof. Alice shuddered. On the bed, facing away from her, sat Richard Warren. He looked smaller than she remembered and she wondered whether he would be able to help her understand some of the thoughts swirling around inside her head. Part of her felt insane for sneaking down into the Ship to speak to a complete stranger, but being forbidden to do so had lit an angry spark inside her.

Alice took a deep breath, pulled back the bolts and opened the door.

'Hello,' she said. 'I need to talk to you.'

The boy looked up and his face opened up in surprise. He got off the bed immediately.

'Alice!' he said, stepping behind her and shutting the door. 'I knew you'd come. Can you get me out of this place and let me go home now? I can't stand being locked up here, it's like a prison. You've got to help me.' He pulled on an Industry issue jacket and moved towards her.

'Richard...'

'I don't have any shoes though; they took mine away. Maybe you could get a pair for me? There were some in the flat where you found me, but it's okay if you can't, I don't mind. There's plenty out there in the shops that aren't too damaged. I found loads of clothes I could use, especially on the higher ground where the animals didn't get to them. I'm so glad to see you, it's been horrendous here.'

Alice's heart sank. A part of her had hoped Richard would be calm, resolute and could provide her with wise advice, gained by the experience of five years above ground. But then she wondered what harm a few weeks under Barnes's care might have done to him, and that worried her. Or perhaps Barnes was right, maybe people who had stayed above ground had been damaged in some way? Pity overwhelmed her.

She held up her hand slowly, looking behind her. 'Richard,' she said again. 'We're not leaving today. I've just come to visit you and talk to you.'

Richard looked at her with a devastated expression on his face that soon turned to anger.

'So, you're still with *them*,' he said. 'After everything that's happened? You know, you can't keep me here, it's illegal. It's worse than being in jail, at least there you know when you're going to get out. I want to speak to whoever is in charge. This is the point at which I should say "I want a lawyer".'

Alice moved over to the bed and sat down. Richard's tone felt so old-world and foreign but at the same time there was something intangible that endeared him to her.

'What do you mean "with them"? Are you referring to Barnes?'

Richard grunted. 'If you mean that crazy woman in the lab coat who thinks she's the Angel Gabriel with a hypodermic then, yeah, her. Her and all the others.'

'Have they told you why you are here? And who we are?'

'Yeah, she's kind of explained the situation. They keep making me watch this crap all the time. And saying you've got the perfect set up in here.'

He gestured towards the screen. 'This nonsense about killer wolves and viruses. It's all rubbish. It's not like that out there – I was just there, I saw it.'

Alice looked up at the screen. 'I saw it too, Richard, remember, I was there,' she said. 'What happened when the rain came changed us all forever – the way we live, who we are and what's important to us. We're rebuilding everything in a different way. We all have to accept that.'

Richard shook his head. 'You don't even *sound* convinced,' he said quietly. 'You've got a load of kids, some underqualified science student, a crow in a black cloak and a vicious old man running the joint.'

It took Alice a few seconds to realise he was talking about Kunstein and Wilson. 'Wilson's not that old,' she said.

'Maybe not,' said Richard. 'But do you know where he was before the Storms?'

Alice paused. 'He... he was in the school,' she said remembering what Filip had told her about how Kunstein had been watching her and felt distinctly uneasy.

'Before that. They chose you, Alice, before the Storms, so he must have known something was going to happen.'

Alice shivered, trying to block out what Richard was saying and focus on her purpose. 'I came here to ask *you* questions,' she said, her voice tight and strained.

Richard stared at her and lowered his voice again. 'Are any of you qualified to do this kind of thing? You're still children – what are you, fourteen? You should be outside, learning, having fun – surviving. This place is diabolical. You see it, I know you do.'

Alice looked away. 'I'm fifteen,' she said. 'I think.' She realised that she had no idea whether or not her sixteenth birthday had passed. 'And anyway, what difference does that make? We're changing things,' she added. 'The world will be different now.'

'You're not even convincing me, Alice. I know you're not convincing yourself.'

Alice felt a strange feeling of unease rise inside of her.

'Look, I'm sitting here, pretending to believe in all this and be a good boy while all the time they're planning this crazy repopulation programme and I can't do anything about it.'

'We *need* to repopulate – there aren't that many of us and the plans, well, we made an agreement that...' Her voice faltered as the words left her lips.

'Oh, Alice, not those plans.' Richard smiled. 'You really don't know the half of it, do you?'

'Then tell me.'

'You have to get me out of here first.'

From outside the room, against the back corridor, came the sound of footsteps and the clatter of a trolley in the cavernous passages.

'We don't have much time,' said Richard. 'They'll be here soon to deliver that disgusting stuff they call food and try to force me to eat it. And they'll be listening.'

Alice glanced at the door. 'Tell me what you know.'

The scratching of the trolley stopped as it moved into a connected passageway adjacent to the infirmary.

Richard dropped his voice again and rustled some papers. 'If you do what I ask then I'll tell you enough about what Barnes is planning so everyone will see what she's truly like. You'd like that, wouldn't you, Alice?

Alice paused 'Barnes?' she said, swallowing hard. 'What do you know about her?

'Like I said,' repeated Richard. 'Get me out of here and I'll tell you. But I think you know already that she's not the fine, upstanding doctor everyone seems to think she is.'

Alice bit her lip, unsure as to whether to trust Richard. 'I know it's difficult,' she said very quietly. 'But the only way you're going to get back topside is to become part of this. If you resist, you're going to be here forever. You have to at least try to believe in this, in the same way that we all do. We're never going to get back what we had before, and the Industry are working very hard to provide the type of life we can all enjoy and be a part of completely. Aching for the old life is only going to create problems for you and everybody else. It may be different to everything you ever knew but it's the right thing to do.' She looked towards the screen on the wall, wondering if anyone could be listening. 'It's the only thing to do,' she said, hedging her bets.

Richard leaned back on the bed. 'Get me out of here,' he said finally. 'And I'll tell you about what Barnes is planning – and about what she's already done. But you'd better be quick, Alice. Friends of yours could be in danger.'

The air felt thick, clouded with a tension that Alice alone could not diffuse. The rattling down the corridor came closer. She felt her hands shaking nervously.

'Do what they say,' she said, her eyes meeting Richard's directly, her words stilted and staccato. 'And I'll work on your release.' She checked the door.

The boy smiled. 'Alice the rebel,' he said. 'I'm guessing you're down here without permission otherwise you wouldn't be so twitchy. So, I was right. You are suspicious of them.' The clanking of the food trolley got louder.

Alice made her way to the door. 'I'll do what I can,' she said calmly, as her heart thumped in her chest. 'Goodbye, Richard.'

*

Emerald leaves glistened in the sunlight and, for a moment, Alice stood and looked around at the beauty of the woodland. What Richard had said swirled around inside her mind. If he did know something of what Barnes was up to then that confirmed her suspicions about the doctor. And if she was right about Barnes, then what if she was right about everything else being wrong? She felt on edge and picked up her pace, hoping no one had missed her whilst she'd been down in the Ship.

She watched the birds scatter across the skyline and the curl of the ivy around branches that were fresh with new buds. Thick rustling from the undergrowth came and went in a second and, as she reached for her gun, a sandy-coloured rabbit the size of a cat hopped across the pathway.

It looked at Alice for a moment and twitched before leaping back into the treeline. She watched, her mouth open as it disappeared across the path and out of view, tiny white feet leaving a trail of dust across the weedy path.

'Why didn't you shoot it? I thought we were supposed to kill all animals on sight? Alice jumped and spun around to see Marcus slink out of one of the concrete shelters and stand facing her on the path. His pellet gun, clenched in hand, was raised and pointed at the bushes. He lowered it slowly and held it still, tight at his side.

Alice's heart still beat hard in her chest. 'Why didn't *you* kill it?' she said, thinking fast. 'And besides, why aren't you at the Barricades? I thought I told you this morning where you needed to be today.'

Marcus hesitated and walked slowly toward her, the gun slightly out of step with his movement. He debated which question to answer first.

'I…' he paused for a second, watching a crow hop from one foot to another in the branches. 'Rabbits… I… kind of like them. Even though I'm not allowed to. I used to have a one once – when I was little.' He waited to gauge Alice's reaction before continuing. 'But I don't like them now, honest, I would have shot it only…'

'It's okay,' said Alice, softening, and beckoned the boy closer. His face was smeared with tracks of dirt, red around the eyes. He came closer and put his arms around her. The midday sun shone through the strands of his long, straggly hair, making them glisten like golden threads.

'I was on my way over to the Barricades and I fell and hurt my arm. Everything looks the same out here and I got lost. I could hear things in the bushes and Izzy says that there are monsters out here. I just want to play football in the park again, and see my mother.' The sobbing started slowly and then built up to a huge crescendo. Marcus, interlaced in her arms, felt a lot less like an undersized nine-year-old boy and more like a very young child, desperate and alone.

'You need to stick to the rules,' she said, gently, not knowing what else to say. 'That's why we made them, so you wouldn't get lost. Who are you supposed to be on duty with today?'

'Kelly,' he sobbed. 'Kelly and Jayden. And Quinn, I think. But I couldn't find them. I don't like it here, Alice; I want to go home.' The tears came again and she gently sank her knees down until they were both half-lying, half-sitting on the path. She put one arm around the small boy who felt like part-son, part-younger brother, even though there were only a few years between them. There was a tenderness to Marcus that made her feel so protective of him that it hurt her.

'It's okay,' she said, running her hands through his hair and gently cradling him until the tears stopped. 'It's okay.'

'You won't tell Filip, will you?' he said, wiping his face with his sleeve. 'Or Izzy – please don't tell Izzy.'

'Of course I won't,' said Alice. 'We can keep a secret, can't we?'

'Yes,' said Marcus, 'but I don't like secrets. I'm always afraid I'll forget and tell someone.'

'What do you mean?'

'Kelly has a secret but she told me I can't say anything. I like her, she's kind to me and she says that one day we're going to get out of here and we're going to live far away, somewhere without Kunstein and Wilson and Barnes and it's going to be like before.'

Alice felt hairs on her arms prickle. The way he spoke was so similar to Richard. 'Marcus,' she said. 'Our home is here now. This is where we live. What secret did Kelly tell you? You know we can't have secrets in our new family; it's not the way it works.'

Marcus pulled away from her. 'I promised I wouldn't tell,' he said, his voice wavering. 'I promised... please don't tell anyone, please. Please. I don't want to get into any trouble. Please.' The tears started to roll down his cheeks again and Alice pulled him back into her.

'It's okay,' she said again. 'It's going to be okay. I'll take you up to the Barricades and we don't have to tell anyone.' She paused, thoughts Richard filling her head – and then of Marnie, the woman in the crowd and the way she had been silenced.

'You need to stop thinking about the old times, Marcus,' she said. 'The old times have gone.'

The sun had just tipped over into its afternoon height by the time they reached the Barricades, glinting bright white shards across the open grassland dividing the Community and the Deadlands. A few crumbling buildings lay scattered across the plain, deserted and dark against the backdrop of the searing sun. Kelly sat on a high wooden construct, gazing out at the bleak landscape, her eyes fixed on the distant horizon.

Kelly turned around and smiled, deep and genuine. 'Marcus!' she said with enthusiasm. 'We wondered where you'd got to. Jayden has just gone to get some water; he'll be back really soon.'

Marcus hugged Alice and climbed up onto the wooden scaffold next to Kelly.

'Have you seen anything exciting today?' he said. 'Has there been any...'

'Nothing,' replied Kelly quickly, glancing at Alice. 'Nothing at all so far.' She put her arm around the boy who looked fragile and small up on top of the platform. 'We might be in for a quiet shift.' She called down to Alice. 'Are you going to stay a while? It would be great if you could.'

She shook her head. 'Sorry, no, I need to get back to the main site – we're reviewing whether or not we can repair the old hospital so that our sick and injured don't need to go down to the Infirmary in the Ship.'

Kelly squinted in the sun. 'That's great. I'm assuming there'll be a maternity wing there too?'

'Yes, of course.'

'And will Barnes be running it?' Her voice sounded nervous, a little gravelly. She cleared her throat and looked across at Alice.

There was a second of tense silence before Marcus climbed to the highest point of the scaffold and whispered loudly. 'Look! Look, out there – can you see it?'

Alice let her eyes scan the horizon again. 'What are we looking for, Marcus?' she asked urgently. 'Is this your secret?'

Marcus half-nodded before Kelly called out.

'There it is,' said Kelly. 'They're out there.'

'What? What is it?' As her eyes grew accustomed to the shadows and brightness across and out into the Deadlands, for a second, Alice thought she saw a flash in the distance.

'It's just the light reflecting on glass,' she said after a while, relieved. 'It's nothing.'

'It *is* something,' said Kelly in a whisper. 'I'm sure of it. I've seen it before. There are other people out there, Alice.'

Alice moved closer towards the Barricades and shielded her eyes from the sun. 'Have you said anything to anybody about this?' she said. 'I haven't seen anything in the official Watch records.'

'I was going to,' said Kelly, 'but I wasn't sure exactly what to say. And how people would react.' Marcus mouthed something to her and she nodded. 'I'll put it in tonight's update,' she said firmly. 'I'm sorry, Alice, it's just with everything that's been going on recently, I...'

'You what?'

'I'm just worried about Quinn,' she said, finally, trying to change the subject. 'I never really see her any more and she's different...' Another flash glittered across towards the Barricades, this time from a group of outbuildings on the other side of the valley. Marcus gasped and grabbed Kelly.

'There, there!' he shouted and they all turned their attention across in the direction of the broken brick shacks. Crows scattered over stones and bushes, cawing in the distance. And then there was silence. A cool breeze blew in across the Barricades, bringing with it the stench of decay. Alice squinted into the sun. No one else could have survived the Storms, surely? She thought about what Richard had said. And then she thought about Hutchinson and the other threats outside the confines of the Barricade. Her head felt thick with confusion.

'Let's be on the safe side,' she said finally. 'So, make sure it goes in tonight's report, okay?'

Kelly nodded and shrugged. 'You won't stay?' she said. 'For a while, with Marcus and me?' Her voice was sad, pleading almost.

'I can't,' said Alice, wondering whether maybe she could confide in Kelly about what Richard had said. 'But why don't I come to see you later. Maybe this evening? We can have a proper talk about things, if you'd like?' Her voice was genuine.

Kelly's face broke open with a wide smile. 'I'd love that,' she said. 'I really would.'

The old hospital on the east edge of the Community was one of the better-preserved buildings internally; while it had been stripped of the majority of the old, rusting equipment and dirty furnishings, both storeys were intact and required little repair.

'It was more of a special care facility, from what I can see,' said Filip, heaving out the last of the personal goods that had been stored in the cupboards of the private rooms. 'But it has got a theatre and some larger rooms we can use as wards as well as plenty of lab space for research and development.

As they walked the length of the dusty corridor, Alice ran her finger through a line of dirt on the wall. 'It'll need disinfecting,' she said. 'Before we even start work on it.'

'Agreed,' said Filip. 'There's a team coming up tomorrow, specialist hygienists, to begin the process.

'Supervised by Barnes?'

Filip nodded. 'This is *her* facility,' he said. 'When it's fully equipped, she can move up here permanently – she's asked for her living quarters to be incorporated here too, so that she can spend all of her time monitoring progress. It's going to have all the latest technology. Barnes really, really cares about our future – about all our futures.' He put his arm around her waist. 'It might not be finished in time for our first, but in future, the new babies will be able to be born above ground, out here in our new world.'

'I'm not giving birth in the Ship!' Alice turned to him in horror. 'Can you imagine climbing down those ladders, nine months pregnant? What if there was an emergency – you know the lifts only work half of the time. I'd rather wait.'

'We're *not* waiting,' said Filip coolly, moving to one of the shattered windows. 'We have to be one of the first. I've told you that before.'

Alice shook her head. 'It would make a lot more sense to wait a few months – to delay until we have this facility up and running…'

'We're not waiting,' repeated Filip. 'And besides, we'd agree a successful transition to the Infirmary a long time before the due date – for *all* expectant mothers. Barnes's Community replenishment programme suggests that no risks at all should be taken.' His voice was calm and measured, while Alice herself felt like screaming. She felt her anger rising – how dare he tell her what to do? How, all of a sudden, did he get to make those kinds of decisions?

'This is a discussion for another time,' she said, finally. 'But I can assure you that I will not be giving birth in the Ship. This is my body and, whatever we agreed before, it was *not* that I would go back down there. The priority is to have a functioning medical centre *above* ground.'

Filip put his arm on her shoulder. 'Alice,' he said, calmly, 'in a very short time, you will be expecting our child and the priority is to keep you both safe.'

The thought of a baby actually growing inside her gave Alice a dark chill that felt very different to the intense, exciting nights of strategic planning in the Ship in the weeks before they had formally settled back topside. Back then it had all seemed so distant, so far away from the current reality.

'I'm not a bystander in this, Filip,' she said, seriously. 'This is my decision.'

She felt his strong arm clamp down on her shoulder. 'Of course, Alice,' he said. 'This is *our* decision. And we will do what's best for our family.'

Still angry with Fillip, Alice set off across the square. By the time she reached Quinn and Kelly's house, almost exactly the same as the one she and Filip had chosen, a misty film of rain had started to drizzle through the evening clouds creating the gloomy veil of a dismal evening.

When she opened the door, Quinn looked startled. Her usually sleek, manicured hair looked ruffled and unkempt and her face tightly guarded.

'Is there something wrong?' she said, pulling the door behind her. 'Is there an emergency?' The door was old and warped, creaking around the edges with sad, peeling paint.

'No,' said Alice, confused. 'I told Kelly I'd come and visit this evening.'

'What for?' Quinn's eyes narrowed. 'She didn't say. And besides, she's sick.'

'What do you mean sick? Is she okay? Can I come in and see her?' Alice craned her neck to look inside the house as Quinn rubbed her eyes and stepped out into the street. A light covering of rain formed on the fronds of her fringe.

'Not right now. She will be okay but she needs to rest – she's in bed asleep. It's just some sickness. She was feeling a little unwell when she got home from her shift.'

'What's wrong with her? Does she need anything? Maybe I could...?'

'We'll be absolutely fine, thank you, Alice. Look...' She held out her hand to feel the soft, dewy rain, '...it's getting late and the rain has started already.' She stepped back into the doorway. 'I'll tell her you called around, okay?'

'Maybe I could talk to you about her then, she said...'

'She just needs to rest at the moment – she will be absolutely fine tomorrow. Don't worry, I'll take good care of her.'

A dark crackle of thunder sounded in the distance as the rain became heavier and Alice shrugged.

'Good night then,' she said and turned to leave.

Quinn smiled and pushed the door open to step back into the house. And, as she did, Alice caught a glimpse of something out of the corner of her eye. Lying across a chair was a bright, white lab coat.

Chapter Six

The Reasons

Carter

Carter looked up from his book and got to his feet, determined to get the truth from his mother once and for all.

'I know my father is dead,' he said as Jacinta busied herself, preparing a drink. 'But why didn't you tell me about Samuel earlier? What's going on here?'

'Hello, son,' she said, pouring herself some tea, avoiding his gaze. 'How are you feeling?'

'Annoyed, frustrated and not in the mood for pleasantries,' said Carter. 'I need some answers. And now. What exactly happened to my father? And why didn't you come back for me?'

Jacinta took a deep breath. 'Your father Nikolas was a pioneer,' she began, 'a true pioneer – who wanted to make things different. His grandfather – your great grandfather – Richard Warren was one of the survivors of the Storms. Two of the first Scouts found him out here on one of their first voyages after the waters had fallen and took him with them into the Catacombs. He knew things, Carter, things about what had happened in the outside world while the rest of them

were underground. But more than that, Richard knew things about
the Industry.'

'What sort of things?'

'While he was in the Catacombs, he learned about what the plans
were for the new world – the terrible plans that they intended to enact.
He planned to stop them.'

'But what about my grandfather, Milton?' said Carter. 'He was
always supportive of the Industry – he hated the old world.'

'And he hated who his father, Richard, had been,' said Jacinta.
'He felt it made him less-Industry than everyone else because he'd
been born outside. Your grandfather was raised by his mother and
her partner – a dreadful woman who caused much of the heartache
your people have had to endure. She was one of the people who
developed the stratification – the Descendants, First Gens, Second
Gens and Lab Made society that you were brought up in. Your great
grandmother developed the Lab Mades deep underground with her
nasty little assistant. She portrayed herself as a doctor, a scientist and
someone who was changing the world for the better. She poisoned
Milton against his own father and the world he had come from. This
made your grandfather very hateful of what lay beyond the Barricades.'

Carter felt an anger rise inside him, a thousand questions about
his past circling in his mind, as if everything he had ever known had
been a lie. He motioned for Jacinta to continue.

'Milton believed all that was wrong with the old world and the
way it had turned his own father against the Industry. His mother,
that evil woman, was very senior in the Industry and she made sure
he was brainwashed into believing in their manifestos. Milton was the
one person in our family who made it difficult for us to plan our next
steps. But you idolised him and he kept you safe. I knew that I could

leave you with him and he would keep you close to the Industry until we could come back to get you.'

Carter frowned. 'So why *didn't* you come for me? What was *your* great plan? And why did you leave me behind?' The words he spoke tripped over each other, angry and frustrated.

Jacinta took a long drink and cleared her throat, her eyes still fixed on the wall. 'Your father and his friend Rufus Delaney had other plans.'

'Rufus Delaney? Isabella's uncle?' The memory of Isabella remained a sweet sorrow for Carter. He remembered hot summer evenings spent exploring the almost forbidden areas of the Community with her, while his father and her uncle buried themselves away in detailed discussion, unable to be roused to go to search for them as the twilight gathered above the glinting Barricades. Since their first days in the Academy, he had known that he would have done anything he could to change the Community so that he and Isabella could be together. She had made his young teenage heart beat fast and his dreams all fit together, despite the regulations that would keep them apart. His father and the high-spirited Rufus Delaney had been the closest of friends since their school days.

'Yes. Your father and Rufus thought they had it all under control. From when they were very young, they had known that they wanted to get outside the Barricades, to find out what was out there for themselves. Even before they found the books they suspected that there was more. Some people are born with an innate curiosity – it's something the Industry couldn't eradicate, as hard as they tried. They wanted to end the division between First Gens and Lab Mades and make the society more equal. They knew there was more to life.'

'What do you mean *more*?'

'More to what happened after the Storms than the Industry taught in their Academies. More to life than what they learned from within that stranglehold of an isolation tank they called the Community – so they set about finding out. At first, your father thought he could become Controller General, change things from the inside, and do it that way, but he and Rufus were never *Industry* enough for that. They were educated enough and were descended from original Scout blood, but they just couldn't be convincing enough to pass for real Community proponents. So, they decided to work towards an uprising. That was when the Industry found out about the books.'

Carter thought of what Isabella had said to him about his father and her uncle before he had left the Community and ached to be able to hold her and, as much as it pained him, tell her that she had been right. To tell her that he was sorry.

'The books,' he said, quietly.

'You told your grandfather about the books you'd seen in the Delaney house and, although Milton knew it would be the end of this family, he felt he had no choice but to tell the Industry. Luckily, he went to Mendoza first, which bought us enough time to make plans – but not long enough to save Rufus.'

'The Industry killed him.'

'They had to – he was more prominent than your father, although he'd have been next. In some ways, he was. And I was scheduled for the Catacombs.'

'But you were pregnant – they couldn't do that.'

'They can do whatever they want. Especially if they could prove that my baby would not survive to be as healthy and as... perfect as those that had gone before. That's what they *do*, Carter.' She gritted her teeth. 'The synthetic food, the fertility drugs they force women to take – it all causes genetic abnormalities in the children who are born. And then they eradicate those who are different. That's the world they have created.'

Carter looked across at the canvas on the wall at the boy, younger than him in the picture but with the same determined, cocky smile. He thought of the stretch of webby skin between his toes.

'Silas,' he said.

His mother nodded. 'Samuel. Silas was the name your father and I had wanted for him before we left the Community. When we thought we should be able to fight this from the inside. But we couldn't stay. I couldn't let us all die in there. We needed a different plan.'

Carter stretched his fingers out in front of him. They were covered in speckles of dirt from the journey, tiny flecks of blood lingering underneath his fingernails. He picked at them carefully.

'What did your plan change to?' he said, his tone slightly bitter. 'What were you expecting to happen? You could have taken me with you.'

Jacinta handed him a damp rag. 'Here,' she said. 'Wash your hands and face with this.' She poured some more tea. 'Your plan didn't change, Carter. Well, not exactly. You were always destined to be Controller General. I put my faith in your grandfather and I followed your movements as much as I could. Especially in the early days when Mendoza was able to communicate with us.'

Carter looked at her directly. 'You were in touch with the Community? With Professor Mendoza?'

His mother nodded. 'It was difficult, but there are some ways of maintaining communication – although it got a lot worse when Bobbie Alderney and then Anaya Chess came into power. Without Mendoza or Isabella, it's going to be almost impossible, but there's still Lily. Although even that's now going to be difficult.'

Carter squinted at her. 'You think she will help us?'

'Lily is on our side,' said Jacinta sharply. 'She was doing what she was told to do.'

'Then who killed my daughter?'

His mother shook her head, silencing him. 'We had good people looking out for you after we were forced to leave, some of whom gave their lives for you. You are a threat and a danger to the Industry now and anyone supporting you is also at risk. But these are risks that I – and they – were prepared to take for something bigger than us, Carter. Mendoza believed that if you thought we had been killed at the Barricades, it would make you even more determined to defeat whatever was outside and a stronger candidate for Controller General. And Lily made it seem like she'd betrayed you, so you would stay away from the Community and make your way to us.'

'Then I was your… your what? Your *experiment*?'

Jacinta shook her head, looking at him directly. 'No. Not at all,' she said. 'But you must know this by now – some things are bigger than the individual, bigger than you, Carter. We couldn't stay – and leaving you with your grandfather, under the watchful eye of Mendoza, was the best I could do to give you and the rest of your Community the chance of something more. I just didn't bargain on Mendoza getting caught.' Her eyes looked glassy for a second but she quickly moved on. 'Mendoza wouldn't have had it any other way,' she said, quickly. 'The future of the next generations depends on us.'

Carter shook his head. 'Mendoza. What happened to her?'

'The Industry got to her. She clearly played her last card with that girl you got pregnant. Her plan was to make sure that the Industry knew that you had no intention of being with Isabella – having children with another Descendent would have been enough to give you a chance to still be Controller General.'

Carter winced as he remembered the promises he'd made to Isabella and his heart ached for just one more conversation with her.

'It wasn't what I wanted,' he said slowly. 'But I did what Mendoza told me.'

Jacinta shook her hair from her face. 'They never told us her name but we knew she was a Davenport – Mendoza said that would add to your credentials. And *twins* – who could have anticipated that? We didn't hear any more from Mendoza after that. The whole thing broke Isabella's heart, you know – she adored you.'

Through the window came the faint smell of lavender, and the dull slow sound of the beat of a drum. Carter breathed in deeply and let the feelings of nostalgia sink into his bones. He thought again of Isabella and his heart sank. Inside his bones he could still feel her, still taste and smell until she permeated every pore of his body in the way that only the deepest of loves could. His mother's words cut deep and he wondered how many times in the fifteen years he'd been underground had she thought of him.

The drumbeat boomed again, slow and deliberate.

'What's happening down there?' he said.

Jacinta pulled a shawl around her shoulders and hurried towards the hatch.

'They've returned,' she said.

'Who? Samuel and his gang? Where have they been?'

Jacinta pressed her palms against the wall of the room and breathed deeply.

'Carter, I'm sure you have noticed that there are things that are different about the people you have met here so far.' she said. 'Things that are different to people in the Community.'

Carter thought back to Angel and her deep, silver eye. The man with the sticks. The boy with no ears.

'They're…' he hesitated. 'There's something wrong with them all.'

His mother shook her head. 'There's nothing wrong with them, Carter. Many of them came from the Community.' She paused, watching the bewilderment in her son's face.

'The Community?'

'Yes,' said Jacinta, firmly. 'They were born too different in the eyes of the Industry. Many of the children born in the Community are – especially those that are Lab Born but as we know, even the First Gens aren't spared. In the early days they created hundreds of babies and used steroids and hormones to speed up development. The synthetic foods increased the sterility levels, and caused birth defects. Without Mendoza and some of the others, these people would not exist. The children are the ones cast out by the Community and left to die in the waste facilities. These are the lucky ones that made it to us.'

Carter felt sick. 'They all came from the Community? You mean, Mendoza brought them out here?'

Jacinta bowed her head. 'A fraction of them made it. And she couldn't bring them herself, it was too dangerous. But some of the babies were stronger than we imagined and they made it to us alive. We did everything we could to keep them with us. During the winter months very few survived – and some of the early caskets they travelled in down the river weren't the most robust, but every single one that came to us was treasured and loved.'

Carter started at her in disbelief. 'Are you serious? That *cannot* be true. The Community believes that life is precious.'

'Life *is* precious, Carter, more precious than the Industry would have you believe. They are looking only for perfection. But to the Industry, some life is more precious than others. No one here is disposable. Everyone has a part to play and a contribution to make. You should ask Angel to tell you her story someday – she was one of our first.'

Carter watched as his mother's face turned a dark shade of grey. He walked back towards the window, catching the beautiful strains of a stringed instrument as the sounds floated through the air.

'I didn't even get to know my *own* children's stories,' he said. 'And your grandson is still in there.' His head felt heavy. 'I can't leave just him in the Community,' he whispered. 'He needs me.'

'What do you believe happened to the girl?' Jacinta's face was hard and fixed in place. 'After we lost Mendoza and you were sent underground, we didn't get much information.'

'My daughter Lucia came to me when I was first released and told me to go and see Isabella. Then she went missing and I didn't see her again until I found her body in the tunnels as we were leaving. Her wrists had been cut.' Carter closed his eyes tightly. 'Then Lily told me she had killed her.'

His mother shook her head. 'I understand why she told you that but that wouldn't have been her. Someone killed your daughter and left her there for you to find. It was a message.' She crinkled her forehead. 'Someone who wanted you to fail – and that could be any number of people.'

'But someone who knew I was a threat.'

'Exactly. Can you think of who that might be?'

Carter replayed every moment of his short tenure in the Community. There had been Alexis, his housemate. He'd been surly but not aggressive. He shook his head.

'What about your competitors? The other contenders?'

Carter thought back to the sessions with Controller General Chess. There had been two others – the shy and nervous Jenson Jeremiah and the girl, Elizabet. He breathed deeply. 'There was someone, a girl. She was... determined and...' He struggled for the word. 'Strange.'

Jacinta looked at him closely. 'Name?' she said.

'Elizabet. Elizabet Conrad.'

His mother smiled wryly. 'A Conrad?' she said shaking her head. 'I didn't know there were any of them left. Don't you know your history? They were a very troubled family.' She placed her hand on Carter's arm. 'I think you have your answer there. If she's the one they're installing as Controller General then they must be desperate. She is just pure evil.'

Carter shivered. The thought that his daughter, Isabella and others had lost their lives because of him made the pit of his stomach grind. And the thought of Elizabet being in control while Ariel was still within the Barricades made him even more determined.

'Ariel,' he whispered, finally.

Jacinta sucked air in sharply between her teeth. 'From what I hear, he's Industry to the core. Takes after his other grandmother, Jescha – she was behind Mendoza's death, I'm sure of it. But there's too much uncertainty and communication is unclear.' She paused. 'If only we could get establish clear links again, we could get a real idea of what's going on in there.'

'My son is in there.' Carter's voice became raised. 'I care about what happens to him.'

'It's not about caring,' said Jacinta calmly. 'It's about the greater good. I did what was best for you – and for everyone else at the time. But now it may be time to address things that should have been taken care of a long time ago.'

Carter picked up the cup of herb tea that still held faint traces of warmth. The music outside had stopped and had been replaced with a soft chanting that undulated up and down through the sunshine.

'That's where Samuel went? To rescue a baby from the Community?'

His mother nodded lifted up the hatch. 'Yes, he did. But it looks like this little one wasn't lucky enough to make it to us,' she said. 'The drum means that the news is not good...' Her voice tailed into the sound of the rhythmic beat. Carter leapt to his feet.

'I want to come too,' he said. 'I want to understand.'

'I don't think that's a good idea,' said Jacinta. 'Your presence down there will be even more unsettling this evening. Let the people grieve. It's only because you're my son that they've allowed you to stay in the Village. The Industry have done so much damage to us. Each unsuccessful retrieval is very difficult and painful. As one of the Community, you have to understand that they resent you too. Until you prove yourself otherwise, you are part of that regime.'

'But I...' Carter felt sick. 'How was I supposed to know that the Industry... do things like that?' He furrowed his forehead in disbelief.

'That's just one of their terrible, terrible crimes,' said Jacinta. 'Why do you think their hospitals aren't all above ground? I'm assuming that there are still several "Infirmaries" in the Catacombs? That's where some of the worst crimes take place.'

'The infirmaries are below ground for safety, so that...'

'Carter, Carter...' Jacinta put her arm on his shoulder. 'There's so much that happens on those lower levels, those ones that only the very privileged are allowed to access. So many hidden things. Experiments that you would not be able to imagine.'

Carter shook his head. 'It can't be true.'

'It's horribly true. You need to stop being naïve and face facts. Some of those people taken down to the Catacombs will never come back. The things we found at the sluice gates are beyond comprehension.'

The sound of the drum grew louder and then momentarily stopped. 'You don't have to believe any of this but it's been happening for years.

This is why they must be stopped. And like it or not, you have a part to play in that.'

Carter moved to the window where a procession was forming in the clearing. The children he had seen earlier in rags were all now clad in white, holding bunches of lavender and were singing bird-like in a harmonious chorus. Their voices blended beautifully in wordless song. The chorded sound echoed through the trees and out into the sky.

'I have to go,' said Jacinta. 'They're expecting me to speak.'

'I want to come,' said Carter. 'Please. I want to understand.'

Jacinta hesitated. 'Like I said, you're not very welcome here at the moment,' she said. 'Out of respect, I suggest you don't, although...'

'Although what?'

She looked out of the window. 'It might actually do you good. But stay close to me,' she said. 'And make sure you hold this.'

She handed him a freshly cut bouquet of lavender from a cloth bag. 'And please, do not say anything to anybody.'

In the cut-back clearing, a small fire had been lit in the centre that steamed a sweet-smelling smoke through the Village. Most people sat cross-legged in concentric circles around the fire, their hands full of flowers and branches that they each, in turn, placed into the flames. The sound of a strange uncoordinated singing lilted through the forest, each person with their own tune that seemed to blend imperfectly into the next, creating a rhythmic hum. Angel stood at the centre, next to the fire, her hands interlinked with Jacinta's until she raised her hands above her head and all noise stopped. Samuel stood behind them, his eyes firmly fixed on Carter.

'Friends,' Jacinta began. 'Today is another sad day, a day in which we will commit this beautiful child to the earth.' Her voice was calmed and measured as if she were well practised at such an event.

A soft, blossom-filled breeze slipped in between the trees and around the flames of the fire, making them glow more brightly. As Jacinta continued to speak, each person in the crowd bowed their heads.

'And for each of these children we mourn – but we must not forget how fortunate we are that we don't believe in borders, that we don't believe in hate, and that we believe in unity. Before we say our final goodbyes, I would like to call upon those of you that have been saved, to remind us that while this is a terribly sad occasion, we have much to celebrate and so much to be thankful for. The saved ones – please come and join me now. Lazarus, Joshua, Victoria… come on.'

When she finished speaking, several children rose from the audience and made their way to join Jacinta and Angel – some with missing limbs, others with faces that were different. A boy with one limp-looking arm that hung uselessly by his side was guided to the front by an elderly woman. Angel kissed each one in turn and cleared her throat.

'For each one we save, we give a thousand thanks,' she said in a clear, proud voice. 'For each one of you that makes the emotionally terrifying and physically dangerous journey, we honour you. And for those inside the Barricades that help us to do this while risking their own lives, we adore you.'

Carter sat quietly, taking in her words. He thought of the people of the Community – good people that he loved and looked up to that had known about this. He thought of those who had tried to protect him. Could he have sanctioned this as Controller General? Could he have stopped it? He wondered what would have happened to Lucia and Ariel if they had been born differently. And how their lives might have turned out if their tiny twin bodies had been imperfect in the eyes of the Industry and they had been forced to make the journey to the world outside.

'It can't be true,' he whispered to himself in disbelief. 'It just can't.'

A woman sat next to him turned, her face lined with grief. 'You were supposed to change all this,' she said. 'I believed you were different, not some coward who would run.'

'I didn't run,' whispered Carter, shaking his head. 'And I am different. I didn't know about any of this. Listen, I have children of my own. A child, A… I…' His voice faded into the fire. 'What can I do now?' he said, mostly to himself.

The woman turned her body away from him and focused her eyes on the flames. Carter watched as Angel carried the body of the tiny baby, wrapped in a white cloth away from the crowd and handed it to a couple who disappeared into the woods.

'They would have been her new parents,' said the woman, her eyes glazed with tears. 'Like many, they have not been blessed with the ability to have their own. While others…' She looked at Carter in disdain and said nothing further.

The crowd drifted out into the forest and gathered around the burial hole. Carter held back, his throat choked with a thick lump of tears as they sang again – that strange low hum that reverberated through the whole Village. An air of serene peace descended as the humming stopped, and the small body was lowered carefully into the ground before there was complete silence where not even the sound of birdsong could be heard. Every head in the clearing was bowed and those in the woods lowered their bodies to the floor. Carter closed his eyes and felt the quiet of the moment hold him and somehow, without meaning to, he felt himself join them in mourning.

When he opened his eyes, there was much movement. Angel and Samuel were carrying large wooden crates of ripe fruit and vegetables into a clearing. Platters of meat and what looked like whiteloaf were placed on flat, topped tree trunks that had been hauled into the open space.

'And now, we celebrate!' said Angel, beckoning the crowd to join her at the tables. Together they rose, kissed and hugged each other and joined hands as they approached the feast in front of them.

'It is not our difference that drives us apart,' Angel continued, 'but our love that holds us together. Today, as every day, we put those differences aside and become one people.' She gestured to the woman next to Carter who stood and embraced him briefly with a cold indifference, then motioned towards the piles of food.

'Join us,' she said. 'You are here now and maybe there is something you can do to right these wrongs.'

In the quiet of the house in the trees, Carter sat motionless, his stomach full and his mind whirring. A stack of books was piled next to him that he'd voraciously devoured in the hours since he'd left the feast. Within the past few days, he realised he'd learned so much more than his days in the Academy and it scared him. His life and everything he knew before was different – even in his imagining, it now felt cold, sad and a distant dream. A terrible dream in which he felt like a naïve and manipulated bystander.

It was late, and the moon cast thin shadows across the wooden floor, shapes that moved and drifted with the clouds overhead. Suddenly, the planks parted and a tired, pale face entered the room.

'Your presence today certainly caused some consternation,' said Jacinta as she hauled herself through the floor hatch, Angel and Samuel behind her. 'But your compassion at the ceremony has won you a little less hostility.' She looked at his, concerned. 'This is just the start of the journey, Carter. You still have to win the trust of the council – and the rest of the people.'

Carter looked deep into Jacinta's eyes. 'I do believe you, but it's…' he paused for a moment. 'It's all too much. Too dreadful.' He shook his head. 'I understand the rules of the Industry better than I ever did. In a horrible, terrifying way, it makes perfect sense. They are experimenting with people's lives in there.'

'Experimenting? They would have killed me,' said Samuel, his teeth gritted tightly together.

'And they will kill us all,' said Jacinta, as she poured each of them a large, herby drink, 'unless we stop them fast. Which is why you're both going back to the Community.'

Chapter Seven

The News

Alice

'Congratulations.'

Ellis Barnes held out a coloured stick to Alice and pressed it into her hand. She watched as Alice's face paled. 'You're around four weeks pregnant.' The broad flash of a smile was there momentarily. 'So, it looks like you *will* be one of the first.' Barnes had the air of someone much older than her years and there was something about her that made Alice feel increasingly uncomfortable. Something more than jealousy.

'*One* of the first?' She watched Barnes as she crossed the room, a makeshift doctor's office on the ground floor of the new hospital.

'Yes,' said Barnes. 'As I said before, there are many trying at the moment and we have one other recently confirmed.' She looked out of the window and watched as a group, led by Izzy dragged a tree by the roots across the square. The office afforded little privacy and Alice leaned back so that she couldn't be seen through the glassless holes in the wall.

'Who?' she said. 'I should know who the other is. It's Kelly, isn't it?'

Filip put his arm around her and squeezed her tightly.

'What does that matter?' he said, grinning. 'We're going to have a baby!' He high fived Marcus who looked distinctly embarrassed.

Alice held the thin strip of paper in her hand and turned it over. 'Are you sure?' she said. 'I don't feel any different…'

Barnes looked at her closely. 'You won't – it's too early for you to feel anything – but you will.'

Alice sat in shocked silence.

'You'll be fully taken care of, Alice. As you know, I didn't complete medical school before the Storms but I've studied more cases in five years in the Ship than most doctors see in a lifetime. And yes, I'm sure. It's a positive result. And you *will* be ready.'

Alice felt the pit of her stomach rise and fall in anticipation and she rubbed the palm of her hand across her skin.

'There'll be a lot more tests,' said Barnes to Filip with a wide smile, 'but there's no reason to believe that, with the right care, it won't all turn out just fine. And if it doesn't we shall keep trying.'

Alice wasn't sure what version of fine she was looking at but there was no denying that the growing mass of cells inside her was going to change the course of her life forever. She could hear voices talking over her head – Marcus asking when the baby would come, Izzy who had darted into the room, probing Barnes for the details of the pain of childbirth, and Filip questioning the security of life above ground.

'Should we reduce Alice's workload?' he said, fervently, 'I don't want her to take any risks.'

Barnes paused and smiled at Izzy. 'I'm sure this little one could help pick up the household tasks – and she's certainly shown an aptitude for young leadership. Quinn too – I'm sure between us we can all cover Alice's tasks so she can get plenty of rest…'

Alice baulked. 'No, you will not,' she said, punctuating each word clearly to stop her voice from shaking. 'Absolutely nothing changes. Women have been having babies for years and continued to work.'

'Nothing is without risk,' said Barnes, putting a hand on Filip's shoulder and ignoring her. 'While I may not be obstetrics trained, I'm the best you have right now, so I would suggest you take the advice that's given. I'm sure Kunstein would agree.'

Alice scowled across at Barnes. 'Would you mind talking to me?' she spat. 'This is my body and my baby we're talking about.'

'And mine,' said Filip gently. 'Come on, Alice, this is the most important and exciting thing that's happened since we spotted dry land.' His eyes were bright and shining with an enthusiasm that Alice had never seen before. He looked proud to the point of regal, almost. She turned to Barnes.

'Kelly is the other one, isn't she?' she demanded. 'Kunstein told me she and Quinn were trying. And the other night…'

Barnes narrowed her eyes and shook her head. 'I'm afraid I can't tell you that. You'll have to wait to be told.' She shrugged her shoulders. 'Doctor–patient confidentiality,' she added and flashed a face-wide smile. 'Now, let's look at a treatment plan.'

Alice scowled. 'I think I should also get to know exactly who is bringing new life into this Community.'

Barnes shook her head. 'I'm afraid not. Repopulation is my business and certainly not before we've done some preliminary checks to ensure that the foetuses are developing as expected. A huge amount is riding on this next generation and it's my job to ensure that each and every person brought into this new community is fit and healthy from both a physical and psychological perspective. As you know, we just don't have the facilities to deal with any… well… complications. We have enough threats all around us on a daily basis – we need to focus on creating something pure and perfect within these walls. Something better than what we had before. You of all people should know that, Alice.'

Even Marcus and Filip were nodding. Alice felt her heart beating strong inside her chest.

'I do. And thank you so much, Barnes,' she said with a bitter tone, rising from her chair. 'I think I need to get some fresh air now.'

'Are you okay?' said Filip, rising with her.

'I'm fine,' she replied, smiling and patting his arm. 'But I need a little time to absorb the news. It's happened more quickly than I expected. I won't be long.'

As she walked out into the partly broken street, freshly cleared of undergrowth, the smell of the cut back lavender felt reassuring and familiar. Above her, high in the sky, tiny speckled white birds formed a protective circle around her as she walked, slowly and with any deliberate purpose towards the edges of the outside world and out towards the Barricades. Her frustration with Barnes and Filip itched underneath the surface of the skin and she longed to speak to someone about it. Kelly would be on watch time now and hopefully alone.

As she crossed into a line of trees, the pattering sound of soft shoes on the dirt track behind her dragged her out of her reverie.

'Marcus, what are you doing here?' The boy was crimson-faced and puffing heavily. He smiled and bent his body, catching his breath.

'I wanted to check you were okay, you know, with the baby thing.' The sentence came out a few words at a time. 'I thought Barnes was a bit mean to you.'

Alice stopped for a moment wondering how much the small boy understood. He looked at her, his eyes filled with genuine concern – a concern that had been distinctly absent from Filip. They stood together for a while taking in the deep green scent of the forest. 'Of course I'm okay with it, Marcus, it's what we want, isn't it?' She kept her eyes fixed on the treeline, avoiding Marcus's gaze but put a hand on his shoulder, feeling an undeniable warmth for the small boy.

'Is it a boy or a girl?' said Marcus, his hand wavering over her stomach.

'We don't know that yet.' She put her arm around the boy and tousled his hair. 'It's going to be a little while before anything happens – these things take months.'

'How big is it? Can you feel it moving yet?'

Alice smiled. 'No,' she said. 'That won't happen for a few months yet. I'm only a few weeks gone…' As the words tumbled out of her mouth, she realised that she actually knew very little about what would happen when, or had any idea of what the next eight or so months would be like.

He looked at her stomach. 'My mum was having a baby,' he said.

'Your foster mother in the Ship?'

'No, my real mother. The one from before.' His eyes welled with tears. 'I know I'm not allowed to be sad but sometimes you remind me of her a little bit.' His shoulders shook but he held the features of his face tight. 'I was excited to have a new sister,' he continued. 'That was before I knew what sisters were really like.'

Alice smiled. 'Is Izzy bossing you about a bit too much?' she said softly. 'I can have a word with her if…'

'No!' Marcus looked up, horrified. 'It's all right, Alice, really. Don't tell her I said that, will you?'

'Of course I won't,' she reassured him. 'You know, I didn't have any brothers or sisters, but I really wish I did. It's okay to not get along with Izzy all of the time, you know. That's what happens when you…'

Marcus's lower lip began to quiver. 'Are they... are they going to take you back down to the Ship to have the baby? Izzy said that Barnes said they might. I couldn't stand it if you went away, Alice.'

'They're not going to take me anywhere, Marcus.' She squeezed his hand tightly. 'The Industry are just trying to make sure everything goes according to plan and getting the topside hospital functioning properly is a priority. The Infirmary is no place to bring new life into this world.'

'But Barnes said...'

Alice swallowed deeply. 'Well, as for the doctor, she's a bit bossy but it's her job to keep us all safe, isn't it?'

Marcus shrugged. 'I don't like her,' he said, as they started walking again.

As they approached the perimeter, the golden sun arced over the Barricades and the silhouettes of the Watchers stood stark against the glinting metal fence. They reminded Alice of the pictures she'd seen in history books of the great wars. They moved in shifts, guarding the edges of their world carefully. She stood mesmerised, watching them, watching the world, scanning the face of each one for her friend.

'I'm glad it's you. You came to find me. You're the other one, aren't you?'

From behind one of the stone shelters, Kelly stepped into the path. She held out her hands in greeting, and Alice was sure she could feel them shake as they embraced.

'Yes.' Alice stopped. She wasn't sure exactly what she wanted to say to her but her simple company made her feel more relaxed than she had in a while.

'You *are* pregnant though?'

Kelly guided her over to a clump of mossy rocks overlooking the Deadlands and they sat, hands still locked together. Alice nodded.

'Everyone's trying,' said Kelly. 'We all said we would. Barnes was insistent that she get to try out her new techniques and ideas for repopulation as quickly possible. Quinn volunteered me. But so far only you and I tested positive for eligibility, though I think there are more underground who qualify. Quinn says she has some ambitious plans for regenerating the Community – along with the freeze-thaw theory, between them, she and Barnes think they can take over the world.' Her face was etched with sadness.

'Was she there the other night?' Alice paused. 'The night I was supposed to come over to see you, were you... were you sick?'

'I felt awful,' said Kelly. 'I thought it might have been something to do with the baby, but it's too early. I don't really know. Quinn wanted to call Barnes but I asked her not to – I fell asleep and I don't remember much. But she's over at our place all the time to talk about the Model and the resettlement plan.' She paused. 'At least that's what she says.' Kelly picked up a stick and scratched her name into the ground.

Alice took the stick from her. 'What do you mean?'

'I don't know. Quinn says I'm just over-emotional because of this.' She patted her thin stomach. 'I'm excited, don't get me wrong, but I feel... well... I'm not sure I'm ready. I've got a strange feeling about the baby. Quinn's been acting differently and...' Her voice broke off. 'And I kind of wish it was just the two of us, like it was in the Ship,' she continued, stumbling over her words. 'I'd like it if we could just go away somewhere, just for a while... I've thought about it, you know. Just getting out of here.'

Alice put her arm around Kelly's shoulders, smoothing her soft blonde hair, her heart pounding. Her own thoughts felt muddled, confused. With the recent news, her plans to talk to Kelly about Richard seemed less significant and urgent.

'But we can't though. That's not what we planned,' she finally said, although a part of her wanted so badly to agree.

'We said and did things we didn't understand,' said Kelly. 'It's not all bad out there. I know it isn't. The Industry don't know everything, Alice.' She picked some leaves from a bush and balled them in her fist. 'The truth is, I'm don't think I'm ready to be a parent. I'm not as grown up as all of you – and I'm scared.'

'You're not much younger than us...' Alice's paused as the words came out of her mouth. 'I mean, you're fourteen...' She looked into Kelly's bright, innocent eyes that were full of fear and apprehension. Her frame was small for her age, and, in that moment she looked a great deal more childlike than she had appeared to Alice in the coolness of the Ship where they had all been desperately keen to grow up. She imagined Kelly on one of the brightly coloured swings in the Simmons Street playground that Alice herself had loved so much when she was younger.

'In the old world, none of us would have been ready, but this is a new chapter,' she said, softly. 'We agreed, remember?'

Her voice sounded strong, reassuring against the rush of cool breeze and the cawing of birds in the distance. She repeated the words to herself over and over, trying to make it sounds believable. She remembered what she had promised but it all seemed so very long ago.

Kelly sighed and nodded. 'I remember.' She paused. 'You know the babies... Barnes says they might not be, well, perfect. There might be contamination from the waste that came from that nuclear plant, Drakewater – and we've not been getting all the vitamins we need. She says we should be taking her extra supplements. And that frightens me too.' Kelly's voice reduced to an almost whisper and her eyes were pooled with an anxious haze. 'I don't know what she's giving me half the time.'

'It's a chance we have to take,' said Alice, a lump in her throat. 'And we have to be strong. We will love them regardless. It's what we both agreed.'

'Aren't you scared?'

Alice struggled to find the words. 'I'm going to be strong,' she said finally. 'Whatever it takes. I can still be who I am, the leader that I want to be, and a mother. I am going to be strong,' she repeated.

'That's what Quinn says. She says that weakness won't be tolerated any more. Not in the new world. Is that true?'

In that moment, Alice felt weaker that she ever had. 'It won't be tolerated,' she said, taking Kelly's hand. 'We have to stick to the plan. It's what we agreed.'

Kelly nodded nervously, then paused and moved closer to Alice, her voice almost a whisper. 'I have to tell you something. There *is* someone out there,' she said slowly, her eyes fixed on the distance. 'I've seen them.'

Alice swallowed deeply. 'What do you mean, you've seen them? Do you mean the flashes of light that we saw the other day?'

'No, it's not just that.' Kelly hesitated. There are others. Other people. In the bushes and the trees. They saw me too.' Her voice was wavering and uncertain as an unexpected bone-chilling wind whipped through the trees.

Alice looked at the girl, eyes bright. She'd always been the one with the most vivid imagination, the most colourful dreams of the future. The one who was most prone to exaggeration and fantasy, even though she'd proved herself to be one of the smartest girls in the Ship. Alice had almost thought of her as a little sister when they'd first come above ground. The girl who thought she'd seen a tiger roaming in the outbuildings at the edge of the woods, which was quickly dismissed as a wolf.

'Are you absolutely certain?'

Kelly paused again, gauging Alice's reaction. 'They were quite far away but I'm sure they were there.'

Alice's eyes narrowed. 'What do you mean? How close did you get? Kelly, you need to be careful. They could be dangerous... you shouldn't...'

Kelly put her hand on Alice's arm to stop her. 'If they were dangerous they'd have killed me already. I think they've seen what we're doing here and maybe they want to know more. They're not hostile. One of them waved at me and I waved back.' She paused. 'I think we should speak to them.'

'We can't,' said Alice, firmly. 'Even if we wanted to, remember what we agreed, our life is in here now. Nothing of the past. Nothing. That could jeopardise our whole existence. What if they're...' Her words trailed off and her chest felt tight.

'What if they're like us?' said Kelly, her eyes cast downwards. 'What if the world isn't such a bad place after all? What if we've got more to fear in here? These are real people. Human. Like us.'

Alice scanned the horizon and turned to Kelly. 'Who have you spoken to about this?'

Kelly shrugged. 'Only Marcus and Quinn,' she said. 'And Quinn said the same thing as you. That we need to remember what we agreed. No outsiders.' She paused. 'And that if I saw anyone again, I should shoot them.'

Alice nodded. 'That's right,' she said, although there was a slight strain in her voice.

She felt her mind spiralling in different directions. 'I'll raise it with Kunstein,' she said, finally.

'No,' said Kelly sharply. 'Let me talk to Quinn again, please?' There was a pleading tone in her voice and her eyes started to water with tears. 'Maybe I was wrong,' she added reluctantly.

Alice smiled gently. 'Okay,' she said. 'But you know what we agreed.'

'But what if what we agreed was wrong?'

'We weren't wrong,' said Alice, opening her eyes wide, her tone intending to be reassuring enough for the both of them as she turned to leave. 'Things may not be perfect but we have to all work together to fix them.'

'I don't know if I want to be a mother, Alice, but I will try to be the best one I can be.' Kelly's eyes seemed frightened but glowed with a tiny glimmer of happiness.

Alice was struck by how much younger than the rest of them that the fourteen-year-old looked and sounded, her pale skin blemish-free and only just starting to earn the colour of the sun from spending her days in the fresh air. In less than a year's time, the child would be a parent herself and the thought of it worried Alice a little, gnawing thoughts biting at her conscience. *What if she were too young? What if they were wrong when they picked Kelly to go topside with them? What if Richard were right?*

She turned and kissed the top of Kelly's forehead and picked up the trail heading away from the Barricades.

'We weren't wrong, *but maybe we weren't entirely right*,' she repeated to herself, running her fingers across the edges of her still flat belly, as she walked slowly back through the sun shadows towards the cluster of houses that made up the Community.

Chapter Eight

The Meeting

Carter

The next morning when Carter awoke, he could hear the high-pitched chirping of a bird somewhere in the branches above him, while the early sun streamed through the window. Samuel begrudgingly nodded in his brother's direction in greeting.

'Good to see you boys getting along nicely,' said Jacinta. 'Now, we need to talk about our next steps regarding the Industry.' Her tone was brusque and direct as she continued. 'There was an early meeting this morning and there's been some good news – the council have voted and agreed that you can stay – if you want to, of course. But there's a lot of work to do to prove to the Villagers that you're on our side before you can go back to the Community.'

Carter got up and poured a drink. 'Of course I am. But overpowering the Industry is going to be a challenge.' The juice was warm and sweet in his stomach. 'There are thousands of them and just a few of us.'

Jacinta nodded. 'Yes,' she said. 'But this is not about numbers. This is about exposing them – proving to everyone in the Community who they really are.' Her voice was determined and strong.

'And you know a way to do that?'

'We think we do, yes.'

'We don't even know what's in there,' interjected Samuel.

Jacinta motioned for him to sit. She turned back to Carter. 'Deep within the catacombs is an area called Chamber One,' she began.

Carter shook his head. 'I've never heard of it.'

'You wouldn't have. Chamber One is said to contain significant amounts of information that can bring the downfall of the Industry and its exact location is not known to us. We were told about it by one of our people who came from the Community. Both Mendoza and McDermott were able to confirm its existence. Neither had security clearance to go that deep into the Catacombs and risk jeopardising their positions. It is a secret passed from Controller General to Controller General – which is why, Carter, the plan had been to put you in that position so that you would find out.'

Carter took a sharp intake of breath. 'But how did you know I would...'

'You're your father's son, Carter. You were exceptionally talented and we knew you'd be chosen. And we also knew that when you found out the truth, you'd work with us. So now you're not there to do that, you're going to have to find another way.'

Carter looked from Jacinta to Samuel and then back to Jacinta. Since he first started at the Academy, his whole life had been about preparing for the position of Controller General. About changing everything so that he and Isabella could be together. But what his mother was saying meant that his fate – that decision – had been made simultaneously by his parents and Mendoza for completely different reasons. He channelled his confusion and anger at their deceit towards the Industry, focusing his energy.

'I'll find it,' he said quickly. 'I'll find Chamber One.'

'I'll go,' said Samuel. 'We don't need him.'

'None of us have been in there for over ten years and he…' Jacinta pointed her finger at Carter, 'will be trusted by the people in the Community.'

'I'm going,' said Carter decisively, ignoring Samuel's glare. 'They know who I am and when I return it will become clear that the Industry have lied about my death. I was a respected figure – a Contender – and what I have to say will be important. People will listen to me.' Carter felt his excitement mounting. 'We should leave in a few days, when we've planned the route.'

Jacinta smiled a little but shook her head. 'Not quite yet. The council here have sanctioned your return, but on the condition that you prove yourself to be one of us – that you are on our side against the Industry. Right now, there is still a lot of suspicion and concern that you'll turn against us. They won't support a mission until they are sure that you won't compromise the situation.' She looked up as Angel came into the room through the door in the floor. 'Angel will help you, but none of us can do this for you.'

Carter watched as Angel pulled back her hair and started to tidy the shelves. 'You're going to need to show us your skills and learn how we do things so that you can contribute in some way.' She smiled. 'If you're not Controller General, who are you?'

Carter raised his eyebrows. 'I have skills,' he said. 'I'm sure there's something I can do.' He wondered how population control, censomics and synthetic food production might help him succeed in a village that was this simple.

'Samuel and I have work to do,' interjected Jacinta. 'We will see you later.'

As they left the house in the trees, a warm, gentle breeze blew in through the window and shifted the delicate pages of one of the books, *Principles of Dentistry*, that Carter had been reading.

'You're going to have to prove yourself to them,' said Angel.

Carter looked at her intently. 'Yes,' he said, finally. 'I know I will.'

'Then let me take you somewhere,' she said. 'Show you a little bit of what life here is like. Part of being here is about learning how we live and you're going to need to fit in. And then you'll have a better idea of how you can be a part of our Village and what you can contribute.'

The cascade of the waterfall deep in the forest was, without doubt, the single most incredible thing that Carter had ever witnessed. Dark green fronds stitched the sides of slate grey rock while the water pounded into a clear pool at the base of the falls. A silver mist of spray covered his face as he got closer to the water. Angel pulled at his arm.

'I guess you've never seen anything like this before, have you?' she said, leading them towards the shallows of the pool.

'Is it…?' Carter looked down at Angel's bare feet. 'Is it dangerous?'

She laughed. 'Not at all, as long as you know how to swim – which you probably don't, do you?'

Carter shook his head. 'Swimming was against the rules. And besides, there was no open water except the Black River – and being anywhere near that was against the rules too.'

Angel motioned for him to take off his shoes.

'It's safe enough, for now,' she said. 'Just stay within the barrier area.'

'Why?'

'Because there are areas for swimming, areas for washing and we use some of the tributaries for drinking.'

Carter looked down at his feet. 'That's disgusting. You drink this?' He turned at her, horrified. 'Have I drunk this?'

'It's clean now,' said Angel, watching the water torrent down in the distance. 'But a few years ago, the Industry diverted pollution in here and drove waste from the Community out into our water supply. Everything became infected and all the fish were poisoned. It took two years for the water to clear – they were hard, hard years. We don't know if they did it on purpose – or whether they could do it again.' She ran her fingers through the water gently. 'We lost some good people,' she said.

The water thundered downwards, a soft spray of mist landing dew-like on Angel's cheeks. 'Then last year there was the fire in the cornfields. We don't know exactly how they managed it but the whole crop was destroyed. All we found were fragments of metal in the dust. The worst thing is the not knowing. Not knowing what they will do next,' she continued.

'Then why don't you leave?' said Carter. 'Go somewhere far away from here and start again.'

Angel shook her head. 'We can't leave here without somewhere to go. Not all of our tribe would make it. We've worked hard to build what we have here. And besides, there's the contamination out there. We don't know where exactly is safe and where isn't.' She rubbed her hand over her eye. 'Few people have been left untouched by this over the years. And besides, it wouldn't matter where we went. This is our home.'

She threw a stone into the pool and Carter watched the ripples of the water unfold and spiral outwards carefully. Suddenly she got up and shook away the conversation as quickly as it had started.

'I didn't bring you here to talk about that,' she said. 'I brought you here to show you how to swim. Just deep enough for you to feel what it's like. Don't worry.'

Carter wasn't entirely sure what he should be worried about, but there was something about Angel that he trusted completely. He rolled up his trousers, took off his shoes and stepped into the icy coldness behind Angel, who was already knee-deep. The pool was so clear he could make out her toes sliding through the soft mud underneath the water. There was something so liberating about the water all around him that he could barely speak.

'This is unbelievable,' he said, finally.

Angel winked her one eye and then disappeared beneath the folds of the water. Carter waited for her to resurface but the cold still water yielded nothing but a tiny piece of wood pushing up through the ripples. Seconds turned to minutes.

'Angel!' he shouted. 'Where are you? I can't follow you.' And then desperately, 'I can't swim. I don't know how to do this.'

From the other side of the pond the skinny reed glided along back towards him. Angel's head broke through the water and she took a deep breath, shook her hair and laughed. She held the reed tube up in front of Carter.

'We use it to breathe underwater. It's like, well, ventilation. It takes the air from above and lets me use it below the surface.'

Carter felt relief flood his body. 'Don't do that again,' he said. 'Teach me by telling me first.'

'I'm sorry,' said Angel, laughing a little and then turning serious. 'It must be so strange for you after being in the Community. I mean, I've heard stories about how terrible it is there. The whole First Gen versus Lab Born system and how they get treated. Is it true that Lab Mades aren't allowed to get senior positions in the Industry? And they're not allowed to have relationships with anyone not in their inferior class?' She scrunched up her forehead. 'That's wrong, Carter.

That whole class system was one of the dreadful things about the old world that I thought your people were trying to eliminate. Instead you just recreated it.'

They sat drying their feet on a grass bank, watching the birds that came and went between the branches of the trees. They'd been there less than an hour but, to Carter, it felt like a lifetime.

'What's he like?' he said. 'Samuel, I mean. Given that he knew I was his brother he wasn't exactly friendly.'

Angel smiled, her eye twinkling in the sunlight. 'He's a good man – he's been an incredible strength to this place and helped build so much here in the last few years. He's moody, bad tempered and sometimes disappears for days on end but he adores his mother and would do anything for her. He's a talented artist – he drew that picture of your family and sketched you and your father just from the description your mother gave. He's smart, but he lacks any real emotional awareness – he can't bear to be around people for that long.'

Carter pictured the rough, brutish man he'd pinned to the floor. 'Right,' he said, nodding. 'He can be pretty nasty when he wants to be. He hates me. When I imagined Silas coming into my life it wasn't like this.' He paused. 'I was so excited to have a brother when I was a child – he was going to be my baby brother.'

Angel bit her lip hard. 'Things have never been easy for Samuel,' she said. 'The first few years here were very hard on everyone. It took a long time for this place to develop. And almost as soon as he could walk, Samuel was relied upon to help build these houses and hunt for food. He never knew your father like you did, and he never knew what Jacinta was like before – in the days when she was happy. Or at least when she had your father with her.'

'That must have been hard.'

'Yes, and with you appearing suddenly, it's been difficult for him.' Angel stretched, revealing the long curve of her neck. 'All his life he's lived in the shadow of an idea of someone he's never even met and then, to have to face you for the first time… well…' she broke off. 'It was a shock for him to meet the brother he's never known. You look so alike.'

He leaned over and looked at his reflection in the water – at first glance, he couldn't look any more different to Samuel, but there was something about the shape of his face, his nose and mouth that was similar. There was no mistaking that they were brothers.

'Tell me about the babies,' he said to Angel. 'Tell me what happened to you all.'

Angel hesitated. 'Apparently the bad stuff started quite soon after the Community people first came above ground, but they managed to keep most of the terrible things they did secret for a long time. Anyone who challenged them was silenced. Your parents—' she trailed her hand through the water '—they knew something needed to be done. Jacinta was able to help so many – along with Mendoza.'

'They would have killed Samuel if he'd been born there.' Carter shook his head; the control and security of the Industry, the safety of the insides of the Barricades made him feel sick to the very core of his stomach.

'Yes. Because he didn't conform to their perfect anatomical standards. You've been told about the so-called supplements and the synthetic food. Being underground with all that stuff impacted fertility and, up here, we suffered too with the lack of food, contamination and clean water. Many people died and fertility levels dropped. But when your mother came here, she was determined to try to change whatever she could. She was able to set up a basic communications system. Mendoza had a contact in the infirmary who was able to let us know when there might be a baby our people could save. The contact would put them into the waste containers still alive, rather than inject them with final sleep serum as she was told to.

'When they first went to the sluice point there, they found years' worth of decay. They'd hide a whole day – sometimes more – in those filthy, wet dumps, waiting for the Transporters to come and drop off their loads of waste. Sometimes they'd hear the crying and dig for hours in the pits until they found them – in whatever state they were in.' Angel stopped and wiped her eye.

'It was terrible. Over the years we've saved some – we've saved many. Between them, the rescue teams do what they can to revive them, feed them and keep them warm and then bring them back here to the Village. The whole thing is disgusting, heart-breaking. We lost way more than we were able to bring back and some of them—' she looked at Carter '—most of them were just a little bit visually different, nothing else. Like me. They saved so many, Carter, so many people that were just not perfect enough for the Community.

'But the communications between here and the Community weren't always the best. There were times when we'd be told there were two, but only find one – or times where the messages didn't get through at all. In the times where we lost contact completely, a few of the team set up a camp there, just in case. We'd have people stationed there for days at a time, sometimes and they'd wake up in the middle of the night to the sound of dreadful, painful wailing and have to sift through all the synthetic food and human decay in the dark with their hands. It was dangerous work.'

Angel paused for a second and looked Carter directly in the eye. 'That was when we knew that we had to change things. The Industry may have saved a lot of people during the Storms, but afterwards the damage to humanity was irreparable. That sterile ugliness those creatures created – nothing natural can survive in there. Not in a way that's worth living.'

Carter felt her words sinking into his bones. The horror and sadness of what the Industry stood for – what he himself had aspired to – ached through into his soul. Anger, desperation and defiance overcame him, coupled with the guilt for all those he had left behind.

'We need to fight them,' he said, finally, and placed his hand on her arm. 'I want to make this happen and I need to know everything I can to destroy what they have done.'

Angel smiled; a sad, hopeful smile 'Then I'll take you to the person who was there. The one who knows about Chamber One. I want you to talk to her.'

As the late evening sun slunk silently behind the tops of the trees and people of the Village melted away for the evening, Angel led Carter through a small thicket to a clearing at the south end of the Village.

Even sat cross-legged next to a fire, Carter could see that the woman was exceptionally small, her features clearly defined in miniature with jet black hair and piercing blue eyes. He looked her up and down. She looked about the same age as his mother, maybe a year or two younger, and spoke with a nervous tone, her eyes fixed on the flickering of the flames.

'Elvira Maddison?' he said. 'Pleased to meet you.'

The woman nodded quickly. 'Yes,' she said. 'I escaped from the Community a year before your parents. And as much as I don't ever want to see those dreadful animals again, I'm the one that can get you in there. Animals. Too good a word for them.' Her words came like bullets, fast and in staccato punctuation. Her face was coloured with a venomous anger.

Carter nodded slowly. 'So you know that my brother and I are going to go back to the Community,' he said. 'And we're going to need your help. Any knowledge you have at all about Chamber One or about how we can get in there will be incredibly helpful.'

Elvira nodded as Angel spoke. 'Elvira was one of the main architects of the tunnel network and she helped to build some of the second-generation Transporters. She'll be an asset to our team.'

'I'm the product of a First and Second Gen,' said Elvira. 'By the time I became a teenager, I had stopped growing but by then it was too late for them to do anything about my size.' She paused. 'If I'd been Lab Made, they'd have had me tested over and over and probably sent me to the Catacombs.' She coughed a dry laugh. 'And I certainly wouldn't be here to tell this tale.'

Carter nodded slowly. 'There are less formal checks on the First and Second Gen hybrids once they've passed ten years old,' he said. 'Their genetics are believed to be… established.' As the words came from his mouth he began to feel uncomfortable.

Elvira ignored him and continued. 'I studied engineering in the Academy,' she said. 'I knew nothing about cryonics or genetics but building things was where I really excelled.

'At first we used some of the old London underground tunnels where possible – and then we needed to dig. The Industry rounded up as many Lab Mades as they could and, when that wasn't enough, they brought frozen people out of storage, just for that purpose. They made the older ones work hardest: the ones who they said they were never going to wake up, the ones over thirty-five, the ones from the time before the Storms that remembered the old world. They said: *these are the ones that have no use. They've been frozen down here for years. We can't rehabilitate them. Let's give them a use.* They worked them fifteen hours a day, sometimes more.' Her eyes clouded over, the sparks of the fire dancing in her pupils.

'The outgoing Controller General, Pinkerton, wanted to leave a legacy, his Contribution as leader – and the extension of those tunnels was it. Those poor people...' Her voice drifted off into the smoky darkness.

'Those people,' she began again, shaking her head. 'They kept themselves alive by singing, even when they were told they were not allowed to sing: all kinds of songs.' She started humming, her head drifting backwards and forwards. 'Songs from the old world.'

'What happened to them?' said Carter. 'Did they escape too?'

'Oh no,' Elvira laughed sadly to herself and drew a circle in the dust with her finger. Carter noticed it was the only finger remaining on that hand. 'No, they died – not all at the same time, but one by one. When the first of them collapsed – and it took a lot longer than you'd think – others followed. The human spirit is very strong, you know, even in the most extreme of conditions.'

'You did what you could,' said Angel in a soothing voice. 'You did what you could.'

'I told Nikolas and Rufus,' said Elvira, speaking into the fire. 'And we talked about how we could let them out, free them somehow. But it was not possible then. I knew only about engineering, not saving people. I tried to help them, to give them food.'

She spat at the flames and they sizzled angrily. 'But they hated me for not doing more to help them. Hated me for being one of the Industry. I told them I was not. That I was like them. But they did not believe me. And they were right. They saw me as their enemy. And I couldn't help them. I was different. There was nothing else I could do. I was too weak, back then.'

Carter felt further sickened by the awfulness of the place he had, for his whole life, called home. 'But you got out,' he said, finally. 'That must have taken a lot of strength.'

'I suppose, yes,' said Elvira. 'But strength of a different kind. I knew that treating people that way was wrong but, in some ways, they *were* different to me. They were unable to see that we couldn't just continue as before. I was brought up to believe that the Industry was the saviour of humanity; that by providing food and shelter and education you have the right to do with people what you want to. But I know now that is not true. None of us are owned. Not by anybody except ourselves.'

'So how did you do it?' said Carter. 'How did you escape?'

Angel held her hand out to Elvira. 'This is your story,' she said. 'You don't need to say anything that you don't want to.'

The others sat around the fire, listening intently, although Carter assumed they had heard the story many times before.

'I went to your father,' she said. 'I told him what was happening and it made him even more determined to leave and do something. But without contacts high enough up in the Industry, there was no way we could get those people out. They were all tagged, you see—' she pointed to his arm '—just like you were.' Those in charge started doing that after a while so that they could track where everybody was. But I knew I had to go. And soon, before those people tried to kill me with their bare hands. They were desperate – as were we all.

'What did you do?' said Carter, slowly.

'One of the men, his name was Jacques, was a giant of a man but he worked like an animal. He was two or three times the size of the next biggest person but for hours every day that man toiled, without food or water. He would do the work of maybe four men and allow the others to rest while he continued on and on without stopping. And, at night, while the men and women of the old world screamed through their nightmares, he slept softly. Not one sound until next morning.

'Jacques was one of the few that never gave anyone any trouble. He was huge, bigger than any man I ever saw. He never shouted, never complained – he never spoke a word. He just accepted that was the way of things. He gave his rations to the weaker ones while he worked himself harder and harder. But not one word left his lips. Until, one day, he came to me.'

Carter felt a shiver run down his spine. 'What did he say to you?' he asked.

'His English wasn't very good – he was from overseas somewhere – Spain or France, I think. He told me that he knew something – a secret.' The flames of the fire rose higher as Elvira struggled with her words. 'He told me that he had been given something in the years before he had been frozen.'

She held up a thin piece of plastic, just like the identity card everyone in the Community held, but this one was blank and smooth. Carter took it from her and ran his fingers across the edges.

'He'd hidden it in one of the old Morristown Row houses – he begged me to go and find it. I had to pretend I was doing some structural reviews to get access to the house. I was lucky.' She smiled wryly. 'The Industry trusted me.'

Carter handed the card back to Elvira. 'What has this got to do with Chamber One?' he said.

'Jacques was scared – terrified. He spoke just that once, in a jumbled, strange way. He told me that this—' she held the card up in front of the fire '—was *tres* important and the key to everything.' She pulled her lips together tightly. 'Then he said that there was something else buried deep in one of the chambers in the Catacombs that I needed to find, that it was important. He mentioned something about a promise he had made and became very animated – frantic even. It was very difficult to understand him.'

Carter put his arm on hers. 'Did he say what it was? Did he say where?'

'I kept asking him but he didn't say another word and we were never alone again. And then, one day, when we were unloading some supplies, his heart just stopped.'

Elvira looked up at the stars. 'I cannot stop myself from thinking of what happened to him every single day, even now, over twenty years later, I will never forget the sadness of that man. If it wasn't for him I would never have got out.'

'He helped you escape?' interrupted Carter. 'If his heart stopped, how did he...?'

Elvira rubbed her finger in the dirt around the fire. 'In a way. Maybe I could have saved him, I don't know. But it was over very soon and he didn't suffer. I just watched him die. Lily too, although no one ever suspected she was on the side of the rebellion; she was very Industry on the exterior. It took three of us to cut up and load his body into the waste Transporter and then I climbed in next to him, curled up like a dirty little insect. Without his death, I would never have made it.'

She paused and Carter stared at her, open mouthed.

'I wish there was something I could have done,' Elvira continued despondently. 'I felt so guilty, I should have called a medic but they wouldn't have helped him, he was already unlikely to see daylight again. And by the time I'd have got someone there, he'd have died anyway.' She sighed heavily. 'Not a day goes by that I do not feel guilty.'

Carter shook his head. 'That's terrible,' he said. 'So awful. But you're right – there was nothing you could have done to help him.'

Elvira nodded. 'And it wasn't just that. Back then, the Industry injected synthetic protein trackers into our fingers when we were born. You never knew which one because it never left a mark. They grew inside you until they were the size of a fly and buried into the outside of the bone, getting their power from your marrow. You never felt it, but when you saw it, you knew.'

Angel shuddered and held Elvira's full hand tightly. 'Lily had to remove three fingers and a thumb before she found my tracker,' she said. 'Before telling Pinkerton that she'd had to terminate Jacques for attacking and killing me.'

She didn't cry but her face became hard and discoloured in the pale firelight. 'She got promoted for that. And poor Jacques.' She stopped for a moment. 'Poor Jacques became a monster of legend – and a justification for the decisions they had made for keeping those people underground and never letting them see the sun. After Jacques's death, I believe the tunnel workers were kept in chains.'

Carter couldn't quite believe that it could have got any worse. 'Did they… did they never ask to see your body?' he said finally.

'Lily told them she wrapped me separately and put me safely in another carriage with some lime so that I would return to the earth more quickly,' she said. 'She's an exceptionally good liar. But she is on our side.'

'My mother thinks she didn't kill my daughter.'

Elvira shook her head definitely. 'No,' she said. 'It wasn't her. You have always been key to us getting back into the Industry and I can think of a hundred people in there who would destroy anything that was important to you to get you to stop. Your mother had absolute faith in you and your abilities, which is why Mendoza, Lily and the others have been trying to protect you. Getting you in position has always been a priority. Your mother just thought it would be as Controller General when you were presented with the information in Chamber One. Before I came out here, Lily gave me this.' She held up a crumpled piece of paper that on one side looked like a hand drawn map, scratched with roads and tracks on one side and, on the other side, a detailed blueprint criss-crossed with tunnels and passageways.

'Tell me more about Chamber One,' said Carter.

Angel chewed at her fingers. 'Let Elvira finish her story first,' she said.

The small woman hesitated, her eyes bright with tears.

'I was in shock and a great deal of pain. But I knew that unless I moved quickly, there would be no hope for me. I had to battle on, despite the agony and the terror of what might happen next. When the body waste – mine and Jacques' – was pumped out into the pits on the edges of Drakewater, I buried my fingers so that the locater would never be found. The waste tunnel is so small that they cut up the bodies and flush it through with acid twice a day to dislodge the bigger parts, those that don't get forced the small hole by the pumps. It's only because I'm the size I am, that I managed to squeeze through – I just made it through and out into the open pit in time. Then I crawled through the old sludge until I made it to the Tower.'

'Unbelievable,' said Carter, his eyes wide. He felt his heart harden, every sliver of the truth sinking like ice into his bones.

'I was lucky not to drown in that filth or die of infection,' said Elvira, holding up her hand. 'Lily may be a good liar, but she's not the best surgeon. Although she did what she could. The only thing I took with me that survived was the blueprint and that card.'

She held up the small, square piece of plastic again. 'I tried this on every door in the Catacombs that I could get to – and it opened them

all. It's a master key – an old one. Whatever is hidden in Chamber
One has been there for a long time. Jacques had been frozen for many
years so whatever he knew pre-dates any of us. It's from the early days.'

Carter sat open-mouthed. 'But how do you know whatever it is, is
still there? Did Jacques even mention Chamber One?'

Elvira put the card into Carter's hand. 'After he gave me the key
card and I had exhausted my search I knew I needed more information.' She pointed to the blueprint. 'All along these outside walls are
air ducts that run in a pattern around the outside of the Catacombs.
They widen out in some places, but mostly they are quite small. They
run past each of the rooms. There is a door on each level, hidden in the
panelling that you can open and climb inside. Not many people know
about these passages because they drop steeply in some areas and are
dangerous.' She paused. 'Because I was responsible for the construction
of the tunnels, I was able to get hold of the architect plans. Lily made
this copy of them with the added information about the overground
road on the other side.'

Carter scanned both sides of the map.

'So, did you go into these ducts?'

Elvira nodded her eyes dark. 'I'll never forget what I heard that
day,' she said. 'That was when I knew I had to leave.'

In the quiet darkness of a hidden stairwell, Elvira pried open
one of the small panels right at the back of the Catacombs
and climbed inside at the Control Room level. As she crawled
through the ducts, she passed many Chambers, all the same
square, boxy shape filled with electronic equipment or stock –
and some filled with sleeping people. Each of them lay silent,
hundreds of them, and of all ages. As she made her way forwards,

a metal grille, smaller than the others, cast a thin ray of light that flashed intermittently, reflecting the coloured screens that came from the room beneath her. Elvira peered into the Control Room, watching the charts rise and fall across the screen, almost scared to even breathe. Aside from the projections onto the wall, the room was still and silent. She pulled at the grille and it came out of its placement hooks easily, falling through into the room with a clatter. The shock made her withdraw back into the room quickly, hands shaking and her heart beating like a drum. But, after a few moments, when no one had opened the door, she glanced back through the hole in the wall. The drop was minimal and she knew she could make it.

Elvira squeezed herself through the grille space and landed noiselessly in the Control Room. Bright lights flashed on the consoles. Screens and keyboards covered every available surface. She tried every system but all were password-protected and impossible to decode. Along one side of the room, a large oak cabinet straddled the wall reflecting the slowly moving graphs and flashing map projections. Although the right side was stuck fast, the left-hand door slid across easily. Elvira took out two small bundles of paper and thumbed through the documents inside, scouring for something that would make sense of what Jacques had told her. But there was nothing, just blank pages with the occasional list of standard engineering structures she had seen before. She felt around the catch of the opposite door and, using all her strength, heaved the other door open. But that too was empty, except for an old pamphlet that had been distributed by the agency in the early days. Elvira scrunched it into a ball and cursed.

Then, from outside the room there came a click as the door slid open. The sound of voices floated into the room and Elvira pushed her body into the small cavity of the sideboard, pulling the door closed from the inside.

'I told you I was right,' came the authoritative voice of Controller General Pinkerton. 'Unfreezing those dark ones has really boosted our productivity in the tunnels.'

Elvira strained to hear who he was speaking to, but when she spoke, she knew it was the incoming leader, Bobbie Alderney. 'The dark ones?' he said.

'Well, we knew they'd never see the light of day again!' boomed Pinkerton. 'Thought we'd have to terminate, but having a bank of fodder underground has proved to be absolute genius. Using their desperate strength and my superior knowledge, I'll make sure they finish the Transporter tunnels – and that is how I shall be remembered.' He gave a hollow laugh. 'Now that is something I would suggest you consider when you take charge.'

'An underground army is what we've always discussed,' said Alderney. 'That's not news. Increasing the Lab Mades and making our population more compliant is always one main way to increase our power.' Elvira heard him clear his throat. 'But what I have to offer will be just as impressive, Pinkerton. The FreeScreen will ensure we have surveillance inside every home and can monitor all types of chatter and dissonant behaviour. Anyone considered to be a rebel will be destroyed.'

'And you think people will want this?'

Alderney laughed. 'Want it? They'll love it. We'll sell it to them as a demonstration of full communication and openness – the majority won't even question why we're doing it.'

Elvira shivered as Pinkerton's footsteps came closer and she felt the weight of his body plump down onto the sideboard. She held her breath and pushed her body as closely into the corner as she could. The pair continued talking for a while, trading tactics for population control, then Pinkerton lowered his voice until she could barely hear. 'You've not heard about Chamber One yet, I assume,' he said to Alderney.

'I've heard the rumours, of course.'

'As part of your Controller General initiation, it falls to me to show you. We'll go down to the Ship after your inauguration ceremony. And you'll see exactly why it must remain a secret.'

There was a silence. 'But what's in there?' said Alderney.

Elvira felt her mouth grow dry.

'Something that could tear this whole place apart,' said Pinkerton. 'Something that can never be revealed. Something that could destroy us all.'

Carter watched as Elvira shrugged off the reverie and came back to them.

'Then they started talking about the Model and more general things and, soon after, they left. I was terrified but I searched the whole room. The only thing I found was a bunch of papers that looked like they'd been written by a child, hidden behind a false panel of the sideboard I'd been in.'

'What did they say?' Carter leaned in towards Elvira. 'Did they say anything about Chamber One?'

'No,' she replied. 'It was just rubbish – maybe from before the Storms. Pictures of monsters, people rising from the dead like zombies.'

'How did you know it was kid's stuff?'

Elvira shrugged. 'The paper was yellowed and the script curled, like the way children were taught in the old schools – you know that writing is discouraged today. Part of it looked like chemistry homework – maybe early cryonics or genetics, but it didn't mention Chamber One so I put it back. It had to be a child, no adult could have opened that false panel.'

Carter shrugged. 'So, what did you do then?'

'I climbed back into the vents and made my way back to the tunnels. That was the day that Jacques died and I had to make my escape.'

'And you didn't find out exactly where Chamber One was or what was in it?'

'No,' said Elvira. 'All I know is that they'll do anything to keep it secret. I looked, I really did, but I had to leave before I could find it. Before they killed me.'

'Chamber One,' said Carter softly to himself. 'We need to know what's in there.'

Angel reached for Elvira's hand. 'But like Jacinta said, you need to prove yourself to our people first. To fight this together, they need to trust you completely and you need to trust them – to trust us. You have to understand who we are and what we're about, and we must be united. Our ways of life, to this point, have been very different. To become part of our group, of our Village, our fight, you need to be a part of us.'

She smiled at Carter. 'You can start by helping me in the healing clinic. If people see you caring for them, they'll know you're one of us.'

Chapter Nine

The Incident

Alice

Hidden inside the depths of a boarded attic space, Alice flicked through the pages of the thick sheaf of papers obsessively, and then threw them to the edge of the rusted bed she was sitting on. At some point, the attic had been converted to make a small child's room, but they had long since cleared the brightly coloured plastic toys away. In the corner of the room, a spider was making its web, weaving sticky threads across uneven bumps in the peeling wallpaper. She racked her brains as to how she could get Richard above ground. He knew things about Barnes and about what was happening down in the Lab that were important. But convincing the very person he could expose to do anything she wanted was proving incredibly difficult.

'Alice!'

She ignored the calls and watched through the broken window frame as soft golden threads of sun twisted through the clouds, lighting the sky with an incandescent glow. Across the way she could hear the construction team clearing the houses and securing the next batch of homes trudging waste to the outer edges of the new community for destruction.

She went into the other houses sometimes, to think; to remember. It had been almost six weeks since the meeting with Barnes where she had received the news. Six long weeks. The sickness had started, but as yet there had been nothing too wretched and she had refused the offer of calming herbs from the doctor. She pressed her fingers around her stomach.

'Where the hell have you been? I've been worried about you.'

The sound of Filip's voice echoing through the room made her jump, but she kept her eyes focused on the cracks in the wallpaper, the intricate, faded flowers that swirled upwards towards the sky.

'Alice?'

She turned around slowly, slipping her hands into her pockets. 'Hi Filip,' she said. 'You don't need to keep checking up on me, you know. I'm fine.' His face looked lined, strained even.

'Where have you been?' he repeated.

'I need space. Plus, I needed to go through the plans and the manifesto. You and Kunstein have made quite a few changes to the papers and I wanted to be sure...'

'I know,' said Filip, 'but you can't just wander around without letting anyone know where you are. I need to know where you're going – even if it's just to one of the other houses. It's still dangerous. Especially now you're preg—'

'This place is worse than the Ship, at times.' Alice traced her finger across the flowers on the walls. 'It's beautiful and wonderful that the rain stopped but I can't *breathe*. I need my space.' She accentuated the last two words as strongly as she could bring herself to.

Filip looked at her carefully, a glint of the sunshine catching his eye. He paused and watched the outside world with her before speaking. 'I understand,' he said, putting his arm around her shoulders. 'I really do.

We all need alone time now and again, it helps us to think and plan. It's just that until we have the full Barricades up around this place, there are still animals – predators – waiting to destroy everything we have built up, everything we have worked for since the rain started to fall.'

'I can hold my own,' said Alice, nodding to the gun that sat on the bed.

'You can – if there's just one or two and if you see them before they see you,' said Filip. He reached out and touched her hand. 'It's only because I want to take care of you that I traipse all over town each time you go running off somewhere. It's not because I don't trust you. Things are changing, Alice, and things are going to be difficult – but they will be okay, I promise you. I will always take care you.'

Outside the clattering of movement had ceased and the world felt serene. Filip brushed his hair from his eyes and smiled at Alice. She breathed deeply. Back in the Ship, she had felt so much more in control – Filip and the others had seemed to look up to her and now she felt she was hurtling through a tunnel on a darkened tube train at night, distinctly unaware of what the final destination was likely to be. Part of her desperately wanted Filip to lift her off that train and take her somewhere else. And part of her was terrified that if the carriage doors opened, whether she would have the courage to step outside of them.

'Do you ever wonder...' She rubbed a smudge of dirt from the wall. 'Do you ever think we might have been wrong? That maybe we made some snap judgements about what's on the outside? That we could have done things differently?'

Filip shook his head. Creases formed across his brow. 'Do *you*?' he said, looking deep into Alice's eyes as she closed them tight. His voice was determined – threatening almost. He grabbed her hand and held it so tightly that it almost hurt.

'No,' she mouthed, scared. 'Not for one second.'

He moved towards her, his fingers circling her stomach, kissing her neck. 'Well, that's good then. Because we have a family to prepare for – and Kunstein has called us to a repopulation meeting in the Ship tomorrow.

The following evening, Kunstein was already in the Ship when they arrived.

'We need to talk,' she said, her face stern. 'There's been an incident.'

'What's wrong?' said Alice. 'What's happened?'

They moved straight to the control room that whirred and clicked into action as they stepped into the room. Thin glass screens covered the walls, some operational and others dulled into a faint grey that flickered occasionally. Alice remembered the first time she'd been allowed into the control room with Kunstein and watched as a shoal of google-eyed fish swam around through the aisles of a supermarket before the waters had fallen.

Quinn sat at a terminal next to Barnes and Wilson, scanning the screens.

'There was an occurrence,' she said, 'earlier, at the Barricades.'

'What sort of occurrence?'

Alice pulled up a chair in front of the screens, her mouth dry.

'There was an intruder, someone from the outside. They tried to break through the perimeter. Just after you left to come down here we got a report from the Watchers. It was human – if you could call it that.'

'What?' Alice turned to face Quinn. 'Who was there? Did they say anything?'

'Not a chance,' said Quinn cutting in, her eyes still on the screen. 'And besides, the Watcher said the person looked crazed, kind of manic. No one got a close look at all.'

'And unfortunately, we didn't manage to catch anything of what happened on camera,' said Wilson. 'We need to up the surveillance some if we're going to ensure that this doesn't happen in future, you know. That rests squarely with you two.' He pointed at Alice and Filip.

'What happened to him... her...?' said Alice. 'Who was it?'

'One of the Watchers got it in time,' said Quinn. 'And luckily none of our people were hurt. But we can't take any risks.'

Barnes nodded. 'Who knows what sort of infection that creature could have brought into our Community?' she added. 'Very lucky we got it.'

'Got it?' Alice's brow furrowed. 'What do you mean?'

'Shot it. Killed it. Good thing too.'

Alice creased her eyes. 'Were they hostile?'

'Absolutely.'

Kunstein nodded in agreement. 'Work on any remaining chinks in the Barricades will need to increase at a faster rate now the boundaries are fully agreed. We cannot allow creatures of any kind to infiltrate our world. We can't risk it.'

Alice looked at them both, thinking of Richard. 'That creature was a person,' she said, slowly. 'Someone who has had to witness some things that no one ever should. How ever they managed to survive out there is a miracle.' She thought of what Kelly had said. 'Surely we should at least have tried to speak to them. They could tell us about the dangers out there. That creature is someone just like us, just from different circumstances.'

Wilson looked at her, shocked, and shot a sideways glance at Kunstein. 'Oh Alice,' he began, 'that's just the point. These people are no longer like us. We have changed and they have changed. It may have been only five years, but in reality, so much more is different. This person came out of that dead village to the north with weapons that they made themselves. They were not coming in peace, nor carrying something they had picked up along the way for defence.'

He paused.

'We are lucky none of our people were hurt. They were there to attack – there was no mistaking it. Had the Watcher not been so quick with their expert marksmanship then I'm sure many of our people would have suffered. You're forgetting about disease, too, Alice. It's our biggest weakness.'

'But what if...?'

'No buts, Alice. No exceptions.'

Barnes pushed past Alice and settled herself in front of one of the other computers. Tapping a series of numbers and then swiping the screen a few times, she brought up a map of the surrounding area, districts inked out with red and blue blotches. She zoomed the screen outwards and then in again with electric precision and pointed at an area of deep crimson.

'Movement was seen coming from around two miles away in this area, known to be where a number of decomposing bodies were found in the first few weeks of our exploration. Tissue samples taken revealed that they contained traces of a serious virus.'

'We don't know that these people had a virus though, do we?' said Alice carefully. 'I mean, maybe they could tell us things, teach us about what else is out there...'

Quinn tapped a screen. 'Alice – nothing, absolutely nothing can come between us and survival now. We've done so much, tried so hard and been given the greatest gift by the Industry that could possibly be given. We checked the outsider – all the physical symptoms were visible – agitation, unsteadiness on the feet, unintelligible speech, loss of hair, nausea...'

'You could tell they were nauseous from that distance?'

Quinn's eyes were glassy with irritation. 'What are you trying to say, Alice?' she asked sourly, lifting her eyes towards Filip and Wilson. And then: 'You tell her.'

'The Watchers had a scope set on the area,' said Kunstein. 'They saw it running towards our boundary, screaming with all the signs of something carrying some sort of infection. If we hadn't shot when we did, the Watchers could have been in danger from anything airborne. Quinn's right. We – you – have a new life to create here, one free of the constraints of the past and threats from outside are more than just physical. Remember what it was like when we first came up here, why we burned everything? We just run the risk of returning to the type of existence we had before. We agreed this would be different – the only way to make this work would be to change the rules. That's what we all agreed.'

'Of course,' said Alice, wanting to change the subject. 'Was Kelly still at the Barricades when the intruder came? Marcus?'

'Yes, Kelly was there but not Marcus,' said Quinn. 'Who knows where that boy goes to sometimes? Kelly won't give up her role as a Watcher for anyone right now, even though she's been told to take it easy. She's committed to complete security – as are we all. There's no place for sentimentality – after Jonah…' Her voice drifted away.

'I'd like to ask her about it,' said Alice. 'I'll speak to her later today.'

'No,' said Quinn, firmly. 'She's under enough pressure already. I won't have you upsetting her further.

'Hold on…' started Alice, 'Kelly is my friend and I don't need your permission to speak to her. I want to know what happened from her perspective.'

'And may I remind you, Alice, she's fourteen years old and pregnant. She doesn't need any further harassment from you.'

Alice felt the rage erupt from her face. 'Exactly,' she said, loudly. 'She's fourteen. Don't you think that maybe this may all be a little too much for her? She's not like us!' By the time she had finished her sentence, Alice was almost shouting.

The whole room looked at her in silence. Filip stepped towards her and placed his hand firmly on her stomach. 'Please excuse Alice,' he said. 'She's not feeling herself at the moment. She's not sure what she's saying – are you, Alice?'

'I…' began Alice, breathing quickly but the others were nodding and Kunstein began again.

'Quinn is right, as always. We need to manage the threats from outside as well as from inside. It's about balancing what works for us as individuals with what will make our Community work long term.'

The team nodded in agreement, all except Alice who bit the edges of her fingers and closed her eyes, her stomach knotted with discontent and her mind resolute to speak to Kelly.

When the others left the room, Alice moved to sit next to Wilson as he flicked the screens between differently angled shots of the new community. His command of the control panels, the switches and curved levers was that of a master craftsman; it reminded her of something she couldn't quite explain – like a teenager on a Playstation console.

'Can I go and see Richard?' she asked, watching Wilson's eyes move from screen to screen.

'Not today,' he said without looking at her. 'He's going to be busy with Barnes doing some more tests and answering some questions. He is proving to be very valuable, you know. And Barnes knows exactly what she's doing. And I believe you've got more important things you should be focusing on.'

Alice drummed her fingers on the desk. 'Do you sit here all day doing this?' she said as he moved from screen to screen, each etching out the same dull grey scratchiness of people topside, carrying boxes and cartons from one place to another.

Wilson glared at her. 'Not all day,' he said. 'I eat and sleep – I teach some of the younger classes in censomics as well – Population Management. I majored on it at university in the seventies, you know, when things first started going out of control. I always wanted to save the world...' He looked wistfully at the screens and switched a few dials. 'My parents indulged me, of course, and when Paradigm Industries were looking for researchers I was their first choice given the work I'd done with the Russians and the Chinese. I bet they wish they'd kept me there now.'

'Censomics is a funny business. Fascinating stuff. Although I think Quinn has a natural gift for it. She seems to know exactly how this will all work – she's run simulations for me hundreds of times and each one is perfect. Again, a smart one – a good choice. Although, of course, I never imagined being able to put it all into practise. I suppose the Storms were the making of my career.'

He cracked his fingers and they watched as Izzy darted across the screen again, this time her arms empty but her eyes scanning the corners of the square, as if she were looking for something.

'That one needs some guidance too,' said Wilson. 'She brilliant – but a bit of a wildcard.'

'I know,' said Alice. 'But why did you choose her – what made her so special? What made both of them special?'

Wilson kept his eyes on the screen. 'Father was useless and the mother was an addict,' he said tartly. 'But that's a story for another day. You know, you were on my radar for some time. I set Kunstein out to look for someone like you.'

Alice shook her head. 'You could only have done that if you knew what was going to happen, if you knew about the Storms and you had this planned all along. Unless…'

Wilson interjected. 'Unless we created the Storms? Come now, Alice, Paradigm Industries has been a powerful force in this country – and overseas – for many years but strong enough to create this…?' He flipped a switch and waved his hand across the screens that showed landscapes full of devastation, rubble and death.

Alice gazed at the screens for a moment. It was unthinkable that Wilson had really been behind this. She looked at him calmly and slowly shook her head. But there was something in the depths of his eyes that frightened her.

'The Storms made me choose between my wife and my work,' said Wilson, curtly. 'Sometimes there are terrible choices to be made and there is no right answer, only the answer that you know will work. This is not something I would have designed.'

Suddenly, on the control panel, one of the emergency buttons flashed an urgent red. Kunstein and Quinn raced into the room and, as she switched the monitors back to surveillance, Alice heard the anger welling in Quinn's throat.

'Wilson!' she shouted. 'What were you both doing – why weren't you watching?' She turned to Alice. 'Were you distracting him? This is your fault.'

Before either of them had a chance to answer, the screen to the above ground control room slipped and Alice saw in the background the familiar bunk beds that she and Filip had slept on during their first night outside of the ship in five years. Quinn flicked a dial and sound filled the room, a desperate, breathless sound that came from the communication system between the two worlds.

On the screen, streaked in blood, was Marcus, his hands shaking. 'Alice, you've got to come quick,' he said. 'Something terrible has happened.'

Alice moved to the front of the camera. 'What is it?' she snapped. 'Tell us.'

Filip, Barnes and Quinn gathered closely, pushing together to see the screen.

The boy looked directly into the camera. 'Just you,' he said. 'Just you, Alice.'

'No,' said Filip. 'Tell us all. What has happened?'

Marcus, his face tear-streaked and filthy looked away and started shaking.

'Tell us,' said Alice. 'We're on our way back up to you now.'

Marcus rubbed his eyes, blood and dirt smearing together across his face.

'It's Kelly,' he said quietly, sobbing uncontrollably. 'I'm so sorry. She's been shot.'

Chapter Ten

The Villagers

Carter

Within three weeks, Carter's stomach had almost become accustomed to the natural, nutritious food and before the month was through, he had read most of the books that lined the walls of Jacinta's house. He avoided Samuel as much as possible. Determined to prove himself to the Villagers, he spent his time with Angel around the trails and paths within the forest. He learned which plants were edible and how they were combined and diluted to make different tinctures and potions.

At the end of the fourth week, the itchy rashes and spots from insect bites had stopped appearing and he'd trekked through most of the areas of the woodland with Angel, collecting seasonal herbs and drying them out in the afternoon sun.

'I used to work in food production, when I was there,' said Carter, stripping rosemary from thick stems and placing it into a plastic box. He had mostly stopped referring to the Community by name, and it felt a lot longer than the month or so since he'd left.

'Forget everything you ever learned,' grinned Angel. 'It won't help you here.'

The clinic was a small wooden ground hut with two large oak beds and a flow of people that came in and out, requesting a variety of potions and ointments that Angel prepared on a daily basis.

'Are lots of people sick?'

Angel looked up from the herbs she had been preparing. 'We have quite a few asthmatics – do you know what they are?'

Carter shook his head but Angel continued. 'And many people in the early years of the Industry were born with weakened hearts. Although most of them were not allowed to survive. You can't always tell on the outside, Carter.'

As Carter scanned the jars of creams and pills, an idea formed in his mind. 'We can do better,' he said. 'We can do more than this. Help them more. I have an idea.'

There was a stack of medical journals that someone had carried for many miles from a library on the outskirts of the city, piled high in one corner of the clinic. Much of the text had been water-bleached and notes had been pencilled on the pages to add the missing detail. Carter had read them all, more than once, and had practiced an appendectomy on a rabbit that Jay, one of the hunters, had handed him when he'd asked her to bring back a specimen. She had flung it on the ground, already dead, and walked out without saying a word.

Angel watched him intently as he delicately sewed up the creature with slow, deliberate stitches.

'You have a real gift,' she said. 'Where did you learn how to do that?'

'I'm learning now,' said Carter. 'I read all the books that there are here that are related in any way – and some that aren't – anatomy, sports injury, botany, needlework and even books written about things that aren't true – fiction, you call it, right?'

Alice smiled. 'I'll get Jay to bring you more material,' she said. 'And in a few weeks' time you'll be the most accomplished doctor that there is.'

'We need more,' said Carter, one afternoon over lunch at Jacinta's house in the trees. 'You can't function out here properly without a working infirmary. Your people – our people – need hospital care when they get sick. More medicine, equipment, that kind of thing.'

'And I suppose you're going to be chief surgeon?' scoffed Samuel. 'You've been here six weeks and you think you can tell us what we need?'

'Leave him alone,' said Angel sharply. 'He's working really hard to do something to help and all you can ever do is criticise.'

Samuel got up, shoved his chair backwards and shot Angel a dark glance. 'I'm going back to work – real work – hunting, getting food for people and not just picking flowers, stitching up rats and making... whatever it is you make. I thought you were supposed to be something special.' He slammed down the hatch behind him and his steps could be heard on every wooden rung of the ladder as he descended.

Angel shook her head. 'Ignore him,' she said. 'Jacinta, that hospital to the west – do you think we could take an expedition there to pick up some extra supplies – and maybe some medical equipment?'

Jacinta, who had been swirling the thick liquid around in her cup looked up. 'It's possible,' she said. 'But only you are to go. Under the current terms of his residency, Carter is not yet permitted to leave the perimeter of our area. Some individuals on the council still have their reservations. Angel, you are to be back within twenty-four hours.'

Carter opened his mouth to object, but closed it again promptly when Angel kicked him underneath the table. 'That's fine.' She smiled and then turned to Carter. 'You can cover for me in the clinic whilst I'm gone. Let's make a list of the things you think we may need and I'll set off tomorrow morning.'

The next day, the late evening sun cast arm-like shadows across the clearing when a small boy slunk his way across the clearing and rapped on the hard, wooden door of the clinic. Carter opened it, and the boy walked in and sat down on one of the pristine white beds, his dirty shorts leaving dust marks as he shuffled uncomfortably. In one hand he held a small flute.

'Where's Angel?' he said. 'I'm Patterson. I need my medicine.'

Carter eyed him and smiled. 'I'm Angel's friend.' The boy nodded and scratched his finger along the edge of the wooden flute as Carter prepared a concoction of garlic, turmeric, ginger, rosemary and cumin seeds in a watery cup.

'I know who you are,' said Patterson, eyeing Carter curiously, his breath a little wheezy. 'I just need my medicine.'

'Well, I have just the thing,' said Carter and handed the boy the cup and a crumbling tablet that Angel had put aside. Patterson knocked it back and belched loudly.

'They say you don't have music where you come from,' he said, holding up the flute. 'I can play this, you know. Angel says I'm really good.'

Carter took the cup back from boy. 'Would you like to show me?' he said, and the boy nodded enthusiastically. Carter watched as he put his mouth to the wooden tube and moved his fingers quickly over the holes, creating a beautiful, melodic tune that reverberated around the hut, echoing and repeating itself over and over. When the boy finished, Carter clapped, as he had seen the others do.

'That's very good,' he said. 'Is it difficult to learn?'

'Not really,' said Patterson, flexing his digits. 'I can teach you if you like?'

By the time the boy was ready to leave, Carter had managed to almost master the same tune he had heard played across the Village and had promised to get a flute himself so he could practise at home.

'You can borrow mine.' Patterson smiled and skipped across the clearing whistling, the high-pitched sound sailing through the air.

Carter leafed through the medical magazines that were piled in the corner of the hut. Many of them were of cosmetic procedures that he understood how he might perform but could not fathom the function of. People who weren't sick having bits added to or removed from their body in order to make them more attractive. He traced his finger across the pictures, confused, and pored back over the medical journals, most of which he had tried to memorise, alongside the herb combination notes all scrawled in Angel's beautiful script.

A piercing scream echoing through the clearing disturbed the peace, and within seconds there was a hammering on the half-open door as Patterson spilled back into the room.

His face was moon white and streaked with dirt.

'Please' he said, breathless. 'You've got to come. It's Sephora. She's fallen from the walkway. You've got to help her.'

The girl sat with her arm twisted, shaking, with her mouth fixed in a tight line. A group of adults had gathered around her and blood was pooling around her knee.

One man had his arm on her shoulder and eyed Carter suspiciously as he approached.

'Let me see her,' said Carter. 'It looks like she may have broken her arm.' His hands started to shake a little but the group parted, letting him make his way through and he knelt down next to her. The girl was weeping gently and moaning in pain.

'Are you a trained medic?' said one of the women. 'Do you know what you're doing? Where's Angel?'

'Angel isn't here,' said Carter, his voice measured, and he examined Sephora's arm gently. 'Now, I'm going to take her into the clinic to bandage her arm – whoever would like to come is welcome.' He took the girl into his arms as the small crowd that had gathered watched, and carried her into the clinic.

'You're being very brave,' said Carter as he laid her on the bed. 'It looks like it's broken, but not badly, so I'm going to bandage it and put it into a sling.' Sephora smiled through quiet tears.

'It hurts a lot,' she said. 'And it's my good arm.'

Carter looked down and noticed that her other arm ended in a smooth stump near the wrist.

'I know I'm not supposed to swing on the ladders,' she added and glanced up at a woman who was standing next to her. 'I'm sorry, Mama.'

The woman looked at Carter. 'Can you fix it?' she said. 'Can you help her?'

'It's just a small break,' he replied, tightly wrapping the girl's arm with a gauzy material he'd found on one of the shelves in the clinic. 'In a month or so, she will be fine.'

Sephora's mother smiled a little, her lips in a tight line but underneath, her face looked gaunt and afraid.

'She'll be okay,' said Carter, his hand gently touching her shoulder.

When he'd folded and strapped up the broken limb into a sling, he pulled out a small crumbled tablet from a blister pack and handed the girl's mother a vial of the painkilling liquid he'd been preparing earlier in the day.

'She can take this before sleeping to manage the pain,' he said and smiled at the girl. 'And no more climbing.'

'Thank you,' said Sephora's mother. 'Thank you, Carter.'

When the small group had left, Carter put his head back on the desk and smiled to himself. It had only been a small injury but he'd done it, he'd really done it. A wave of satisfaction crept over him.

'Well done.' He looked up to see the outline of Jacinta in the doorway. 'I've heard you did some good work this evening,' she said. Her eyes looked somewhat different, proud even.

'Thank you.' Carter smiled but his mother's face remained granite firm.

'I think the people of the Village are ready to believe in you,' she said, before turning to leave the clinic. 'We will speak to the Council at the end of this week.'

By the time Angel had returned, Carter had scrubbed clean the wooden clinic and recorded the details of Sephora's injury in the incident book that was worn with yellowing pages.

'You did a great job last night,' she said, wheeling a barrow through the door. It was piled high with packaged goods marked STERILE and a heap of books in various stages of decomposition. 'It's the big news of the morning.'

Carter beamed. 'It wasn't much,' he said. 'What did you manage to bring back?'

Angel started unloading her bounty. 'The old hospital is almost empty now, but there was a chemist in a village that we passed through that still had some drugs and bandages. I'd never been there before.' She shrugged. 'The medicines will be expired now but there might be something we can use.'

Carter watched as she unloaded each item carefully and categorised it on the shelves, putting the pills into the cabinet on the wall.

'These are great,' he said. 'But we need more. And better. We need technology to be able to manufacture things. And chemistry.' He paused. 'I have the knowledge but I don't have the raw materials. We need the type of medicine the Industry has in the clinics underground.'

Before Angel could reply, the door opened and Samuel's shadow appeared.

'Welcome home,' he greeted Angel. 'Are you coming back to the house for some lunch? Jacinta has prepared some soup.'

'I'll be along soon too,' said Carter. 'I just need to—'

'I was talking to Angel, not you.' Samuel turned his back on Carter and leafed through the book on the table. He stopped on the final entry. 'Quite the hero, aren't we?' he said, smirking. 'They're talking about you all over the Village.'

'I was in the right place at the right time,' replied Carter. 'Anyone would have done the same.'

'Not everyone would have been able to,' said Angel, rubbing his shoulder. 'You've learned more about the health profession in a month than most doctors learn in a year.'

Samuel sniffed. 'Well, some of us have real jobs to do, not just stand-in trainee nurses,' he said and turned to Angel, waving his hand at the shelves. 'You've got yourself a good haul here.' He pocketed a small bottle of pills.

'Hey, those are for the clinic,' said Angel.

Samuel rattled the bottle. 'I might need them. I'm going to have to go away for a day or two – there have been some sightings of cattle we may be able to domesticate out in the west forest. It could be dangerous so I'm going to take precautions – just in case.'

Angel narrowed her eyes. 'Cattle? Really? Do you think we can get them here? The last ones didn't last very long.'

'That's because we didn't take care of them properly.' He patted Carter on the back a little too hard. 'And I'm sure if anything untoward happens to them, my brother here will be able to bring them back from the dead.' He laughed heartily and strode out of the clinic.

'When will you be back?' Angel called after him. 'We've got the meeting with the Council in a few days to discuss how we approach the Industry and to get their backing to enter the Community.'

'I'll return in plenty of time,' he shouted. 'I leave in a few hours.' He trudged his way across the clearing.

'Ignore him,' said Angel. 'He's got his own issues.'

'Has he always been this… unbearable?'

Angel sighed. 'He's always been a loner. He likes things to be done his way. Your mother pretty much let him do what he pleased from a very early age – as long as it was to benefit the Village.'

'He has got a point though,' said Carter, deep in thought. 'I've read through all the books about animals in Jacinta's house. As much as I still find it strange, we could raise livestock here – if we knew a bit more about what to do with them. We could even create a – what were they called again? A farm?'

In a moment of surprise, Angel hugged him tightly and Carter felt all the air leaving his body.

'What was that for?'

Angel shrugged her shoulders, and her cheeks flushed crimson. 'I don't know,' she said. 'Just that it's a great idea and it would make such a difference to us if we were able to expand what we do here. Sometimes, people can be so defeatist even though we live free and wonderful lives.'

Her enthusiasm made Carter smile. 'I wish my children could have grown up here,' he said. 'My daughter, Lucia, was a really talented artist – I saw something she had painted on a wall.'

Angel frowned. 'I thought art was banned there,' she said. 'No painting, no singing, no dancing.'

Carter nodded. 'That's true,' he said. 'But she was part of the uprising. She was different. Even though it wasn't allowed, she still did it.'

'Brave,' said Angel. 'It takes a lot to be different. Especially in there.'

'I wish I could have known her.' Deep inside himself, Carter ached to have been able to spend just one day with the twins, to learn more – anything about them.

'What about your son? Angel looked at him intently. 'How old is he?'

'It's strange to think about it but we're the same age, pretty much,' said Carter. 'I was underground when the twins were born – I didn't even know they existed until I was unfrozen.'

Angel whistled. 'That's just weird,' she said. 'Really weird.'

'Things are different in there – time is different. You kind of get used to the changes in generation and the ageing process.' He stopped for a second. 'I guess you don't question it too much. You're taught not to question anything the Industry tells you is right.' He shook his head. 'I guess that was part of the problem.'

'I heard about the freezing process but…' Angel's voice tailed off. 'I never thought about things like that happening.'

'I'm not sure that many people come above ground to find out they have twins though,' said Carter. 'Apparently they were the first to be born in the Community.'

'I'm sorry about your daughter,' said Angel, putting her hand on his arm. 'But tell me about your son.' She smiled. 'Does he look like you?'

'A little, I guess.'

'Tell me more.'

Carter shook his head. 'I don't really know, I only got to meet him briefly, but I liked him. I wish I'd had more time with both of them – had the chance to watch them grow up.'

Carter turned around to Angel, his face suddenly taut with determination. 'I'm going in there to get to Chamber One. But I'm going to get him too.'

The next night, Carter gathered with the Villagers. Samuel had returned sulkily, with no sign of cattle or anything other than a grunt when he had strolled back into the Village. But even with Jacinta and Angel's backing, Carter had to persuade them that he was trustworthy, and that their plan to go back to the Community was a good one. Even though the small wooden stage in the clearing was raised almost a metre from the floor, he felt very low on the ground in comparison to the group of men and women in front of him. Most eyed him suspiciously as they spoke.

The Villagers were a mixture of ages. Some had missing limbs with replacements fashioned from wood, blotches on their faces, pale skin with bright pink eyes and no hair – or eyes that seemed to look in every direction except the way their heads turned. Some he recognised from conversations he'd had in the last few weeks – Sephora's mother nodded at him. Carter tried hard not to stare and smiled even though he felt more nervous than he ever had in the Community.

From the front of the stage, Jacinta started to speak. 'Brothers and sisters,' she said. 'For years we have known that the time would come for an opportunity to remove the threat posed by Paradigm Industries and their Community. That moment has now arisen.'

Some members of the crowd cheered, others remained silent. As she pursed her lips to continue, a call came from the back of the group.

'We're doing okay without them,' called the woman at the back. 'If they leave us alone then we leave them alone.'

Jacinta hesitated and Samuel moved in front of her. 'But they don't leave us alone,' he said. 'Remember what happened to the pools two years ago? In almost ninety years since the Storms we haven't moved on. We don't have the resources to continue living like this, not knowing when they might poison the water or send out people to kill us. If we want to grow, we need more knowledge of the world that's left. It's time for us to be in control of own destiny and stop living in fear.'

A round of applause rippled through the clearing and Carter watched as a few people stood to commend his brother.

'I know that there are some of you with distant relatives in there and you want to know if they are still alive,' Samuel continued. 'And others of you that just want to see justice done and believe that the people of the Community deserve to live freely, just as you do. Our plan is to release them all, to unfreeze them and to allow them to come and stay with us, as our family and brethren.'

The crowd erupted in another small cheer.

'My great great aunt is in there,' shouted one woman. 'She was in the Ship and I don't believe she ever came out!'

'My great grandfather too,' called another. 'He worked for Paradigm Industries and he was one of the crew.'

Carter felt his blood run cold. There were hundreds, no, thousands of people stored underground. He waited until the crowd died down and then stood up, even though he felt his legs would fail him. As he did, the clearing fell silent, the strangled strains of a night bird drifting down into the gathering. Their idea would never work.

'Friends,' he began. 'Simply unfreezing everyone is a dangerous plan. Without a full understanding of how many individuals are there, what status they are and what censomic makeup is there, we may not be able to provide them with what they need. Some of the people that you love and care about may not be equipped to a life outside of the Barricades – not straight away.'

The woman sat next to him turned around and snarled. Carter recognised her as one of the patients from the clinic that he regularly prepared medication for to regulate her heartbeat.

'What do you know?' she said. 'Who do you think you are to tell us what we should be doing? You don't know anything.'

'It's a difficult decision,' he said calmly. 'Life – and people – inside there are different. We are just going to need to be sure that we can provide them with what they need before we bring them all out into a life they are not ready for.'

'Hand out a few pills and think you're a doctor,' she scoffed and turned away.

Jacinta cut in. 'My son has been here for over a month, and he has already proved that he can be a valuable asset to us – if we give him a chance. And also, he has a point. As most of you will know,' she continued, 'intelligence inside the Community has advised us that there is information – key to exposing them – that is hidden within the Catacombs. Information that is ours.'

Someone else called out from the crowd. 'I heard Chamber One was empty. I still vote we unfreeze everyone and let them choose.'

Carter looked around. There were nods of appreciation around the edges of the clearing. He stood up again.

'I don't know a great deal about Chamber One, but what I do know is that most people living within the walls of the Community – both underground *and* overground – truly believe in the Industry. Until I saw for myself some of what you have shown me—' he looked at Angel '—I would never have believed it.' He paused. 'You may think that you are helping those people but you need something more – something that they too can believe in.'

Samuel turned to him, his voice uncharacteristically cordial. 'So, what do you suggest?'

'Well, I suggest that we don't unfreeze everybody in the Catacombs and create the next biggest famine and housing crisis since the Storms – not to mention civil war. We have to understand what size of population we're going to be dealing with.'

Carter thought back to his training, to the Model and the simulations he had run with the other Contenders. He shuddered at the memory of how quickly everything could disintegrate. 'If Chamber One does contain any proof of the Industry's wrongdoing or a secret that they want to keep hidden, then it will be fundamental to your – our – survival. And when we know the scale of what we're dealing with, we will be better placed to overcome the Industry. But the main thing is to find out what the Industry are planning against us next and how we can expose them for who they are.'

A man at the back stood up and walked to the front of the clearing.

'And how do you propose to get this information?'

Carter lifted up his arm to show the scar where the tracker had been. 'I know the Catacombs better than anyone. If Chamber One exists, then I can find it. I've been there recently and I also am the only one of us qualified to work with the Model. I've been to the Control Room. I can find out how to manipulate the systems to find the chamber and also how many people are underground and how we can best help them, when we're ready. I know the Industry better than anyone here.'

'What information are you looking for?' shouted a woman from the back. 'What if Chamber One is a hoax?'

'Well, firstly, regardless of Chamber One, I want to know what they know about us and what they intend to do next. Secondly, we are looking for anything that can discredit the Industry,' said Carter. 'Anything that can prove and corroborate what I've learned since I've been here. There will be records of the horrors they've committed and, when we're ready, we can use this against them. Also, within the Catacombs, there are detailed surveys of what they call the Deadlands that include safe non-infected areas, sources of power and scientific equipment that will help you treat the sick and injured out here, increasing your ability to develop something sustainable. With the information in the Control Room or in Chamber One, we will have what we need to plan our next stages.'

'It's too dangerous.' One of the men on the stage stepped forward. 'We've lost too many people at their hands. Most of us wouldn't have been allowed to live if we'd stayed inside those walls. And too many more of us have died at their hands. I'm sure you all remember Company Five. They were headed in that same direction – and they were some of our strongest.'

Samuel's face flared crimson and he squared himself defensively to look at the man. 'That was over a year ago,' he said. 'We know more now and we're better equipped.'

'Even so,' said the man. 'It's a fool's errand.'

Jacinta stepped between them. 'Samuel feels guilty every single day about what happened.'

'True,' said the man, 'but I'm not prepared to risk the lives of more good people.' He stared at Samuel. 'I lost my brother that day.'

'That was not my fault, Jakob,' Samuel said in a low voice. 'What do you suggest we do?'

'Leave well alone, we'll be fine here.'

Carter watched as a number of people in the crowd took to their feet to get a closer look at the altercation and to rally behind the different sides. Samuel's face flared with anger and as he was about to respond but, before he could, Carter saw his opportunity and leapt back up onto the wooden platform to address the crowd, his arm on Samuel's shoulder.

'Firstly,' he began softly, addressing Jakob, 'I'm sorry for your loss.' A quietness descended over the clearing at the mention of Company Five and there were nods of respect.

'From what you've said today and what I've heard from others, you are reaching breaking point here,' he continued. 'You have the waterfall but that's not enough. What if they poison the river again?'

He watched Jacinta's eyes seem to sharpen with a level of respect. 'Exactly,' she said. 'What's to stop them poisoning us again?'.

'They can't force us to live like this,' added Samuel. 'We can't move out of this area for fear of attack. We're just as much prisoners inside our Village as they are within that so-called Community.'

There were shouts among the crowd, as agitation and disagreement broke out among small groups.

'We could continue here,' said Carter, quickly, looking at his mother, careful to include himself in the debate. 'But for how long? Another two years – five at the most. I know the way the Industry works and with a strong company, I believe we can do this. With my knowledge and yours we can plan this operation with precision. We can ensure we all get what is rightfully ours – the chance to exist in peace, with the resources we need to sustain ourselves. And, in time, release those in the Community to live a free life. But we must plan carefully. We don't have the information we need right now. That must come first.'

Jakob did not look convinced, but some of the others in the crowd did, so he let Carter continue anyway. 'Our company will be small and Samuel will lead until we get beyond the Barricades. Then, once we are within the Community, I will take control.'

The crowd listened intently. 'We know that the appointment ceremony for the new Controller General will be soon,' he continued. 'There will be a significant celebration party – there will be lots of preparation and concentration on making this a successful event. The Industry will use this opportunity to assert their power, to quash any thoughts of a secret rebellion. If they're smart, they'll use my supposed death to signal to everyone who thought that I was going to lead this revolution that it's over. They will turn it to their advantage.'

His mother nodded and put one hand on his shoulder. Carter strengthened his jaw and continued.

'And for those in the Community who believed I was the best candidate, it will be the Industry's opportunity to show that the new leader they have chosen is even more worthy than me. If Lily has done what you all think she's done, and made sure they believe that I died – that she killed me – out here in the Deadlands, then we have a chance of searching for what we need while they're focused on the ceremony.'

Carter paused. 'We can't change the world unless we know what we're dealing with. Information first, rebellion later.'

Through the crowd he saw people nodding in agreement.

'Then it's settled,' said Jacinta. 'We will send a small company into the Catacombs to gather the information we need, led by Samuel and Carter.'

There was a ripple of applause and Angel, half way back and listening intently, smiled. The crowd dispersed into smaller groups, some chatting animatedly while others wandered back towards the trees.

'Well, it seems you *are* both going back to the Community then,' said Jacinta, dryly eyeing both of her sons.

'Yes, we are,' said Carter, watching as Samuel caught the attention of a group in the distance and disappeared. He turned to Jacinta. 'And I may not like him but some things are more important than either of us, correct?'

'I didn't leave you because I didn't love you or care about you,' said Jacinta, her eyes fixed on Carter. 'I left you because I knew you would be an asset to me – to both me and your father. We needed to separate – but I absolutely believed I would see you again. Things happened this way because it was planned.'

Carter nodded. 'I know that now,' he said. 'I might not agree with the way you did it, but I think I understand why. You believe in taking down the Industry more than anything, don't you?'

Jacinta nodded her head firmly. 'I do,' she said. 'You are no longer a child, Carter – in this world you are a man. And your part in this is pivotal. Samuel has his weaknesses but he also has his strengths – you will need to harness those – and between you, I am certain you can do this.'

'So am I, Mother,' said Carter, his gaze wandering to where Angel stood smiling. 'So am I.'

Chapter Eleven

The Goodbye

Alice

As Alice had requested, Kelly hadn't been moved from her position near the Barricades and still lay there, a trickle of blood thickening in the dusty afternoon sun. A thin breeze blew a veil of dirt across her eyelids as the group sat there in silence beside her still body. Marcus held his hands up towards the sky while Quinn scanned the horizon. A line of Watchers pointed their guns outward at the desolate lands to the north. Filip stood motionless behind them.

'How did this happen?' said Alice. 'Who was here with her?'

Marcus let his hands slip to the ground and ran his fingers through stony gravel. 'The shot came from behind that small building there,' he said and pointed towards a hut in the distance. His long hair, streaked with blood and dirt hung limp across his face that was wrought with devastation. He clung to Alice for support. 'I didn't see them until they ran. I tried my best to make her better. I'm sorry.'

'You don't have anything to be sorry for,' said Alice, her voice breaking. A single tear dripped from her cheek into the stony dust before her chest heaved and she began gulping back torrents of hot, wet sobs. Her hand moved instinctively to her belly as she looked at Kelly, her hand too, cupping her stomach,

Quinn softly, a light wavering in her voice, but her words were clear. 'It must have been a revenge attack – I expect they're building an army. These murderers must die,' she said. 'Those outsiders will pay for this.'

'They will,' said Filip. 'We'll make sure of it.'

'An eye for an eye will make the whole world blind,' mouthed Alice to herself, looking into the treeline that bordered the Community. For a moment she thought she saw a flash of metal, glinting against the sunlight but when she looked again, it was gone and there was nothing except the faint scent of lavender in the air and the heavy feeling of sadness.

Quinn kneeled down next to Kelly and took her hand.

'There will be no mercy,' she said, her eyes glistening with tears. 'We will build these walls so high that no one will come close again. Death to all outsiders.'

Alice shook her head. 'We don't know all the facts,' she said.

'This is fact enough,' spat Quinn, pointing at Kelly's stomach. 'They killed *my* child. And they *will* pay.'

Another electric white flash between the trees and the horizon caught Alice's attention again. 'They're still out there,' she said quickly. 'We need to move.'

Quinn and Filip reached for their guns.

She touched Marcus gently on the shoulder. 'There's something you can do to help Kelly and Quinn. Go and tell Wilson we need a new batch of Industry Watchers up here to patrol the Barricades – the latest trainees. Filip, you go with him.'

Quinn looked up into the light. 'And get them to bring more guns,' she added.

As Marcus and Filip disappeared into the distance, Alice put her arm around Quinn. 'I'm so sorry,' she said. 'We should have listened to her.' She felt Quinn's muscles stiffen hard against her arm.

'What do you mean?' she said. 'What did she tell you?' Her eyes were diamond hard and angry.

Alice paused. 'She'd said she'd seen people out across the Deadlands. I was there myself and I didn't see anything – just some glass reflecting in the sun. She'd been so worried lately I thought she might have been imagining it. But she said she had told you, that she was going to speak to you again.'

Quinn pulled away from her, her face blazing with anger. 'Well clearly, she didn't say anything to me – do you think I'd have done nothing? Didn't you think for a second that *you* should have reported it? That maybe you should have spoken to me, or Barnes? Or Kunstein even? We had a right to know. Did you tell anyone at all?'

Alice ran her fingers through the dirt. 'No,' she said quietly. 'No, I didn't. But I came to you and you sent me away.' She remembered the night she had called at Quinn and Kelly's house. Her stomach ached with sadness. Was there something she should have done? Could she have been more determined to tell Quinn what she knew?

'And Marcus? Did he know about this? He's been spending a lot of time with her?'

Alice felt immediately protective of the small boy and shook her head slowly. 'No, he hasn't said anything to me. Quinn, I know you're angry and upset but she said she'd told you. You must feel…'

Quinn picked at the undergrowth around them, wrenching the leafy plants from the ground. 'You have no idea how I feel,' she said. 'I have lost my chance at helping to bring new life into this world. And keeping secrets from me, Alice, is very unwise. You could have saved her. You seem to be making a habit of this.'

Alice could feel herself shaking in anger. 'You know that's not fair.'

'Life isn't fair,' said Quinn as she covered Kelly's face with a blanket of ferns. 'And guilt is something that never goes away.'

Using a makeshift stretcher, they carried Kelly back towards the main square, Jayden and Alice on one side, Quinn and Filip on the other. It felt so horribly similar to when they had moved Jonah from the Deadlands, after the water from the Black River had sent him delusional: horribly similar and yet, frighteningly different. Alice felt her stomach churning over and over.

'We'll need to burn her, won't we?' said Quinn, glancing at Barnes.

Alice ran her fingers along the side of the stretcher. 'We need to agree a way of… dealing with these kinds of things. Up here, we need to have a form of… disposal.' She chewed on the side of her mouth, trying to choose the right words. 'We don't have the space to make graveyards any more, not if we're to keep this space sustainable.'

Barnes moved forwards. 'Quinn, you know as well as I do that we're going to have to set the fires. Okay?'

Quinn looked straight ahead, glassy and calm, almost ignoring Alice. 'Yes, it's the right thing to do,' she said, emotionless.

Alice's sniffing turned into silent sobs and she dropped the corner of the stretcher. Jayden moved quickly to catch Kelly's left leg that flopped aimlessly over the side – slender, pale and useless.

'Keep it together, Alice,' said Filip. 'Not even grief can be what it used to be.'

Barnes stood in the background, almost respectfully silent, the gold edges of her coat flapping in the breeze.

'You should have told us,' said Quinn. The group closed around her and held her close, their shoulders rising and falling in sadness.

'From here on in, no one goes anywhere alone,' said Filip, putting his arm around Alice tightly and rubbing her stomach. 'No one.'

They took Kelly's body to the west, into a hidden small wooded copse and covered her body in thin twigs and bracken. Quinn placed a spring of lavender in each of her hands and they each took turns in saying a few personal words.

'I know it's wrong, but I wish you still had that violin,' said Jayden to Quinn. 'Kelly loved the way you played that night we said goodbye to Jonah. She said it was the most beautiful thing she had ever heard in her life.'

'That night we said goodbye to a lot of things,' said Quinn, sharply. 'It wasn't just Jonah. I knew that would be the last time I ever held an instrument and played like that.' In the evening light, Alice thought her face, like granite, looked almost unrecognisable from the passionate, loving girl she had known in the Ship.

'These are the parts of the old world that we have to forget,' said Filip with solemnity. 'They caused more heartache than joy. We have attached too much meaning to these simple things – when we bring the rest of the new community topside, how easy would it be to slip back into the old ways if we allowed everything to be just as it was before? How much of our time has been wasted on the idleness of hobbies that don't create anything, on religions that tear our world apart and on sports teams that serve only to set communities against each other. Unity will come, only when we work towards the same thing: when everyone is equal.'

Alice felt her chest grow tight and a knot form in her stomach as the heat behind her eyes grew stronger. She was the last to speak and, as she moved towards Kelly's body, she struggled to find the words she wanted to use.

'I will miss you,' she said, finally, tears running down her cheeks in thick rivulets. 'You were quiet, innocent and beautiful. You saw the best in people and you had dreams of a future that I wish you could have fulfilled. I will miss you.'

'I'm glad we could do this one privately,' said Quinn, crushing a sprig of lavender between her fingers. 'Our new world has little place for grief and emotion when there is so much to do. But she deserved something more, being one of us original Scouts. Unfortunately, it was probably her ability to see only good in people that contributed to this tragedy.' She threw down the lavender and moved back to stand with Barnes and Jayden.

'I couldn't bear it if we'd had to put her on one of the trash pyres or send her down to the incinerators in the infirmary,' said Alice in a choked voice.

'That's enough, Alice,' said Filip, his arm weighing heavy on her shoulders.

'Aren't any of you even *upset*?' Alice spluttered the words out, so incongruent against the calmness of the others.

'We won't be able to do this for everyone,' continued Filip, watching the breeze lift the bracken slowly and then settle it again against the cloth they'd wrapped Kelly in. 'But Quinn is right, she was special, one of the first and she deserves to be recognised. Our sadness must become our strength.' He stood up and picked a sprig of lavender from a nearby bush, scattering the petals over the body. He handed Quinn the fire-maker.

'It's time,' he said.

They watched as the flames slowly died to a calm flicker and everything was burned before carefully pouring on the water. Jayden and Izzy stayed to bury the remains and between them, dug up the lavender bush and planted it on top while the others watched from a distance away.

'We can celebrate her life with lavender,' said Alice, calmer now the ceremony was over. 'Burn it to signify love and the promise of something better.'

'Yes,' said Filip. 'And just as Jonah's death helped us to understand the threats of the old world, Kelly's will force us to remember that the lands outside of our Community are devoid of anything that will enrich or sustain us. This will serve as a warning to others.'

The Industry elite that Wilson sent to complete the Barricades exacted their operation with almost military precision. They took it in turns to build thick metal structures and watch over the Community every hour of every day. Within days it was finished: thick metal fences that surrounded them on all sides, cocooning them from the dangers of the Deadlands loomed up towards the sky. With the exception of the Industry Watchers, Alice was the last to leave, and she watched the others trudge off silently southwards towards the Community.

'It's good we have the emergency access out here on this one side,' she said to the workers. Then added 'But it will need to be guarded at all times.'

'Right you are, Davenport,' saluted one of the women, her features almost indistinguishable. Alice wasn't sure if she'd spoken to her before or whether she was a different officer. There was something weirdly unsettling talking to the Industry professionals – they were almost mechanistic in the way they pooled information and knowledge: it felt like accessing a hard drive. She marched off in the direction of the

Barricades and shouted something to two of the others who were fixing metal plates to a wire frame. They high-fived and laughed, their voices disappearing as Alice became aware of something in the background, a sparkling that came from the hillside to the north. The same flash of light she'd now seen too many times for it to be a coincidence.

The Watcher saw her turn her face and raised her gun.

'Where?' called the woman Alice had spoken to. 'Co-ordinates, Davenport – or a direction at least.'

'To the north and slightly west,' called one of the other Watchers. 'There on the outcrop, a flashing light.' They all watched in silence as an eagle circled around the outcrop and then down into the valley. It curved gracefully across the skyline and then back up towards the clouds. Then the flash came again, quickly.

'Do you see it?' shouted the first Watcher. 'There, near those two trees.'

'Negative,' said two officials in harmony. 'Nothing in the trees.'

'It was there,' said a man, pointing. 'I saw it.'

The eagle swooped back downwards, spying something in the grass. Skidding across the plain, it elevated again clutching something small – a rodent – in sharp talons. Alice kept her eyes marked on the spot she'd last seen the flash.

'There it is!' she whispered. Three shots rang out from across the Barricade, hard clear tones ringing out into the Deadlands and something moved within the trees before everything was still. The eagle dropped like a stone from the sky. Alice felt time slowly wind down: and then stop. The woman's voice cut through the ringing in her ears.

'I reckon we got whatever it was,' she called. 'There's nothing there now. And that thing in the sky was in our way so we bagged that too.' There was more laughter between the shooters.

In the distance, Alice could just make out the shape of the eagle, one errant wing flapping with the breeze. And out of the corner of her eye, she thought she saw something shining.

Dinner that evening was quiet and sombre. As they sat around the table, Marcus pushed his carrotina around the plate. Izzy had long finished and asked to be excused. Alice felt sick to her stomach but thankful in many ways to be back within the four walls she called home. Although something felt different; concerning, unsettling after what had happened at the Barricades. Her attempt at a smile felt more forced than she imagined it would.

'Why are you in such a rush to leave?' she said to Izzy.

'I have to write up my Contribution,' the girl replied brightly. 'Barnes says I'm ready to move up another grade and I can start doing some practical work in the Lab. Can I go now?' She giggled and jumped up from her chair.

'Okay,' said Alice, exhausted and ruffled her hair. 'And not too late to bed tonight, all right? You can take some time to study tomorrow.' But the girl whispered something to Marcus and was gone before Alice even finished her sentence.

'Izzy seems to be dealing with the whole thing with Kelly well,' said Filip finishing a mouthful of chicker. 'She's very resilient for an eleven-year-old.'

'Yes,' said Alice, thoughtfully. 'It's a lot to have to deal with.'

'She wasn't even there,' said Marcus, circling his fork around the plate. 'She didn't have to deal with anything, did she?'

Alice pulled her chair next to the boy. 'What exactly did you see, Marcus?' she said. 'Where did the shot come from?'

'Leave it,' said Filip, sharply. 'The boy has been through enough.'

'I told you,' said Marcus. 'I was looking out at the Deadlands and it came from nowhere. One minute I was talking to Kelly and the next she was lying on the floor with blood coming out of her head.' His hands started to shake. 'It was horrible. She was telling about the baby and how your baby and hers would be like brother and sister. And how...' He started to sniff and his mouth quivered uncontrollably. 'I liked Kelly,' he said. 'Much more than the others. She understood stuff.'

Alice handed him a tissue from the table. 'Did you hear anyone? See anything across the Barricade? Maybe a flash of light like the sun catching on something?'

'No,' wailed Marcus, 'there was nothing there; I swear I didn't see anything. It was like a sniper or something.'

'It's okay, Marcus,' said Alice. 'It was more than likely just a one-off – someone probably hiding in the clump of trees just outside the boundary. We've cleared everything close enough to hide in now, nothing like that will ever happen again.'

'We need to be vigilant though,' said Filip. 'Who knows what threats are out there?'

'Who knows what threats are in here,' said Marcus quietly sobbing.

'What do you mean by that?' said Filip. 'Explain yourself.'

'Nothing.' Marcus pushed his plate away. 'It's just that now we're trapped in here with no way out. The Barricades are locked down so there's no way into the Deadlands, even if we wanted to go there.'

'Why would you want to go there?' said Filip. 'You've seen for yourself the dangers that the outside world could pose to use – there's contamination, radiation, all kinds of poisons in the Black River and then there's a few people who might kill you without even asking if you mean them any harm. Do you think Kelly deserved to die like that?'

'Of course not,' said Marcus, wiping his face with his hands. 'I just feel trapped in here. It's like we spent five years underground in that prison just to come up to another one. It sucks.'

The pattern of his hair flopped over his eyes and the way he tried to make his voice deeper, more masculine when he was so desperately upset reminded Alice so much of Jonah. She held his hand tightly.

'You have to remember that this is how things are now,' she said softly, but finding it difficult to convince herself completely. 'The Industry has taken care of us and now we need to take care of ourselves. We're creating a new world out here and things are going to be different than before. It's going to be tough but you're going to have to fit in.'

Marcus pulled back his hand sharply and stood up. 'What if I don't want to?' he said. 'This isn't fair. I hate it here.' The heavy stamping feel of his feet on the stairs as he went to his room remained in the kitchen longer than the sound itself.

'He wasn't ready to come up here,' said Filip, shaking his head. 'I blame myself. Barnes mentioned to me the other day that she had concerns about him.'

'How can any of us be ready for such a transformation of the life they knew before?' said Alice. 'We all just have to get on with it. He'll get there, in time. We all will.'

'No,' said Filip slowly. 'I think Wilson was right – and Barnes too. Marcus needs more than we can give him here.'

'What are you suggesting?' said Alice, her hands fiddling with the plate.

'I'm not sure,' said Filip, 'but there are people underground who can help with this kind of thing, they're trained in the ways that we aren't. People who work for Barnes for example – she's doing great things with Richard – dealing with his trauma. I don't want Marcus to become another sad story we have to tell our children. He's nine years old, Alice – he spent over half his life in the Ship but still he remembers too much. We need to have a process for this, you know, when things – *people* – don't adapt in the way they should.'

Alice stacked up the food containers and wiped down the table. 'I don't know, Filip,' she said, a tight ball of worry in her stomach. 'Maybe we should give him some more time – he's your brother after all. And if Richard is such a great success then maybe he should be above ground with us.' She watched for a reaction.

'He's only been my brother for the last five years,' said Filip, ignoring her thoughts on Richard. 'And it's for his own safety. Maybe they can work with him down there. He's becoming erratic and over emotional; I don't want that influence on my baby.'

'Our baby,' Alice corrected. 'And he's excited about having a younger brother or sister. I think it will do him good. And besides, he won't want to go back, he hated the Ship.'

'He doesn't have a choice; I've already spoken to Barnes.'

'You spoke to Barnes without talking to me first?' Alice slammed her hand down on the table. 'I've been taking care of him for months and you make this decision without me?'

Filip put his arms around her shoulder and stroked the top of her arm. 'It's for the best,' he said. 'They can make a space for him tomorrow when we take Izzy underground for her tests.'

'No. I won't have it.' Alice shook Filip's arm from her shoulder. 'You can't just make decisions like that without me. He's my son too.'

'He's not your son – he's—' Filip took a step closer to Alice, his height towering over her '—he's a member of this Community just like everyone else. And if his presence here isn't working, then we take steps to remedy that. We're in the early stages, Alice, we can't afford for things to go wrong. You know that.'

Alice shook her head. 'It's not right, Filip,' she said. 'He's just a boy, he needs a chance.'

'There will be plenty of other chances,' said Filip, firmly. 'It's just that, for Marcus, now might not be the right time. We need to make sure that we give people the opportunities that best fit them. It's cruel to keep him here before he's ready. There are others who won't make it on their first attempt – we've known that all along. That's why the resettlement programme Barnes is developing is so important.' Filip sounded so calm and measured against the cascade of anger that was building up inside Alice.

'We can help him,' she said, steadying herself. 'I'll help him adjust.'

'No,' said Filip, firmly. 'Your work here is to help repopulate with new life. And to lead those people who are ready. Our mistake with Jonah cost us a lot as a community. We can't afford for that to happen again. Not with anyone.'

'I can't agree to it.'

'You don't have to. He doesn't belong here and that's clear. His safety and wellbeing overrides any personal decisions we may want to make. It's a decision we can't avoid. You don't want to put him in jeopardy, do you?'

Alice felt the guilt like a knotted knife in her stomach. 'When will he come back?' she said quietly, pleading almost.

'When he's ready,' said Filip, his arm back on her shoulder. 'Alice, we need to be strong. He won't be the last to leave us for a short while but we agreed that we would do whatever it took to transform what life means to us, for the sake of future generations.'

Alice rubbed her stomach. 'Would you do this if it were our child?' she demanded and pressed against the tiny being inside her.

Filip smiled at her. 'Our child won't know anything of the old world and therefore, it won't happen. It's impossible.'

'Would you do this if it were our child?'

'I'd do it to save anyone's life. That's what we're doing here, Alice, we're saving his life. You know what happens when people don't belong. Jonah went crazy believing that the old world still existed, desperately trying to find his sister – swimming across the Black River. You didn't forget that did you?'

'No,' said Alice reluctantly. 'I'll never forget that.'

As she climbed the stairs, legs heavy, Alice could hear a gentle sobbing coming through the door to Marcus's room, even though it was tightly closed. She stopped for a second before crossing the hallway to Izzy's room where the little girl sat reciting her homework, working out range and directions aloud, and setting up the targets in her room.

'Time for sleeping,' said Alice in a half-breaking voice as she came through the doorway. 'You've got another big day ahead of you tomorrow.'

'Can I have another ten minutes?' said Izzy. 'Please?'

'Not tonight,' said Alice, sad and irritated. 'If you want to be ahead of all the others, the most important principle is sleep.'

'*Marcus* isn't asleep,' said Izzy. 'He's still crying in his room.' She set up another target and pretended to aim. Alice felt her heart ache.

'Marcus is hurting,' said Alice, sitting next to her. 'He saw something that made him feel a lot of pain.'

'Marcus is weak,' said Izzy, bluntly, in a voice much older than her years. 'And he's worried you won't like him any more when you have the baby. Because it'll be yours and we aren't really your family.'

Guilt spread through Alice. 'What makes you say that?' she said. 'Did you hear us talking before?'

The girl fiddled with the sharp tip of an arrow, the thin blade piecing her finger until a sliver of blood dripped onto her bed. Quickly, Alice reached for a piece of cloth that had held the arrows and wrapped it tight around Izzy's finger.

'There you go,' she said and the girl smiled sweetly, the traces of the hard, indifferent child seeming to melt away.

Alice sat down on the bed and held the little girl close to her and felt the skinniness of her bones dig into her sides. 'I know how it feels to be alone,' she said. 'But even though I'm not your mother, I'm your family now – do you know what that means?'

'It means you're in charge of me,' said Izzy. 'Doesn't it?'

'It means I'm never going to leave you,' said Alice, trying to connect with Izzy's emotional side. 'We're going to take care of each other, whatever happens, okay?'

'I guess.'

Alice paused. At times, the girl reminded her so much of the frightened, insular soul she had been as she wandered from room to room in Prospect House, a lifetime ago. She watched as Izzy jumped up and lined the targets squarely in front of her. And, at other times, they were so desperately different.

'You're very good at that,' she said. 'You fit right in here, don't you?'

Izzy smiled. 'Yes, I am,' she said. 'I can lift a crate of books all on my own and I don't even look at all the old toys we find. Marcus does. Sometimes he picks them up. I saw him put a metal car in his pocket once.'

Alice smiled weakly, her heart splintering into tiny pieces.

'Maybe Marcus should go back to the Ship where he belongs.'

Alice, surprised at the pragmatism of the girl, baulked a little. 'He belongs here, with us, Izzy. We're a family and we take care of each other.' She held the girl's hand, her heart tight in her chest. 'But sometimes we all have to do things we don't want to, don't we? But often, those things are the best for us, right? Even if we don't know it at the time. And it may be that Marcus will have to go back to school underground for a while. Just for a little while.'

'Yes, I know. Barnes says we must be brave.'

Alice shook her head and wondered how true those words were and whether taking Marcus back into the Ship really was the best for him – for all of them. Whether they could really make a difference with him and how many more people would come to the surface only to feel like they were in another version of the Ship, just with more sunshine and less comfort. She shuddered at the thought of any future versions of Jonah – but worried more about having to lie to Marcus over breakfast and the betrayal he would feel when he knew he was staying below ground.

She pulled back the covers and tucked the girl into bed. For the first time she felt some sort of connection between them; the constant knot of antagonism had, it seemed, to have loosened itself a little and for that, she was grateful.

'We can't say anything to Marcus,' she whispered. 'Nothing at all, okay?'

Izzy chuckled and put her finger to her lips. 'I can keep a secret,' she said. 'I know lots of secrets.'

Alice patted the pillow down and took a serious tone. 'Secrets can be fun but you know you can always talk to me about anything, don't you? There's a fine line between secrets and lies.'

Izzy nodded and closed her eyes and, as she blew out the candle and looked out through the window, Alice watched the moon, crisp and bright, high in the sky until Izzy's regular breathing confirmed her sleep. In just a few months' time, she thought, there would be another child sleeping in this house and her heart skipped in a mixture of terrifying anticipation and hopeful excitement. In her mind, she saw herself cradling the infant, pulling him or her close and something inside her warmed.

As white stars glittered through the sky, she touched the crown of Izzy's head and kissed her on the cheek wondering whether, in a different world, there would be any space for secrets in the sleeping girl's dreams.

Chapter Twelve

The Plan

Carter

In the well-ordered, intricate house in the trees, Carter and Samuel sat facing each other. Each was holding a cup of a thick liquid that smelled strongly alcoholic, like the chag that Carter had once seen his father drink.

'Drink,' said Samuel, smiling a little. 'This will make you a man.'

'I'm a man already,' said Carter. 'And technically I'm ten years older than you *and* a father of twins.'

Samuel rolled his eyes but didn't rise to the challenge. Since his return from the fruitless cattle venture, he had appeared to be making some element of effort, conciliatory and unsettlingly cordial at times.

Carter took the drink and swilled it around his mouth.

'Not bad,' he said, chinking his glass against Samuel's. 'Not bad at all.'

Samuel nodded and clapped his shoulder. 'A drink with my brother, how civilised,' he said smiling, making Carter feel distinctly uncomfortable.

He nodded back. 'Let's get on with this, shall we?' he said.

*

They sat at a table, lit with flickering lamps as Carter pored over the crumpled paper that Elvira had given him while Samuel made notes with a thin piece of charcoal.

'This is incredible,' said Carter turning it over and looking at the tunnel blueprint. 'It's old and out of date, but still...'

'Leave it this side up,' said Samuel. We need to keep working on the overground routes in and out before we look at the Catacombs. We don't have much time.'

Carter flipped the paper over. 'This road here has been closed for some time,' he said. 'And this—' he drew a small circle on the paper with his finger '—this area has been developed since whoever drew this map was there.'

'Any other changes?' Samuel kept making notes with the charcoal and poured himself and Carter another drink.

'He was only there a couple of days,' said Angel from the other side of the room, 'how much do you expect him to remember?'

'I remember everything,' said Carter and took the charcoal from Samuel, making some annotations of his own. 'Okay, I think this is about it.'

Samuel turned the map over. 'Now for the Catacombs,' he said. 'How much of that is stored in your photographic brain?' The other side of the map was a tangle of corridors and chambers, scored with crossings out and amendments.

Carter scoured the page and frowned. 'This is all wrong,' he said. 'The corridors are here—' he scratched a mark on the page '—and here. It was very different coming up to when I went down to be frozen. I thought they'd taken us a different way but it's more likely that they've built and excavated down there. And these shafts I've never seen before. They're not tunnels – they must be used for something else. This area here—' he circled a small section that was almost identical to every other on the plan '—is different structurally – look how there is a double wall here.'

Angel let out a low whistle. 'How can you see that? That's impressive,' she said. 'You do know your stuff.'

Samuel shrugged. 'I'm sure my brother will prove his worth even further when we're there, won't you, Carter?'

Carter narrowed his eyes. 'I'm sure we both will,' he replied coolly.

They carried on working and by the time Jacinta returned, the amendments to the map were almost complete. She nodded and hummed in agreement as Carter took her through the new roads, developments and the increased security at the Barricades. Her questions were short, direct and pointed. Carter's responses were the same and they transacted in almost military fashion as they moved from one end of the map to the other.

'Well, this all seems to be going well,' she said, finally.

'Has there been any news from McDermott yet?' said Samuel. 'We need to know if we can count on her.'

'Nothing concrete yet,' said Jacinta. 'But we have had an indication that a Controller General has been agreed upon.'

Even though so much had changed, Carter felt his heart ache a little. He'd been training his whole life, destined to take that role. If he'd known the truth he could have made a real difference. And, although he no longer wanted it, he felt the loss of something he could never have hit him bitterly as a pit formed in his stomach.

'Who is it?' he said, the sadness rising in his throat.

Jacinta shook her head. 'There's been no confirmation of who it is, just that the decision has been made. The formal announcement will be made in a few days' time.'

'Tough luck, brother,' said Samuel. 'Must kill you to know the job went to a better person.' He picked up a piece of fruit from the counter and bit into it.

Carter turned his head away. 'I could have made a difference,' he said. 'If I'd known before, I could have stopped it from the inside.'

'Leave him alone,' said Angel, turning to Samuel. 'Don't you think he's been through enough since he's been here? The two of you need to start collaborating and decide how you're going to get into the Community and what you're then going to do when you get there.'

Samuel bowed his head in acknowledgements. 'Sorry,' he conceded. 'Force of habit.'

Carter turned to Angel. 'It's fine,' he said. 'This is going to take some time. But we're going to get there, aren't we, Samuel?'

Samuel looked at Jacinta. 'I guess so. We're brothers, aren't we?'

Carter picked up his drink and took a sip. 'Tell me about Company Five,' he said. 'How come you survived?'

Samuel looked out of the window and scowled. 'I don't want to talk about it,' he said.

'Tell him,' said Jacinta. 'It will help.'

Samuel walked to the other side of the room. 'It was the middle of the night,' he said. 'I'd climbed up into one of the higher trees – I've never been able to sleep at ground level, feels unnatural to me. I tied myself to one of the flat branches, like I always do, and sharpened a spear for a bit. I could hear the others around the fire; I remember there was some sort of bird that they were pointing at and talking about. The next time I opened my eyes, it was morning and everyone had gone. All of our stuff was still there – the tents, the food, the weapons, everything. It was like they had just disappeared. There were no signs of any attack and all the food was still there, so it can't have been an animal.'

Carter eyed him. 'You didn't hear anything? No cries for help?'

'Not a single sound.'

'Maybe they just left? Wanted to start up their own group from scratch?'

'You don't understand, Carter. They wouldn't have done that.'

'Why not? Perhaps they thought they could make it more easily on their own, without having to be a part of something bigger?

Samuel interrupted him. 'They wouldn't do that by choice,' he said. 'They wouldn't just leave. I'll tell you why, Carter Warren. Because our people stick together, always.' He chewed his lip.

Carter ignored him. 'I propose we take a different route to any that has been taken before. If, somehow, the Industry did attack Company Five then they must somehow have been watching you.'

Samuel scoffed. 'If they'd been watching us, I'd have seen them. I can track an animal miles off and I know when I'm being…'

Carter held up his hand to silence him. 'This was recent, right?'

'Less than a year ago.'

'It wasn't your fault. It was a drone.'

At his first training session with Lily, after coming out of the Catacombs, he remembered the trilling of what he had thought was a bird but had turned out to be an Industry night drone, collecting information on dissident conversations. And how quickly Lily had moved them on from their conversation about his daughter and the rebellion when they had heard the mechanical buzzing. She had been trying to protect him.

'Drones?' said Angel. 'You mean like…'

'They made the one I saw look and sound a little bit like a bird; probably with a camera and a sound recording device.' He tried to remember exactly what Lily said but realised she hadn't said very much at all. 'That must have been how they knew they were there. It's probably how they set the cornfields alight as well. What happened after that is anybody's guess but the drone probably missed you as you were in the tree. We need to take a different route.'

Samuel looked stunned as Angel joined their conversation. 'So how do you expect to get in?' she said.

Carter flattened out the map of the Catacombs. 'If this blueprint is correct, then these shafts are air vents and they lead all the way to somewhere on the north-east side of the old city.'

He squinted at the paper and then pulled out another, larger scale version from one of the shelves. 'It looks like this structure—' he ran his finger through several squares on the old map '—runs all the way up to the east of Drakewater. He paused for a second. 'That's where they were getting some of their power, wasn't it?'

Samuel nodded. 'Yes.'

Carter looked at the map again. 'If they were depositing waste near there by Transporter, we could go through the tunnels.'

'Not possible,' said Jacinta. 'The only Transporter tunnel in or out is the one you told us about, the one Lily went though. The rest of the waste goes deep underground. The Transporter tunnel is so heavily guarded you'd never make it. The Transporters run across magnetised tracks towards Drakewater, empty their load into the pits and then return. There's no way of getting inside them, under them or on top of them. The sensors would track you the minute you enter the tunnel. They expect there to be human waste on the outbound journey, but not coming back in.'

Carter shivered at the thought of the babies. 'The team needs to be small,' he continued. He walked over to the shelves of books, picked one and flicked through it. 'How long will it take to get to the Catacombs?'

'Depending on the weather, maybe two or three days. Also depends which side we want to get to, exactly.'

'Then we'll leave tomorrow.'

'You still haven't told us how we're getting in there, or where we're headed to, boy genius.'

Carter held up the book from the shelf and placed it in front of Samuel, opening the pages at chapter three, looking at Angel all the while he did.

'Smart,' said Jacinta. 'Mechanical Engineering – Chapter Three, Principles of Ventilation.'

'The Industry takes air from above and uses it under the surface,' said Carter, glancing at Angel. 'Now all we need to do is work out who knows where the vents are. And how to make our way through the shafts.'

'Elvira knows,' she replied. 'She'll come with us all the way. She knows every inch of the initial construction. She knows how the insides of the Transporter tunnels were built, remember. She was there.'

There was a knock on the underside of the floor and Elvira climbed monkey-like into the room.

'I hope you're ready,' she said, breathy from her journey. 'The council have just made contact with Lily. We didn't manage to communicate for long, but she's fine and still in position. Everything is going accordingly to plan and they will be ready for our arrival in a few days.'

Angel smiled. 'Did you agree any other volunteers to come with us?'

'We don't need anyone else,' said Samuel sharply. 'The four of us is enough.'

'Aaron and Lisa,' nodded Elvira. 'The cooking brothers. They have asked to be a part of the mission.'

'No,' spat Samuel. 'I won't allow it.'

'They're honest and trustworthy,' said Angel. 'The way they've dedicated their lives to making our people healthy and our Village a better place to live is admirable.'

'They know the lands around here quite well too,' added Elvira. 'In their search for new vegetables and herbs, they've travelled more than most. And they're strong and very capable'

'We don't need them,' grunted Samuel. 'There's more than enough of us.'

'They will come,' said Jacinta, decisively. 'You need more people and the brothers will provide additional security.'

Samuel frowned and said something unintelligible under his breath, tutting and huffing in Angel's direction.

Jacinta turned to Carter. 'This boy of yours – do you think he will be an ally? There's an indication he has some affiliation with the Industry.'

Carter thought of his son, who looked so very much like him, the boy he wanted to know and care for. 'I don't know,' he said. 'I hope to be able to bring him back here – maybe not straight away, but I want him away from the Community so he can live a free life.'

Jacinta cleared her throat and looked upwards at the sky as the stars melted into blackness. 'I know what it is to leave a child behind,' she said. 'But don't let that cloud your judgement. There is more at stake here than the life of one boy.'

Her words cut Carter deep. 'I know,' he said, through gritted teeth. 'But I've already lost Lucia – nothing can prepare you for a loss you didn't even know you could experience. I won't lose my son too. No one deserves to live those lies – not Ariel and not any of the others.'

'Do nothing hasty,' said Jacinta, firmly. 'I lost a part of myself the day I left the Community but, if I had stayed for you, I'd have lost a whole lot more and all this—' she spread her arms wide, gesturing to the Village '—all this and all these people would not be here.'

'I know,' said Carter, again. 'But I won't leave a part of myself behind.'

'You'll have to.'

Carter straightened his back and cast his eyes out across the dense thickness of the forest.

'On the contrary, Jacinta,' he said. 'Rather than leave a part of me, I intend to bring a part of myself back.'

Chapter Thirteen

The Catacombs

Alice

When Alice awoke, the rain that had hammered through the night had stopped. Filip, Marcus and Izzy were already up, the sound of breakfast preparation floating upwards through the floorboards. Her stomach churned and she rushed to the bathroom, the first wave of nausea sweeping over her. As she sat there on the floor, her hair lank against her face, she picked at the tiles and then threw up all over them.

When she finally made her way downstairs, she saw that Marcus looked less upset, if a little sullen, but Izzy held her usual chirpy excitement as she always did on the two days per week she returned to the Ship for socialisation and Academy classes.

'I'm going to be top of the class again today,' she said as she ran through the house, stopping in open corners to perfect a handstand against the wall.

'Not in here,' said Alice as she came through into the living area. 'Be careful you don't kick something over, Izzy.'

The girl grinned upside down. 'I won't,' she said. 'Look, Alice, look. My balance is perfect.' She tipped her legs backwards and walked the length of the room on her hands. 'See,' she said. 'I bet you can't do that.'

'No, I can't,' said Alice. 'You're very clever. Now get your things together, both of you.'

Alice watched as the young girl tore through the house and out of the door with boundless enthusiasm. Her resilience seemed unshakeable – Alice wondered if having spent almost all her life in the Ship had created something in her that was a new, different human trait.

Marcus picked at a piece of whiteloaf and pushed it around the table.

'You look tired,' said Alice, wiping crumbs from the counter. 'Did you sleep okay?'

Marcus yawned and cupped his hand to his mouth. 'You know in a few weeks the baby will be able to do that too – yawn, I mean.' He smiled weakly and looked sheepish. 'I read that in a book I found, sorry.'

Alice pressed Marcus's hands against her stomach. 'I think she's a girl,' she said. 'I really do.'

Marcus nodded. 'I'd like that,' he said. 'A different sister – a baby one that's all new. I'd like that, Alice.'

As the four of them approached the Industry headquarters there were two guards on patrol, clad all in black with guns wrapped in leather holsters around their waists.

'Good morning, Davenport. Good morning, Conrad,' said one of them. 'You here to take the kids down?'

'Yes,' said Alice. 'Why all the security? What else has happened?'

'Nothing yet,' said another. 'Barnes's orders. Until we can ensure complete safety above ground, we're not going to risk any breaches down there. Access in and out of the Ship is now strictly by appointment and agreement with Barnes, Wilson or Kunstein.'

Alice frowned. 'Do you really expect anyone to make it past the Barricades, through the Community and down here into the headquarters without being recognised?'

'We're taking no chances,' said the first guard, her eyes trained on a point way beyond Alice. 'We watch for everything. Have a good day now, won't you?'

As they got into the elevator, Marcus fingered the edges of the buttons anxiously. The whirr of the mechanics started and, as the doors closed, he looked through the gap until they shut tight. Izzy giggled and poked him in the chest.'

'Please don't,' said Marcus in a weak voice, turning away. He rubbed the side of his face and looked at Alice. 'I don't feel very well,' he said. 'Can I stay home today?'

Filip turned out his pocket and produced a fresh bar of fauclate. Snapping it in half, he gave some to Marcus. 'Eat this,' he said. 'It'll make you feel better.' The boy put it into his mouth and crunched down, sucking out the sweet taste between his teeth.

'It's not as good as chocolate,' he said, sulkily. 'It tastes bitter.'

'It's better than chocolate,' said Filip. 'All the nutrients and vitamins you need.'

Izzy jumped back upright and pulled on Filip's sleeve. 'Can I have some?' she said. 'Pleeeeease?'

'No,' said Filip. 'You have your trials today and you've already had breakfast. You can have some later when we get back.'

'I still don't feel well,' said Marcus and sat down in the corner of the small metal box as it descended downwards into the depths of the Industry.

When they arrived, Wilson was there to greet them with a wide smile, teeth like tombstones in a mouth that had always seemed to Alice that was too big for his face.

'Welcome,' he said. 'I hope your journey here wasn't too laborious – that elevator is running on slow speed to conserve energy until we sort out Drakewater. We're mostly only using it for goods these days, as you can imagine.'

'Have you ever seen the sun?' said Izzy. 'You look paler than Marcus does.' She giggled and the boy smiled weakly as Alice shook her head.

'Sorry, Wilson,' she said, feeling a little sick herself. 'This one's a bit over excited at the thought of the trials today. I thought Kunstein would be here to take her to the sports arena.'

'All in good time,' said Wilson dismissively. 'Spirited, isn't she?' He bent down until he was face-to-face with Izzy. 'Barnes says you're a very good worker,' he said, 'committed to the cause and making the most of your time topside.' The girl nodded and looked at Filip, her eyes wide.

'I've no doubt that this one will rise high in the ranks, just like you both,' said Wilson to Alice and Filip. He patted Izzy on the back, hard. 'She has something very… special.'

The conversation outside the lift was cut short by the crashing sound of Marcus collapsing against one of the ventilation grilles that ran along the bottom of the wall. The force of him falling was hard that the grate almost dented. He lay on the floor, his breath shallow and his eyes rolling. Alice rushed to his side.

'Get him to the Infirmary, now!' shouted Kunstein from down the corridor. She swept up, the wings of her cloak flailing, flanked by two officials who lifted Marcus by the arms. With Kunstein in front, they heaved him onto their shoulders and made off towards the Infirmary.

'Marcus!' shouted Alice, panicking. 'I'm coming.' She forced Izzy's bag into Filip's hand and fled down the corridor, her blood running cold. Desperation and terror coursed through her as she shouted back to Izzy and Filip.

'What is happening to him?'

Her pace increased as she darted towards Marcus. 'It's okay,' she repeated to him as she attempted to wipe the sweat from his face and support him from behind. Guilt spread through her as the small boy faltered.

'Leave him,' said Kunstein, her face darkening. 'We can move quicker if you let the officials do their job.'

But instead of the Infirmary, the officials took Marcus through a side-corridor and down deep into the heart of the Industry head-quarters. As they marched through the tunnels, the quality of the air changed from being a pure, conditioned breeze to a heavier, dank heat that pushed down oppressively into Alice's lungs. The walls were no longer painted the soft azure of sky but were a solid grey, the colour of a miserable day and even the floor sloped downwards in a spiral towards what Alice believed could only be the centre of the earth.

'Where are we going?' she said to Kunstein, panicked. 'I don't think I've even been down this deep before – we must be…' she looked upwards. 'We must be even lower than the swimming pool here, right?'

'Correct,' said Kunstein. 'We're taking him to the specialist Infirmary.'

'In the Catacombs?'

'Yes.'

Her chest heaving, she kept moving ahead, deeper into the heart of the underground. The tunnels within the Catacombs were laid out in thick strips, carved in the bedrock with perfect precision. On each side of the tunnel there were boxy chambers with small grilles in the doors, some wide open and others bolted shut. Each had a number on the door. With Marcus carried over the shoulders of the guards, they walked up one, down another, took two rights and then a left turn and through past a small bay where technicians were busily pouring liquid from one flask to another and mumbling in voices so unintelligible that Alice couldn't understand a word. Then another corridor with chambers as far as Alice could see – hundreds of them – many occupied with the lights dimmed low with a calm humming sound seeping out from underneath the doors. After another loop through the tunnels Marcus groaned and opened his eyes, sweat pouring down his cheeks. Alice felt as though her heart might break.

'Don't you think we should get him to a doctor?' she said, breathless. 'He needs a doctor – what's happening to him? Can we take him back topside? The fresh air might…'

'We're almost there,' said Kunstein. 'And don't worry about him, he'll be fine.'

Within another ten minutes they reached one of the cells in the wall that looked no different to the others. Inside there the chamber it was perfectly square and there was little furniture – just a light, a squat table and a raised bed that the guards placed Marcus on, attached to the wall. They undressed him swiftly and placed him in a thin plastic suit.

'Thank you,' said Kunstein, nodding her head and they left to be replaced by Barnes who seemed always to appear from nowhere.

'Hello, Alice,' she said in her familiar, curt tone.

Alice nodded. 'It was the fauclate, wasn't it? Filip knew he wouldn't come down here willingly. It was drugged, wasn't it?' A combination of sadness and anger overwhelmed her.

Kunstein ignored her and straightened the collar of Barnes's jacket, rubbing some dust from the shoulder.

The doctor stepped back just out of her reach and readjusted her coat carefully.

'Thank you, Kunstein,' she said. 'I can take things from here.' She nodded out towards the gloomy corridor.

'Oh, yes, okay. I'll leave you two to get Marcus settled in then. Would you bring Alice back to the Control Room when she's ready please? I find this place a little inhospitable and I do need to check in with Wilson. Please excuse me, both of you.'

'Of course.' Barnes smiled again and the cloud hanging over the room lifted, but only slightly. Marcus rolled over onto his back and opened his eyes for a moment, blinking at Alice and then closed them again. Barnes pulled out a bag from under the bed filled with a variety of medical instruments and began checking Marcus thoroughly from the toes upwards.

'Can't you do something?' said Alice in desperation. 'You're a doctor, aren't you?'

'He'll be absolutely fine,' said Barnes, calmly. 'No damage at all, just a little sedative to ensure his safe transfer here. Keeping him awake for the journey would have been cruel and stressful. He's already been under a lot of pressure topside and from what I hear he's not adjusting that well.'

'He's been doing just fine,' said Alice, adamantly. 'We've all had to adjust to the new world and some of us will adjust in different ways.'

'As I've said before, on many occasions, we don't want another incident,' said Barnes. 'It's my job to see that everyone is fully ready to adjust to the new world before they get there. His safety rests squarely with me. As the Original Scouts, you never had to undertake the routine tests because we didn't know what we were going to encounter but with what's been happening recently, it really is for the best that we ensure everyone is both physically and psychologically fit to perform.' She looked at Alice. 'Maybe we *should* have tested you Scouts.'

She tapped Marcus's chest and then listened intently through a stethoscope.

'Physically perfect,' she said. 'Now all we need to do is deal with his attachment to the old world and work out a resettlement plan. It sounds easy in theory but can take quite a long time to get absolutely right.'

'I want to take him back up.'

Barnes looked at Alice with incredulity. 'You're going to have to start rethinking your ways, Alice. You were much stronger before you went topside, we all thought you were ready, but…'

'I *am* ready.' Alice felt her hands begin to shake but she held her ground, her eyes fixed on Marcus.

Barnes flashed her wide, white teeth, her accent sharpening. 'I know this is difficult for you but, in the circumstances, you and Filip have done absolutely the right thing. Marcus would have become a disruption on the surface and that's something the two of you don't need right now, am I right?' She placed a cold, heavy hand on Alice's stomach. 'Especially with the baby,' she added.

Alice stepped backwards. 'Marcus must be taken care of. He's done nothing wrong. He should be with me.' A maternal, protective surge filled her chest.

'You're right,' said Barnes. 'He's done nothing wrong. But he might. And for that purpose, he's in the right place, with the right people now. We need to ensure he has none of the empathy that poor Kelly displayed towards those creatures on the outside of the Barricades.'

'Quinn said that the *person* that approached may have been infected with a virus,' said Alice. 'How much of a threat do you think that really is? Do you really think the outside world poses such a serious threat of disease?'

The doctor opened her mouth to answer and stopped as a sharp buzzing and then the tinny sound of a voice that sounded miles away came through a grille.

'Barnes to the Control Room when you're ready, please.'

'That sounds like Wilson,' said Alice, puzzled. 'How…'

'Yes,' said Barnes, sighing. 'He's asked the technicians to rig up an intercom system down here so that he can communicate with us whenever he feels there's something important I need to know. So, I'd best be on my way…' She slipped the first, thin needle quickly through the plastic cover and into Marcus's arm before Alice could say any more. The boy groaned and opened his eyes.

'Is that sleep serum?' said Alice in a sharp tone. 'I didn't say it was time yet.'

'Not your decision,' said Barnes, holding up the needle to the light. 'I have to do what's right for my patients.' She touched Alice's arm gently. 'All of them.'

Alice shivered and watched as Barnes injected Marcus with the second complex cocktail of chemicals that started the freezing process and prepared the body for the next stage of stasis. Marcus opened his mouth and licked his lips, which were dry, although his skin was still damp and clammy.

Alice felt her mouth becoming equally dry. 'I'm going to stay with him until he falls asleep. And then I'll make my way up top.'

Barnes paused. 'Yes, all right,' she said pulling her lab coat around her and packing up her bag. 'Of course, you must.'

Alice stepped backwards as Barnes pushed past her towards the door.

The doctor looked Marcus up and down. 'If he starts calling out or mumbling, don't worry – it's just the effects of the serum. My lab is just around the corner there, on the right. I'm sure you remember the way – I've heard you have the most acute sense of direction there is. He should be out in less than three minutes so I'll expect you back there.

'Fine,' said Alice, glancing over at Marcus. 'I'll be there when I'm done. Then I'd like to talk you about Richard Warren while I'm down here.'

'Sure,' said Barnes, 'although I really don't think he's up to visitors yet, he's still… well… confused, to say the least. But that's what I'm here for.' She smiled and left the room. 'Just on the right, remember.'

As Marcus's eyes flickered open and close, Alice fondled his head gently trying to find the right words to say but struggling as she did so. A number of times he opened his mouth to speak but then closed it again without saying a word.

'It's okay, Marcus,' soothed Alice. 'We'll all be waiting for you when it's time.' She hesitated. 'It won't be long, I promise and I'll come to visit you whenever I can.' Guilt anchored her feet to the floor but the desperate need to leave the confines of the four walls was almost unbearable.

The boy smiled, his skin cooler than before, the effects of the sleep serum beginning to take effect. Alice felt thankful that he no longer looked uncomfortable or in pain. She pushed the long strands of hair from his eyes.

'I…. have to tell you… something,' he said, his voice breaking and faltering with every word.

'You don't need to speak,' said Alice, choking back tears, 'just close your eyes and dream of the beautiful trees and the sunshine and everybody outside who loves you very much.' Her own voice was breaking as she spoke as the boy just a few years younger than her, who had become like a son, drifted off to sleep.

'No,' he struggled. 'I really…'

'Just sleep,' said Alice. 'It will all be okay. I know that you knew about the people outside. You're not in any trouble. Filip and I will be…'

'Don't tell anyone,' mumbled Marcus. 'Don't tell anyone I told you.'

Alice continued. 'Filip and I will be waiting for you – and Izzy – she adores her little brother, you know.'

Marcus struggled to sit up but his limbs were limp and useless. He opened his eyes as widely as he could. 'Izzy...' he said slowly. 'Izzy...'

'Izzy's taking her trials,' Alice said, smiling, teeth gritted. 'She's absolutely fine.' Her chest tightened and she felt a sickness rise in her throat.

'No!' Marcus looked almost angry, his eyes rolling and hands shaking. 'Izzy...' His eyes started to close again. 'Kelly....'

Alice rubbed his head softly. 'Calm, my sweetheart,' she whispered. 'It's all okay.'

'Alice!' Marcus's breath came in short, sharp bursts as he struggled desperately to talk. 'When... Kelly...' He paused for a second. 'Izzy knows. She was there.'

And with that Marcus was asleep, and Alice was left holding his limp hand as his breathing slowed to a steady pace.

Chapter Fourteen

The Company

Carter

As the day closed down into night, the rest of Company Six made their way into the trees to sleep. Aaron and Lisa had barely spoken throughout the whole evening but nodded in agreement at everything that had been said.

'I don't know why we need the brothers,' hissed Samuel. 'We can do this without them. They'll hold us back – there are too many of us.' He hesitated. 'This wasn't in the plan.'

'They're the right choice,' said Carter with confidence, remembering the earlier conversation with Elvira. 'Who knows what we're going to find when we get there.'

Samuel shook his head. 'Don't you think we can do this alone?'

'They're coming,' said Carter as they made their way back up the ladder and into the house in the trees.

Jacinta turned to Carter. 'Your failed escape caused significant upset within the Industry and your death has been widely broadcast, which is good for us. Although you have been deemed somewhat of a traitor by a handful of the rebels – which is not so good. They are ready for trouble. You should stay away from the general population and especially from anyone you know. Get the information we need and get out. That's all you need to do.'

Angel joined in. 'Can't Lily speak to the rebels? Get us some help on the inside?'

'Most of the rebels don't know that she's working against the Industry – but she will do anything she can, if we can get any messages to her.' Jacinta turned to Samuel. 'Have you packed everything? There's no going back now.'

He nodded and clapped Carter on the back.

'We're ready,' he said. 'And when we get to the Catacombs, we access the Model, find out exactly how many people are there, understand what their next move is against us and find out what the Industry has stored in Chamber One, right? No heroics.'

'Yes,' said Jacinta. 'It's all we can hope for.'

The next morning came cloaked in a thin, ugly rain that leaked into the bones of everyone in the Village who turned out to wish them well. They had salt-baked fish, wrapped in coarse paper and cloth, different coloured fruits and juices that Jacinta had bottled for them. Angel carried a bow and arrow, spears, and the only handgun that the Village owned.

'We'll try to send word that we've arrived,' said Samuel. 'But there's no guarantee we'll be able to reach you.'

'Focus on getting there and doing what you have to,' said Jacinta. 'We will wait for your signal to find out what to do next and how many of us you need to join you.'

She hugged both of her sons briefly and kissed them with an efficient fondness.

'Stay with the rest of the Company, Samuel. I shall be thinking of you both,' she said. 'Keep safe.'

For the first few miles they followed the trail, patterned with leaves through the darkness of the forest that sheltered them completely from the falling rain. Samuel selected the path carefully, leading the way, with Lisa and Aaron stopping every half an hour or so to pick some plants or fruits that grew in luscious crops in the corners of the wood.

'We'll take the trail past Outposts One and Two before we head north-east,' said Samuel. 'That way we know we'll be able to rest safely if the rain gets heavier over the next day or so. After that we'll find a safe route around the back of the Drakewater plant, staying clear of the main city, and start looking for entry points on the east side.'

'Isn't Drakewater supposed to be radioactive?' said Carter. 'How close are we going to get?'

'We're not going directly into the plant,' said Angel. 'Well, that's not the plan. It's dangerous, yes, but Drakewater isn't just a reactor, it's a whole town, built on higher ground like a castle. You know what a castle is?'

Carter thought of the books he'd read back in the Village. 'Kind of. A safe place, from the old world.'

'Yes. Built up high with walls around it. Drakewater is a bit like that. Most of the waste was contained before the real heavy rain set in, back during the Storms. The reactor was shut down way before any real damage could be done. Some people made plans, Carter. They weren't all stupid.'

He looked at her, wide-eyed. 'But there must have been some leakage otherwise the mutations wouldn't have happened to the animals and the...' He thought about Angel's eye, then quickly looked away.

'There were no animal mutations,' said Elvira. 'The Industry told you that to keep people from trying to escape to the outside. It's true that fertility was affected to some degree and there has been some increased susceptibility to certain illnesses. But that wasn't because of any nuclear spillages. Inside the Community, what happened to the babies, well, that was due to the food that was being served – those synthetic supplements and all the so-called nutrients people were being served. And some of the methods they used to make the babies. Nuclear mutations? It's all another lie.'

Carter remembered what his mother had told him. He was getting used to revelations about the Industry, but it was still a shock each time he was reminded of their awful acts. Angel smiled gently.

'And, remember that out here, we don't have access to the Infirmary care that your people do so if someone gets an infection, sometimes an amputation is the only way. A sickness or a fever that can't be treated early can cause damage to the brain. We do everything we can to give our people the best quality of life. We don't dispose of people like the Industry does.'

Carter felt a flush of embarrassment as Angel continued.

'Very few if any real doctors or scientists survived the Storms, and so much of their work was experimental, especially in the early days. They did some terrible things, Carter, that still impact people today. Some people, before your parents, managed to get away. And for those who make their way here, well, we don't always know how to help them, which is why the work you've been doing is so valuable.' She smiled gratefully.

'We had an agreed exclusion zone around Drakewater,' she continued, as they started to move again. 'Just in case, but now we don't have any real reason to believe that the levels of toxicity in the soil and water are necessarily nuclear.

'Before the Storms, Lisa and Aaron's great grandfather worked at a similar plant in Wales. They shut down operations well before the rain started to fall and the reactors were built to withstand significant weather interference. But the other waste from the city – all the oil and sewage and industrial matter – *did* have an impact on the environment, and it took a long time to get over and for the earth to recover enough to grow edible food.'

'Keep up,' said Samuel in gruff voice. 'We don't stop to eat for at least another hour.'

The thickness of the wood gave way to a paved path and the remnants of an old village that wound its way up a small hill banked by trees on either side. In the distance, Carter could hear the constant trickle of water punctuated by birdsong. Any trace of rain had disappeared; the air felt fresh and warm. Ochre bell-shaped flowers burst from green vines that wound their way around the houses, some making their way through the glassless windows and inside the rooms.

'Outpost One,' said Elvira. 'We're here.'

Aaron turned to Carter. 'This is my favourite outpost,' he said. 'When we were younger, I would bring Lisa here to learn about all the different types of plants that grow here – there's much more variety than our side of the forest.' He smiled. 'Lisa's real name is Lee but when he was little we found this book in that house over there.' He pointed into the distance. 'It was about an orphaned girl who grew up in a treehouse – and she was called Lisa.'

'Are your parents…?' Carter stopped mid-sentence.

'They're gone,' said Aaron. 'They both died very young of malnutrition and stomach complications. As you know we don't have great amounts of medicine and even until recently our knowledge of nutrition and healthcare has been limited. So, when we lost them, Lisa wanted to do something to help people. We set up a food programme and learned everything we could to bring a balance to what we eat in the Village.'

Carter looked into his earnest, thoughtful eyes. 'You've done an incredible job,' he said with sincerity. 'The people of the Village eat wonderful food and you've taken such great care of Lisa.'

Aaron's eyes gleamed with pride. 'Thank you,' he said. 'We just want to help people.'

As they moved towards the first house, Angel pushed down on the handle and the heavy wooden door creaked open. Inside, there was an old, salty smell that emanated from the mismatched furniture and roughly painted walls.

'It's one of the older villages,' she said. 'Most things are original and far enough – and high enough – that it didn't get as damaged as some of the others. It was underwater for a time but the drainage here is good and some of our people stayed here for a while before we built the new village. Samuel fixed this door on,' she added proudly, swinging it on its hinges.

Lisa stepped past her and into the house, beckoning Aaron and going straight into the back room where there was a fire pit, complete with a stack of dry wood and a curved hole in the ceiling covered with tarpaulin. From above them, Samuel peeled it back and sunlight flooded into the room.

There was clanging and scraping as Lisa moved things around the kitchen. 'Let's get cooking,' said Aaron, rearranging the wood and sparking the flames into action.

Carter watched as Lisa laid the plates carefully onto the large table in the kitchen. Steaming vegetables of different colours and shapes, baked fish and bowls of chopped plants decorated the surfaces.

'Help yourself,' said Aaron handing him a plate. 'It's better while it's warm.'

He took some fish and a selection of vegetables, piling them high. Now that his system was used to real food, he'd grown a taste for it.

There were carrots, potatoes and fish with salad. Angel sprinkled some herbs from a small pot over her fish.

Carter copied her then loaded up a fork with some fish and a potato. The warm softness crumbled in his mouth. 'It's delicious,' he said, amazed, his mouth full of food. 'You learned how to do all this from books?' It was even better than the plates of food he'd had back in the Village.

'Nobody cooks for themselves in the Community,' said Elvira to Lisa and Aaron who were watching Carter with amusement. 'Everything comes pre-packaged – and it's all eaten cold. The food is grown in a lab, manufactured by machines then cubed up by the workers. Usually a week's supply is delivered to each home.'

'Ugh.' Aaron wrinkled his face. 'That's disgusting.'

'They don't believe in fresh food,' explained Angel.

Aaron turned to Carter. 'Like I told you before, it was difficult to get things to grow in the early days and our people ate what they could find. Now we have so much more and when we travel further afield there are surprises that nature brings us. In the winter it's difficult, but we store what we can and preserve some foods using the old methods. The forests are full of nuts and berries and we have learned what's good and what isn't. The Outposts each have a wild area where things grow.'

'I picked these in the gardens this morning,' said Samuel, waving his hand over the vegetables. 'But it's hard work feeding people, Carter. Especially when the fields of corn you depend upon are set alight by your enemies.'

*

As the others were packing up to leave, Carter wandered through the other rooms of the house slowly, drinking in the details of the pictures, furniture and ornaments of the old world. It was all on one level – no upstairs – which was different to the house he'd broken into through the cellar and out into the kitchen with Lily. He remembered the feeling of bizarre wonderment at the intricate complexity of the splinters of life before him.

Above the fireplace there was a note, yellowed with age.

If you are reading this, you will have survived the Storms that raged for over five years and destroyed much of what was real to people. We have also survived and welcome you to join us – we are friendly people and unlike those to the south. We return here often and you may stay here as our guests. We ask that you ensure that this note remains here for others. If you would like to join us, we are close and we will likely find you before you find us. Do not approach the barricaded area under any circumstances. You will find no shelter there. Travel safely.

'Leave it there.' Samuel's voice rang through from the kitchen as Carter folded the note carefully and placed it back where he had found it.

'Who wrote this?'

'We did,' said Angel, appearing next to him. 'We have one at each of the outposts. That's how some of our people came to us.'

'Don't you worry about others coming to your Village that might not be as friendly as you are? People that might want to attack you.'

'We'd see them coming,' said Samuel, wrapping up the rest of the food. 'Track them until we can work out if their intentions are good.'

'How can you be sure?'

'We saw you, didn't we?'

*

As they made their way east, Outpost One disappeared into the distance with just a faint trail of smoke drifting into the empty nothingness of the miserable grey early afternoon cloud. The landscape changed quickly, becoming stony and dotted with weak plants as they moved through the rocky gulley with its intermittent derelict and damaged outbuildings. Lisa picked at the empty branches and shook his head towards Aaron. There was nothing to collect that was of any use to them.

As the afternoon wore on, they headed further north, where the undergrowth became denser, a thick tangle of brambles hugging the paths, offering bleached unripe fruit out on thorny limbs.

The thought of revenge for Isabella and Lucia, and his remaining son, Ariel, drove Carter onwards and blotted out the recurring images of what the Industry might do to them in retaliation for his desertion. He sighed heavily.

'He'll be okay.' It was almost as if Angel had crept inside his head and untangled the mess of thoughts and emotions that lay crumpled in his mind. She smiled. 'I know you're worried about Ariel, but we'll get there and work out a way for you to help him.'

He smiled back at her, but her words of comfort couldn't entirely remove the worry he felt for his son.

Company Six hiked mostly without talking, the thin whistle of birds breaking the silence as the afternoon slunk on into early evening. They moved at pace; mostly in single file, Angel occasionally passing a water carrier backwards down the row, each slurping at the neck. Aaron and Lisa picked at branches as they moved – sniffing and sometimes tasting the different fruits and plants in the woodland as creatures scuttled in the bushes around them.

After several hours, when they rested in some old stone buildings, Carter sat down on a wall, exhausted. Samuel climbed up onto the roof of the building and scanned the horizon.

'We move away from the normal route,' he said, craning his neck higher. 'We should avoid Outpost Two today.'

'Why?' said Carter. 'Can you see something?'

'It's not what I can see, it's what I can feel,' said Samuel dismissively and jumped down from the roof. He took off his boots to pull out a stone, flexing his webbed toes before he squashed them back in.

'Samuel feels things instinctively,' said Angel. 'Just like I do. When you've survived out here for long enough you become accustomed to things – certain sounds, smells and the way the air feels. It's like our instincts are heightened because you don't know what could be around the next corner or under a bush or what might fall from a tree. And most of the time, we're right.'

'Where will we eat?' said Lisa. His brother nodded with equal concern. 'We need to stay strong and alert,' he added. 'Especially this one,' pointing towards Carter.

'There are two villages we should pass through before nightfall,' said Samuel. 'The facilities won't be as good as the outposts and I can't guarantee there'll be extra food but it's better to take a path through the thicker forest. I don't want another Company Five situation.' He looked up at the falling sun and then nodded east. 'We have two hours of daylight. We'll need to move fast.'

The evening light had turned to a pale grey by the time they reached the three or four brick buildings clustered around a tiny courtyard in the middle of the thick wood. Two tall streetlamps, blind and unlit, towered above them. Aaron and Lisa took a torch and started foraging for food amongst the undergrowth while the others went inside one of the bigger two-storey buildings, searching for signs of animals and securing a place to sleep. The house was loaded with a thick dust that rose up into clouds as they moved from room to room and then settled back down in patches on the floor and furniture.

'I'll set the fire outside,' said Samuel, running his finger through the dirt. 'There will be a lot of smoke and this place is filthy enough.'

Lisa returned with two skinned rabbits that he and Aaron wrapped in green leaves and roasted over the fire on their spears. Carter was less sure about the rabbit than the fish but it still tasted better than anything he had ever eaten in the Community.

Lisa nodded towards him. 'We don't tend to eat much rabbit in the Village as there's never enough to go around,' he said. 'But it was one of the first meats I learned to cook when Aaron brought me out here.' He gave a wide smile. 'It's my favourite.'

In the light of the fire, the outside of the old house looked beautiful; it had a small balcony overhanging the front porch that looked out onto what might have once been a meadow, Carter imagined. Samuel was on the roof, looking out into the stars.

'We should make it by tomorrow evening – or the morning after at the latest,' he called down. 'If we leave early enough and get a full day's walking we can get ourselves to Drakewater and start the search for a way in.'

'How can you tell where we are?' said Carter. 'There's barely enough moonlight to see what I'm eating.'

'He can just tell,' said Elvira. 'He just knows this whole area better than any of us.'

Back in the house, they checked each room one by one. When they got to the front bedroom, Samuel stopped.

'We should sleep here,' he said. 'It's the best-preserved room and there's a balcony overlooking the garden.' He dragged a small mattress from one of the other rooms and opened the glassless doors, pushing it out put it out onto the wooden platform. 'I can keep an eye on things from here if anyone – or anything – approaches the house.'

'We'll take the landing,' said Lisa, beckoning to his brother. 'That way we've got the stairs covered.'

Carter nodded. 'Seems sensible,' he said.

'Will you stay with us?' said Elvira, looking at him. 'Please?'

Carter felt the air gently breeze into the room as he pushed a pile of old blankets out onto the floor. He placed one over Elvira who was already curled up in a corner. Next to him, he could hear the regular rise and fall of Angel breathing, her head turned slightly away from him. He watched the paleness of her skin in the moonlight, so delicate against the bulk of his brother's large shape through the balcony doors.

'Goodnight, Carter.' Samuel's voice was stern, commanding almost. 'Make sure you get plenty of rest, we have a big day ahead tomorrow.'

'We sure do, brother,' said Carter, closing his eyes tightly.

Sleep came to him quickly and with it, dreams of the Catacombs, the Industry and his mother. That night, she looked younger than she was now, soft and unworn, eyes shining like the glint of the sun on water. And with her came visions of Isabella, bright ivory hair and the sharpest of blue eyes. They each picked up a hand of his and rocked him gently and immediately he was ten years old again, innocent and unaware.

Then, suddenly, something sharp and a hissing came from outside his dream and jolted him awake.

'Carter, wake up!'

Angel's voice was urgent, desperate and as he opened his eyes he could see Elvira moving around the room, gathering things together quickly and in complete silence. He jumped out of bed and leaned for his spear at the side of the bed.

'What's happening?' he whispered. As he did so, two gunshots rang out in the darkness.

'There's someone downstairs,' she said, and he could see through the moonlight that her hands were shaking.

'There's someone downstairs,' she repeated, frantically, 'and they're asking for you.

Chapter Fifteen

The Sleepers

Alice

Alice closed the door behind her and it locked shut. As she looked through the grille, watching the rise and fall of Marcus's chest she realised that the dull, rhythmic pull she felt in the tunnel synchronised exactly with his breathing. The corridor outside hummed with what should have been the reassuring heartbeat of the Ship but as Marcus's words and Barnes's half-threats rang through her, for the first time in a long time Alice felt more than unsettled. She felt genuinely scared.

She watched him sleep, his face free of the creased lines that had mapped his forehead in previous days. Her heart felt heavy and sad and, although she knew it was too late, she wanted to shake him awake and hold him tightly, to bring him back to her. Guilt mixed with anger coursed through her. Filip's deception was unforgiveable – and now, in so many ways, the world seemed different to Alice, like she was viewing it through a frosted window. She reached her fingers through the grille towards Marcus, but she could stretch only a small way into the room and the door was bolted shut. Guilt at betraying the boy snuffed out her anger and her head hung down, limbs weighted and heavy. Regret cut her like a knife and, for the moment, she tried to blot out the words the boy had said.

Alice left the door and walked to the next chamber. Inside was a man, possibly in his early thirties, in the same plastic casing, sighing in time with Marcus. The next was a young woman, hair tied back, but recognisable as one of the substitute mothers from the Ship. She peered through each grille, watching silently and feeling more ashamed with each one she observed.

Everything inside the lab was spotlessly clean and shining white. The temperature in the room was perfect. The disarray she'd seen the last time she was there had been beautifully ordered.

'Where is Richard Warren?' demanded Alice.

Barnes looked up from a microscope and smiled her disingenuous smile. She went back to her microscope, moving one plate away and putting another in its place.

'How did Marcus go down?' she asked, sliding plate after plate in front of the scope. 'I'm actually a little worried about him, you know.' This time, when she looked up, there was no smile.

'What do you mean you're worried about him?' Alice sat down next to Barnes and tried to peer into the scope. All she could see over her shoulder was a gooey red mass of nothing on the slides. She worked hard to let her concern mask the sadness and fear inside her.

Barnes wiped her hands clean on the tail of her lab coat. 'This is the blood I just took from Marcus as part of the routine procedure. Here—' she waved her hand over the microscope '—you can see some small irregularities. Nothing much at this stage but it's worrying.'

'Worrying, how?'

'Well, it's very early but...' Barnes lowered her glasses and tightened her lips. 'Did you notice anything unusual in the way Marcus was behaving in the last week or so? Has he said anything unusual or acted strangely in any way?'

'He has been upset since the incident with Kelly,' said Alice, 'but that's normal, that's to be expected. Isn't it?'

'It might be but it's worrying nonetheless. Plus, his reaction to the sedative in the fauclate, along with whatever he said to you – what did he say to you?'

Alice smiled, keeping calm, her hands shaking. 'Nothing important,' she said. 'Probably just his brain letting go of things before the sleep. That would be right, wouldn't it?' The tension between them was palpable.

'It would be,' said Barnes. 'Although what worries me more is that he may have the early traces of a viral infection – probably caught from whoever attacked poor Kelly up at the Barricades.'

'I thought they said that the shot came from some way away,' said Alice. 'Is there a virus that contagious and airborne to have infected him from there?'

'There's still a lot we don't know about the illnesses on the outside,' said Barnes as she leant over the slide again. 'A great deal – which is why so much of my time is taken up researching it and, of course, supervising Quinn's censomics work. But I will do some more tests on Marcus, just to be sure. We need to be very careful with the boundaries, Alice, very careful.'

'Of course,' said Alice, trying to keep her tone casual, heart beating fast. She kept her eyes clearly averted from the side door. 'Now, where is Richard Warren?'

Barnes nodded. 'He's in there,' she said, pointing towards the room where Alice had been only a few weeks before. 'I like to call it Infirmary Two. This and Infirmary Three are where the majority of our rehabilitation takes place. It's where we keep those who are almost ready for resettlement but still require some intervention and retraining.

'So, everyone apart from me, Filip and the other Scouts has been through your programme?'

'Yes, everyone who has made it over ground so far – except the children. Wilson thought that as most of them had spent the majority of their lives in Industry company that they might not need that level of immersion. For children over ten I think we may need to reconsider that. For all Industry employees it is standard practice – they have their own programme, which is relatively similar, and you Scouts, well, you had a very different education and intensive training that covered the core elements. Clearly it was not enough.'

'What do you mean?' Alice kept her eyes fixed on the door.

'Well, there's nothing wrong with understanding and compassion – but we can't let that cloud our judgments any more. I just wonder whether the information you received in the Ship made you hard enough to deal with the realities that you will have to face. Kelly, for example. We don't know exactly why she was targeted or why she felt it necessary to make peace with her aggressors. Or to try to let them in here.'

'She wouldn't have done that,' said Alice, still looking ahead, her gaze unflinching. 'She knew the rules.'

'Well, whatever the circumstances, we do need to take this opportunity to strengthen our boundaries and maintain our power in this area.'

'You starting to sound more like a chief of staff than a doctor.'

There was a sharp silence before Barnes smiled tightly. 'Oh goodness no, Alice,' she said, her face breaking into a lukewarm glow. 'My goal is simply to protect and provide a safe place to bring new life into the world. New life just like yours. Your baby will be with us in around six months Alice – we don't have much time.'

She reached out to touch Alice's stomach but the girl moved away – and so, instead, Barnes pointed to the screen in her room that had returned to the Deadlands footage. 'Look how far we've come already – we just need to maintain that now.'

Alice shivered as she remembered that first terrifying journey out of the Ship and into the bright sunshine that she hadn't seen for over five years. The crumbling destruction that had faced them and decaying remnants of the life they had left behind. A life to be forgotten. A future to be excited about.

'I want to see Richard now.'

'I'll take you through.'

Alice looked around the lab. 'If he's fit for visitors, why hasn't he been sent topside sooner?'

Barnes scowled. 'He was pretty disappointing and very disruptive with the others – talking about the old life before the Storms and whipping up trouble – especially at the beginning. It was as to be expected, but he spoke with a *fondness* that we just can't tolerate, I'm afraid. I wondered for a while if we'd make *any* difference with him, but Kunstein urged us to continue and I suppose he became a bit of a project for me. There has been *some* improvement of late.' Barnes looked particularly proud of herself, leading Alice towards a door but partially blocking it as she continued.

'It's only been in the last month or so that we've seen any real changes in behaviour, but they are positive; it seems you can teach an old dog new tricks.' Alice didn't laugh.

'He's recovered then? He's ready?'

'As I have said,' Barnes accentuated her words in short staccato. 'For some people, Marcus for example – and hopefully this Warren boy – a short spell asleep and then some intensive therapy when we've perfected the process and they'll be fine. But others… those who were on the Ship, less so…'

Alice tried to peer past Barnes and around the door but she failed to see anything other than a huge version of the screens that were in the main room.

'What happens to them?' she said. 'When do they get to resurface?'

'Well, that all depends.'

'On what?'

'A number of things – general health, age, elasticity of the brain, functioning parts, exposure to the old world – those kinds of variables, in the wrong combination, can be very… destructive. We aim to find a use for everything and everyone in this new construct, recycling is key but when the mind has completely gone, there's so very little we are able to do about it.'

Colour drained from Alice's face but her cheeks felt distinctly hot and prickly.

'Do we actually *dispose* of them?' she said. She couldn't quite bring herself to use the word kill but as the words left her lips she felt like she was part of some sort of mafia conversation from a film she'd seen as a child.

'Goodness no!' said Barnes, surprise-smiling. 'We stand them down until there's something we can do for them in the future. Or rather, something they can do for us. You seem to be forgetting, Alice, this is what we agreed. Everybody, even you, must make a functional contribution to this new world. We simply cannot allow ineffective passengers.'

Anger rose in Alice again, but she dampened it down.

'Let me in please, Barnes.'

The doctor moved her hand from the doorframe so that Alice could see into the room and, although the last time she'd seen him he'd been pale and semi-conscious, there was no mistaking the shape of Richard Warren sprawled on the bed, leafing slowly through an Industry briefing pack.

'Bear in mind that he may be a little confused and possibly aggressive,' whispered Barnes. 'You're the first real visitor he's had – although he *has* been asking to see the girl who saved his life. I'll give you a few minutes with him.'

She stepped completely away from the door and ushered Alice inside. For a moment she stood there watching him before he acknowledged she was there.

'Any chance you can change the TV channel?' he said, without looking up. 'Or better still, can you let me out of here? Failing that, I'll talk to that Alice girl. I kind of like her voice.'

Alice smiled at Barnes. 'I'll take it from here,' she said and waited until Barnes had left the room before she started talking.

'Hello, Richard,' she said softly. 'I don't have long so we need to keep it brief.'

The boy sat flicking through a well-thumbed copy of an Industry manual. At the sound of Alice's voice he turned around and put down the papers, his face breaking into a wide smile.

'Alice,' he said, 'finally you came back.'

The girl put her finger to her lips and whispered. 'Barnes is in the next room and I don't want her to know I've been here before.'

'Okay,' Richard mouthed, still smiling.

'I think I can get you out of here, but you need to keep doing what we agreed. Whatever they ask of you.'

Richard nodded. 'And how will you do that?' he said quietly.

'I don't quite know yet, but I will. Is there anything you can tell me that would help me to get you out of here?'

'I was sad to hear about Kelly,' he said quietly. 'You could have stopped that.'

Alice felt her heart thump harder. 'What do you mean? You know who killed Kelly?'

'I hear everything,' he said in voice that sounded half-threatening.

'But that was someone from outside,' she hissed. 'Who was it? Someone you know?'

'Not until you get me out of here,' said Richard, his eyes gleaming. 'And then, I'll tell you. Everything about what you're already having doubts about – Kelly, Marcus, Barnes – all of it. But think about this – why are they using children to carve out their brave new world? What do you Scouts really know about what's happening down here in the Labs?' He paused. 'Get me out of here, Alice.'

'I'm going to try,' she whispered, fiercely. 'But you have to promise that you'll do everything that Barnes says; without question. I'll make it happen as soon as I can. You have to trust me on this.'

Richard handed her his copy of the Industry manual and lay back down on his bed. 'Then I won't be needing this any more,' he said, smiling before his face clouded and his voice became more urgent. 'But you'd better make it quick, Alice – before it's too late for all us.'

Chapter Sixteen

The Messenger

Carter

'Carter Warren, if you are here you should identify yourself. We have a directive calling for your arrest.'

The voice came from outside, gruff and angry.

Carter looked around the room. In the pale morning light, he could only make out the shapes of Elvira and Angel. He motioned for them to keep low and move to the side of the wall behind the window.

'Where are Aaron and Lisa?' he whispered. 'And Samuel?'

'Aaron and Lisa went downstairs to see what was happening,' said Elvira, her lip quivering. 'Samuel wasn't here when we woke up.'

The voice came again, this time more insistent. 'We've shot your friends, Carter. I think it's time you came with us. We can arrange safe transport home for you and any others that you have with you can return to where they came from in peace. This offer won't last for long though, so I suggest you come down immediately.'

'They've killed them,' said Elvira, covering her face. 'They're both dead.'

'Do you know who it could be?' Angel crept to the edge of the window and peered out over the balcony.

'Get back,' said Carter. 'Of course I don't know who they are.'

'What do they want?' snapped Elvira. 'If they think you're alive, the Industry is going to be much more vigilant. I thought you were meant to be dead as far as they were concerned.'

'I am,' said Carter. 'At least that's what I thought.' He edged to the window and peered outside. As the light filtered over the tops of the other brick buildings he could make out the shape of two bodies lying still on the grass outside. A third person, standing upright and wearing a hazard suit, stood facing the house, gun in hand.

'Carter Warren,' said the man, 'You're needed back at the Community. It's your son, he needs you. We're willing to forgive you for your indiscretions out here in the Deadlands – if you come in now we can decontaminate you and will make arrangements to have the news about you corrected. It's important you come now, Carter; for your son's sake.' His voice was threatening.

Carter pressed his body against the wall and closed his eyes tightly. A dark, slithering feeling gathered in his stomach. Ariel. Every inch of his body was wracked with sickness and despair. What could be wrong with Ariel? It couldn't be true.

'He's using your son,' said Angel nervously. 'He doesn't need you.' She peered around the edge of the window. 'Can you see Samuel?'

'Samuel's not there,' said Carter, glancing again. 'I can't see him anywhere. I don't think whoever that is knows he's not in here either.'

'The Industry wouldn't have sent just one person,' said Elvira. 'There must be more in the trees. I can't believe they've sent anyone out this far at all. You must be pretty important to them.'

'It seems I am,' said Carter, looking around the room. 'Where's the gun?'

'Samuel had it,' said Elvira, her eyes full of terrified tears. 'It might be out on the balcony.'

'I can't see it – he must have taken it with him.' Carter ducked down below the level of the window and crawled through the frame of the door that led out onto the overhanging balcony. A small stone wall running around the edge kept him out of sight of the man with the gun.

'Your son's life is in danger,' shouted the man. 'He needs you to come back with me now.'

'I need time to think,' said Carter to himself. 'I need time to think.' He looked through a chink in the wall. The man was still there, pacing backwards and forwards, looking agitated.

'I know you're in there,' said the man. 'Don't let us have to come in and get you.'

'If you go with him he'll kill us anyway,' said Elvira. 'Don't do it. Please don't leave us.'

'I have no intention of going with him,' whispered Carter. 'But he's not going to leave unless I do something.'

'We can wait,' shouted the man from outside. 'However, you should remember that the offer on your friends expires shortly. I will kill them all if I need to.'

Carter sat with his eyes closed tightly, thinking. He hadn't seen the man very clearly – he'd been wearing a bio-suit, was of medium height and spoke clearly. What else? The man knew he was a refugee from the Community. But Elvira was right; the Industry wouldn't have sent just one person. If he was important enough to capture – or kill – they would make sure the job got done properly. He motioned for Angel and Elvira to be quiet.

'I'll come with you,' shouted Carter. 'But before I come down, I have a few questions and some conditions of my own.'

The man on grass looked up towards the balcony and raised his gun. To the west, the faint rays of the morning sun filtered through the trees and cast sad shadows across the bodies of the brothers. Carter felt sick – the kind, eager-to-please food foragers and expert cooks were gone, just over a day after leaving home. Inside the guilt pained him: Isabella, his daughter Lucia, even Mendoza – all gone trying to protect him and save the people of the Community. And now, his son was in danger.

'Don't go,' mouthed Elvira. 'He'll kill you. And then he'll kill us.'

'He won't,' said Carter. 'At least not yet.'

'Hurry up, Carter,' said the man loudly. 'We don't have all day. We have to be back before the new Controller General is established otherwise the deal could be off the table and then I'd have to kill you.'

'Like I said,' shouted Carter. 'I need to have a little more information first. What's wrong with my son and why does he need me to come back?'

The man shielded his eyes. 'You know, we could have this conversation down here, it would be much easier.'

'I'd prefer it if we did it this way, for now,' said Carter. 'Who are you and what's wrong with my son?'

'My name is Saul,' said the man. 'I work for the Industry.'

'What's your position?' said Carter. 'Who do you work for?'

'I'm an Elite Scout,' said Saul. 'Should I remind you now that you're a dead fugitive, guilty of treason and murder?'

'Tell me what's wrong with my son. And why it's so important that the Industry sent you all the way out here to find me.'

The man paused. 'If you don't come out here immediately I will come in there and shoot the women you are with,' he said. 'I know they are in there.'

Angel's hands started to shake. 'Carter, what are we going to do?' she said. 'Where is Samuel?'

Carter reached out from the balcony back into the room and tried to remain calm. 'It's okay,' he said. 'Don't worry.'

'If you tell me why you need me, I'll come out and we can leave these people in peace,' he shouted back out into the garden. 'What is wrong with my son?'

'He's sick,' said the man. 'A genetic disorder. He needs material from a blood relative. Had his sister still been alive, she would have been perfect but, of course, your actions put paid to that. Your family and the Industry are willing to forgive you and we can offer you work within the Industry Headquarters – a privileged life – as your skills and knowledge could be well utilised. You may still be able to change the world, Carter Warren.'

'Really?' said Carter. 'Sounds like a deal too good to be true.'

'As I said, it is a one-time offer,' said Saul. 'Your family are keen to see you come home and the Industry would welcome your insight on what you have experienced out here. You would, of course, have to remain within the Headquarters for a while so as not to disrupt the appointment of the new Controller General, or you could have the option of being frozen again and awoken at a time of your choice.'

Carter sifted through Saul's words in his head. 'Why is *Andrew* so important to you?' he said, clearly, looking to see if the man corrected him. 'He's just one person. I've never heard of so much being made of one life.'

The man didn't hesitate. 'He's like you, Carter,' he said. 'The Industry has great plans for him. He has solved synthetics problems we didn't even know we had. He can reconfigure the Model without using a computer. And any chance we have to save him now, when we need him, we will take. He's your son, Carter, and you're the one person that can help him. We wouldn't be here if we weren't desperate.'

Carter raised one hand above the balcony. 'How do I know you won't shoot me if I come down?' he said.

Saul held his gun high in the air. 'I'll throw this onto the ground,' he said. 'Then we can talk properly. But not until you have agreed to return to the Community.'

'Okay,' said Carter slowly, edging back into the bedroom, away from the balcony without standing up. 'I'll do it for Andrew. But you'll need to give me some time to get my things together here.'

Elvira reached out towards him, hooking her one finger in his jacket. 'Don't do it,' she said. 'Don't go with them.' Her voice was desperate and pleading, her eyes raw with tears.

'I know what I'm doing,' whispered Carter, 'It's okay. It's what needs to be done.'

'You have five minutes,' shouted Saul, 'and no longer. Otherwise these friends of yours will die, you will die and your son will die. You will be guilty of all their deaths.'

'I'll be down there shortly – faster if you stop threatening me.'

'If the Industry knows you're still alive then Lily is in danger,' whispered Angel. 'We have to warn her somehow.'

'We can figure that out later,' said Carter. 'First of all, we need to get out of here.' He fingered through the bags that they had brought with them and stuffed what he could into his pockets. He inched his way back onto the balcony.

'One more thing before I come down,' he shouted to Saul. 'Why can't his mother provide whatever material is required? Surely Isabella is a match in the same way that I am?'

'No good,' said Saul gruffly. 'Not a match. They say it's a father-to-son thing.'

'Convenient,' said Carter under his breath. 'Stay here,' he added to Elvira and Angel. 'If anything does happen to me, go back the Village, tell them they're not safe and to run.'

He quietly made his way to the entrance to the cottage, within the safety of the doorframe, and stood there watching Saul standing in the grass in the old gardens. Outside the light was beginning to shine more brightly through the trees, illuminating the cool morning and the uneven hillocks made by animals in the grass. The air felt fresh and warm as a light breeze caught the plant blossom and carried it in the air, and, even now, when he and his friends' lives were in danger, it struck him how beautiful it was.

'I'm here,' he said. 'I need to see you throw the gun – in the direction of the house.' There was a dull thump and a crackle as the metal landed in the bushes near the path that led to the house.

'Come on,' said the man. 'We don't have much time. Your son's life depends on this.'

In the upstairs window beyond the balcony, Carter could see the shapes of Elvira and Angel watching Saul, as he moved towards him. The crushing sound of the biosuit he wore got louder as he came closer. The man's shoes were old and worn down. He stamped hard through the long grass and bushes, tracing a path that sprang back up again swiftly as he passed.

Carter motioned to Saul and smiled. 'Take the path to your left,' he said. 'The weeds are less there – it should be easier to get through. '

Saul grunted and shuffled his way towards the left and, in doing so, caught his foot on part of the uneven ground made by the molehills, staggering a little to one side. It was all that Carter needed. He rushed towards him, catching Saul full in the stomach and pushing him roughly to the ground.

From the upstairs window he heard a gasp and clatter as Elvira and Angel ran out onto the balcony. He sat astride the man, punching his face hard until his nose cracked and broke, blood pouring down his cheeks and he screamed in pain.

'Who are you?' shouted Carter. 'What the hell are you doing here?'

'Sc-Scout,' spluttered the man. 'Let me go, you'll pay for this.' He struggled underneath Carter, twisting his legs desperately in an attempt to break free. Carter ripped open the flimsy biosuit to reveal old, filthy clothes that reeked of sweat and days of wear. He looked in his mid to late thirties.

'You're *not* Industry,' spat Carter, holding the man down with all his strength. He pulled at the tatters of the suit. 'You're too old to be a Scout and they'd never send you out wearing this – it's old issue, years old and half of your facts are wrong. First of all, my son's name is not Andrew and his mother is not Isabella. Now tell me who you are before I destroy the rest of your skull.'

He grabbed Saul's hair with one hand and smashed it down onto the stony grass. The man shrieked in pain and lurched to one side, kicking his legs upwards, unseating Carter who fell over onto his back.

'You're a dead man, Carter Warren!' He tried to get to his feet, stumbling in a daze towards where he had thrown the gun before Carter brought him down again, grabbing his legs just below the knees and flooring him completely. He forced the man onto his stomach and sat astride him again. The man lay still for a moment, groaning and pulling his hand up towards his head. There was a rustling in the bushes and they both looked up.

'Are you here alone?' said Carter, his hands circling the man's neck. 'Tell me the truth and you might live to see the end of today.'

'There are others,' said the man, struggling to wrap his tongue around the words. 'They will come for me. Other Scouts.'

'I know you're not a Scout,' said Carter, firmly, glancing up at the house 'Tell me who you are and how you know about my son. Who sent you? Tell me now.'

Saul gurgled something and spat out a tooth onto the ground. 'You don't know anything,' he said, breathing heavily. 'Let me up and I'll tell you.' He lifted his body up with his bloody hands, using all his strength to push Carter to one side, but he wasn't quite strong enough.

'You *will* tell me,' said Carter, pulling one of the small serrated knives from the inside of his pocket, holding it to the man's throat. 'I will protect those I am with and I will not let you go until I am sure they are safe. Now give me the answers I need and I will let you live. You can leave and tell whoever it is that you never saw me – or any of us. Now who are you and who are you working for?'

The man coughed and rolled onto one side, the knife still danger-ously close to his neck. He was old, unfit and scarred on every patch of skin Carter could see. His eyes flickered open and closed.

'Last chance,' said Carter, letting the blade touch the man's skin, his hand shaking. 'Who are you working for?'

'I'm a Messenger,' said Saul, slowly. 'I work for myself. They told me some details about you and told me I had to take you prisoner. That's all I know. Let me get up, please.' Blood poured down his face and Carter let him struggle to sit upright.

'Who are they?' said Carter. 'Who sent you to do this and how did you find me? If you tell me the truth I'll let you disappear as long as you never come near me again.'

'You'll let me go?' said the man. 'I have a child, you know, just like you do.' He moved his hand inside the biosuit and started to fumble around in his pocket.

'Tell me who they are.'

A single gunshot rang out cleanly through the gardens and Saul slumped dead onto the blanket of course grass and stones. Upstairs, from the balcony there were two screams; the first in horror and the second of joy. Carter heard Angel's voice ring through the aftershock of the bullet that had hit Saul. His body lay limp, warm and pouring with hot, sticky blood.

'Samuel! I thought you were dead – what the hell happened to you?'

Carter sat there, next to the body in shock while Angel and Elvira flooded out into the garden, each embracing him and Samuel in turn. They crowded around the body in silent disbelief. Samuel broke the quiet, opening his mouth in a grim smile.

'He would have killed you,' he said. 'He had another gun in his pocket, I'll bet. Or a knife. Who was he? Did he tell you?'

'Where were you when all this was happening?' said Carter. 'How did you manage to get out of the house?'

'You can thank me later,' said Samuel. 'I was out on the balcony and I heard someone coming across the grass – that suit made one hell of a racket. I climbed up onto the roof to get a better look and before I could get back down, Lisa and Aaron had already gone downstairs. I heard the two gunshots and then I saw him leave the house so I thought the best thing I could do was approach him from behind. I slid down the pipes at the back of the house and out into the trees. You okay, brother?'

'Who was he?' said Elvira. 'What did he want?'

'He said he was a Messenger,' said Carter. 'That the Industry sent him to kill me.' He wiped the blood from his hands onto the grass, leaving sticky traces in between his fingers.

'That means someone inside the Industry knows you're still alive,' said Angel.

'Someone, but maybe not everyone,' said Samuel. 'This Messenger could have been acting on old information, from when you first escaped the Community. In the early days they were usually hired discreetly to kill leaders from other villages. I've never met one before or heard of this happening in my lifetime.'

Carter looked thoughtful. 'He knew some details about me,' he said. 'Some of what he said was interesting.' He pulled open the man's shirt and checked his pockets.

'But you knew,' said Angel. 'You knew that he wasn't an Industry Scout when you went downstairs, didn't you?'

'Of course,' said Carter. 'Firstly, there are no Scouts any longer and if there were, they wouldn't act alone. The Industry may hire Messengers as Samuel has said, but Scouts don't exist any longer as far as I am aware.'

'Lily managed to get out,' said Samuel. 'How do you know there aren't more like her? Rebels with a grudge against you?'

Carter ignored him. 'Secondly the suit – you could tell that was old issue. And then thirdly, he didn't correct me when I said that the twins' mother was called Isabella. Everyone in the Community knows their mother was called Samita. And he didn't challenge me when I said Andrew, rather than Ariel either.'

'Well, now he's dead, we may never know,' said Elvira, looking across the lawn at the bodies of Aaron and Lisa. 'But we need to be extra vigilant, especially now that there are only four of us.'

For a moment, Carter had almost forgotten the loss of his two new friends, who had taught him the value and beauty of food – something he had never known.

'We may never know,' he said, looking at the man's broken face. 'Unless, of course, there's something that tells us who he is.' He pulled the man's hand out of the pocket he'd been reaching into when Samuel had shot him.

'Told you,' he said as Carter pulled out a small army knife from the man's trousers. 'He'd have stabbed you the minute you let your defences down.'

'There's something else,' said Carter. Saul's balled fist was still tightly clasping a scrap of paper. 'Maybe there's information that will tell us where he came from or who hired him?'

Angel helped him uncurl the fingers and open the palm, releasing the crumpled note. They opened it out, smoothing the corners down and teasing the wrinkles until the picture inside was visible. Elvira gasped as Angel touched the face etched into the paper in charcoal.

It was a hand-drawn sketch of a little girl.

Chapter Seventeen

The Second Generation

Alice

Back up in the Control Room, Alice felt her head dancing uneasily with a million questions. How could Richard possibly know about Kelly? And Marcus? Deep inside her stomach she felt the dullest and saddest of heartbeats. She stopped twice to retch, her stomach queasy and sea-like. She had walked back alone, despite Barnes's attempts to arrange an escort.

'It has been an unsettling morning,' Barnes had said when she got back to the lab. 'What with Marcus and now Richard – you have to understand that not all of the survivors of the Storms are as strong as we are. That's why Wilson and Kunstein chose you, I am sure. It is only the strong who will survive. And only the strongest who will lead us. You're one of those, aren't you, Alice? Now, let me call a guide for you. Or perhaps you'd like to stay a little longer and we can arrange your next set of appointments? I have something that will help you with that morning sickness that Filip mentioned...'

She pushed Alice down onto a chair and stood towering over her. 'It might even be better for you to stay here awhile, maybe a day or so?

That'll help you adjust to the environment again for when you return to give birth. We could make you up a bed...'

Alice turned to face her. 'No. I am not staying here. Not now, and not when the baby comes.'

Barnes narrowed her eyes and the pair of them squared off. The doctor, the taller of the two, stood firm. 'I know you'll do what's needed for the good of the Community, Alice. And for the good of the baby.' Her tone was threatening and she put her hand on the back of Alice's seat, blocking her exit.

Alice stood and pushed the chair backwards, feeling the weight of Barnes's overbearing shadow encroaching closer. 'Doctor Barnes,' she said, an element of strength returning. 'I may be pregnant but I am still Alice Davenport and I still – we all still – have a say in how things are run here. I'll be going now.' She moved backwards and away from the doctor. For a second she opened her mouth to talk about what Marcus had said about Izzy, but then thought better of it. They locked eyes silently, intently, for a second before Barnes smiled widely.

'Of course. It was just a suggestion to help you feel more comfortable. Now, would you like me to come with you?'

Alice shook her head. 'No. I'd just like to take a walk alone,' she said. 'It helps me to clear my mind and to prepare for what's next.'

Barnes nodded. 'If you prefer. Would you mind taking this up to Kunstein?' She handed Alice a thin sliver of plastic card she took from a stack on the side of her table. It reminded her of the stack of hotel room keys her mother used to keep lined up on the living room table.

Alice turned it over in her hand. 'What is it?' she said.

'Something I've been working on with Quinn,' said Barnes, her pride evaporating the tension of the seconds before. 'Swipe one of these over any tablet screen in the facility and you'll be able to get a copy of the whole population here, medical records and sleep status and open any door you need to. Quinn and I designed them to automatically update remotely. Kunstein asked for a copy to be sent up today for her to test. The next phase of our development is imminent.'

'It sure is genius,' said Alice, smiling sweetly. 'Is that your buzzer again?'

And, as Barnes looked up to the wall at the array of light signals, and as Wilson's voice bellowed through the grille again, Alice lifted a spare plastic card from the top of the stack and pushed it deep into her pocket. *Easier than stealing watches at the market*, she thought to herself.

Rather than take the lift, Alice climbed through the tiny panelled door that led to the side stairs, hidden away in the side walls of the Ship. Even though she'd never been down as deep as she was, she knew that the structure was exactly the same on every level. Kunstein had caught her there once, when she was much younger, and scolded her severely.

Sometimes when she had wanted to be alone in those early days, Alice had crept through the panels and onto the stairs, or into the air ducts that ran through the length of the Ship. It was a sure way not to be seen and also to spy on everyone else and find out what they were doing. Being in the air ducts or on the escape stairs never made her feel lonely. The edges of the Ship made her feel safe. She pulled the plastic card from her pocket and ran her finger over the edges and then slipped it inside a gap in the panelled wall, pressing her hand against it hard until she could feel the vibrations of the ventilation system pumping freshness down into the dark of the Catacombs. She wondered if she should hide it there: '*Thieves always get caught, Alice*,' he mother used to say.

She thought about what Richard had said – he knew things. Things that he shouldn't. There was something about him she trusted; something horribly compelling and terrifyingly real. The kind of reality that only came after an unusually lucid dream, the kind that usually quelled the heartbeat of a nightmare. But there was something that he had said before that had made her feel almost ashamed and she couldn't shake off. *Are any of you qualified to do this kind of thing?*

She shivered.

The Industry manual Richard had given her had her picture on the front. It was about two years old, taken when she was at the height of her training, long hair scraped back and her arms faded and pale from being underground for years without sunlight. She opened the cover and read through some of the text, letting the words leap from the page and into her mind.

Monsters. Virus. Murderous Assailants.

Everything about the world outside the Barricades had seemed so threatening back then – so alien and so very different to what she had imagined going back out there to confront. And now – now it was simply unknown. Dangerous, but unknown. That was how Marcus had felt about the Community.

She tore off the front page of the manual, folded it in half, then absently folded it again until she found a paper aeroplane in her hand. Without thinking, she held it high and let it sail down the stairs, where it sat unfolding like a splayed bird. Then, more determined than before, she pulled the card back out of the gap in the panelling, pushed it into her pocket and began climbing.

The Control Room was empty when she arrived, but it wasn't long before Wilson returned. His eyes narrowed when he saw Alice.

'How was the boy?' he said. 'Was the freezing process followed?'

'He's fine,' said Alice, avoiding his gaze and fiddling with some of the dials on the panel. She switched the cameras from one view of the Community to another. 'What are your plans for Richard?'

'Richard?' Wilson looked at her intense with suspicion.

Alice steeled herself. 'Richard Warren, the boy Filip and I brought back from the Tower with us. He's been down here for months now and he's not like the others, he could come and live topside with us – teach us about what the world outside has become. He could come back in here for his therapy sessions with Barnes, until the hospital is finished, if she still thinks they're needed but he'd be much more of an asset if he were outside.'

'The boy you brought back with you from the Deadlands…? Oh yes, I remember now.' Wilson looked at Alice closely for a long time. 'Well, I don't see any problem with that. Have him make those fences around the outside, those Barricades. Another pair of hands would probably get the job done a hell of a lot faster.'

Alice felt the tension leave her body for a second and relief washed over her until she saw Kunstein standing in the doorway, her black cloak wrapped dramatically around her.

'Alice,' she said sharply. 'Resettlement conversations should always be held with Barnes present,' she reprimanded. 'Do not try to bypass her by going direct to Wilson.

'I understand,' said Alice, thoughtful. 'But Barnes seems to think she has it under control with the programme she's developed in the Infirmary. I'm sure she'd appreciate not having to supervise Richard constantly.'

'True,' said Kunstein, 'and she herself is keen to move topside full time for her own reasons and would like to speed up the process if possible. However, I do not want that to be at the expense of doing this properly.'

'So why not let Richard be one of the first of the next batch? I've been down there to see him; he trusts me and we could learn so much from him if we give what he needs right now. If Barnes agrees, of course.

Which reminds me, Barnes said to give you this.' Alice held out the plastic key card, keeping her own copy tightly clasped in her hand.

'Thank you,' said Kunstein. 'The master key. This is exactly what we need. I thought you might have forgotten to give it to me.'

Alice felt a finger claw of paranoia scratch at her insides. 'So, Richard?'

'We do need more people on the surface urgently,' said Wilson. The Second Generation will need to be brought up immediately. The building work is going too slowly.'

Kunstein nodded. 'Fine. We'll get Quinn or Barnes up here and confirm the next steps.' She flicked a switch on the dashboard and spoke loudly into the microphone, calling Quinn to the Control Room.

Anxiety raced through Alice – she was moments from getting agreement to Richard's release and now Quinn could change all of that. Things between them had been particularly frosty since the ceremony for Kelly.

'She's only down in the Lab so I'm sure she won't be long,' said Kunstein. 'But we're installing these receivers everywhere. Down in the Catacombs, outside in the main square and in most of the houses.

'Including mine? When was someone in my house?'

Kunstein smiled. 'Oh, Alice, there's no need to be so territorial. We're a Community now, remember. And the plan is to put in screens too – but that will take many years to perfect. I wanted you to be the first to see it. And, when it's transmitting, this whole room becomes a soundproofed sanctuary, the doors automatically lock so that there can be no interruptions.'

'Hmmm,' said Alice, irritated. 'What about when my baby comes? I won't want just anyone coming into my home.'

'Your baby will be part of the Community,' said Kunstein. 'We will all be a part of its life.' She touched Alice's arm. 'I can understand you becoming a little protective but you really do need to start to amend your thinking.

Quinn breezed into the room holding a tablet and stylus like a clipboard.

'Sit down,' said Kunstein. 'We've been discussing the next phase of repopulation and looking at the numbers. From a logistical perspective, we're ready to take a few more and—' she lowered her voice to a respectful tone '—given what has happened with Kelly it might be good to establish a number of old timers up there to start to normalise things a little.'

Quinn shifted in her chair without acknowledging Alice. 'It could work,' she said. 'I think Barnes should be one of the first to be given a permanent space. Her quarters in the hospital are already being developed.' She paused for a moment. 'The next group we release will be the Second Generation and their ancestors will be the final set of important people who help to build our society. We need to ensure that we give them some recognition for that – to differentiate them from the people that come afterwards.'

Alice looked at her strangely. 'I understand that the ten of us First Scouts came out here before anyone else. But surely everyone will be descended from us and the others, the First Generation of settlers who are here now – or the Second Generation who will be out shortly? What do you mean the people that come afterwards?'

Quinn smiled. 'Alice,' she said with a patronising tone, 'as much as we would like to repopulate our world with people who are just like you and me, as you know, our stocks of people who are able to procreate effectively are just not enough.' She glanced across at Kunstein. 'Barnes is making significant progress with some experimental methods that will allow us to speed up the process of life creation.'

'She's going to make babies in the Catacombs?' Alice thought back to the chilling papers she had found in Barnes' laboratory. 'Clones?'

'Don't be ridiculous,' scoffed Quinn. 'We will be using our genetics engineering to improve the processes. We need to ensure we have enough people to sustain our new Community and that the brightest and the best are selected to lead. The Descendants of us, Scouts, will provide the leaders for the next generations. That's what we decided, Alice.'

Alice nodded slowly. 'So, isn't it time we brought our Second Generation to the surface? There aren't that many of the First Generation of settlers – less than a hundred including the Watchers. We won't be able to repopulate the whole Community ourselves. Plus, we need to start bringing our Second Generation up here or they're going to go crazy knowing that there's sunshine and trees and the beauty of what's left here just above their heads.'

Kunstein looked thoughtful. 'What does Filip think about this?' she said, then addressed Quinn. 'And do you have everything ready?'

'It's ready,' Quinn replied. 'And there are a few that the Model would recommend.' She tapped at a keyboard and brought up a list of names. There were a number that Alice recognised from the Ship as she scanned through them.

'Filip will agree with me,' she said looking directly at Kunstein, her excitement building. 'We need to make sure Richard Warren is added to this list.' She turned to Quinn, nervously. 'How soon can we start?'

'Tomorrow,' said Quinn. 'But the new arrivals need to be monitored by Barnes and if there are any individuals that struggle to readjust, we'll take them back to the Catacombs for further therapy, agreed?'

'Agreed.'

Alice felt a wave of relief wash over her that she'd managed to get what she wanted. She strangely felt more like herself than she had in many months. Whatever information Richard had would be hers sooner than she had anticipated.

The level of enthusiasm in the Control Room rose considerably when Filip returned later that afternoon, his cheeks flushed.

'Izzy is doing really well,' he said, grabbing a chair and scanning the monitors. 'She's going to have to stay an extra day to finish off but she came first in shooting and…'

'Agility,' said Alice, the anger she felt towards Filip very present in her voice. 'Top of her class. Marcus is fine too, by the way. You should have told me about the fauclate.' She glared at him, her cheeks burning with rage.

The air in the room felt heavy as the colour darkened in Filip's cheeks. 'Let's talk about that when we get home,' he said, fixing his eyes on the screens and changing the subject fast. 'So, what do we have here, the Second-Generation participant names?'

'Yes,' said Quinn, holding up her tablet. She ran through the list of names on the screen.

'I want Richard Warren housed with us,' said Alice, firmly. 'Just to start with so that we can keep an eye on him. He can take the room Marcus used to have.' Although the anger sat deep inside her, something forced her to remain calm. She masked her frustration the best she could.

'He can help us turn it into a nursery, in preparation for the baby.'

Alice heard her voice tail off into the thickness of the room that fell silent with the anticipation of agreement. Filip chewed his lip over and grunted his thoughts, the whirrs and buzzes of the computers underscoring his indecision until finally he shrugged and nodded.

'Okay,' he said. 'But any trouble and he's back underground.'

Quinn turned to Filip. 'We'll have them ready by late afternoon so you'll need to sort out the housing allocations and jobs for them all to do,' she said. 'We can probably sort out the housing allocation now, if Wilson can pull up the most recent development plan,' she said.

The screen flickered on and the homes already prepared for habitation glowed green.

'Most of these I know,' said Filip. 'Barnes has picked a great crew here.' He ran his finger down the list.

'This one I don't know,' he said, stopping at name on the list. 'Jacques Therack.'

'What's his profile like?' asked Alice.

'There's not much on him in the records – good worker, quick learner, able to reproduce. Not in the best physical shape but he's been picked by the Model so, as long as he's been through evaluation, he gets to prove himself topside. Apparently did a stint in the military when he was much younger. We could make him a Watcher?'

'Yes – and put him in a house in Morristown Row,' said Filip. 'And make it the one opposite us. That way, when we're certain Richard is ready, he will have somewhere to move into and our new friend Jacques Therack will have some company.'

Alice smiled tightly and nodded. Having Richard topside would, at least, help her to get closer to some of the answers.

Chapter Eighteen

The Township

Carter

They buried the bodies quickly and with little ceremony, turning over the hard ground as fast as they could, leaving three small mounds in between the trees. Carter uprooted two small rosemary bushes and planted them where Lisa and Aaron lay, shaking his head sadly.

'The rabbit was wonderful,' he said quietly. 'Thank you.' His heart filled with sadness at the loss of the brothers, two young men who had tried to make a real difference in the world. He placed his hands on the earth and waited for a second.

'We should go,' said Angel, placing her arm on his shoulder. 'We honour them by moving forward with what we have to do.'

Carter nodded and pushed the picture of the little girl deep into his pocket while none of the others were looking. He holstered the gun he had retrieved from the long grass into his belt. They packed up the rest of their belongings and headed out through the trees towards the darkness of Drakewater that loomed in the distance.

The road widened out into thick tarmac trail that was peppered with bursts of colour as determined plants thrust their way through the asphalt. By the time they had eaten and got started, it was late morning and, as they twisted their way north-east, the sun was high above them, blazing through the cloudless heat. As Carter walked, he turned over the events of the night in his mind. The man said he was Industry, but who had truly sent him? His heart ached that yet more of his friends, Lisa and Aaron, were dead because of him.

'We'll be there by nightfall,' said Samuel, looking up at the sky. 'If we head around the back we should make the east side of Drakewater late this evening.' He stormed off ahead, mumbling something to Elvira who ran to catch him up.

'I couldn't bear it if something happened to Ariel,' said Carter. 'But I knew that man wasn't telling the truth.' He rubbed his eyes, trying to shake the image of the twins lying dead in the grass.

'Your son really means something to you, doesn't he?' said Angel.

'I'm not sure what,' said Carter. 'He's genetically my son, but I've never known him – I've only really met him a couple of times. It's just strange to think that he's a part of me that I don't have any control over but I desperately want to be close to, even though I can't.'

'Sometimes that's what being a parent is about,' said Angel. 'Or, at least, it used to be. Your mother talked about you often. She always spoke about you with love and she did everything in her power to keep as close to you as she could. She's a strong woman and so determined.' Angel smiled. 'In some ways you are quite alike.' She touched Carter's hand. 'The Village – and our survival – means everything to her.'

Carter nodded. 'Sentimentality is frowned up within the Community,' he said. 'The Industry believes it's an old-world emotion. But I missed her and my father so much when I was younger. And part of me resented being left alone. But a part of me understands now – at least some of what she's gone through and what her cause means to her.'

They trudged along the path, Samuel and Elvira winding ahead of them.

'So, who are the Messengers? I had assumed that everyone outside the Community lived with you,' said Carter to Angel. 'Are you telling me there are others? And how do you think one of them would have had details about me – but details that were wrong?' He shook his head. 'It doesn't make any sense.'

Angel picked an orange flower and pushed it into her hair. 'I didn't know for sure that there were any Messengers left,' she said. 'Especially not those that worked for the Industry. Back in the old days, just after the Storms, anyone who was outside the Barricades was seen as an enemy by the Industry. I don't think they imagined that anyone could have survived outside the Catacombs for those five years and, when they did, the magical formula of a new life they'd devised seemed, well, threatened.'

'The risk of infection was real though,' said Carter. 'There would have been all kinds of diseases and the psychological damage of people who'd had to endure that would have had a massive impact on the Community. They would have been too... different.'

Angel twisted her fingers through her hair and the flower fell onto the floor. She bent down to pick it up and shook her head.

'Many people tried to make contact with the Community – some were starving, begging for food and others just wanted to be part of something real, something more like the old days. But the Industry wouldn't even entertain the idea of negotiations. Once they had established the Barricades, it became impossible for anyone to even approach them. Anyone who tried was shot on sight.'

Ahead, Samuel and Elvira were beating a new path to the right, hacking blows with the long knives cutting a track north.

'Don't lag behind,' shouted Samuel. 'We could use some help up here with these branches.'

As Angel moved forwards, Carter grabbed her arms and pulled her back.

'Wait for a moment,' he said. 'Tell me more about the others. What happened when they couldn't join the Community?'

Angel hesitated and looked at him. 'When people realised that joining the Community wasn't an option for them, they started to form their own groups. Smaller ones at first and then some joined together to form real societies, like ours. Most fizzled out after a few years as their members died – they got sick or were just too small to grow or sustain – and the remaining members joined us. Now, there are just two main groups outside the Community – us and the Township.'

Carter looked her in disbelief. 'There are *two* groups outside the Community?'

'It makes sense that there are probably more,' said Angel. 'But up north, not around here. We – us and the Township – tend to keep ourselves very separate now. They hold the land to the north and around Drakewater, the Community is to the south, and we are to the west.'

'And what's to the east?'

'They say that the land to the east is deep marsh and beyond that the sea, but nobody I have ever heard of has been there. It's too dangerous to travel on foot and impossible by boat. Where the river opens out onto the marshland it's treacherous. Or at least that's what we're told.'

'Do you have any contact with the Township?'

'Not exactly. They're a different people to us and they have no interest in the Industry. Their policy from very early on was to reclaim the land to the north, rather than descend south into the Deadlands around the Community. The Messengers are not affiliated to the Village or the Township, they're independents who trade information or work for food and then move on. People who don't want to fit in anywhere.'

'But they work for the Industry too?'

Angel shook her head. 'I've never heard of that,' she said. 'The Industry has enough of their own people that they consider expendable to use outsiders. We usually use light signals, a sort of code from the tower block to communicate with the Community – very occasionally Messengers, but they'd never approach the Barricades, it's too dangerous for them.'

She looked upwards at the sky.

'The Messengers are loners, they don't have families or friends and they always work alone. I don't understand who this Saul could have been, Carter. I'm sorry.' She looked at him directly, certainty in her eyes.

For a moment they stood there, in silence until a flash of light distracted them as Samuel raised his knife high in the air. 'Are you two coming to help?' he said, sharply. 'Or do Elvira and I have to do this alone?'

They took turns with the long knives, carving the route until they came to a clearing in the forest. Broken brick buildings covered in moss and lichen were scattered around the edges, remains of an old village, cracked and desolate. A row of small houses curved into the sunlight, windows free of glass, silent and empty. Crows cawed from the rooftops, their wings gleaming in the sunlight. Although it was deserted, Carter could tell straight away that it had been lived in since the Storms, but not any longer.

'I don't like it here,' he said. 'It's eerie, something doesn't feel right.'

'This is the old Township.' Elvira scraped away veined ivy leaves from the corner of a sign. She read out the words slowly, tracing her fingers over the words. '*Welcome to Woodford Hatch.*'

'The old Township? Why did they leave here?' Carter looked at the buildings more closely. He could tell that many of them had been repaired and patched up since the Storms but were now being reclaimed by nature once more. The dark shadow of Drakewater loomed to the east. Remnants of broken bottles still littered the streets, some overgrown with plants and others still stony and partially clear. A battered surfboard, faded and scratched lay incongruous across one path.

'This was where the trouble happened and the factions broke off after the Industry found them, wasn't it?' said Angel to Samuel, who nodded briefly. 'They uprooted from here and took their settlement a little way north, years ago, but not too far if I remember. If we keep moving we could be at the new Township early evening. We should ask them for hospitality for the evening – at least we'll be safe.'

Samuel wrinkled his face at her. 'What do you think they'd say?' he jeered. 'Come and join us for dinner? If they know we're planning to confront the Industry there's no way they'll let us in. They don't want any trouble and, from what I've heard, they've managed to escape any further attacks from the Industry since the very beginning. I think we should avoid them.'

'You seem very keen for us to stay away, Samuel.' Carter eyed him suspiciously. 'Have you upset them, too?'

Samuel looked exasperated. 'They are not our people and this is not their business. I just think—'

'Well, you're not always the one who makes all the decisions,' interjected Carter, quietly. 'Elvira, Angel – what do you think? How much do you know about the Township? Could you get us there?'

They looked at each other. 'I'm pretty sure I know the way,' said Angel, 'with Elvira's help, but I don't know how they'll receive us. Samuel is the only one who has had any contact with them.' She looked across at him. 'They're good people, Samuel, peaceful people. If we head north from here then we can make the Township by nightfall. But we all go together, in agreement, or we avoid it and head around their settlement.'

'I've had no contact – not for years,' Samuel muttered.

'I vote we go there,' interrupted Elvira, speaking quickly and enthusiastically. 'I'd feel safer there overnight and they're not enemies of ours – it's just that they're not really friends.'

'We're taking a big risk,' said Samuel, sharpening a thick stick with his knife. 'We keep our lives separate from theirs for a reason. They might not be very welcoming.'

'But what we're about to do will affect them too,' said Angel thoughtfully. 'Maybe we should let them know what we're planning.'

'They'd see that as putting them in danger,' said Samuel. 'No, it's not right.'

'They'll be in even bigger danger if they don't know. They're a peaceful group. We should at least warn them.'

Samuel shaved big chunks of bark from his spear in silence, shaking his head. 'It's not their battle,' he said, stripping the wood until the whitened point was sharp and defined.

'But it's the right thing to do.'

Elvira and Angel nodded as Carter turned to Samuel. 'It seems like we're going to the Township,' he said. 'Are you in agreement?'

Samuel aimed the spear into the bushes, letting it glide into the undergrowth. 'Let me do all the talking, then,' he said, reluctantly, putting the knife back into his pocket. 'And don't tell them our business.'

As they continued northwards, the forest thinned out into a mass of overgrown shrubs and scrubland. Houses and outbuildings were scattered across the horizon and they passed through a number of small villages, some that seemed virtually intact except for the sprawling creepers of overgrowth that wound their way through every building crevice. Rabbits darted into bushes as they passed, some stopping to check out the travellers, their noses twitching at their scent before they moved on. As the afternoon folded into early evening, the four that were left of Company Six stopped near a crumbling bridge that forded a brook, and watched the sun glide slowly over the backdrop of the sprawling mass of what was once outer London.

'We should take something,' said Elvira, refilling her water canister in the cool, chuckling spring. 'We should take a gift for the Township.'

Carter nodded. 'Good idea,' he said, watching Samuel skimming stones across the surface of the water. 'What do you suggest?'

Pulling back on the bow, Angel shot straight and true, spearing two rabbits with a simple twang of the string. She trussed them up with plaited vine and wrapped the package in sycamore leaves with bunches of rosemary and thyme that she picked from a field on the other side of the river. Her movement were deft and exact. The sight of them made Carter feel sad, Aaron and Lisa almost a distant memory.

'I think this should do it,' she said. 'At least it shows them we mean them no harm.'

'We could have just eaten them ourselves,' Samuel grunted. 'What if they decide not to give us any while they're harbouring us for the night?'

'Then we go without,' said Carter. 'It's more important that we're hungry and alive than dead and full of food.'

As the stars started to prickle through the night sky, they arrived at the gate to the Township. Around the border edge was a high wooden fence with thick posts driven deep into the ground, but no sentries sat on top and no guns pointed at them. The heavy gate was dragged open from the inside as they approached.

'Who goes there?' came a voice from inside the gate. 'Identify yourselves and make the Township aware of your business today.

'We are residents of the Village,' said Samuel, speaking on behalf of them all. 'We do not offer any trade or business with you; we simply request a safe place to sleep for the evening and perhaps some food. We plan to continue with our journey before sunrise tomorrow.'

A woman wearing all black stepped out of the shadows. Her hair was long, and flowed around her cheeks in dark, feathery curls. As the moon slipped out from behind a cloud, Carter could see that her face was painted with intricate patterns; tiny grey and black spirals that danced outwards from her eyes. She smiled at the Company, eyes twinkling in the evening light.

'Welcome,' she said, holding out a flaming torch to inspect them. 'There was a rumour that some of your people were making their way out here. You *are* a long way from home, aren't you? What is the purpose of your trip – are you out here looking for new lands? You do not need to be reminded that everything from here north, up to the river, belongs to the Township – anything directly to the south is really not the safest of territories. I'm sure you, of all people, do not need to be reminded of what *they* would think of your trip.' She smiled at each of them individually and tucked some of the flowing curls back behind her ears.

'We have brought you a gift. Please take these for your trouble.' Angel held out the package of rabbits to the woman and stepped backwards as she took them.

'Thank you,' she said without opening them. 'Now what is your business here?' The swirling patterns on the woman's face seemed to move in the flickering torchlight, making her face more dynamic and threatening that it otherwise might have seemed. Carter spoke as softly as he could, mirroring the formal tones of the conversation.

'As my brother mentioned, we are looking for shelter for the evening and we will leave your Township before the morning arrives. We do not wish for any discord, simply a place to stay for the night and for you to accept our gift of friendship.'

The woman looked each of them up and down in turn. She stopped at Samuel. 'This one, I recognise,' she said. 'You are a frequent traveller. And you—' she pointed at Angel '—you have also been around these parts before. But the other two are not familiar to me. Are you a part of that Village?'

'Yes,' said Samuel immediately. 'They are both residents that are not familiar with travel and tend to stay within our boundaries.' As he stopped speaking a thin mist of rain drizzled downwards, making the woman's torch fizzle and spit.

She raised her eyebrows. 'Then why do they travel this evening? And so far from home? What about your own Outposts?'

She looked past them and into the forest as she continued. 'You could have eaten alone, stayed in one of the old villages on the track,' she said. 'Why do you choose to come to us?'

Carter spoke, interrupting Samuel. 'Last night our Company was attacked,' he said. 'A man, armed with a gun, shot two of our people with no explanation or motive. We would like to spend tonight in safety, in the company of people who can be trusted.'

The rain picked up pace and the pattering that had begun turned to the thudding of bulbous drops on wood. The woman nodded.

'Violence against any other human is something that our people do not tolerate,' she said, with a serious, grave tone. Pellets of rain sank into the soft earth around her. 'It is because I know him—' she pointed at Samuel '—that I will allow your entry on this occasion. But do not assume that this will be a regular occurrence. And there are two conditions – firstly, we will want to know exactly what business brings you here. Secondly, all weapons are to be left at the gateway. We do not allow any form of aggression here within the Township.'

She pointed to a long wooden box just inside the gate and the Company dropped in their spears and guns. Samuel held onto his knife for a long while before reluctantly tossing it inside with the other weapons. The woman spoke quietly to two men that stood in the shadow of the gatepost and they nodded to her in agreement. She ushered the Company through the gate and past another set of sturdy wooden entrance panels before they found themselves in a large clearing surrounded by oaks. Squat brick huts were arranged in perfect symmetry throughout the area, lit with bright torches that glowed warm in the darkness. The woman guided them to the largest of the buildings in the centre of the clearing.

Despite the majority of the smoke escaping through a large opening in the domed roof, the room was still clouded with the breath of the crackling fire in the middle of the room. Around it sat a group of men, women and children of all ages, laughing and talking merrily as the Company entered, their faces all covered with the same beautiful, decorative swirls. The joviality stopped and whispering started as they caught sight of the Company stepping into the room.

'These are people of the Village,' said the woman loudly, above the crackling of the fire. 'They are our guests for this evening and they have brought a gift for us.' She held up the rabbits to which there was a faint cheer from the back of the room. 'However, we are still interested to know why they are here. They have dispensed of their weaponry at the gatepost and have assured me that they come in peace.'

She raised her hand to silence the protests that began.

'We will eat together and seek first to understand what their plans are, before making any judgement.' The woman passed the rabbits to a couple who were skinning other chunks of meat and forcing them onto skewers.

The people of the Township nodded in agreement, making room around the fire for the Company to sit with them. As they shuffled around, some of the children got up and took bowls from a table, filling them with nuts and berries and handing one to each of the travellers. Carter found himself sat next to an old woman, her eyes blue-grey and sleepy. She smiled at him and tapped his shoulder as a little girl passed across a bowl brimming with fruit. He held it with both his hands.

'Thank you,' he said and picked out some of the squashed red berries, pushing them into his mouth, realising how hungry he was. It was only when the girl turned away from him, coughing heavily, that he realised in sick horror that he had seen her before. There was no mistaking the dimpled smile and curly dark hair that stared back at him – it was the glassy-eyed girl pictured in the sketch he had found in the dead Messenger's pocket.

Chapter Nineteen

The Newcomers

Alice

By the time they left the Control Room, ascended the lift and got back out into the main square, the sun had dipped behind the trees, trailing ribbons of silver and pink across the evening sky. Filip put his arm on Alice's as they walked into the near dusk.

'Don't.' She moved away from him and walked ahead, her heart still aching from the thought of Marcus alone in the Catacombs. Filip caught up with her quickly and grabbed her hand tightly.

'Marcus is in the best place,' he said definitively. 'For anyone who doesn't fit up here right now, the Catacombs is our only option. You know that, Alice.' The tone of his voice was threatening almost and Alice shivered, her hand entombed by his.

'But Marcus was one of us, one of our family,' she protested, her eyes gleaming with tears. 'It's not right.'

'It's not just right, it was the only thing to do.'

'No, it wasn't. We could have helped him.'

Filip pulled Alice around sharply, so that they were stood face to face. 'I don't want to hear this talk from you,' he said, angrily. 'We are the two people who must embody the values of the Industry. Our survival as a Community is more important than the individuals within it. If you don't believe in that any more, I can't protect you.'

'Protect me from what?' Alice felt a cold chill run down her spine. Her hand moved to her stomach, cradling the tiny life inside her. She had hoped so desperately that she was wrong about what was happening in the Community she had helped to build, but she knew that all that Richard had warned her about had substance and it terrified her. And there was something about the tone of Filip's voice that terrified her too.

'I can't protect you from yourself,' he replied. 'Do you understand that, Alice?'

Biting down her anger and her fear, she watched as everything she had ever found attractive or endearing about Filip melted out into the night. Richard would be here soon and she would be able to discuss it with him, to get some perspective – support even.

'I understand,' she said quietly, attempting to inject some remorse into the hard, angry tones that came from inside of her.

'And you're aligned with what we're doing here?'

Alice bit down hard on her lip. 'Yes,' she said.

'So, what's caused all this behaviour?'

Alice felt her cheeks smart. How dare he call *her* out on her behaviour? She kept her jaw strong, unable to trust her reaction but unable to trust Filip more. She hesitated. 'I just feel that in some ways, since we've come back out here, things have started to change. And not in a good way.'

'What do you mean?'

'Well…' Alice waited for the owl hooting a deep bassoon-like call to stop, her heart beating fast. 'Things seem different. Marcus is gone, Barnes seems to be making all the decisions and I'm not sure this is what we agreed.'

Filip let go of her hand and pushed his hair back from around his face. 'Things were always going to change, Alice,' he said. 'Different people are destined to lead and direct different parts of this journey. Some people provide hope and others provide control. At the moment, you seem to be providing neither and I'm not the only one to have noticed it.'

Alice stifled her anger and swallowed deeply. She thought of all that Richard had said and closed the conversation down. 'I think I've just been a little emotional over Kelly,' she said finally, clawing for an excuse. She half-smiled. 'I'll be back on full form soon, don't worry.' Her heart sank at her own compliance but she knew, at this stage, it was for her own good.

'You'd better be.'

Filip's arm felt unusually heavy and cold as it grasped her shoulder and guided her back home to the house on Morristown Row. As she slipped into bed and beneath the covers, although she knew it was too early to be the baby, something inside of her moved. And it was something that terrified her.

The following evening, Kunstein was the first to emerge from the Industry headquarters building, ahead of the party that had been selected to join the Community. Her long coat flapped delicately in the breeze that accompanied the light rain pinpricking its way through the covering of grey clouds. She nodded to the guards outside and made straight for Alice and Filip.

'Barnes has done a thorough job of the assessments,' she said briskly, 'although we can't guarantee they will all be successful in this first real batch of newcomers. We will need to monitor them closely to ensure they are ready for this next phase. Any irregularities must be reported immediately so that we can make the appropriate adjustments both out here and as part of their rehabilitation package.'

'Absolutely,' said Filip. 'Have you assigned the mentors?'

'We have,' said Kunstein. 'As discussed, you will have Therack and Warren and we'll put Therack on Watcher duty and Warren on food distribution. Since your little chat, he seems to have adjusted exceptionally well. What exactly did you say to him?'

'Not a lot,' said Alice, trying to remain normal. 'Just explained to him some of the advantages of the new world over the old one – not everything is made that simple in the manuals. Sometimes you have to appeal to the human element inside people – they're not all machines.'

Kunstein smiled. 'Well, it certainly did the trick,' she said. 'We may have to get you working alongside Barnes down in the labs.'

'I think Barnes is doing just fine,' said Quinn who had appeared over Kunstein's shoulder. 'Shall we get the Second Generation out here then?'

They dribbled out of the doors in pairs, eyes wide and fixed on the sky. Alice watched as each one of them breathed deeply, drinking in the fresh air and scanning the new world in a state of equal wonder and terror.

'The air,' said one of the men, 'it's so… fresh.' He opened his arms wide and wheeled around a circle, letting the faint drops of rain fall on his tongue. A woman bent down and kissed the floor; two teenage boys hugged each other and started to cry. Another woman moved towards her, holding out her hands.

'It's Alice, right?' she said. Her long blonde hair was damp with the rain but her eyes were shining bright. 'Congratulations. I hear you're having a baby.'

Alice frowned. 'You did?' An arc of birds flew overhead and fluttered into the distance. The woman watched them carefully, then her eyes turned back to Alice.

'It's a beautiful thing,' said the woman. 'The love of a child is like nothing you'll experience. They're so dependent on you and yet...' her voice tailed off into the sky '... and yet you'll love him – or her – in a way that's indescribable. Tears glistened in her eyes. 'I miss my girls,' she added. 'The day the rain fell I tried so hard to find them but I never did. I only hope they didn't suffer. And I won't forget them. But I know that this new life is going to be different. Maybe one day I will be as lucky as you are. Being topside again makes me feel like anything is possible. It's everything I imagined.'

Alice felt a churning in her stomach and a hard lump form in her throat. 'I remember my first time outside,' she whispered, and smiled as the woman walked back off into the crowd. And she did – the wondrous, exciting empty feeling that anything was possible. A feeling that was very much in the past for her.

The crowd stared to stream forwards and Alice caught a glimpse of Richard Warren somewhere near the back of the group. Filip grabbed her hand and they climbed a small flight of stairs that led to the building opposite. As soon he raised his hands, the crowd fell silent and turned to Alice and nudged her arm. 'Go on,' he said. 'Inspire them.'

A cheer rang up and out into the mist of rain cloaking the evening sky.

'Welcome,' she started, 'to the new Community. Don't worry about the rain, this is just a shower.' Laughter filled the air – a desperate, strained laughter that scared her a little. As she looked at them she felt a sadness, something akin to pity, that she couldn't dare explain to them. She strengthened her voice and pulled back her shoulders, her eyes fixed on Kunstein.

'This evening is very special to all of us,' she continued. 'The world now is very different and while you will have all received briefings underground, there's nothing that can fully prepare you for life in the new Community...' She paused for a second. Their lives from this point onwards would change irrevocably in a way she could not possible vocalise to them. She wanted so badly to tell the young girls that strained their necks to catch her eye that soon they would be paired with others who would be encouraged to fill them with children, whether they wanted to have them or not. Because this was what she, Alice, had agreed in the depths of the Ship only months before. Sickness and guilt filled her stomach. She licked her dry lips, watching Barnes at the edge of the stage who nodded and smirked an ugly grin. Filip nudged her to continue.

'Carry on,' he whispered but Alice looked blankly ahead at the crowd. She started to speak again but then stopped. The words just wouldn't come out. Not the words she was supposed to say.

Filip took over. 'I know that some of you will have left friends and loved ones to be here today and that the period of adjustment will be different for each of you, but we have done all we can at this stage to make you feel as comfortable as possible. Your homes have been prepared, and the day after tomorrow you will start your new roles in helping to make this Community a place we can all work and live together.

'We only really have one rule out here and that's to follow the Manifesto to the letter. If you have any questions, please do ask me, Alice or Kunstein. And you all know Barnes, of course. We're going to take a walk to the Community now, so that you can all get settled into your new homes.'

'Is it safe out here?' called a man from the front. 'I've heard someone got killed.'

Filip nodded. 'Sadly, we have lost one of our people recently. But that was because the rules were not being followed as they have been designed. Since that incident, we have established a boundary to ensure our security here is not compromised – there's plenty of space for you to explore but I suggest that until you're familiar with your surroundings, you return to your homes before dark. And stay away from the Barricades.'

'And what about the rain?' The man held out his hands, feeling the drops land softly on his palms.

'All of the houses are being significantly reinforced and, while we can never be one hundred per cent sure, our weather warning systems don't indicate anything of immediate concern. Now, let's move before we get drenched.'

As they stepped down from the podium, Filip turned on Alice. 'What happened to you?' he said. 'You were supposed to give them encouragement. This is all new to them.'

'I… I don't know,' said Alice. 'I'm not feeling too great.' They melted past the crowd and into the shadows of the square.

'If you're not up to your duties, you have to tell me,' said Filip. 'I can always get someone to take your place. It's you they want to see, of course, but you must keep your focus if you still want to be a part of the team. If you need to rest, because of the baby then…'

'I'm fine,' interrupted Alice. 'Just a little morning sickness.' She smiled weakly at Filip, hoping he believed that the dull ache in her stomach was fuelled by her hormones rather than the desperate sadness she felt for the innocent and desperately hopeful Second Generation.

The tour of the Community was brief and, within the hour, all of the newcomers had settled into their new houses. Most stood out on their doorsteps until long after the moon had climbed in the sky, drinking in the cool night air. Richard Warren was one of them, holding tight to the doorframe, he swung in and out of the house, breathing deeply each time he pulled himself back.

'We should talk,' he said. 'About how I can get out of this new prison.'

Alice looked behind her into the house. 'We can talk,' she said. 'But not tonight. Filip is inside and you all have a big day tomorrow, getting to know your way around here so you can start on the food delivery programme. Then you can tell me about Barnes.'

'Nobody asked me if food delivery was what I wanted to do,' said Richard, stretching his legs high. 'I was training to be an electrician before you dragged me in here.'

'You were dying of an infection before I dragged you in here,' said Alice. 'We've all had to make changes and you were, what, thirteen when the Storms started? You'd barely started senior school. I doubt you were very far through the qualification process.'

Richard laughed. There was something mischievous but kind that reminded her of photographs she had seen of her father when he was much younger. 'You're funny, Davenport,' he said, staring out into the blackness. 'You're like my brother. He's out there, you know. I can take you to him. You'd probably like him.'

Alice shook her head. 'Get some sleep,' she said. 'We've got a lot to talk about, but not tonight.' She glanced behind her into the house. 'There are too many people around.'

'I'm not like Jonah, not deluded about my brother having survived. I know he did,' said Richard in a low, deliberate tone. 'He was there with me until I got sick. He went to the others to get help. That was when you came – I thought at first he'd sent you.'

'How do you know about Jonah?' said Alice, her mouth dry. 'That's classified information; only the Scouts and Kunstein know anything about that.'

'And Barnes,' said Richard. 'She knows everything. You think Barnes is as equal as everyone else? You know she's not.'

'Keep your voice down,' hissed Alice, agitated. 'You'll be sent straight back down to the Ship if anyone else hears you.'

'If you didn't think there was at least some element of truth in what I was saying then you'd send me back down there yourself.'

He smiled and swung himself past her and through the doorway.

'Get me a way out of here, Alice. And if you've got any sense, you'll come with me.'

When Alice opened her eyes the next morning, a cool light streamed through the window and the space in the bed next to her was equally as cold. She touched her stomach and shivered, pulling the blankets closer to her. Richard's words were still floating around in her head when she finally pulled herself out of bed and got dressed.

'Filip's gone to collect Izzy. He said he'd be back this evening and he was going to try to check on Marcus while he was there too.'

Richard was sat at the table, helping himself to a slice of whiteloaf covered with lickerspread as Alice came down the stairs.

'Save some for Izzy,' she said, retrieving the tub from his grasp. 'That's her favourite.'

'Oh yes, Izzy, the new Industry hotshot. Well, maybe I can get us some extra when I'm your takeaway delivery boy.' Richard grinned, crumbs of whiteloaf all over his jacket. 'I can't wait to get some real food again – all this synthetic protein rubbish is disgusting.'

'It's all we've got,' said Alice, feeling irritated. 'This is what we eat out here.'

'You mean, you're not growing anything yet? There are rabbits out here, birds, rats even. They have to be better than this.'

'I didn't get you out of there to talk about food. How do you know about Jonah? And what about Barnes?'

Richard laughed. 'Barnes, for her lack of genuine psychological training is a pretty good talker, especially when she thinks no one is listening. You do know they've got something going?'

Alice pulled up a chair opposite him. 'Quinn and Barnes?' She shook her head. 'Not so soon after Kelly…' She heard her own voice drift into a chord of disbelief that was tinged with the sick feeling of knowing something after the event.

'Oh yeah, Kelly,' said Richard. 'They pinned that on someone from outside, didn't they?'

'It *was* someone from outside. Marcus said it was…' Alice's words trailed away as she remembered what else Marcus had said.

Richard raised his eyebrows. 'You don't think that's a coincidence? So soon after the so-called intruder?'

'The intruder was shot trying to attack us.'

Richard shook his head. 'Kelly knew the people outside weren't violent. She wanted to let them in.'

'How do you know that? Did Barnes know they weren't a threat?'

Richard nodded, his mouth full. 'Yep,' he said. 'She ordered them to be killed.'

'Tell me.' Alice moved her face close to Richard's and grabbed his hand. 'Tell me everything.'

He wiped crumbs from his face and shrugged. 'You've got to help me out of here first. I need to find my brother. You saved my life, now I'm going to save yours.'

A sharp rapping on the door cut the conversation dead and Alice felt her legs weaken as she got up to answer it. When she did, there was a large man – the biggest man Alice thought that she'd ever seen – in his early thirties, with short dark hair standing in front of her, his eyes filled with tears.

'You are Alice Davenport, no?' he spluttered, his hands shaking. He grabbed at her clothing, almost pulling her off balance and out into the street.

'Er… yes, and you are…?'

The man looked around the door and into the house.

'Hi Jacques,' said Richard, smiling. 'Come on in.'

The three of them sat around the table, Jacques hunkering over the side with great dollops of tears dripping down onto the floor.

'They have told me I cannot speak my language,' he snivelled. 'No more French, only English allowed in the new Community.'

'It's not like you really had anyone to speak it to,' said Richard, patting him on the back. He turned to Alice. 'I mean, I tried with the little bit I remembered but as you so kindly reminded me last night, I'd barely joined senior school when the Storms started so I couldn't do much more than ask for a train ticket to La Rochelle.'

Jacques started to cry again. 'Why is my language so offensive to people?'

'It's not that it is offensive,' said Alice. 'It's just that now, we're living in a different way. We're all one Community, with one aim, one culture, one purpose…'

'And one language,' finished Richard. 'Back in the nineteen forties there was another leader who had similar thoughts.'

Alice knew she should feel anger but only sadness echoed in her voice. 'This is meant to unite people, Richard, not divide them.'

'But they don't see anything wrong with it? You're like a bunch of kids playing Risk. Only this time it's not a game.'

Jacques wiped his nose on his giant sleeve. 'Can you talk to them?' he said. 'Make them see that I am not trying to cause trouble. I just want to be able to speak my own language.'

Alice held her hands out towards him, avoiding the sleeve. 'Jacques,' she said softly. 'Try to think of it this way – everyone being able to communicate with each other on the same level with no confusion or complication. Nothing separating us from each other and no difference in nationality or religion that keeps us apart or pits us against each other. Everyone being equal.'

'That's bullshit,' said Richard. 'The things that make us different are what make us human.'

'They are also what made us inhuman,' said Alice, watching Jacques's tears fall. 'This levels the playing field.'

'There may be a playing field, but no games to play,' said Richard. 'Your Manifesto sucks.'

Jacques started to sniff again and pulled a package of whiteloaf from the bench and balled it in his hands before swallowing the chunks whole. Alice watched the crumbs litter the floor and felt a cool wash of helplessness drain through her.

Richard looked at her intently. 'Do you feel safe here?' he said. 'Is there anyone in here you trust. Completely, and with your life? That you could trust with a secret that might change everything?'

Alice thought for a moment. There was Kunstein, Filip – in the past, Kelly and Quinn. But certainly not Barnes, William Wilson or any of the others. And not Filip. Not after Marcus.

'Kunstein, I guess,' she said slowly.

'What about Filip? Not the father of your child?'

Alice paused. 'Why?'

'I think you are in danger.'

Alice bit her lip hard. 'What makes you think that?'

'I'm only out here because I did what you told me to do,' said Richard, ignoring her question. 'So did Jacques, didn't you, monsieur? We complied with your rules.'

'I do what they tell me,' said Jacques, wiping his tears. 'No more France.'

'French,' said Richard, correcting him. 'No more French.' He patted Jacques on the arm. 'Go and get ready for your shift on the Barricades and I'll keep you company in a while.'

Jacques pocketed another slice of whiteloaf and slid off the chair. 'Au revoir,' he said then quickly covered his mouth with a paw-like hand. 'I am sorry. I am sorry.' And then with a sniff and a gulp, he was gone.

'You *really* think that's okay?' said Richard, rolling his eyes. 'He's harmless. A real gentleman. You know, he never spoke a word of English until he entered the Ship. One of the nicest guys I've ever met in my life. He used to teach history, back in France and he was an accountant for a while – before that the military. They had him shifting crates in the Ship – effortlessly, to be fair to him – the man is like a machine. His strength underneath all that bulk is unbelievable. He speaks three languages, just never got around to learning much English. Do you *really* think it's okay to pretend his whole culture never existed in favour of this new-fangled nonsense?'

Alice pulled Richard towards her. 'Before Jacques came in you were going to tell me what happened to Kelly.'

'I'd tell you, but I'd have to kill you.' Richard grinned, feigning a Russian accent and rocking back on his chair, a mock smile spreading across his face. He even sounded a little like Barnes.

'Who was it?'

His face turned serious all of a sudden. 'I know about Marcus and why he was taken into the Catacombs – and I'm fairly sure I know who your people murdered out there at the Barricades. The same person who killed them, killed Kelly.'

'How do you know all this?' Alice felt the room spill outwards in circles around her.

'Do you really think you can trust Kunstein with what I'm about to tell you?'

Alice paused. 'I'd need proof. She won't believe me without some sort of proof – I'm sorry.' She shook her head. 'Your word just isn't going to be good enough for her.'

Richard smiled wryly. 'I can get you proof. And lots of it. Proof that your world here isn't what it seems, and that your Scouts and your Watchers are telling lies. Kelly knew, which is why she had to die. Come out there with me. Let me show you the people that live in what you call the Deadlands. They're good people, kind people that want a new kind of life just as much as anyone else – except that they're doing it without force and without the need to make everything that happened before wrong.'

'Going into the Deadlands is forbidden now, you know that. And besides it's dangerous.' Alice rubbed her stomach, her mind in splinters.

'If you don't get me out of here, you'll never know what happened to Kelly and what your people are up to – I *can* prove it. But I need you to help me find my brother. And if you don't, I'll find my own way out. Do you want your baby to grow up in a world full of lies? You know this place is corrupt.'

Richard jumped up on his chair and starting poking into the corners of the ceiling.

'What are you doing?'

'Just checking they haven't got around to installing all the houses with two-way listening yet.'

'The speakers are only one-way at the moment,' said Alice. 'At least that's what I was told.' She paused. 'Do you think I'm in danger?

Richard shook his head. 'Possibly. They suspect you're going to cause trouble, that you're already doubting what's happening. It's in your nature.'

She shivered. A tiny black spider inched its way across the floor towards her.

'Listen, they're going to call Izzy back into the Ship for her final trials soon.'

'Yes,' muttered Alice, her eyes fixed on the creeping legs. 'We're supposed to spend the weekend in the Ship.' She had been dreading the thought of going back there again – it no longer felt like the sanctuary it once had but more like a nagging, toothachy threat.

'Don't go. Frankly, you *can't* go. You'll never come back – Barnes will see to that. Izzy will be gone all weekend and so will Filip – he's already lined up to be her chaperone. Most people will be down in the Ship watching the trials and Jacques is lined up to be the solitary Watcher on the main gate and you...' he paused. 'You won't be feeling very well.'

'I don't feel well,' said Alice. 'My stomach hurts and I'm exhausted.'

'Well, you need to keep that up for another week or so.' Richard leaned back in his chair. 'This is important, Alice. I need to get out of there. And you need to see the truth – so you can at least save yourself. When they leave for the Ship, you'll stay at home. Then, you can take me out into the so-called Deadlands that weekend and I'll show you something that will blow your mind then, if you still want to come back to this awful place, you can.'

Alice felt the plastic card she had stolen from the Ship digging deep into her pocket and held it tightly, her mind thick with indecision.

She had a feeling that her habit of the theft of things lying around was about to pay off.

'I'd be putting everything at risk.'

'Oh, come *on*, Alice, you're already putting everything at risk if you stay here. You want to change the world? Then be brave enough to see it for what it is.'

Alice paused, her skin feeling hot and clammy. 'I guess we all do,' she said. 'But there are some things that…'

'Things that don't feel right? Things that you don't know?'

Alice shook her head. 'How do I know you're telling the truth?' she said. 'You've already proved you can lie well enough to get yourself out of the Ship.'

Richard stared her directly in the eye. 'You know those communications systems Kunstein and Wilson are putting in?' he said.

Alice nodded. 'Yes.'

'Well, when they were installing it, I started talking to the electrical engineer. Just like Barnes, he loved to show off his knowledge. We talked about the circuits and where they ran to – blah blah blah. Then, when I was taken for one of my many psychological evaluations in the lab, I switched the wires to the one in my room so that it was constantly on – even when Barnes thought she had flipped her switch off.'

'How did you know…?

'It really was very simple. Barnes leaves stuff lying around all the time and like I told you I was training to be an electrician – my father was one before the Storms and he'd take me out on jobs with him. I just prised open the box, reconfigured the circuit and it was done. The engineers were so organised, they even labelled all the wires and switches with the room names. There were plenty of medical tools in the drawer too. Barnes made it really easy for me – all she needed to do was leave the room for a moment and it was done.'

'So, you could hear everything from your room?' Alice felt sick.

Richard looked smug. 'Everything that was said in the lab, yes. Visits from Quinn, discussions about your pregnancy, what happened with Kelly, the plan to bring Marcus to the Catacombs…'

Alice stood open-mouthed, her heart beating fast as she remembered the boy, terrified and traumatised, her guilt raging inside her. She made an attempt to ask Richard a question but no words came out. 'I've told you more than I should have already,' he said, watching her. 'Now do we have a deal? This could be your only chance to find out the truth, Alice. I won't tell you anything else until you get me out of here. You do want the truth, don't you?'

'We have a deal,' she said, her hands still shaking. 'But until then, you do everything I or anyone else asks of you and you keep Jacques in line too. Okay?'

Richard stood up and mocked a salute. 'Okay, *ma cherie*,' he said, and showed her a toothy grin as he bit into the last slice of whiteloaf.

Chapter Twenty

The Betrayal

Carter

'Why are you out of bed, Maya?' said the woman and carried the little girl Carter had so suddenly recognised towards the door in her arms. The little girl watched them as they left, her mouth slightly open as she sucked her thumb, her breath unsettled and wheezy.

Carter stared at the little girl as she was carried away and pushed his hand into his pocket, feeling the scrap of paper with her picture on it between his fingers. A wave of dread washed over him. He rubbed the paper as if to erase the memory of the incident with Saul from him mind. He glanced at Samuel, who looked away; Angel licked her lips nervously and pointed towards the food by way of distraction.

The rabbit meat was seasoned and grilled to perfection on the open fire and it was complemented with a fruity mead that had been sweetened with pieces of honeycomb that bobbed in the cups as they drank. The conversation flowed beautifully, with the people of the Township teasing the children with wild stories of fantastic, mythical monsters that roamed the Badlands – their name for the Deadlands – at night; giant eagles that would swoop down and steal them away to nests filled with juicy fruits, and tiger-bears with twelve feet that could run as fast as birds could fly.

Carter watched as even the smallest of the children danced around the fire, bounding into the arms of the nearest adult and laughing until tears twinkled in the corners of their eyes.

For a brief moment, he forgot about the little girl and thought of the Community and how he had grown up only to work and learn – to be productive and thoughtful, strong and brave. He ached for his own childhood, to have been able to be free to swim underneath the waterfall and to play by the fire, eating succulent foods caught in the open wilds.

He listened as they each took it in turn to sing, closing his eyes for a moment as the cadences climbed up and tumbled down, losing himself in the delicacy of the tune. He knew then that his idea of taking music and art back the Community as his Contribution to becoming Controller General would never have worked. The Industry would never have allowed it – it would have been the start of something they couldn't have stopped. They would have imprisoned him in the Catacombs at best – or killed him. Lily had undoubtedly saved his life and sent him back to his family.

He shivered and focused his thoughts back to the girl from the drawing. Suspicions were beginning to form in his mind. He needed to talk to the others. The children were all still playing, and the woman who'd carried the girl out came back into the room and smiled, passing around another bowl of berries.

Carter looked away, trying to catch Angel's attention, but she was busy talking with the man next to her. Elvira twirled around in front of him, dancing with a man equally as short as her, and Samuel sat staring into the fire, helping himself generously to the bottle of mead cradled in his arm.

'Samuel,' he called across the laughter. 'I need to talk to you.'

'What do you want?' said Samuel. 'I'm listening to the music.'

'It's important,' said Carter. 'It's about the Messenger. Come outside with me for a moment.'

As they made their way back inside the hut, Samuel grabbed his arm tightly. 'Whatever you do, don't say anything to anybody about this. These people treat any violent acts very seriously – especially against their own people. They've lived generations now with no fighting – between themselves or others – and no violent acts have been committed towards them either.'

'It's a delicate equilibrium,' said Angel, who had appeared next to them. 'Elvira and I had already seen the girl. We need to be very careful here. We may not have known that he was one of their people, but that will make no difference to them. Neither will the fact that he shot two of our people – they won't believe it.'

'So, what do we tell them?' said Carter. 'Surely they deserve to know that one of their people is buried in the forest and the father of one of their children is never coming home?'

'Telling them that will not only endanger us but everyone in the Village,' said Angel. 'You both need to keep quiet until morning.'

When the three of them walked back into the hut, the music had stopped and a stillness had taken over the atmosphere. The woman with the dark curly hair stood near the front of the fire and welcomed them inside.

'Good to see you are all back with us,' she said softly. 'Now that we have provided you with the hospitality you requested, one of you can tell us what business you have travelling through the Badlands towards Drakewater with very little equipment or food. Let's start by you telling us a little more about this attack you encountered last night.

The leftover members of Company Six remained silent, listening to the crackling of the fire, all intently staring at the woman.

Carter started, his voice faltering a little as he began. 'We were camped up in a house not far from here,' he said, 'about seven hours to the south, south west. When we awoke in the morning, two of our men had been—' he hesitated, conscious of his audience '—had been attacked and killed.'

There was an audible collective exhalation from the group. The woman held up her hands for them to be quiet. A ripple of whispers travelled through the room.

'Continue, please,' the woman said to Carter. 'What happened next?'

'I…' Carter began before Samuel interrupted.

'When the rest of us came downstairs, whoever had attacked our Company had disappeared. They had taken some of our food and clothing. We buried our men in the forest and continued on our way. It was probably a lone traveller, some sort of explorer from the north, desperate for a meal.' He took a glug of mead and looked at the woman. 'I'm sorry to have burdened you with our troubles,' he said finally. 'I know you don't like to hear of any violent acts and this… assailant… well, he is probably far away by now.'

The woman looked at him closely. 'So, you know it was a *he* then?'

'To have overpowered two of our best men, I can only assume,' said Samuel.

'This troubles me greatly.' The woman stood up, walking around the fire that had begun to reduce itself to glowing embers. 'There hasn't been one recorded incident of violence in these parts in many generations. But what concerns me more is that one of our people, my partner, has not yet come home from his plant collection duties. This is very unlike him.'

Company Six sat in silence.

'Maybe there was an accident?' said Samuel, draining his cup.

'That would be a remarkable coincidence,' said the woman. 'More likely that he has met with the same assailant you claim has killed two of your Company.'

'We should leave,' whispered Elvira to Carter. 'This is not going to end well for us if we stay here.'

'We have to tell her,' said Carter. 'We have to be honest with them.'

'No,' hissed Angel, 'we can't.' Samuel shot him a look of fury.

Carter stood up, his legs feeling weak at the knees. 'We have something else to tell you.'

When he finished speaking, he handed the woman the sketch of the little girl. Her eyes remained dry but behind them, she looked desolate and empty. She ran her fingers over the lined paper, straightening out the creases and looking upwards, out through the hole in the roof and into the delicate pattern of stars above them.

'You expect me to believe that my husband came from nowhere, knew things about you and attacked your Company when he had absolutely no reason to? That he was working for the *Industry?*' She spat out the last word with contempt.

'I can only tell you what happened,' he said. 'I cannot guess as to his motives or who he was working for – but I do know that he shot and killed two of our Company and, if my brother had not defended me, I would have been next. He lied about being an Industry Scout and he lied about my son being ill.'

The woman whispered to a man next to her, who had been nodding gravely throughout Carter's speech. 'This is Saul's brother, Eli,' she said. 'He will deal with proceedings from here-on in. I need to be with my daughter now.' Her feet crunched on the gravel as she left.

'I'm sorry,' said Carter. 'I am truly sorry for what has happened.'

The woman turned to him, her face so close that he could smell the lavender flowers pinned to her cloak. 'You have an honest heart,' she said, softly. 'That is admirable – but when it is paired with such vengeful anger, you will not be successful in whatever it is you are trying to achieve. I do not believe that Saul was working with the Industry – there is no way he would do that. Look within yourself and your Company to find your own truths; that is what I need to do now.' She glided slowly out of the hut, not looking at any of the other Company members.

Eli waited until she had disappeared and then addressed Samuel directly, the crowd silent. 'As you know,' he said, 'we cannot condone nor tolerate any kind of violence whether it is perpetrated by our people or against our people. You claim that Saul attacked and killed two of your people, but there is no evidence other than your word – which, at this point, is not held in particularly high regard with our people, given your attempts to lie. He had no access to weaponry, has been schooled in the customs of peace and had no motivation to work for the Industry.' He cleared his throat. 'How can we be sure that you did not just murder Saul for your own means?'

'We had no reason to,' said Carter. 'We have no argument with your people and we had no idea that Saul was from the Township. We would not have come here and asked for your hospitality if we had known he was one of your people. We all deeply regret the incident, but we were acting in defence of our lives.'

Eli looked at them each in turn. 'You carry weapons, you expect violence,' he said. 'You are on a journey to disrupt the fabric of life as we all know it. For many years we have worked to create a different type of life here, one free of violence and oppression. Everyone here subscribes to that notion or they leave, it is very simple. People come to your Village because you invite them, you want to grow and recreate the old world. We do not. We wish to live simply. Saul was part of our life here.'

He turned to the group of people left in the room who were sat silently, shock and disbelief on their faces. 'You may all leave,' he said to them. 'Our guests will be detained until we can establish the truth.'

Shaking their heads, the group stood up one by one, and left.

'We should run,' whispered Samuel, looking at the others. 'Now!'

Carter looked at his brother, his suspicions building, as several guards closed around them. Eli looked on and continued his orders, as each member of Company Six was seized.

'You will all stay as our guests until we have understood exactly what Saul was doing out there in the Badlands and how much of what you have told us is the truth. You will remain separate from your brother until we have completed our investigations.'

Carter felt his heart beat fast as his arms were bound behind his back. 'Friend,' he said, trying to remain calm. 'I appreciate your need for closure in this matter but we have urgent business to complete on the other side of Drakewater and it is time-critical. I promise you that on our return we will pass through here again and we can discuss how we resolve this matter between our two groups of people.'

'Out of the question,' said Eli. 'This matter is too serious. We will discuss further in the morning but, for now, you will receive our hospitality once more.'

'But—'

Eli held up his hands. 'No arguments, I insist that you stay. I bid you goodnight.'

*

In the darkness of the grain store, only a single cube of dim light filtered through the single stone window onto the straw mattresses that had been shoved through the door by the people of the Township before they had barricaded it shut.

'Why did you tell them?' said Elvira. 'Why didn't we just avoid this place?' She threw herself back onto the mattress and sighed heavily.

'I told the truth because it was the right thing to do,' said Carter.

'How were we to know that Saul was from the Township?' said Angel, twisting a piece of straw through her fingers.

'There was something not quite right about him,' said Carter, moving next to her. 'His information was wrong; his clothes were wrong. He wasn't working for the Industry, I'm sure about that now – but he was working for someone.' He took the straw from Angel and held it in front of the light, watching the shadows it cast on the floor. His mind furiously worked through the possibilities. He could come to only one conclusion.

'Do you think...?' began Elvira and then stopped herself.

'Do I think it was Samuel?' said Carter, slowly. 'Do I think my brother somehow convinced that man to threaten me so that he could get me alone and kill me himself without you knowing?' He felt Angel stiffen in the darkness. 'I've thought about nothing else since I met the girl when we arrived. That man was not a mercenary. He was acting under duress.'

'You think he's not violent just because he had a daughter?' said Angel, the tone rising in her voice. 'You saw Aaron and Lisa dead on the grass. He killed them, didn't he?'

'I don't know, maybe. Perhaps he was coerced, possibly he panicked.' Through the night air came the sound of doors closing and the desperate shouting of Samuel to be let out. 'Maybe he wasn't expecting them to be there,' he added.

Elvira stood up and walked around the edges of the circular grain store. 'We need to escape from here,' she said. 'If we don't, we run the risk of missing the only opportunity we have to break into the Community and take back what is ours.'

'I can't believe it was Samuel.' Angel's voice sounded thin and broken. 'Why would he do such a thing?'

Carter looked up at the square of light high above his head. 'Jealousy?' he said. 'Maybe something more. I can't quite believe it either but Elvira is right. We need to get out of here tonight if we're going to make it into the Community before the new Controller General is in place and they regain the stability that's been disrupted since I left. What I need to know is whether I can trust you both.' He reached out his hands to Elvira and Angel, touching them both gently.

'You can,' she said. 'You can trust us both.'

He sat there for a moment, before looking back up at the tiny window. It was roughly square and free of any covering. He released his grip on them both and looked at Elvira.

'Do you think you could get through that and drop down the other side without hurting yourself?'

She stared upwards and blinked into the moonlight. 'I've got through smaller,' she said. 'But you're going to have to lift me. Both of you. I won't be able to hold on long.'

Balanced on Carter's shoulders, Elvira contorted her body through the rough block gap and dropped with a soft thud onto the earth below. There was the scrape and clack of the bolt to the grain store being pulled back and then they were out, into the darkness.

Carter paused and looked across at the other grain store, which had fallen quiet momentarily. He felt an anger rise through his body, a cold sweat forming on the back of his neck. A desperate banging came again from behind the door.

'Leave him,' Angel said, disgusted. 'He may be your brother, but he could have got us all killed. He as good as murdered Lisa and Aaron.'

Carter gritted his teeth. 'He has betrayed me – betrayed us all with his actions. Lisa and Aaron are dead. He has created a rift with these people over Saul's death...' He broke off, his voice wavering. 'But we won't get there without him. He's the only one of us who knows the way from here. Unless you...'

'No,' said Angel, reluctantly. 'But we can find it, if we just...'

'Wandering for days out here, in the dark?' Carter shook his head. 'We need Samuel's expertise. As much as I wish we didn't, we need him.' He cast his eyes towards the grain store. 'And he is my brother – I need to know why he's done this.'

'He's no brother,' said Angel, angrily. 'He betrayed you. You'd never have done that to him.'

'No, I wouldn't have.' Carter straightened his jaw and looked out into the darkness. 'But we can't leave him here.'

Elvira shook her head. 'But what if he attacks you? What if he tries to kill you in your sleep or while we're in the Catacombs?'

Carter laughed curtly. 'He wouldn't dare,' he said. 'If he'd had the guts to do it himself, he wouldn't have hired Saul. And besides, now you both know what he's tried to do, there's no way he'd attempt anything else.'

Angel let out a heavy breath in the night air. 'I don't trust him,' she said. 'But I do trust your judgement.'

Carter crept to the grain store and tapped on the door.

'Samuel,' he whispered. 'I'm going to let you out and you're coming with us. But we know what you've done.'

'Let me out,' said Samuel, banging on the door. 'I had my reasons.'

'Shut up,' whispered Carter sliding back the bolt and dragging his brother through the door. 'We *will* talk later. If you want to get out of here, we need to get leave quietly – and before they realise we've gone.'

Samuel grunted in agreement. 'I…' he began, but Carter held up his hand. 'Don't say another word.'

They slipped back into the brick alleys of the Township, signalling to Elvira and Angel to follow. Carter pushed Samuel in front of him and, silently, they crept with their bodies pressed against the sides of the wall, pushing into the shadows and away from the intermittent torches that lit the paths with a dull flicker. Ahead lay the gateposts, the heavy oaken door unguarded and framed with trees on either side.

'Quickly,' whispered Angel, 'there's no one there.'

They picked up pace, treading lightly, breaking into a near sprint when they reached the gate. Carter pulled back the bolt and teased it open with a loud creak, cringing as he did so. As they slid through, light flooded onto the path as the woman with the curly hair stepped out behind them with a torch in one hand and Carter's gun in the other.

A shard of moonlight glinted off the metal barrel.

'I would have thought you'd be needing this where you're going,' she said, waving the gun with a confident smile, then pointed it directly at Carter's temple.

Chapter Twenty-One

The Outsiders

Alice

Izzy turned three somersaults through the hallway before ending up with her legs against the counter in the kitchen. She kicked herself over to stand upright again and bowed in front of Filip and Richard Warren, who sat eating breakfast. Richard clapped slowly and then ruffled her hair.

'You're smart, aren't you?' he said.

'You don't have to be smart to do agility but, yes, I am that too.'

'I thought you might be. Hey, Alice, are you feeling okay?' Richard touched her arm gently as she breezed past him, smiling brightly.

'Of course,' she said, 'just a little morning sickness, that's all. Izzy, no more acrobatics in the house, please. You're good enough.'

'Are you *sure* you won't come?' said Filip. 'I'm sure there will be plenty of breaks and Izzy would love it, wouldn't you, Izzy?'

'I really don't feel great,' said Alice. 'I'm going to get some rest here, if that's okay with you all.'

'You should be there.'

'Not this time, Filip.' Alice stopped herself from glancing across at Richard and rubbed her stomach softly. 'I'm going back to bed.'

'Should I call Barnes? Perhaps it's best that you come with us for an examination?'

'Filip, it's morning sickness, nothing else. It's normal. I'm not coming to the Ship and I'm not going to see Barnes. You wanted me to rest so I'm going to rest.' Alice tried to hide her exasperation as best she could.

Izzy wrapped her arms around Filip. 'Just us!' she exclaimed, 'Just us!' and then cart-wheeled around the kitchen. 'Can we go see Barnes?' she added.

'Yes,' said Filip. 'Now come on or we're going to be late. Richard, keep an eye on Alice, won't you?'

'Indeed,' said Richard, munching through his chicker and whiteloaf. 'I'll make sure she gets all the rest she needs.'

They had been gone less than half an hour before Richard came downstairs with an empty bag, sweeping the remains of the food parcel from the counter into it with a smile.

'I saved some extra too,' he said. 'From the delivery rounds. Just in case this takes a bit longer than we think and you've forgotten how much you like the taste of real food.'

Alice shook her head. 'You still think this is the right idea?'

Richard nodded unequivocally. 'Absolutely. We stay here and you're going to either end up getting brainwashed into believing them or something bad is going to happen to you. I don't know what's worse. You've not changed your mind, have you?'

'No,' said Alice. 'But if we get caught…'

'If we get caught, then we run,' said Richard. 'Assuming we make it through the Barricades. That card of yours opens doors as well as spills the beans on whether we all had the measles when we were four, right?'

She pulled it out of her pocket. 'If anyone knew I had this, they'd send me down into the Catacombs for sure. And even I wouldn't see the light of day for a long time.'

Richard smiled. 'Then leave it here. All we need to hope is that Jacques can complete his Watcher shift handover smoothly and can let us out of the gate without anyone else seeing.'

Alice scowled at him and pulled a faupple out of his bag. 'For some reason, I can't get enough of these,' she said, biting into it and spraying the acidic juice all over the table. 'I don't know why you had to involve him – if we get caught then at least we can explain ourselves – or at worst escape – but Jacques is risking his life. And he's not the smoothest of talkers in a difficult situation.' She placed her hands over her eyes and felt the coolness of her palms on her skin.

'And that's exactly why we're using him,' said Richard. 'All he has to do is look away when we open the gate and do exactly the same when we come back in on the same shift tomorrow. Easy.' He looked happier than Alice had ever seen him.

'I genuinely don't feel great,' she said, sitting down heavily into one of the chairs at the table. 'I actually wasn't pretending when they were here. I was sick this morning. What if I get worse while we're out there? Maybe this *isn't* the best idea...'

'It's the only idea,' said Richard. 'You're probably nervous. If I were you, I would be.'

'Why aren't you?'

'Because I know what's out there.' Richard handed her another faupple. 'And I can't wait to see it again. Being away from this toxic, terrifying environment will change everything you think you know about the Deadlands. And you've been fed so many lies, you don't know which way is up. Don't you want your baby to grow up in a safe, honest environment?'

Alice ignored him. 'What if we get caught?'

'Then we deal with the consequences. Sometimes, Alice, you have to take a risk to get to the truth.'

Alice shook her head. 'All I know is that there's something very wrong here. And I need to know how to resolve it.'

'*Bonjour!*'

Jacques held up his hands to greet them as they approached the old copse near the north gate, his voice booming through the silence of the trees, deep and infectious.

'Ssh!' said Alice, quietening him, although the innocence of his happiness and enthusiasm filled her with something not unlike excitement and, for a second, made her forget the threads of worry that embroidered her.

'There is only *un*,' he said, holding up one finger. 'Nice man, much further along the fence. I talked to him already. He went to Paris once, with his wife.'

'Ooh la la,' said Richard, patting him on the back. 'You know the plan, right?'

'*Oui*,' said Jacques. 'He is leaving the shift soon and I take over, shoot any bad people that come out of the Madlands.'

'Deadlands,' said Richard. 'But no, you don't need to shoot anyone – that's just what the Industry tell you to do.'

'I know, I know,' said Jacques laughing. 'And the same time tomorrow. I close my eyes for *un, deux, trois* and back in you come. Simple.'

Richard put his thumbs up. 'Perfect,' he said. 'Exactly right.'

Jacques looked serious. 'What if you don't come back? I will be all alone.' The jollity in his face was gone.

Alice felt the key card burn deep in her pocket. It would be no use to her on the outside – if she lost it, or it were taken from her, the one chance she had of accessing any areas of the Catacombs might be gone. And if she and Richard failed to return for some reason, Jacques would have no way to escape, no way to survive in the Community. He already knew too much. But he would never make it on the outside alone. He would need an ally, someone to help him.

'Jacques,' she said, 'When we have gone through the gate, I'm going to throw this key back over the Barricade and I need you to keep it for me – somewhere very safe. If something – anything – happens to me, you must use this card to escape. Do exactly what I'm about to do – click the card on the gate and it will open. And then you will need to run – very, very fast.'

The man nodded solemnly as Alice continued.

'But you need to have someone you trust to help you,' she said. 'Someone you trust completely. Someone you trust with your life. Even if you have to wait a while to find the right person.' She paused. 'Do you understand?'

Jacques nodded. '*Oui*,' he said seriously.

'This key opens everything,' said Alice, her hands shaking. 'Do not give it to anyone or tell anyone about this unless you are sure about them. If you cannot be sure, do not trust anyone.' She smiled as his face clouded with worry.

'It's okay, Jacques,' she said. 'We'll be back.'

Jacques nodded again. 'Is it true that there are other people out there?' he said. 'Good people living happy lives?'

'We don't know,' said Alice, an uneasiness in her stomach and her smile fading. 'But we will find out. Are you ready?'

Richard nodded. 'Okay, let's go,' he said.

There was a slight metallic click as Alice slid the card over the receiver plate that filled her with a terrifying relief. Over her shoulder, the large shadow of Jacques watching her every moment obliterated the shadow of the Barricade, as she and Richard darted through, heaving the small gate closed.

Alice tossed the small piece of plastic over the metal fence and they ducked behind a large bush.

'Jacques!' she hissed. 'Do you have it?'

'*Oui*,' whispered Jacques loudly. '*Au revoir*!'

'Make for the trees to the east,' said Richard. 'There may be someone coming. Run quickly and don't look back.'

They darted across the plain, the thin grass making a fast surface for travel, Alice hitting the trees first, Richard covering her as they threw themselves down behind two rotting stumps that looked like tombstones rising out of the earth.

'Ugh, said Alice, breathless. 'These smell disgusting.'

'Great, isn't it?' said Richard, digging his hands into the flesh of the wood. 'They smell real.'

Over the top of the Barricades in the distance, they could just make out the shape of Jacques's head, and the glint of a gun trained on the line between them and the hills caught Alice attention.

'Do you think we're safe?' she said, but she didn't look back again.

They moved into the cover of the tree-lined scrub as the Barricade gleamed its warning beacon in the sunlight, getting further into the distance. From the slight incline of the land they had crossed, they could still see the bright reflection of the metal through the outlines of half-broken buildings and torn-up paths. Already, the wiry saplings had begun to reclaim the land, pushing over stones and rubble to form a thin cover of green where, before the Storms, it had been grey.

'It doesn't take long,' said Alice. 'In twenty, maybe thirty years' time this will all be trees again.'

'If the Industry doesn't concrete it over,' replied Richard, wiping his face on his T-shirt. 'It takes an awful lot longer for things to grow than it does for us to destroy them. Don't you think all this—' he cast his arm across the battered landscape '—is so much more beautiful than that dreadful city? Don't you want your child to see real things? Trees, mountains, cities, animals?'

'I want my baby to have the world,' said Alice softly, her hand touching the small bump forming inside her. 'Despite who her father is and what Filip has done – and what she has been born from, it's not her fault. I didn't think I wanted her, Richard, but now…'

He leaned over and touched her arm gently as tears formed in her eyes. She abruptly changed the subject.

'Do you know where we're going?' said Alice.

'Of course.' Richard stopped as the stony path forked into two and feigned confusion before nodding gravely and pointing.

'But how?' asked Alice.

'Easy. If you plot the Community in the centre of everything, which is where the Industry believes it is, then the sun rises in the east, which is clearly in that direction. The tower is north-west of the Community and where we're going is east and slightly north of that.'

'But without following the roads, how do you know? What if we miss it?'

'How do you know we're not following the roads?' said Richard.

Alice looked down at her feet and, through the weeds and stones, she could just make out faded white lines against tarmac.

'You have to remember,' said Richard. 'I might not have been this particular way recently but I was out here a long time, navigating by all kinds of different methods. There are landmarks that you never see when you take them for granted. You have to learn a different way of following things.'

'I suppose,' said Alice looking around at the fragments of buildings around them. 'But how do you do that when everything's covered with water?'

'It wasn't always covered with water,' said Richard. 'In fact, the worst of the weather was over in the first year. The tides weren't helpful, obviously, but after a while my brother and I made a raft and headed for the higher ground, near Drakewater. We assumed that's where we'd find people, although we were scared to go too far in the early days in case the rain came again. We managed to find ourselves these scuba suits – that was great fun. You know we learned to dive from a book?'

A robin hopped onto the path in front of them, bead-black eyes focusing on Alice, head cocked to one side.

'You ate birds,' said Alice. 'We found the trap in the flat.'

'Chicken's a type of bird,' said Richard. 'I'll bet you had no problem with that before. We ate birds, frogs, squirrels, leaves, baked beans, tinned vegetables, anything we could at first – still better than any of that synthetic stuff. Not sure I'd eat a robin though, too many bones.'

He laughed loudly and the bird skittered off. 'I liked the view from the old flat; that's why when I wasn't feeling well my brother took me up there to rest. In the early days, we'd stayed there a lot while we were out scavenging. It had a great view of the city and you could see people coming from miles away.'

'Did my mother ever come back to find me?' The words sprang from Alice's mouth before she could stop them. It was the one question she really wanted an answer to, but had been so desperately afraid to ask – even in her own mind.

Richard kicked his foot against a tree. 'Honestly, Alice, I don't know. A woman and a man came one time we were there but we wouldn't let them in. It was the only safe place that we had at that time and it was in the early days, when people were still angry and a little bit crazy.'

'She could be out there,' whispered Alice. 'She could be looking for me.'

'It's not impossible. It's unlikely, but not impossible.'

'What did they look like, the people that came? Did they say anything?' Questions darted through her, questions she hadn't dared to think about in years.

Richard smiled. 'Alice, if you have this much to ask about the world outside, it's a good thing you're taking this once-in-a-lifetime opportunity to find out some of these things for yourself.'

Alice nodded sadly, her eyes full of tears and regret. So much had happened so quickly that it was almost impossible to work out what she thought she felt and what she knew she believed. A butterfly with silver-tipped wings landed on her shoulder and sat for a second before fluttering across and onto a shattered bus shelter that stood overgrown with thick ivy leaves. The things that would have once been ugly or irrelevant were suddenly eclipsed with an unparalleled beauty that overwhelmed her, and she burst into tears. Richard patted her arm.

'It will be okay,' he said. 'It will. It might not seem that way now but I promise things will come right. You just have to be a part of that too. Life is always better when you have something to fight for.'

A grasshopper with emerald-green legs jumped from one clump of grass to another and Richard held out his finger for it to hop across.

'You will find a way through this,' he said. 'There are people out here who can help you – my brother, for example.'

'What happened to him?' Alice wiped her eyes on her sleeve.

'I got sick, really sick, when we were out searching for supplies. We holed up in the old flat for a while but I kept getting worse. I was drifting in and out of sleep while my brother got food for us both. He went out a few times to look for antibiotics but couldn't find any so he said he was going back to the Township to get help. That must have been when you found me.'

'The Township? Do you mean the Community?'

Richard laughed. 'Hell no! The Township is certainly not the Community. It's very different.'

Alice looked quizzically at him, her eyes still shining with tears. 'Do you think these other people are still where they were before? It's been months – wouldn't they have moved on by now? Or have tried to contact you…'

'My brother wouldn't leave without me. He knows that I'd come back for him. I just hope that he isn't one of the so-called creatures that your people have already killed for trying to communicate through the Barricades.' He kicked the root of a tree hard, causing a shower of tiny orange fruit to scatter around them. He picked one up and handed it to Alice. 'Taste one of these,' he said. 'And you'll remember what the Industry has taught you to forget.'

The fruit was sugary sweet, delicate and melted as Alice closed her mouth. The taste was incredible and reminded her of home. Real home.

Richard laughed. 'Concentrate on how that tastes,' he said. 'Feel how delicious the juice is and now tell me you still crave those disgusting faupples.'

*

By mid-afternoon they reached a stream forded by an old stone bridge, every inch still intact. Richard went first, testing it with his weight, then stamped across, the sound reflecting off the cool walls of the half-standing village on either side of the water.

'That's incredible,' said Alice. 'The houses all around are falling apart but this bridge—' she ran her fingers over the curves of the stone '—it's still perfect.'

'Some things really were built to last,' said Richard. 'There's so much out here that's still workable – and not just out here, in *here*.' He banged on his chest. 'We might not have to reinvent everything. Do you want your child growing up in a world without any history? I don't. In fact, I want to live in a world where I get to choose whether or not to have children at all.'

Alice closed her eyes again and let the tranquil sound of the trickling water wash over her. 'I've missed that,' she said. 'That noise. Not rain, not taps, not anything industrial. Just that.' She lay down on the bridge and folded her hands across her stomach, looking up at the sky, blue and cloudless and empty of anything.

'Can we stop here for a moment?' she said. 'I need to rest.'

They sat there in the ruins of the village, Richard refilling their water canister while Alice let thoughts of the Community and Filip run through her mind and out into the heat of the afternoon. The unbroken, unstoppable flow of the water soothed her almost to sleep before she felt the gentle touch of Richard tapping her arm.

'We need to go,' he said softly. 'If we leave now, we should make it before it gets dark. We just need to keep the line of this brook to our left and it will take us straight there.'

The air cooled significantly once they were inside the wood and the sounds of the evening made Alice shiver underneath her thin Industry-issue suit. Ahead of them, the track wound around the bushes and deep into the trees that looked black and almost impenetrable.

'Careful,' said Richard, taking her hand. 'The roots have taken over the path here and you don't want to fall. Think of your baby.'

Alice touched the outline of her stomach. It still felt so unreal but there was a part of her that couldn't remember what it was like to not have the tiny life growing inside her.

Richard stopped for a moment. 'He didn't... force you, did he? Don't you think you're a bit... well... young?'

Alice felt her eyes prick with tears. 'We did it the new way,' she said. 'With the syringe. I wanted to wait a while, everything was so confusing and so different. But now—' her voice disappeared into the darkness '—now I feel it, I feel her inside me and she's a part of me, however much it scares me. Bur what scares me most is how I'm going to cope with a baby. I want her to have everything, but what can I possibly give her? She won't have a favourite teddy bear a pet kitten or...' Her voice quivered and stalled. 'I'm not even supposed to want that for her, but I do. Maybe I'm just selfish.'

Richard shrugged. 'It's okay to not know what you want all the time,' he said. 'But it's not okay to do what's expected of you just because it's expected of you. You need to be able to choose.'

Alice nodded. 'It feels real and so unreal all at the same time,' she said. 'But more than anything else, it's confusing. I want to make sure that my child grows up in a place that's safe and happy – a place where they never have to deal with bullying or hunger or greed. The old world wasn't somewhere that could ever happen. It was too damaged. People were too damaged.' She looked away. 'I've said more than I ever should have.'

'Some people still are,' said Richard, 'Damaged that is. Take Barnes, for example.'

'At first, I thought I was just jealous of her,' said Alice slowly. 'But then I knew it was something much more.

'She's evil,' said Richard. 'I know you feel the same way about her – I've seen the way your eyes change when her name is mentioned.'

Alice looked past the darkness of the trees and tried to clear her mind. Then, through the branches, she saw something that made her mouth feel dry and hard. She looked again – there was definitely something there; the intermittent flicker of a torch light and the thin grey line of smoke, rising up and out towards the sky.

'Stop,' she said. 'Look. Look up.'

Richard smiled. 'That's it,' he said. 'We're there.'

The smell of wood smoke became stronger as they approached the settlement and, as the wood thinned out and they got closer, Alice could see the outlines of old houses and the spire of a church. As the crack and snap of twigs beneath her feet gave way to the gravelly trudge of a road, she could hear the gentle hum of activity and conversation. Richard put his hands to his mouth and made the sound of a bird, half-whistle, half-trill, the notes ascending and descending in quick succession over and over, then he shouted his own name loudly.

When he stopped, there was silence.

'Hello!' he yelled again. 'Is anyone going to put the kettle on?'

Alice watched as slowly, from out of the house, a group of people gathered and started walking towards them. She felt in her pocket for something, anything to defend herself with.

'I...' she began, but before she could say anything else, the men and women in front of her whooped and hollered, running towards them with their arms outstretched. A teenage boy at the front led the charge, sprinting towards Richard and wrestling him down onto the floor with soft punches.

'Where the hell have you been? I thought they'd killed you. We've been looking for you everywhere.' Tears welled up in his eyes and Richard, covered in dirt and twigs rolled over, grabbing the boy by the hair.

'Thank god you're alive!' shouted Richard. 'I thought it was you they'd shot at the Barricades!'

'Not me,' said the boy, his eyes full of tears. 'Others, but not me.' He held Richard's face in his hands and then looked at Alice. 'And who the hell is that?'

'That,' replied Richard, 'is Alice Davenport. And this, Alice Davenport, is my brother Joe. Welcome to Woodford Hatch – or what we call The Township.'

Chapter Twenty-Two

The Community

Carter

Although every fibre in his body told Carter to run, he kept remarkably still and calm while the barrel of the gun brushed against his forehead. The woman moved next to him, facing Elvira, Samuel and Angel – all five of them hovering in the gateway to the Township.

'We must leave,' said Carter. 'I apologise for deceiving you, but what we need to do is important.'

'Were you already aware that your brother and my husband were known to each other, before the incident this morning?'

'I didn't know when we came here but I suspected something wasn't right. He paused. 'I am not from their Village. I have recently left the Community inside the Barricades.'

'No one leaves the Community – they haven't done in years.' The woman waved the gun at Carter. 'Tell me the truth.'

'I am telling you the truth,' said Carter. 'I escaped through a tunnel that had been dug by the rebels and was found by these two.' He gestured towards Angel and Samuel. 'It is a long story, but this man is my brother. Our mother is Jacinta Warren, the leader of the Village.

But the time has come for me to return to the Community. We must stop what is happening within the Barricades.'

The woman eyed them both suspiciously. 'There is a resemblance,' she said.

Carter paused. 'I believe my brother here hired Saul to threaten me – or even kill me – because he is a jealous, suspicious man. Saul killed two of my friends as well. It is our responsibility – and not yours – to bring Samuel to justice. '

The woman turned the gun towards Samuel. 'Saul had a temper, but he was a good father – and lately he'd been disappearing for days at a time. He had been speaking to someone from your Village but he wouldn't say what about. You must have threatened him, forced him into doing this.'

Samuel kicked at the earth and hung his head. 'That's not how it happened,' he said visibly upset. 'Things got out of hand – very badly out of hand. Lisa and Aaron weren't supposed to die and Saul wasn't meant to kill you. He panicked. He was—' he broke off and covered his face '—he was only meant to keep you away from us for a while. Things were fine until you arrived.'

'We'll talk about the why later,' said Carter with a tone of bitterness. 'But *how* did you get Saul to agree to do this?'

Samuel scratched the side of his face. 'The kid,' he said. 'Maya. She's sick.'

The woman looked deep into Samuel's face and Carter watched as his scar darkened. 'What about Maya?' the woman asked coldly.

Samuel replied, trembling. 'He wanted medicine for Maya in exchange for getting rid of my brother. But when I told him that he would need to bring Carter back to your Township and keep him there for a while, he got aggressive. Aaron and Lisa heard him shouting and came out of the house and tried to overpower him. Then he shot Aaron and Lisa, so I ran.'

Carter felt his anger building. 'Samuel,' he raged. 'You wanted to get rid of me that badly? So badly that you had someone try to kill me?'

'It wasn't like that.'

Carter held himself back from punching his brother square in the face. 'Then tell me what it *was* like,' he said through gritted teeth. 'Tell me.'

Samuel furrowed his forehead. 'It's not fair,' he shouted, his temper exploding. 'You've turned up here after all these years and acted like a long-lost hero while I've been here working hard and looking after our mother, building a life. How could I let you be the one to take down the Industry and take all the glory? I could have done it on my own. I just wanted you out of the way for a while.' He paused, catching his breath. 'It's not fair,' he repeated.

Carter stepped back and swallowed deeply. 'Lisa and Aaron *died* because of you.'

Samuel bit his lip hard. 'That was never meant to happen. I gave him the gun to threaten you, I never meant...'

Carter put his hand up to silence him. 'We'll deal with you later,' he said, his anger subsiding a little. 'There are more important things we have to deal with first – things that are bigger than you and me – and much bigger than your pathetic little ego.'

He turned to the woman. 'Do you have any rope?'

As Angel bound Samuel's hands together tightly, he put up little resistance.

'I'll release you when the time is right,' said Carter. 'When I can trust that you're not going to do anything else to endanger us, our friends or our mission.'

'I'm sorry,' said Samuel quietly. 'I never meant…'

'Shut up.' Carter looked at the woman and the patterns that swirled across her face.

'Where's the girl? Where's Maya?'

The woman who had been listening intently turned towards Carter. 'She's in the hut. Why?'

'Because I may be able to help her.'

The woman looked Carter up and down. 'What makes you think you can help my daughter?'

'He's a doctor,' added Angel, finishing the knots carefully. 'And a very good one – he's read every book we have and fixed the broken arm of a girl in our Village.'

'I can't promise anything,' said Carter. 'But take us to her and I'll do anything I can.'

The girl lay in bed, sleeping soundly. Carter crouched by the bed as her mother described her symptoms. He put his ear to her chest and listened intently.

'I think she has an infection,' he said finally. 'From what I've read and what you've told me, she needs antibiotics.' He looked at Angel. 'Do we have any in the clinic?'

Angel shrugged. 'They'd be a long time out of date but we do have some. But they're back in the Village and we're miles from the nearest hospital and…'

Samuel looked at the floor. 'They're in my pocket,' he said.

Angel fished in his jacket and pulled out a small brown bottle that Carter remembered him taking from the clinic. She threw them onto the bed.

'I brought them with me. I was going to give them to him in exchange for taking you back with him. He gave me his word...'

Carter snatched them from the bed and looked at the faded label. 'How long has she been like this?' He looked at his brother in disgust – he couldn't decide what was worse, Samuel's plot to capture him or using the poor girl's illness to blackmail her father.

'About three weeks, maybe longer.' The woman put her lips to the girl's cheek and kissed her gently. 'We've been so worried about her. It gets better and then worse again. She just doesn't seem to fully recover.'

Carter opened the bottle and counted the tablets inside. 'Keep her in bed, give her plenty of fluids. Raise her head when she sleeps, that will help with the breathing. If you have any honey here, mix it with some warm water and give it to her regularly.' He handed the woman the tablets. 'These will have lost a lot of their potency so give her one every four hours until they're all gone. We will come back this way when we have the information we need from the Industry and I'll check on how she's doing.'

Gratitude spread across the woman's face. 'Thank you,' she said. 'Thank you.' She kissed Carter's cheek. 'My name is Frida,' she said. 'I hope you will find cause to come back here one day.'

Carter ran his hand along the edge of the bed and held the little girl's hand for a moment. 'You are welcome, Frida,' he said. 'Nothing we can do between us here can justify the lies and the deaths that have occurred in the last few days. We have lost good people, both of us, but we must get on with what we set out to do and stop what the Industry is doing. There have been too many lies and too much death already. We need to stop this. With or without your help. For your daughter's sake, and all of those living inside and outside of the Barricades, we must try to do this.'

Frida hesitated, before nodding slowly and motioning for them to exit the hut. She walked with them to the gatepost, handing Carter his rucksack that had been stored there since their arrival.

Frida placed the gun in Carter's hand but kept hold of the other end herself.

'You are a good woman.'

'And I believe you when you say you want to do this for everyone,' said Frida. 'If you leave now, I don't think they'll follow you.' Her hands slipped off the gun and Carter held it tightly.

'We will deal with Samuel, I promise you. Take care of Maya – and I am sorry for your loss,' he said, and beckoned the others with him as they trudged off into the darkness.

They travelled in near silence, night birds hooting and the trudge of boots on damp grass being the only sounds underscoring their journey.

When they were far enough away from the Village, Carter turned on Samuel, the gun still tight in his fist.

'I would never have betrayed you like that.'

Samuel kept his pace slow and steady. 'I didn't mean for it to happen,' he said, regretfully. 'I was just sick of you being the favourite.' He spat on the ground. 'You were always her favourite, even though you weren't here.'

'Jacinta doesn't have a favourite,' said Carter. 'She left me when I was just a child because she believed in something bigger than all of us. Your stupid, petty jealousy has just cost the lives of three good people.' He glared at Samuel, who cut a pathetic figure. 'We need you with us to get to the Community, but you should be ashamed of yourself. You are an embarrassment to our family.' His brother had no idea of how it had felt to have been left alone for years, believing his whole family had perished. He opened his mouth to rage even further at Samuel but decided against it and shook his head in silence.

The road wound upwards, the path getting steeper as they veered further east. After two or three hours on the path, they arrived at a cluster of burned-out houses that backed into the wooded copse that lay between them and Drakewater.

'We should rest,' said Carter. 'It's going to be difficult enough to find our way around the back of the plant in daylight. We can't do it at night and we need to sleep. These houses should give us enough shelter for tonight and we'll leave at daybreak. We continue this mission as we agreed.'

'It's a safe place,' said Samuel in a quiet voice, dropping back to walk with Angel and Elvira.

Angel scowled. 'Don't talk to me,' she said. 'I can't stand the sight of you.'

Exhausted they climbed into the attic rooms and barricaded the door shut with leftover furniture. As he closed his eyes, Carter could hear Angel gently sobbing and he reached out his hand to comfort her. She took it for a second and then rolled over, the only sound in the quiet house as he went to sleep being the sound of the wind outside and the creak of the old wooden floor.

The trek around the outside of Drakewater to the eastern edge wasn't difficult but it took longer than they had expected. They had left the house as the sun crept up between the trees, making their way through the thick wood, keeping the tall expanse of Drakewater to their right. As they got closer, the terrain got harder and steeper, veering upwards at times until they were almost climbing. As they moved through the woodland and into forest, they collected as much fruit and berries as they could carry, stuffing them into their pockets and eating as they went.

Below them, the land dropped away into a hazy blur of heather and bracken that trailed back into the clumps of woodland and forest. Between them and Drakewater, the fences were high but through them they could distinguish the outlines of hundreds of small grey-painted buildings with the large, funnel shaped dome in the centre.

'How are we going to know we're even close to the ventilation systems?' asked Angel, her face flushed from climbing. 'It seems like we could be here for years and still not find what we're looking for.'

Carter pulled the blueprint from inside his shirt. 'Couldn't risk him stealing it in the night,' he said, gesturing towards Samuel who sat on a rock, gazing out at the trees. 'But this is one of the reasons I needed him to come.' He whistled loudly. 'Hey, brother, come here and help us.'

'How can you even bear to speak to him after what he's done?' Angel closed her eyes. 'He makes me sick.'

'The power of a team is much stronger than individuals,' said Carter. 'We need his help to find the Community.'

As Samuel trudged over towards them, Carter unfolded the map and the four of them sat down on a mossy rock near a fence in a pale clearing that let shards of light through. He ran his finger down the right-hand side of the page.

'Are we anywhere near here?' Angel pointed to an outcrop of building plans on the schematic. They looked through the fence and back at the map. Carter untied Samuel's hands and held the gun and the blueprint in front of him.

'I'm giving you one last chance,' he said. 'Do not let me down. Now, are we anywhere near here?'

'Sort of,' said Samuel and pulled the map towards him. 'But this isn't the right set of fences. We need to look in this direction.' He pointed east but cast his eyes into the distance. 'Thank you for bringing me with you,' he said. 'Look, I'm really sor—'

'Save it,' said Carter. 'We can talk when this is done. But until then, we need to focus on getting the job done.'

Samuel sniffed. 'Fine. Then we need to head to the east. From what I know of the area, we're probably about twenty minutes away.'

They carried on walking, and at the junction of two paths carved deep in the forest, Samuel motioned for them to stop. Another long fence, wreathed in thick creepers wound its way across the path.

'We're here,' he said. 'The ventilation duct should be around here somewhere.'

They looked around in silence, eyes straining for any sign of their entrance to the Community.

'There, near that sycamore,' shouted Elvira in excitement. 'Look, there it is.' They all turned their heads and then looked back at the map.

'I think you're right,' said Angel. 'Let's go.'

The squat, unassuming buildings that housed the ventilation shafts corresponded exactly to the location on the blueprint and as they moved closer, the faint whirr of the machinery below was just about audible. The gates were tall but they had been able to scale them after several attempts, and one by one they dropped over the other side into thick patches of brambles.

'You can barely see the buildings from outside the walls,' said Elvira, breathless. 'It's well hidden.'

'It is,' said Carter, picking thorns from his fingers. 'It's in the heart of the forest, nowhere really close to the main plant.'

They cut their way through into a small, paved courtyard, the concrete cracked and broken with flowered weeds forcing their way towards the sunlight. The overgrowth on either side of the courtyard was untouched and wild.

'No one has been here since the Storms,' said Angel. 'At least we know they're not expecting us.'

Underneath the scramble of ivy that covered them, the walls of the building were smooth and featureless, fashioned from some sort of metal that felt and looked impenetrable.

Carter ran his hands over the surface. 'Look for any cracks or spaces that might indicate a door,' he said. 'Anything that's different or out of place.'

They inched their way across the building for hours, sweat pouring from their foreheads, working under each tendril and thick stem of weed. The metal glinted in the sun, reflecting hot rays back at them as they toiled until Elvira, scrabbling across the floor, eventually yelled, 'It's here, this is it! I knew it would be lower down!'

Between them, they pulled away the plant growth until a small square groove cut into the metal walls, less than a metre across, revealed itself at floor level. Samuel kicked at the door then tried to smash at it with a rock.

'We're never going to open that,' he said. 'It's impossible.'

Elvira beamed. 'No, it's not,' she said, pulling the plastic card from her pocket. 'Jacques said it was the key to everything.' She swiped the plastic gently across a keypad with a flashing red light in the corner of the door and it groaned open. Smiling, she handed it to Carter who pushed it deep into his pocket.

'After all these years it still works?' said Angel as they crawled through into a long, dark hallway. Carter pulled out a large candle from his bag, lit it and shone it around the room.

'The Industry created things to work for ever,' said Elvira. 'Although this door wasn't originally theirs and this was never a formal entrance – you can see that by the blueprint – this was just a building they recommissioned to manage the secondary ventilation. They will have made sure they updated their security.'

A low rumble came from underneath the floor, making them all jump; but it stopped as quickly as it started. Along the floor of the corridor room, on either side, were a series of twenty or so long metal grates that each led into a deep shaft that disappeared downwards into darkness. His heart sank as Angel voiced the question he was asking himself.

'How do we know which one to choose?'

He walked the length of the room and then back again, talking aloud. 'Each one must ventilate a different area of the Catacombs but they all lead back here. He placed the blueprint on the floor and stepped backwards, turned it around and looked at it sideways on.

'How did this room not get flooded and drown everyone down there?' said Angel.

Elvira pointed to the map. 'We're on the very edge here,' she said. 'Remember how far we've come outside the immediate area surrounding the Community? This is much higher ground. The main ventilation goes through the central pipe here, which leads through to the domed area of Drakewater. That's so secure that nothing can penetrate it. These shafts are for the outlying Catacombs – they were barely used until after the water subsided. Even at its highest point, the water would probably not have come this far.'

Carter rearranged the blueprint and walked the length of the room again.

'What are you doing?' said Angel, examining each of the grates in turn.

'He's trying to work out which one is going to take us closest to the Control Room, where the machine that runs the Model is stored,' said Elvira. 'If we can get into the Control Room we might be able to find out how to get to Chamber One.'

'All without the Industry noticing?' Samuel shook his head. 'I thought there were hundreds of guards down there.'

'There are,' said Elvira. 'But I can show you how to get through without being noticed. I built the tunnels that connect all this together. I know the way.'

She chose the shaft at the far end of the room and they lowered themselves inside, Carter first, Elvira, then Angel and Samuel. The edges were smooth to the touch and dangerously slippery; there was no way of going back up once they had started to descend.

'Spread your arms and legs wide,' said Carter, 'and move slowly. It's very steep.'

'It's going to get steep at points,' said Elvira, 'but if my memory is correct, we should be able to move out into a service shaft in an hour, which means there may be a ladder or something more stable.'

Carter turned to Elvira. 'I know this will be more demanding for you than it will be for us – physically and emotionally – but if you have any problems, just let us know, okay?'

She nodded. 'I know I'm right about the service tunnel,' she said, gritting her teeth hard. 'And I'm sure I can do this for an hour, even though my limbs really aren't long enough. You don't need to sorry about me.'

'And we need to be quiet,' added Carter. 'Who knows how far sound carries through here.'

Moving through the shafts was painful, hot work and they rested as often as they could, trying to time their breaks when the pipes levelled out and became almost horizontal so that they could crouch without fear of falling downwards. After almost two hours, they were all exhausted.

'I don't know how much further I can go,' said Elvira, breathless. 'My arms hurt too much – at points they barely reach the sides.' She laid herself flat on the cool surface and closed her eyes.

Angel looked at Carter and Samuel. 'What do you think?' she whispered. 'Could we leave her here? Come back to pick her up once we're done down there?'

Carter shook his head. 'You know what might happen to us and then she'd be stuck here to starve to death if she was alone. There's no way we can leave her. We have to take her with us now, there's no going back.'

'I'd like to go upfront,' said Elvira as they set off. 'Knowing what's ahead makes it easier for me to manage my pace and balance. Are you okay with that?'

'I guess so,' said Angel, 'if you're sure.'

'I'm sure.'

'Then let's go,' said Carter. 'We need to make sure that we get level with the Catacombs during the shift change, and have built in enough time to rest and eat.'

As they crawled downwards through the sloping shaft, the heat began to intensify – only abating when the occasional draft of cool air drifted through the ventilation system. Sweat poured from Carter's forehead in the darkness as they moved forwards, feeling the way with their hands in the darkness. He could smell Samuel in the hot darkness, breathing heavily behind them.

'The tunnel splits here.' Elvira moved her body aside so that they could all feel the outlines of the openings in front of them. 'We need to get to the bottom and start looking for the original set of ventilation tunnels – those that existed in the early days – they run to the old part of the Catacombs. The part they used to call The Ship.'

'The one on the left slopes downwards more gradually,' said Carter. 'But it's still pretty steep. Wait a minute…' He felt down for his shoe, picked out a small stone that had become dislodged in the sole and then threw it into the shaft. There was a clattering sound for a while, then silence, then a final thud.

'Sounds like there's a fairly big drop there,' said Samuel. 'It would be okay if we were able to keep our balance against the sides but it feels like tougher work than we can manage.'

Elvira shook her head.

'The other tunnel has a sort of ladder,' said Angel. 'Come.'

Carefully, Carter felt around the edge of the tunnel. It curved around to the right and then disappeared into a hole directly downwards. He lowered his body slowly into the shaft, touching each rung gingerly with his feet as he went, shining a candle into the space.

'There are cabling rungs on each side,' said Elvira. 'Not exactly a ladder, but something to hold onto. These ones here are not too far apart; we should be able to make it here. I can't tell how deep this goes but it joins back up with the air ducts at the bottom.'

'Sounds like the best option,' said Samuel and Angel shot him a glance. He hung his head downwards again and closed his lips together tightly.

'I'd like to go first,' said Elvira, pushing her way past Angel. 'If I can't reach then I can let you know, rather than get left behind.' She waited until Carter pulled himself back up onto the flat surface and then snaked her small body into the hole. Curling the one finger on her right hand into a hook shape, she started downwards moving hand over foot quickly like a tree creature.

'This is much easier,' she said cheerfully, her voice rising up from the shaft in waves.

'We'd better get down there quick,' said Carter with smile, 'or she'll have taken on the might of the Industry alone without us. Elvira, wait!' He felt Angel climbing behind him.

They continued down the rungs in single file, until the silence was broken by a cracking sound and then a single, piercing scream.

'Elvira!' Samuel scrambled past him and downwards. Elvira was beneath them, dangling precariously in the shaft, holding on with the one remaining finger on her right hand, the elbow of her other hand balanced against. He could hear her feet scrabbling for purchase against the side of the tunnel.

'Hold tight,' said Samuel, grabbing at her arm. 'I'll pull you up,'

'My feet slipped,' she said desperately, breathing heavily. 'I smashed my good hand on the side of the tunnel. Help me, I can't hold on any longer.'

'What's happened?' whispered Angel loudly. 'What can I do?'

'Hold on, Elvira,' said Carter, his voicing hiding his panic as he watched her finger peel away from the rung. 'Try to bring your other arm up.'

'I can't hold her,' said Samuel, desperately. 'I'm losing my grip.' His face contorted in stress. He pulled at her clothes and forced his feet into the sides of the shaft but it was no use.

'I'll be quiet,' whispered Elvira. 'I'm sorry.'

The ripping sound of her jacket and a quiet sigh were the last they heard of Elvira as she dropped downwards into the shaft. It seemed like several seconds before they heard her body hit the floor of the tunnel in a sick thump. Angel put one hand over her mouth to stop herself from screaming and Carter felt his stomach turn sour.

'We can help her,' said Angel, 'maybe she's still alive.'

Carter nodded. 'Let's go quickly,' he said. 'We need to keep moving. It's the only way we'll know for sure.'

Chapter Twenty-Three

The Decision

Alice

Joseph Warren looked a couple of years younger than his brother, but he had the same white-blonde hair – although his was long and tied back in a loose ponytail. Alice wasn't sure whether it was this, or the three-quarter length multi-coloured trousers that he wore, that gave him the appearance of someone who'd spent the best part of the day on a surfboard.

'Dude, what the hell happened to you?' he exclaimed, shaking his head back and forth. 'What's with the sack cloth?'

Richard grinned, dusting down his trousers. 'They make you dress for dinner in there,' he said. 'You like?'

Joe shook his head again in disbelief and looked Alice up and down with disdain. 'Is she one of them?'

'She is, but she's okay. She's in a bit of trouble herself. So, what's new?'

The rest of the people of the township took turns welcoming Alice with thinly veiled suspicion and bear-hugging Richard until he could hardly breathe. They melted back into their houses, carrying piles of wood, building supplies, books and cans of food. Others continued to repair roofs and fences or dig the gardens. The walls inside the houses were smoke drenched and filthy with insects crawling across every surface.

In contrast to the pristine cleanliness of the Ship and the reconditioned houses of the Community, the Township made her skin itch constantly. But it was alive and vibrant with children playing, couples singing and a delighted sense of wonder on the weather-beaten faces of the young and the old. As they walked through the Township, the smells and sounds of both wilderness and industry combined into something real, something almost tangible – like the feeling she used to get when the seasons changed. The clinical, stale smell that she had become used to, even topside, had disappeared. The thought of going back sent a stagnant chill into her heart.

Joe pulled a crate full of bottles across to the bench they were sat on. Alice sat on a small stool opposite them, watching the strange young man with the kind face and bright eyes. Richard took a swig of a dark-brown liquid.

'Is that beer?' said Alice. 'Real beer?'

'Sure is,' said Richard and passed a bottle from Joe. 'Want to try some? I bet you've never even tasted alcohol.'

'I have, actually,' said Alice, thinking back to the vodka Hutchinson had forced her to drink. 'But I'd rather not think about that.'

'Sad news first,' said Joe, opening himself a bottle. 'Three of our people are dead.' Jason, Mark and Clara.'

'Let me guess,' said Richard. 'They were gunned down by those animals behind the metal fence.'

'How did you know that?' Joe's eyes were wide. 'Were you there? We went to find you and…'

'I wasn't there,' said Richard, taking a gulp of beer. 'But I heard all about it. I knew it would be you guys coming for me. When Barnes described Clara's outlandish taste in clothes and Jason's New York Yankees cap, I knew it would be them. No one else would be brave enough – or stupid enough to come anywhere close. They said that one or two may have got away – I desperately hoped that was you.'

Alice shook her head. 'You heard Barnes talking about it?' she said. 'She did this?'

Richard knocked back the bottle and handed the empty back to Joe. 'I heard her talking to Quinn and Izzy about it just after it happened. Plus, she told Filip everything,' he said. 'But the worst is yet to come, isn't it Joe?'

'I guess,' said Joe with solemnity. 'I don't even know which bit of this is the worst.'

Richard but his arm on his shoulder. 'Tell us,' he said. 'Tell us everything.'

Joe hesitated and grabbed himself another bottle. 'We wanted to find out where you were – to try and make peace with them. Three separate times. The first time we got close enough, they shot Jason as he approached. He only wanted to try to find out where you were but the minute he called out, one of them shot him point-blank. Clara was a way back and took a graze to the arm but she made it back here okay – just a scrape really. She was lucky.'

'She's a fighter,' said Richard and put his arm around his brother. 'I'm really sorry about Jason. That must have been hard. Were you two still…?'

'Together?' said Joe, taking the bottle back from Richard. 'Yes. The only good thing is that Clara said it was quick. We never imagined they would be so completely hostile.'

'What made you go so close to the Barricades? Didn't you know they were armed?'

Joe shrugged. 'We just naively assumed they'd be like us. There was one girl by the fence – we'd watched her before, from a distance; she seemed kind of nice. She was really good with one of the boys there; he always seemed upset. Clara said that when they shot Jason it was just one sentry and the girl. When Jason reached out to them and was killed, the girl was really distressed and starting shouting and screaming about how it wasn't right and they were murderers and how Jason only wanted to make contact. I think she was pretty shocked. Clara had to run; she was so brave.'

'Kelly,' whispered Alice. 'She knew that it wasn't an attack.'

Richard nodded. 'But having an apparent threat on the outside is a great justification for the Industry. Which is why they made the attack public.' He looked around for another beer. 'And it made what came next, well, all the more chilling.'

Joe rubbed his forehead. 'Clara went back shortly afterwards, when it was just the same girl and the young boy there. We thought it would be okay.'

Richard gulped at the bottle. 'I'm assuming our people were all completely unarmed?'

'Totally,' said Joe, handing him a can. 'We don't even have any weapons here. Unless you count that silver-plated knife set you pinched from John Lewis.'

Richard laughed loudly, genuinely, in a way Alice hadn't seen him do before. He held his stomach and made a deep chuckling sound, dimples appearing in his cheeks and a wicked twinkle in his eyes. He reminded her of her father and the way he'd smile when they'd played together for hours in the garden. Richard stopped laughing when he saw the look of seriousness in Joe's eyes.

'Dude, I can't believe you made it out of there. They're crazy,' he said, then looked at Alice briefly. 'I'm sorry, no offence, but we've seen things. There's kids running all over the place with guns.'

'Just rats,' said Alice. 'They were killing vermin. And they don't do that any more.'

'So, I guess that the nice girl was just vermin too?' said Joe.

Richard narrowed his eyes. 'Tell her,' he said. 'Tell her what her new family are really like.'

'What do you mean?' Alice looked at him darkly and picked up the can, tossing it from hand to hand. The smell of beer was revolting and appealing all at once.

Richard rubbed his eyes with his hands. 'Joe. Tell us.'

Joe screwed up his face. 'It's pretty sick, man,' he said.

'Tell us!'

'When Clara decided to go back alone, to talk to the nice girl – Kelly, you called her? – a few of us went up to the rocks to try and get a better view. I found some pretty cool binoculars in this store a couple of miles away so they could check out what's going on. Anyway, as we're watching, there's Kelly talking to this boy and they're smiling. There wasn't anyone else in sight and they started calling to Clara, so Clara decided to go in and talk to them, you know, to find out if they know where you are. She wouldn't give up on you.

'Then, as they're approaching, the girl starts waving to her and everything and it's all okay, and before we knew it – bang – Clara's dead too. Shot in the head. But not by the girl, Kelly, at the fence. It was someone else. From out of nowhere there's this other kid all dressed up in military gear and she kills Clara. Then there's some shouting from the Kelly at the fence and bang: the kid pops her as well. We saw it all.'

'Kelly,' said Alice slowly. 'The boy, shot her?' She turned to Richard. 'Marcus shot her?'

Joe shook his head, then nodded. 'No. It was a girl – just a little kid – about ten or eleven.'

Izzy, Richard mouthed, as Alice looked shell-shocked.

'Short hair, blonde. She came from nowhere and shot Clara. Kelly was really, really mad that the kid shot Clara and she started shouting again so the kid killed her too. She went to gun the boy as well, only he threw himself down on the floor, hands in the air, crying and everything, hugging the dead girl. The kid – Izzy you say? – held the barrel to his head for a while but then she spared him – dunno why – and then she ran off. And she laughed – this sick nasty laugh. We stayed for a while – we were in shock – and then a load of guards arrived, too many to count. We were about to leave when they shot up into the bushes. They caught Mark in the leg and he bled out.'

Alice shook her head. Izzy. Marcus had been telling the truth about her having been there. Then she remembered the Watchers firing long shots out into the Deadlands just after Kelly's death and the thump of the eagle as it hit the ground.

She stood up slowly. 'I think I'm going to throw up,' she said, and disappeared behind one of the houses. The sky swirled red and blue and black around her as she felt her stomach heaving back everything she had eaten that day and everything she had known the day before. She thought of Izzy, so desperate to please Barnes and then Marcus who had tried so desperately to tell her, who had been silenced all too easily. She made her way slowly back to where the brothers were barefoot, quietly kicking a ball back and forth in the grass, the shush of leather against skin reminding her of better summer days in the garden with her father and Charlie Davenport.

'Why?' she said.

The boys stopped playing and the ball ticked away into the bushes. 'Why Kelly?'

Joe handed his brother another beer. 'I can leave you guys to it, if you'd prefer?' he said, picking up the ball.

'No, you can stay,' said Richard. 'I'll only end up telling you later anyway.' He turned to Alice. 'What would *you* have done if Kelly had told you that the Industry were killing unarmed outsiders who just wanted to make contact? It would have threatened everything Barnes is trying to create. Killing one of your own to save the sanctity of the Community – sounds like quite a Contribution to me. Kelly wanted to leave, didn't she?'

'Yes,' Alice faltered. 'She wanted to go to Spain.' The booming inside her head got louder and then quieter as she stumbled over her words.

'The world they are creating in there is some sick experiment. Everyone has been conditioned to accept that there's nothing left outside and that their way is the only way. Barnes, Filip, you – you'd all become tiny fish in the world's biggest pond. Kelly had to be silenced and so did Marcus.'

'But why would Izzy do that?'

'Because Barnes told her to after Kelly had mentioned to Quinn that the people on the outside were friendly and that she wanted to leave. Izzy saw her chance and took it. The only way to get rid of one of the original Scouts was to make it look like an accident. There was no way they could admit to having made a mistake with someone like Kelly. And then there was the baby...'

Alice shook her head in disbelief. 'She was *pregnant*,' she said, cradling her stomach. 'She hadn't done anything wrong.'

Richard shrugged his shoulders. 'Depends how you think,' he said. 'From what I've heard, unless your babies are perfect, then you've not done a good enough job. It seems like Kelly's baby was, well…' He hesitated uncomfortably. 'Barnes didn't think it was forming right.'

Alice touched her own stomach. 'But why?' she said. 'What happened to it?'

Richard shook his head. 'The precious doctor was trialling various kinds of drugs on Kelly – she'd give Quinn medication to put into her food and then go around there at night when Kelly was asleep and inject her with her experimental concoctions so half the time she didn't even know. She used all sorts – those to help conception, support foetal development and anything else she cooked up in her lab. Kelly suspected she was interfering with her pregnancy, which was the final reason she needed to try to escape.' He clenched his fingers tightly. 'But she's not a real doctor, Alice. The drugs she's dispensing – god knows what they're doing to the babies. She's just playing at being a scientist. And she's stringing others along with her. I mean, look at Izzy. She's what, eleven?'

Alive looked up at the clouds. 'Izzy's just a child,' she said, her voice breaking. 'How could she have become so… so… corrupted?'

'She is a child. But not a normal child. She's had a very different upbringing. She's been taught to shoot since she was six years old and is conditioned to believe that anyone outside of the Industry is evil. It's not entirely her fault.' Richard put his arm on Alice's shoulder. 'And it's not your fault either.'

'Barnes has to be stopped.'

'Exactly. But you need others you can trust. You can't do this on your own.'

'Filip knew all about this.' Alice felt her skin prickle as tiny drops of rain fell from the sky. Where had Filip been when the first shooting had occurred? What was it Wilson had said about him needing to go and get some extra practice at the range? Did that mean Wilson knew too? She shivered uncontrollably.

Joe put a filthy jacket around her shoulders that smelled sourly of mould and damp.

Richard shrugged. 'I'm sorry, Alice. Like I said, he's very aligned to Barnes's way of thinking and he's keen for the power too. Kunstein – from what I've seen of her, she seems pretty decent if a little bit weird. Marcus knew – Barnes knows he saw everything – that's why they had to get rid of him, before he said anything to you.' He took a deep breath. 'When she was taking my samples for insemination she got a call from Filip to say that the deed had been done. She didn't even flinch.' He put his head in his hands.

Joe looked at him incredulous. 'Hey, hang on a second – She did *what?*'

Richard nodded grimly. 'Yup. They took my *sperm*. Gross, isn't it?'

Joe looked shell-shocked. 'Like, how, man? That's some sick stuff they got going on in there. Do you know who they're going to use it with?'

Richard gritted his teeth. 'I have my suspicions,' he said, glancing at Alice but her mind was elsewhere.

'I can't believe Izzy would do something like that,' said Alice, grimly. Her heart sank at the thought of what she knew had to come next.

'So *now* do you believe me?' said Richard.

'I must tell Kunstein. This can't go on.' The coldness of the rain soaked through to Alice's bones.

'I don't think that's wise. You need to stay here with us where we can keep you safe.'

'And let everyone else become a part of this? I can't stay.' Alice shook her head decisively. 'There's no way I can let them get away with this – no decent person would.' She felt her hands shaking in rage.

'I am going back there and I *will* change what they're doing.' Richard smiled at her gently. 'You're a good person, Alice,' he said. 'But you're fifteen years old and…'

'If I'm old enough to have a baby,' said Alice determined, 'then I'm old enough to change the world. Things haven't felt right since we came above ground – in my heart I knew that. I have to tell Kunstein the truth and stop what Barnes is doing.'

You need to think about what's right for you,' said Richard, putting his arm on her shoulder. 'But first we go inside, eat some proper food and rest. Then we can talk about what happens next.'

Joe led them inside a small cottage that had been patched together on the outside using all kinds of different materials to make it watertight and storm resistant, but still there were damp stains down the walls and the rain trickled in. Inside there were brightly coloured paintings, two guitars and a long sofa that ran the length of the entire front room.

'Jason and me dragged this all the way back from the town – it took two days to get it all the way here.' Joe smiled and slapped the back of it, tiny particles of dust rising in the air and catching the light. 'We carried it halfway, slept on it and then carried it again. I never even wanted to bring it back. I didn't think we would manage it but Jason wouldn't let up…'

He moved two surfboards out of the way so that Alice could sit down. 'I don't use them,' he said. 'They're for decoration. They're good ones, really good ones. Way better than mine ever were. Reminds me of when we used to go down to Cornwall, you know, before…'

'It looks great in here,' said Richard, looking around. 'You've been busy while I've been gone. Do you think that there's space for a couple more in here, until I fix myself up with something?'

Joe grinned. 'Course there is, dude. I wouldn't have you stay anywhere else. And your friend is welcome too.'

Alice sat down in the space where the surfboards used to be. 'I can't stay,' she said. 'I have to get back to the Community and sort this all out. We can't build anything new on these lies and deceit. We have to start again.' She folded her hands over her stomach. 'There are consequences to what happened and I need to deal with them.'

'You really want to go back in there? You think you can sort this out alone? Look what they did to Kelly.'

'That life, that problem, is one that I, amongst others, have created,' said Alice. 'People need to know what's out here – and more importantly *who's* out here. That not everyone is a threat and that we can work at building relationships with whoever else has survived the Storms. And there are consequences to what Barnes and Izzy have done.'

'Even so, the principles are fundamentally flawed,' said Richard. 'They're denying everything it means to be human – destroying music and art, denying cultures to coexist, retelling the history of how everything went wrong. It's just not right.'

Alice looked down at her hands. 'How do we make the world a different place if we don't start from scratch?' she said. 'How do we make sure that it doesn't turn out the same way?'

'There's different good and different bad,' said Richard. 'You just need to choose which way it's going to go.'

'I know,' said Alice. 'And I have to go back to make that happen.'

'*Veritas liberabit vos*,' said Joe, smiling.

'What does that mean?' said Alice.

Richard grabbed her hand and pulled her outside and towards the village. 'Come with me,' he said. 'We'll be five minutes,' he called to his brother.

As they walked down one of the carefully weeded paths, through a small alleyway, Richard stopped them at an old building with 'Woodford Hatch High School' in large block letters on a battered sign in front.

'Now look closer,' he said, pointing up the carved stone frontage of the school. Alice scanned the walls and then, over the arch of the main door, she saw it straight away.

'*Veritas liberabit vos*,' she said, slowly.

'We found the school motto when we decided to settle here,' said Richard. 'It means "the truth will set you free".'

Back at the house, when Joe and Richard brought out the plates, steaming with hot chicken and potatoes, Alice felt the pit of her stomach ache desperately. The meat was so tender and tasted sweet and delicious. Her mouth watered as she chewed slowly, releasing the incredible flavours.

'Where did you get this?' she said, savouring every second. 'I can't believe that this is real chicken.'

'Delicious, isn't it?' said Joe. 'We don't have it often, but when we do... damn, it makes me happy!' He slapped his thigh and laughed, turning to Richard.

'I'm so glad you're back,' he said. 'You'll never know how much I missed you.'

He reached up onto a shelf and pulled down a battered guitar, holding it close to his body like a lover and plucked the strings individually, coaxing into tune.

'Play something,' said Richard. 'Anything. I haven't heard music in so long I felt like I was going to die.'

Joe strummed a few chords and Alice let her eyes gently close. The chords gave way to individual notes that blended beautifully together, arpeggios upwards and downwards, and Joe's voice, husky and doleful made its way above the sound of the guitar. The words were hazy and blistered in her mind, and it made her feel a nostalgic ache for something she had never really known.

The next morning, a thin drizzle of rain accompanied Alice and Richard on their journey back to the Community – a misty film that rose up from the ground with a dewy, earthy smell. It stayed with them for most of the morning until just before midday when the sun burned through the clouds and replaced the dampness with a sharp, bright glare.

'I know what you have to do,' he said. 'And I will come back with you – just as far as the Barricades. But I won't come in. I can't go back in there. My place is here with my brother and the people who have become like a family to me. I will never belong in there. But if you want to come back to the Township, there will always be a home for you here.'

'Thank you,' said Alice. 'But first, before I decide what to do with myself—' she shook her head '—with myself and my baby, I need to let Kunstein know what's been going on. If Wilson has anything to do with what Barnes and Izzy have done then he has to be removed too. Kunstein will know what to do.'

She breathed in deeply as they walked through the forest. Bluebells clustered in the corners, fighting for the light with the heavy fronds of dark-green ferns that curtained the path in front of them.

'Do you wish you never came?' said Richard. 'That you never knew any of this?'

'No,' said Alice. 'Not for one second.'

'But I might not have been telling you the truth.'

'But I had to know.' said Alice, in a quiet voice. 'I had to find out for myself.'

As they came through the final row of thick conifers, the scrub of the plain between the Deadlands and the Barricade came into view.

'Well,' said Alice, her hands hot with pearls of sweat, 'I guess it's just goodbye for now.'

'Whatever you decide to do, I will be thinking of you,' said Richard. 'Whether you come back, or you stay – I mean that sincerely. You know where we are. We will always be here for you.'

'I know that,' said Alice, nodding. 'And thank you. For telling me. As hard as this will be, I know it's the right thing to do.' She watched the last rays of the sun fall across the valley and felt their warmth on her skin.

'Every action we take leads us closer to what would have happened anyway. If I hadn't gone back to the tower after the Storms then...'

'Why did you go back there?'

'I guess it was fate. Or something like that.'

She turned to face him. 'I have to go now,' she said. 'But we will see each other again, I promise.' She hugged him briefly. 'You have to promise *me* something now.'

'Anything.'

'That you will go back to the Township now,' she said. 'Don't watch me leave. And don't say another word.'

As she crawled carefully across the bare scrubby grass, Alice kept her eye distinctly on the glint of the Barricade. She had been gone for only just over twenty-four hours but the whole world of the Community seemed so distant and alien to her. She hoped Jacques had managed to divert any attention away from her absence – by previous experience, she had at least a few more hours before Filip and Izzy would return from the Ship.

'It's going to be okay,' she whispered to the growing life inside of her. 'It's going to be okay.'

Most of the verdant tree cover had been razed and there was little to shield her shape as she edged towards the Barricade – but if she could make it to the gate while Jacques was on shift, she could slip through and be back at the house on Morristown Row before lunchtime. She felt a shiver of nervous anticipation course through her and, as she got closer, she could see the shape of Jacques on the scaffold, looking directly at her. A sense of relief washed over her but, as she raised her hand to wave at him, she saw there were more, familiar outline shapes of people sat on the Watcher posts next to him with their guns trained on her.

Her heart sank with a sick, terrified thump and she raised her hands slowly, waving to them and calling their names. She could see that Jacques was crying – big heavy tears that streamed down his face.

'Filip, Kunstein, Barnes, Quinn – it's me, Alice.' She smiled at them weakly but not one of them smiled back. 'I need to talk to you all, just let me back in.'

Quinn disappeared from her post and the click of the entry gate sounded. As the door swung open, she reached out and grabbed Alice, pulling her roughly back into the Community.

'Got her, Filip,' she said, lashing Alice's arms together with plastic rope.

'Don't,' said Alice, 'that hurts... I...'

Barnes put her hand over Alice's mouth. 'Save it,' she said, pulling a hypodermic from her pocket and injecting her in the shoulder. 'You can say whatever it is you need to when we're all back in the Control Room.'

'Easy with her,' said Filip softly. 'Until we know how much she knows.'

And, with that, the sun disappeared behind a cloud and everything in Alice's world turned to the darkest shade of black.

Chapter Twenty-Four

The Discovery

Carter

After another five minutes or so of climbing, they found Elvira's body at the base of the service shaft. She had landed on her side, her head angled cradled in her arms. Carter reached out to her.

'She still has a pulse,' she said. 'It's faint, but there's a pulse.'

They looked at each other in silence.

'What do we do?' said Angel.

'We can't leave her here,' said Carter, examining her injuries. 'She needs medical attention, herbs, daylight – we need to put her legs in splints and get her back to the clinic.'

The shaft was quiet and Samuel looked deep into Carter's eyes.

'No one gets left behind,' Samuel said without hesitation, and gently picked up her tiny, broken body. 'There's going to be more chance to save her up there than there is down here.'

Using some of the clothing in his rucksack, they strapped her body to his back. 'You need to carry on,' he said. 'And I need to do this. For her. I'll take her back to the surface.'

'Samuel, wait,' said Angel. 'How will you get out? Carter, do you still have the key?'

Carter pulled the piece of plastic from his pocket and handed it to Samuel.

'No – you keep it,' he said, pushing it back to Carter. 'I'll find a way out and I'm the strongest one here. I can carry her weight and force anything open that I need to.'

Angel looked at Carter. 'He's right,' she said. 'We should let him go.'

She handed him a candle and, without any further words passing between them, Samuel began to climb back up the shaft, the regular thump of his hands and feet hitting the sides of the metal beating a regular rhythm.

Carter placed his hand over Angel's.

'How did she manage not to scream or call out?' said Angel finally, wiping away the tears from her eye.

'Because she knew it could endanger us,' said Carter, shaking his head in disbelief. 'Because she was prepared to die for this.'

They sat by together for a short while in a stunned silence before Carter took the last small candle from his bag and shone it onto the blueprint.

'This should give us enough light until we get into the Catacombs. A couple more miles and we should be able to get back into the ventilation shafts that run around the edges of the Catacombs.'

The base of the shaft opened out into a small tunnel, almost wide enough to walk upright. They moved as quickly as they could, holding hands for comfort and mapping their way on the blueprint. After a couple of hours, they reached a small grille in the side of the wall.

'This is it,' said Carter. 'We have to be absolutely silent from here onwards.' He pulled open the vent and they squeezed through, back into the same square metal duct structures they had crawled through at the outset. On hands and knees, they moved forwards, the air becoming cooler and filled with scents that were terrifyingly familiar to Carter. Chemical smells that oozed through the pores of his skin and reminded him of somewhere that he no longer called his home. He blew out the candle.

'There's light coming in here,' he whispered to Angel. 'We're getting very close.'

As they turned around a curve in the duct, streams of thin striped light cast beautiful arcs across the way in front of them. Ahead, on either side at roughly two metre intervals were slanted air vents that overlooked the chambers at the very edges of the Catacombs. Carter inched towards the first one, peering through into the dimly lit room.

'What can you see?' said Angel in a whisper. 'Is it the Control Room?'

'No,' Carter responded as quietly as he could. 'We're at the end of the Catacombs. The Control Room is much further up – and on a higher floor, I think. We're too far down. This is where they keep the frozen ones.'

As he squinted his eyes through the thin gaps of metal, he could just make out the shapes of a multi-rester against the wall, four bunks high, filled with bodies in sleep cases. Each was attached to a machine that flashed tiny green indicators.

'There must be hundreds of them,' said Angel. 'Thousands of people that they just don't want spoiling their perfect little constructed world.' She shivered. 'How much further?'

'We keep going until we get closer to the hub,' said Carter. 'Until it's safe for us to start looking for the Control Room.' He pulled out the blueprint again. 'It shouldn't be too far until we hit the centre of the Catacombs.'

As they crawled past the chambers, they peered inside one and watched the sleepers. Each face was barely visible through the sleepsuits in the eerily lit dimness. Carter shivered to think that just a few months ago he was one of them; locked up in a dreamless sleep, unable to wake until the Industry decided that his time was right.

They carried on crawling, past chambers, storerooms and labs. Many of the labs had only security lights on and were empty – others had the odd Industry technician poring over a microscope.

Then, into the tunnel came the sound of muffled voices from one of the rooms ahead. Carter turned to Angel and placed a finger to his lips and they shuffled further towards the grille that overlooked the room. A pale shaft of white light filtered into the duct and they pulled themselves towards the lattice, peering through carefully. Voices familiar to Carter pierced the quiet.

'You're ready then?'

'As ready as we can be.'

'We have two hours until I hand over to you both. It's going to be a tough job but I believe the right choice has been made.'

Carter recognised the first voice – Anaya Chess, the outgoing Controller General. But there were two others, a boy and a girl. The new Controller Generals. Two of them. He strained his eyes to look through the grille and he could just about make out the silhouettes of a couple reading a tablet on the other side of the room. Angel moved closer to him and the shuffling of her feet caught the attention of them both.

'What was that?' said the girl looking up into the grille. Carter pulled back sharply and moved his body out of sight, his head spinning at what he had seen.

'Probably just the vibrations of an excited crowd eager to see us take over,' said the boy, raising an eyebrow.

'It's been a very long time since we had joint Controller Generals,' said Chess. 'But you will make this work. Let's get started.'

Carter felt his heart beat fast and his breathing become shallow. There was no mistaking the voice of the girl; it was Elizabet, one of the Contenders he had trained with. But the boy? He edged his head to the side of the grille and watched as the two of them smiled and nodded at Chess.

He shook his head and swallowed deeply.

It was, without a doubt, his son, Ariel.

Carter leaned back against the wall of the air duct, his breathing shallow and his heart beating fast. The dark metal felt cool against his skin, although his face grew clammier the more he thought about what he'd seen in the room. A wave of relief crept over him before the disappointment took over; even though he hadn't believed what Saul had said, the sight of Ariel alive and well had reassured him. But as joint chief of the Industry? His heart sank again.

'That was your son, wasn't it?' said Angel, moving close to him. 'The likeness is, well, incredible. But who was the girl?'

'Someone I was competing against for the position of Controller General,' said Carter. 'Lily told me she'd dropped out, but I guess that was a lie too. Or maybe she was brought back in after I was declared dead. She was from before the Storms. She's vile. I don't know how Ariel got involved with her though – or how he became a Contender.'

'At least you've seen that he's still alive,' said Angel. 'We knew already that he wasn't sick but at least we know he hasn't been captured as some sort of revenge for your escape. We can find a way.'

Carter felt his hand warm against the cold metal of the gun in his pocket. 'But now things are more complicated. He's my son. I let his sister down – I can't let the Industry consume him.'

Angel held his shoulder tightly. 'We've come too far to let anything stand in our way,' she said. 'Remember what Jacinta said.

This is bigger than Ariel or either of us – whatever happens next, we have to think of what's best for the Community, the Village and the Township. Too many people's lives are depending on us. We will come back for Ariel, I promise you. But now we have to carry on with what we came here for.'

Carter pulled open the blueprint, his hands shaking, pointing to a circular reference. 'There's staircase mapped here at this corner. If we can just move out of this duct and into one of the rooms, we can use the stairs to get up to the Control Room. Everyone here uses the lift so we should be safe until we get there.'

'How are we supposed to find Chamber One?'

'We'll know when we do,' said Carter. 'I'm sure of it.'

The first two rooms they tried to exit through were electronically locked from the outside but the third opened easily, out into the corridor. The locked rooms were both electrical supply areas and Carter stuffed as much as he thought might be useful into the cloth bag, grabbing a handful of synthetic snacks from a bowl on the side counter.

'Try one of these,' he whispered to Angel. 'They used to be my favourite.'

She wrinkled her nose. 'That's disgusting,' she said. 'They make people eat this crap?'

'And they think they enjoy it,' said Carter as the climbed back into the vent to try the next room.

The third room was a chamber, similar to the ones they had seen but the bed inside was empty and the door stood slightly ajar. As Angel peered round the outside, she heard voices and they both backed into room and pushed the door until it was almost closed. Carter could feel his heart banging against his chest as the voices grew louder and stopped almost directly outside.

'They're going to be on soon,' said a deep, booming voice. 'Looking forward to hearing what they have to say.'

'It's going to be incredible,' said another. 'Better security, more structure and a plan to develop parts of the Deadlands – apparently there's some big water structure out there we can harness to get extra power. Might come in useful for the stuff they've got planned.'

'No kidding,' said the first voice. 'It's ambitious. Certainly transformational – anything outside these Barricades won't stand a chance.' They both laughed; deep, hearty laughs that made Carter shiver. He glanced at Angel as the sound of the voices echoed back down the other end of the corridor.

'You're right,' he whispered. 'This is our one chance to make sure that people understand what the Industry is all about and to make sure that we secure some sort of a future – whatever that looks like.'

The staircase at the end of the tunnel wasn't easy to find. Hidden beneath thick wooden panelling that slid across sideways, if they hadn't known for sure it had been there, they'd have missed it.

'This blueprint has been invaluable,' said Carter. 'But without Samuel and Elvira we'd have never have found our way through this place.'

He slid back the doorway and looked upwards. The steps spiralled upwards until they disappeared into the black vortex above them. They were at the very bottom of the stairwell, a small space edged with metal and wood panels, with thin, unlit corridors that ran behind the panelling and away into the darkness. The air coming down past the layers of the Catacombs was laced with the familiar smells of production – chicker, boeuf, fauclate, all of which made him feel sick. The floor was littered with old papers that lay coated in a thick layer of dust.

'Nobody has been up or down these stairs in years,' said Carter. 'This can't be used by the Industry now – they would never let it get this dirty. These must be the vents that Elvira was talking about, the ones from the old days.'

Carter looked along the lengths of the corridor. 'We need to go up,' he said, finally, 'but not too high. From what Elvira described, I think this is the right way.'

Angel combed through the dust. 'What's this?' She bent down and picked up a folded piece of paper that looked like a bird; wings of straight, yellowing pleats covered in writing, with bright vivid pictures. She opened it up and read from the text:

'Outside the Barricades there are animals of monstrous proportions that have been genetically altered by the waste that human civilisation that was left behind after the Storms. Those who have remained in this wasteland have become infected and dangerous – creating a real threat to our society. These creatures are not like normal people; they are abnormal and must therefore be destroyed.'

Carter took the paper out of her hand and turned it over. 'This is very early literature – it's ancient, look how the page has discoloured. And the pictures – these are just after the Storms happened.' He held his light over the wording and scrutinised it carefully. 'There's something else written here,' he said, his heart beating fast. 'Look.'

'The truth will set you free,' said Angel, picking out each word individually.

'Lucia said that to me,' said Carter, confused. 'When I first got released from the Catacombs. She came to find me, to warn me about what was happening and to get me to join with her and Isabella in the uprising. At the time I didn't know what she meant because it was in another language. But it was written on the wall in her room, too, underneath some paintings she had done.'

Angel smiled, her eye glistening in the torchlight. 'It's no coincidence,' she said. '*Veritas liberabit vos*? The truth will set you free? That's the motto of the Township – it has been since they first established themselves. The rumour is that they found it written on an old school sign when the waters first subsided at the first place they settled. They adopted it as their motto.'

Carter passed the piece of paper from one hand to the next. 'The truth will be more important to the people of the Community than they could ever imagine,' he said finally. 'Each and every one of them is living here believing that the Industry is doing everything to keep them safe while, in reality, they're being used.' He paused for a moment and looked at Angel. 'The truth will do more than set them free,' he whispered. 'It will let them live again.'

The steps were made of a soft metal that absorbed the sound of their footprints as they climbed. At regular intervals there was a gap in the stairway that led to a tiny panelled door, like the one that they had come through, that led to the next level of the Industry Headquarters.

'How far are we going?' said Angel, breathless. 'How do we know when to stop?'

Carter hiked the bag up over his shoulder and pulled the blueprint from his pocket. 'I'm hoping we'll know when we get there,' he said. 'But from what I can see here, if we keep going upwards, we should reach the Control Room in another ten to fifteen sections, maybe slightly less.'

They managed another three before they heard a low, humming noise interspersed with periodic, piercing beeps that were head-splittingly high. It came from above them and was accompanied by a string of sliver lights that illuminated the round staircase above them.

'What the hell is that?' said Angel, straining her voice to be heard above the noise.

'I don't know,' said Carter, looking up and down the stairs, 'but I think it's safe to say we've triggered some sort of security system coming to this level.'

'This floor is different,' said Angel, looking at the walls closely. 'There's no door on this side, it's not the same as the others.'

'We need to get out of here,' said Carter, 'as a matter of urgency.' He scanned the height of the stairway upwards and downwards, the blaring of the sirens seeming to increase in volume with every second. Somewhere, high above, he could hear the sound of shouting.

'Carter, what are we going to do?'

'Up or down?' he said, frantically watching the lights as they flashed. The shouting above them stopped.

'Quick!' said Angel. 'We need to move.'

Carter looked desperately around at the platform. 'The door is here,' he exclaimed, his fingers fumbling around the panelling. A door opened higher up in the shaft and a light shone downwards. They pressed their bodies tightly against the far wall, moving one of the panels slightly. 'The door is on the opposite side,' breathed Carter, his heart racing. He slid it across and they dived through into the openness of the corridor. Above them, the lights dimmed to a low frequency and the noise subsided.

'Security,' said Carter. 'We need to find another way to get up there but we can't stand here in this corridor. If the Industry believe someone has breached the perimeter then they'll send people out to find them.' He pulled open the blueprint, turned it upside down and scanned his eyes across it intently, before looking up at Angel, wide-eyed. 'This corridor doesn't even exist on the plan,' he said. 'What does that tell you?'

They pressed their bodies against the side of the tunnel and inched their way towards the end where a dim light flickered. Cables ran across the ceiling, leading the two or three doorways that stood ajar, rooms empty and stale.

'There's nothing here,' said Angel, disappointed. 'Nothing at all.'

'We need to find a way out of here,' said Carter, moving along the corridor. 'We can't go back up the stairs. There must be another way.' They crept further, the walls becoming slightly damp and, around the light, a thin moss had started to grow.

'It's colder here,' said Angel. 'This must be an older part of the structure.'

'It feels different,' said Carter, looking at the dim lights and signs of decay. 'Something is down here.'

As they neared the end of the corridor, Carter could just make out a glowing light that came from about halfway up the wall. The last door at the end of the corridor looked exactly the same as all the others, except that this one was bolted shut. A number one in the shape of a lightning strike had been carved into the wood. Dust had gathered around the edge of the doorframe and a low humming noise came from underneath. Angel pushed on the door but it was closed fast, metal strips surrounding edges that looked old and worn. The shape on the door pulsed virulently.

'Why is this one shut?' she said, trying to look underneath. A tiny sliver of pale light came from the room but there were no signs of movement.

'Can you see anything?' said Carter.

'Nothing. Do you think it could be...?' Angel stopped herself from saying the words.

'Chamber One?'

She nodded and stood up, looking around the edges of the door. On one side, a tiny electronic contact plate glistened in the dim light.

'Do you have the key card?' she said.

Gently stroking the surface across the contact plate, Carter's mouth felt unbelievably dry and his body shivered in the damp corridor. A click echoed through the corridor and, when he pushed the door, it moved slightly. He grabbed Angel's hand tightly and felt the cold metal of his gun in the other. Pulling it out in front of them, he widened the space so they could move through into the room, allowing his head to get an initial view of what was inside.

'You're not going to believe this,' he said to Angel, his hands trembling and his eyes, wide with shock. 'I think we've found exactly what we were looking for.'

Chapter Twenty-Five

The Secret

Alice

'How exactly did you get out?' Quinn's vice was sharp and cruel, through the haze of noise. Alice tried to move her arms but they were strapped down straight at her sides. When she opened her eyes, the light was bright, dazzling even, but she could just make out the outline of screens and flashing red and green: The Control Room.

Barnes paced back and forth in front of her and then turned on Quinn. 'I told you to keep an eye on her, to distance yourself so that you could be objective. She changed the moment she came above ground. You were supposed to be training her. Did you not see this coming?'

Quinn flared back at her, pale white cheeks streaking red. 'I was the one who first warned you – and if you're looking for someone to blame, then her boyfriend might be a good place to start.'

'We're all to blame,' aid Filip quietly, calming them. 'We should have taken action sooner, Quinn was right.'

'Let me go,' she shouted, moving her arms and feeling the room spin around her. 'We need to talk about what's outside the Barricades. I know Izzy killed Kelly. I know what she did for you, Barnes. But I came back here.' She could feel Filip's breath near the back of her head. 'I didn't stay out there, I came back so we could talk about this. So we could make things right.'

Barnes scoffed in derision. 'You're delusional. Be very careful with what you're saying, Davenport. You came back here because you were afraid. You'd never have survived out there alone.'

'Filip,' breathed Alice, exhausted. 'Tell her to let me go. That's not why I came back. She made Izzy kill Kelly.'

'Stop whining, Alice.' His voice from behind her sounded cold, indifferent and not even angry. 'And tell me where Richard is. I am assuming that he forced you to do this and that this was his idea. Tell us how you escaped from him and managed to make your way back home to us. Tell us how he made you do it.'

Alice twisted her neck around. She could just make out the shapes of Filip, Wilson and Kunstein behind her. Quinn stood at the front, eyes blazing.

'Tell us where Richard is,' she said, echoing Filip. 'We need to know immediately. It's for his own good.'

'He's gone back to his people,' said Alice, croakily. Suddenly her mouth felt dry and parched and the brightness of the lights were hurting her eyes. 'Why did you do it, Barnes? And why do you have me tied down here?' she demanded. 'I'm not the one who's done anything wrong.'

'Oh, but Alice you have,' said Quinn. 'You've put the whole Community in danger by going out there into the Deadlands. You more than anyone should know that.'

'It's not like that and you know it,' said Alice. 'The people out there aren't looking to create conflict with us. We—' she turned towards Barnes '—*you* have murdered them.'

'Murder is a strong word, Alice, you should be very careful of who you splutter your accusations towards.' Barnes moved close to Alice's face, her teeth gleaming. 'From what you seem to be saying it was the girl in your charge who committed the crime.'

Alice closed her eyes to stop the room from spinning. Her own voice sounded like it was thousands of miles away. She tried to speak louder. 'Those people just want to be able to live in peace – they were only coming to look for Richard. We had absolutely no right to attack them.'

'From what I understand, their idea of living is nothing like ours,' said Quinn. 'The life they have chosen is not all that different to what almost destroyed our civilisation in the first place. I'm not sure we can tolerate their presence this close to our Community. They pose too much of a threat. And now they know too much about us and what we are doing.' The tone in her voice had changed; it sounded almost mechanical.

'Too much of a threat to what?' said Alice. 'We should help them, collaborate with them maybe. We could all learn things.' She struggled under her restraints. 'Filip – this is ridiculous – tell them to let me out of here.'

'They are a threat to our security and to the sanctity of what we have managed to achieve here.' Wilson walked around to face Alice. 'As Quinn said, we just cannot tolerate it.'

'But we can't tolerate murder either, can we?' Alice was furious, her words spitting out into the room.

'I don't think I heard you protesting when you murdered... who was it, Filip?'

'Hutchinson.'

'... that's right, Hutchinson, when he threatened your security during the Storms.'

Alice bit down hard on her lip. 'You know that was different,' she said. 'He tried to...'

'And what about Jonah,' said Barnes scornfully, stepping out from behind Kunstein. 'You took him out into the Deadlands, knowing that he was unprepared mentally, and that he'd never make it through. You pretty much signed his death warrant, as well as you have Richard's. It's just lucky that we saved Marcus in time. You're a danger to yourself and to others.'

The lump in Alice's throat grew thicker and her eyes pricked with the beginnings of hot, wet tears.

'I didn't kill Jonah,' she screamed angrily. 'I didn't. Kunstein, tell them. I cared about Jonah – you all know that.'

Kunstein remained silent in the shadows at the back of the room, her presence heavy but any words unspoken. Just behind her, Alice could make out the shape of Barnes, her eyes dark and glittering.

'There's nothing Kunstein can do or say right now,' said Filip coming around to face her. Alice realised she had never seen him angry. Not like this.

'Unless she can explain why you lied to us all and stayed out overnight with that *animal* of a man putting everything we know at risk? Putting my daughter at risk.' His words hit her face more with a hard, acidic venom.

Alice's eyes welled with tears. 'Daughter?' she said, her voice breaking. 'How do you know?'

'We had Barnes run some viral tests on your blood as soon as we got back here to the Ship. We analysed it while you were out cold.' Filip's voice was ice-cold.

'I knew,' whispered Alice to herself. 'I knew.'

'You're just lucky there were no signs of infection,' interjected Barnes. 'We've further tests to run but how dare you risk one of our new lives.'

'*My* baby was never at risk. Richard just wanted me to know the truth. And now I do. And I am ashamed of you all.'

'And we, Alice, are ashamed of you.'

There was a stillness in the room as they looked at each other intently. 'I had to know the truth,' she said struggling in her chair and looking at Kunstein. 'You all need to face up to what you've done. This is not how we agreed to live.'

Her hands, tied to the chair, were aching and her eyes hurt too. 'Let me go, Filip. Please, we need to talk.'

'We can talk with you sat there just fine.' He put his index finger under her chin and lifted her head up to the light. 'Barnes is one of our best,' he said, as she stepped out of the shadows. 'And Izzy too. Your accusations are borderline treason.'

'Marcus told me what happened before he went to sleep,' said Alice. 'He was there. With Izzy.'

'Marcus was traumatised by the Storms,' said Barnes curtly. 'He didn't know what he was saying. I should never have allowed his ascent to the surface in the first place.' She looked into Alice's eyes. 'And I'm not sure I should have allowed yours either, following this little escapade. Besides, if it were true, the removal of a traitor such as Kelly would be the most patriotic act a young Community member could undertake. Now that really ranks as a Contribution – she would be an example to us all.'

Kunstein stepped forward, the wings of her cloak forming a semi-protective ring around Alice. 'I can't say I'm in complete agreement with this,' she said. 'And I know that a way forward has been agreed by all of us but it makes me very sad that we have reached this juncture. Before we start this process, are we sure that this is the only decision available to us?'

'Absolutely,' said Filip and Barnes in harmony, their voices blending into a single, decisive blow of judgement.

'We cannot allow her back into the Community,' Barnes continued. 'Her politics have become misaligned with ours.'

'With what's right,' interjected Quinn.

'But…' Kunstein looked directly at Barnes who cut her off.

'Are *you* still aligned?' she said, dangerously.

'Of course,' said Kunstein, in a voice that appeared to Alice to be slightly less confident than normal. 'I don't think you need to concern yourself with my allegiance.'

'Then it's decided. We will need to keep her in a controlled state until the child can be safely removed, and then terminate her. She presents too much of a danger to everything that's important to ever let her back out.'

Kunstein's face was a clock with no hands – blank and meaningless. 'She has always been special to me,' she said, turning to Wilson, 'to us.'

'And sometimes, for the right reasons, those bonds must be broken,' he replied. 'Had she never brought that boy back here in the first place then this may never have happened.' He coughed quietly. 'But we all have own weakness, demons if you like, don't we? Only some are a little more harmful than others.'

Kunstein's smile was the pale weakness of a dying star, circling around itself before burning out. 'We all knew that difficult decisions would need to be made,' she said. 'I just didn't expect this one to come – or at least so soon.'

Between Quinn and Barnes, she looked so small, thought Alice, much smaller than she ever had before. Barnes seemed to tower over them both, her arm around Kunstein.

'You must be finding this hard,' she said. 'Why don't you take the rest of the day to yourselves, you and Wilson go back to the apartment and get some rest. After the trials, you must be feeling exhausted.'

Kunstein shook her head slowly. 'As painful as this is,' she said, 'I choose to be a witness to this. It is the only way lessons will be learned for future generations.'

Alice worked furiously to free her hands, the solemnity and finality of the discussion becoming more unnerving as each sentence unfurled itself. She began to shake with anger and fear.

'What are you doing? What are you talking about?' she screamed. 'You can't be a witness to this – to murder, to silencing the truth, to ignoring what's outside the Barricades! This can't be happening!'

'Silence, Alice,' said Barnes. 'We've heard enough.'

'Filip, Kunstein.' Alice's throat was raw with shouting that was turning to pleas of desperation. 'You can't do this – I am one of you. I am a part of things. I helped create this.'

All in the room turned away from her. Kunstein turned to Filip, her back to Barnes. 'Are you sure there's nothing we can do differently?'

'Not any more. Power can be taken away just as fast as it can be bestowed.'

He turned his back and walked to the other side of the room, his hands trembling. 'You stopped being a part of this when you took your first step outside the Barricades with that outlander. Tell me, Alice, what was so important that you needed to allow him to escape from here... or worse, that you needed to go with him? What was it that was more important that caused you to sacrifice everything we have here? What is so important about *him*?' His voice crackled at the end of the sentence and Quinn looked at him sharply.

'Leave it, Filip. She's nothing to us now.'

Alice wrestled with the cords that bound her. 'I wanted to know the truth. You won't be able to hide from this, Barnes,' she shouted across the room. 'This is wrong. What we're doing is wrong. I came back here to help you make it right. I could have stayed out there but I came back because it was the right thing to do.' She let a single, salty tear run down her cheek, biting out her anger. 'You must remember what the right thing to do looks like, all of you?'

Filip placed a hand on her cheek and wiped away the tear. After a long pause he spoke again, voice tinged with regret. 'I'm sorry, Alice,' he said. 'But we can't trust you any longer. There is no place for deceit and lies within this new world and you have broken something that was very special; something that cannot be repaired.'

He paced around the room thoughtfully. 'Take her away,' he said to Kunstein, finally. 'Allow the child to grow but dispose of her when her use is done, as we agreed.'

Alice's eyes widened, full of terror. 'What?' she screamed. 'No! Let me go, I'm Alice Davenport!'

Kunstein looked at the floor, her cloak still, like the wings of a dead raven.

Barnes, who had nodded throughout Filip's final speech looked at him and gestured towards Alice.

'Yes,' he continued. 'Take her now – down the back stairs so that no one else has to witness this betrayal. We'll let the people of the Community know that she eventually died in childbirth. Send a party of our strongest and most able people to that place north of here where Richard has gone and slaughter everyone there – and anyone within a five-mile radius.' His eyes shined darkly. 'Kill them – men, women, children. Kill them all. Except Richard Warren. Bring him back here alive so that I can do the job myself.'

Barnes laughed; a sickly-sweet chortle that hollowed the pit of Alice's stomach and she felt desperately sick.

'You're actually not going to tell Richard, are you?' said Quinn to Barnes. 'I mean, if we find him and bring him back?'

'Tell him what?' screeched Alice. 'Why can't you just let them go, leave them alone – they won't want to have anything more to do with this place, they'll stay away.'

'It's so very touching you feel the need to defend him,' said Filip. 'But he has everything to do with this place. I'm looking forward to seeing the look on his face when I tell him that his kind donations to the Community during his stay here have resulted in a new life. Barnes is already pregnant with his child, just as you are with mine.'

'We're going to call him Milton,' said Quinn, smiling. 'And he's going to be perfect.'

At this, Alice was stunned to silence, gazing in horror at Barnes' smug expression. So this what they had wanted Richard for – Barnes's sick plan. She started to kick and struggle against the cords harder than ever.

'She's not going to go quietly,' Quinn observed, as Barnes approached and placed a hypodermic beneath her skin.

As darkness descended on Alice, she managed to whisper. 'The truth will set you free,' before consciousness left, and she was gone.

What seemed like hours later, when the room slowed to a steady spin, Alice realised that Barnes, Wilson and Quinn had gone but that the others were still there, talking behind her at the back of the room.

'Let me take her downstairs,' said Kunstein firmly but still with the edge of a question. 'What we're doing here is just unfair. It's time now.' She moved over to where Filip sat at a high chair, his eyes fixed on the control panel and the bar charts of the Model that climbed up and down in front of him. He flicked a switch and scanned through some of the other screens, watching as the charts disappeared and a map of the Community filled the control panel. 'Goodbye, Alice,' he said without looking up. 'Look after our daughter until I can get her back.'

The tight knots that had bound her to the chair and burned dark flowering bruises into her skin loosened, as Kunstein cut the thickest of the cords with a knife she produced from within the folds of her long cloak. Alice flexed her fingers, allowing the blood to flow back through them before Kunstein tied her arms together again, this time in front of her.

'What are you doing?' said Alice, her legs shaking and her head groggy. 'Where are you taking me?'

'The Catacombs,' said Kunstein. 'Stand up, now Alice, we need to leave.'

As Kunstein half-carried her from the Control room, Alice felt a heavy blanket of panic fold over her.

'I don't want to go,' she whispered to Kunstein, finding it almost impossible to move one foot in front of the other. 'What's going to happen to me?'

'I'm taking you down to the labs for some final checks,' said Kunstein, 'and then you're going to be put into an isolation bay so that we can monitor your baby until its ready to be born.'

'But what about me?' said Alice, her voice breaking. 'What happens to me?' They turned the corner of a small corridor and through a door to the top of the maintenance staircase. Kunstein held onto her arm tightly.

'Take the stairs one at a time,' she said. 'It's only a few floors but you need to be careful; we can't afford for anything to happen to that precious cargo you are carrying.'

Alice felt a thread of fear run through her. 'But what about me?' she said again as they wound their way down slowly. 'What's going to happen to me?' she said, her head spinning, but Kunstein remained silent.

With every step downwards, the air felt heavier and more stifling and each step more difficult than the last. Twice she tried to break free but the serum inside her had left her weak and powerless. Alice felt her sniffing evolve into a steady sobbing and then a gulping, shivery cry that left her empty inside.

Kunstein gripped her arm, pulling her away from the thin edges of the steps. 'I'm going to talk to Filip,' she said, whispered, looking around at the walls. 'When the baby has been born, I'm going to talk to him again. When he's a father himself, he might feel more inclined to clemency, maybe even forgiveness. I don't think I can appeal to Barnes, but Filip maybe.'

They stopped on a wider stair that divided the layers between each floor like slabs of geological debris. 'But you're going to need to think long and hard about what you're going to say to him – if he ever allows that opportunity. He needs to know that it was Richard who orchestrated the whole thing and that you were forced to help him.'

She looked long and hard into Alice's eyes. 'And if there's anything or anyone that can demonstrate that you were a knowing and willing party to this, you need to tell me now so that we can have it destroyed or discredited. You need to trust me here, Alice. Filip will never allow himself to look foolish. Is there anyone, perhaps, that knew of your plans?'

As the enthusiastic tones of a French accent twisted through her ears, Alice wasn't sure she could trust anyone, even Kunstein.

'Barnes can't do this,' she murmured. 'I'm Alice Davenport. Isn't there anything you or Wilson can do?' She pushed her hands to the side and tried to get them free.

'He can and he has,' said Kunstein as they stepped downwards. 'The manifesto sub clause stated that you, Filip, and Quinn were empowered to make all decisions regarding law and punishment here in the Community, by majority and overruling anything that Wilson or I had to say. Barnes was added later, given the fact that she's been designing most of the censomics rulings with Quinn.'

Alice shook her head angrily. 'This isn't right and you know it.'

There was the swish of a cloak. 'Alice, this is your last chance to help yourself. What about that man – the one who was on guard? Did he know anything of your plans? What is his name again? You know if you offer him up to Filip, he might consider some leniency. He would be terminated immediately, of course, but I think it's a small price to pay. Did he know how you escaped?'

Alice gulped silently. 'Jacques?' she said, keeping her voice steady and holding her hands together to stop them shaking. Her head swirled with fear and confusion. She blinked back tears and held her head high. 'No,' she said, clearly. 'He had nothing to do with this.'

Kunstein shrugged her shoulders. 'As you wish,' she said, and guided Alice through the small door and out into the Catacombs.

Although she tried hard to concentrate and keep track of where she was, as Kunstein led her though the maze of tunnels she became dizzy and disorientated. It wasn't until the door snapped shut and she was pushed down onto a rester bed that she realised she was in one of the sleep rooms, deep within the Catacombs. Barnes appeared in the doorway, smiling. 'Hello again,' she said brightly and jabbed another needle deep into Alice's arm.

'This won't take long,' she added, her smile piercing. 'Goodbye, Alice, it's been a pleasure. I'll leave you in Kunstein's capable hands.' The flap of her lab coat was the last Alice saw as she marched back to the corridor.

Kunstein glanced up at the grille on the wall and lowered her tone.

'I promise that I will do everything I can to keep you alive, for as long as I have any influence in here. You have my word.'

She untied Alice's hands and undressed her, checking through the clothes and placing her, naked, into a clear plastic sleep suit. Carefully, she folded the Industry workwear and held them close to her face, drawing in the scent, before placing them back beside the rester.

Alice let her limbs and body be moved by Kunstein, unable to lift her arms or get away from the bed. She let herself flop down onto her stomach, cradling the mass of cells inside her. Her lips parted slowly as she tried to speak but the words felt so difficult to form against the numbness that was spreading through her.

'What is it?' said Kunstein. 'Is there anything you want to tell me?'

Alice licked her lips and tried again. This time she managed to let the sounds escape her. 'Call her Jescha,' murmured Alice. 'I want Filip to call my daughter Jescha.'

Kunstein nodded and held her tightly in her arms as Wilson's voice crackled over the speaker system from the Control Room.

'People of our Community, I am delighted to inform you that Elizabet 'Izzy' Conrad, charge of Alice Davenport and Filip Conrad, has been crowned champion of the first annual Community trials. I am sure you would all like to join with me in congratulating her on an excellent performance and outstanding Contribution, which has won her the leading place on and therefore, chair of, the junior board of the Industry Committee. She has made us all so, so proud.'

Alice opened her mouth to speak, lines of pain creasing her face like musical staves.

'This is all wrong,' she mouthed, and then, 'please make sure Jescha is safe.'

'She's perfectly fine,' said Kunstein, her eyes blotted with deep tears. 'Sleep now, Alice.' She kissed her gently on the cheek. 'Goodnight, my girl,' she said, her voice choking with emotion.

But Alice had already lost consciousness, and was gone.

Chapter Twenty-Six

The Chamber

Carter

As Carter pushed open the door, a shaft of yellow light from the corridor partly illuminated the otherwise dim room. Angel slipped through the crack and Carter followed, pulling the door shut behind him with a click. It was similar to the others they had seen from the vent, sparsely furnished with a pull-down rester attached to the wall and a pile of clothes neatly folded up under the bed. Tubes led from the wall to a plastic sleep suit that contained a body, frozen still in an enforced sleep. Angel ran her finger across the thick layer of dust that wasn't just on the sleep case, but coated every surface.

'It's just another room,' she said, disappointed. 'There's nothing in here. It's just another room with just another sleeper. It was all lies – unless there's something in the walls or underneath the floor.' She started searching the room, smoothing her hands down the walls and checking the floor on her knees.

'I don't think it is just another room,' said Carter, slowly, rubbing away the dust from the sleep case. His hands were shaking uncontrollably as each layer of dirt disappeared beneath his fingers to reveal the face beneath the plastic skin of the sleepsuit.

'Where are the books, the papers, the confession – everything we were told was in here?' said Angel, frantically trying to scrape her way through the floor. She was almost in tears. 'This whole journey has been a complete waste of time.'

'It really hasn't,' said Carter, his voice steady as his fingers fumbled for the zip on the side of the sleep case. He switched over the cryonic tubes and steadied the switches, adding a substance from a third tube that stuck out of the wall.

'What are you doing?' said Angel, pulling his arm. 'Why are you waking it up? I thought you said that was a bad idea. Whoever it is will slow us down – we don't even know how we're going to get into the Control Room yet.'

'This one won't slow us down,' said Carter, his voice wavering. The face that was so familiar to him from his lessons at the Academy looked calm and peaceful while asleep. 'I'm sure she won't.'

They waited in a heavy, anticipatory silence, watching the blood flow back into the dark veins of the sleeper and the cold pallor of cryonic sleep slowly start to leave her.

'This has to work,' said Carter, desperately willing her to wake. 'It has to.'

'You sure you know how to do this?' said Angel, as Carter adjusted the tiny valves attached to the tubes.

'In theory, yes, but I've never had to do it in practice.'

Outside in an adjoining corridor came the sound of voices that grew louder and then diminished as people passed through the tunnels.

'Broadcast announcement,' said one voice. 'New Controller Generals' first address. Elizabet and Ariel.'

Angel leaned over the bed and rubbed the girl's cheeks softly. 'Come on,' she said. 'You need to hurry up, we're running out of time.' She turned to Carter. 'We should leave her here and get out while we can. How long does this usually take? Is there anything you can do to speed the process?'

'Minutes, sometimes more,' he said. 'And without any additional drugs, there's not much more we can do.'

Angel shook the body hard in frustration. 'Come on!' she whispered loudly.'

Carter massaged colour into her skin and lifted her eyelids carefully. Very slowly, her eyes peeled open, the paleness of her skin having been replaced with the light-brown shimmer of her body coming back to life. Her gaze shifted from ceiling to wall and then floor, like an animal afraid. She opened her mouth to scream when she saw Carter and Angel.

'It's okay,' said Carter softly, putting his hand over her mouth. 'It's okay, we're here to help you – but you have to be quiet.'

As her eyes became accustomed to the light, the sleeper flexed her muscles and shook the slumber from her body.

'Who is she?' said Angel. 'Who the hell is she and what is she doing here?

The sleeper sat upright, coughing huge clouds of spray from her lungs while her eyes watered and fluids raced through her body. Carter handed her some water and she drank furiously until there was nothing left. He knew as soon as she opened her eyes that she was exactly who he thought she was. She was unmistakeable.

'Who are you?' said Angel impatiently, 'What is your name?'

The girl looked at her directly, an angry tear racing down her cheek. There was a brief silence before she spoke, but when she did, Carter felt his heart beat faster than it ever had in his life.

'My name is Alice Davenport,' she said, her eyes shining brightly with anger. 'Now where is my daughter?'

A Letter from Ceri

I want to say a huge thank you for choosing to read *The Girl in the Storm*. I'd like to say that I enjoyed writing it, but Alice and Carter seem to tell their own stories – I just hold the pen! If you did enjoy it, and want to keep up-to-date with all my latest releases, just sign up at the following link. Your email address will never be shared and you can unsubscribe at any time – and don't worry, I won't pass your details on to the Industry…

wwww.bookouture.com/ceri-a-lowe

I really hope you loved *The Girl in the Storm* and if you did, it would be so great if you could write a review. I'd love to hear what you think, and it makes such a difference helping new readers to discover one of my books for the first time. If you haven't yet read *The Rising Storm*, the first in the Paradigm series, please do check it out – and also keep watching your email and social media for the final instalment in the trilogy. It will be out at the end of the year.

I always love hearing from my readers and getting their views on the end of the world so please do get in touch on my Facebook page, through Twitter, Goodreads or my website. Together, we can conquer the Industry

Thanks,
Ceri A. Lowe

cerialowe

@cerilowepetrask

www.cerialowe.com

Acknowledgements

Many people have shaped the way this book has developed by being part of my world or part of my end of the world conversations but there are a few without whose support this book may never have got finished. To everyone who has been on this journey with me, I thank you.

A HUGE thank my amazing editor Ellen Gleeson for her sterling work in pulling my ideas apart and helping me put them back together again with such precision and care and also Kim, Noelle and the whole team at Bookouture for the incredible work they do.

To Leila 'Friend' Stroud, for always listening to whatever I say and always finding the right way to say what needs to be said.

To John White, David Morgan and Sue Jones for being the best work colleagues money can't buy.

To Jane and Tony, for being an inspiration in the world.

To Pablo & Barney for the constant interruptions, unlimited requests and spontaneous play time.

A special mention to the next generation of my extended family who are already doing things to change the world in their own amazing ways; Alys, Louis, Harri, James, Elizabeth & Christopher. Don't ever let the Industry grind you down. You can be anything you want to be. And I know you will.

To the Lifelongs – Becky, Jayne, Jill, Claire, Janine & Sarah. I loved you then and I love you still.

To my dad – I never stop hoping I make you proud of me; thank you for always being you.

To my incredible sister, Sally, the inspiration behind Alice Davenport.

And, finally, to the wonderful Lara – for believing in me, encouraging me and supporting me every single step of the way.